What Comes After Crazy

# What Comes After Crazy

*A Novel*

## SANDI KAHN SHELTON

*Shaye Areheart Books*

NEW YORK

Published by Shaye Areheart Books, New York, New York.
Member of the Crown Publishing Group, a division of Random House, Inc.
www.crownpublishing.com

SHAYE AREHEART BOOKS and colophon are trademarks
of Random House, Inc.

Printed in the United States of America

*Design by Lynne Amft*

Library of Congress Cataloging-in-Publication Data

Shelton, Sandi Kahn.
What comes after crazy / Sandi Kahn Shelton.— 1st ed.
p. cm.
1. Mothers and daughters—Fiction.   2. Divorced women—Fiction.
3. Single mothers—Fiction.   4. Teenage girls—Fiction.   I. Title.

PS3619.H4535W48 2005
813'. 6—dc22                                                    2004013255

ISBN 1-4000-8295-1

10 9 8 7 6 5 4 3 2 1

First Edition

*To Jim, as always*
*And Benjamin, Allison, and Stephanie*
*Amy, Mike, and Charlie*

I owe huge debts of gratitude for the support and kindness I've received while writing this book. My family has been endlessly patient and understanding as my head was filled with these characters instead of real life. And my friends have lent their insights and wisdom to the long process of bringing this story to life.

Special thanks go to Alice Mattison, Diane Cyr, Mary Rose Meade, Nancy Hall, Leslie Connor, Nancy Barndollar, Kim Steffen, Kay Kudlinski, Jennifer Smith, Melissa Weiner, Mary Squibb, Deborah Hare, and Jane Tamarkin for their suggestions and editing and encouragement.

I couldn't have written this book without the strong women whom I am lucky to have in my family: Helen, Joan, Pat, Amy, Alice, Jennifer, and Gwen. Allison and Stephanie amaze me each day with their strength and their faith in me.

Thanks also to my wonderful writing group, who each month shares laughter, great food, lovely anecdotes, and plenty of advice: Beth Levine, Nicole Wise, Tamara Eberlein, Louise Tutelian, Andrea Atkins, Susan Stewart, Ellen Parlapiano, and Jill Kirchner Simpson. And to Bryan, who, more than once, has saved the whole enterprise from the jaws of the computer demons that threatened to swallow it whole.

And, of course, endless thanks go to my agent, Nancy Yost, and to Shaye Areheart and Sally Kim, for believing in this book and working so hard on its behalf.

What Comes After Crazy

# I

The fact is, I'm in the process of panicking in front of Dan Briggs. We're sitting in my living room late on Sunday night, and although I met him only a month ago and nothing has been said outright, the air has a sudden crackle to it that even *I* know means it's time we decided whether we'll sleep together. We've kissed three times—although not yet tonight—and he's called me on the phone five times, and we've gone for two walks that turned romantic. That adds up to one overdue sexual encounter by today's rules, I believe.

Here's the thing: theoretically I would love to sleep with him, but I can't remember how you get started. It's now been so long since I've been with a guy and had sex as a possibility—I am still technically married, after all—that I can't for the life of me remember how it is that two people can go from having a conversation to passionately kissing. What is the signal that gets sent? And how in the world do the clothes come off? If only I could press the "pause" button on this relationship and call a few friends. What I need to know for starters is this: since it's my house, do I have to make the first move? Or shouldn't he, as the male of the species, simply ease me down onto the floor and start in with some heavy petting? And . . . well, is it possible to have sex without the other person seeing you naked?

Worse, we've somehow stumbled into an endless loop of a conversation about the benefits of whole wheat flour versus white flour, and I don't see how we'll ever get out of it. Dan, you see, is a naturopathic physician who's just moved to town to open a practice, and I'm a baker in a health food store. Or more truthfully, I simply *pass* as one. I'm actually the last person you'd think would be concerned about all that tofu and granola stuff. Really, I just follow a bunch of somebody else's recipes: carob brownies, nondairy tofu cupcakes, carrot-soy bread. I don't even *own* any whole wheat flour.

But then, just as I've resigned myself to a whole evening's two-person seminar on wheat bran, Dan suddenly shifts gears. He reaches over and takes my hand. "Tell me," he says gently. "When you named your daughter Hope, what was it you were hoping for, do you think?" He says, "Do you remember exactly?"

I take a jagged breath, and *that* is when the phone chooses to ring. It's my mother.

"Baby!" she yells into the phone. "I've got *the* most amazin' news!" Not: How are you? Not: What's going on in your life? Not: Is this a good time to talk? She has never asked any of those questions, as far as I can remember. She is Madame Lucille, the fortune-teller, which gives her license to call people at the most annoying times possible.

"Actually, Lucille, I'm just the tiniest bit busy—" I begin. I look at Dan's beige sweater with little nubbly things all over it, and he smiles at me and sprawls out on the rug next to me. He has this shaggy, pleasing brown hair that keeps falling into his brown eyes, and he's long and lean and handsome in that vulnerable, nontraditional, non-model kind of way. Good lines to his face. Crinkly eyes. What I like best about him, though, is a contradiction I've noticed: even though he seems completely put together and way more sane than most people I know, his socks do not match. One is dark blue and one is brown. I love that.

"So," I say to Lucille, looking yet again at the socks and taking a shaky breath. "Busy. Let's talk tomorrow."

"The answer is yes," she says. "Sleep with him. Definitely."

"What?" She is always doing stuff like this, showing off.

"You heard me. Do it. Whoever he is. Sleep with him." She starts clicking her lighter and laughs her wild, cackly laugh. "Oh, never mind. You never take my advice anyway. Listen, darlin', here's why I called. You won't believe this, but I'm bitin' the bullet and gettin' married again."

"What?" I say.

"I'm gettin' married!" she shouts. "*Mar*-ried! Me! Can you believe it?"

Actually, yes. I can. She gets married all the damn time. But you see, this is exactly what I do not want to get into with her. I put my head down. Dan Briggs is so nice and normal, and I'm practically certain he doesn't know how screwed up lives can get. Do I really *have* to let him in on *everything* weird and dodgy about me all at once? It's bad enough that I've already had to explain about Lenny, who left me to go to Santa Fe a year ago saying he was off to earn money for a few months but then never returned—and also about our two high-strung daughters who are barely coping with being left behind. Dan had been more than understanding of all this technically-married-and-have-kids stuff while I was explaining it to him, but—you know how it is. He had that kind of overly sympathetic, textbook way that some people have. Probably there was a chapter in his naturopathy school about the psychological ramifications of divorce on people's immune systems or something.

But—God!—now to have to explain about my crazy mother and her fortune-telling and her life of serial marriages—it's too much. I frown, turn my body slightly away from him, and cup my hand around the receiver, as if that would be enough barrier to keep her words from leaping out of the telephone and landing on him. I'm almost sure he's heard her ordering me to sleep with him. Still, he politely takes the hint and gets up, unfolds himself, and heads to the bathroom. He touches my shoulder lightly as he passes—my nerve endings go *zzzzzt*—and I turn and smile at him. I mouth, "Mother" to him, and he pantomimes back, "What-are-you-gonna-do."

God, he has no idea.

Lucille is still jabbering away, and just from the way she's gone all southern, I can tell that she's in a crowd of people, and that she's sure all of them are thinking she's just the most outrageous, special person they've ever met. She's got the Scarlett O'Hara thing going so hard that I'm afraid that honey will start dripping into the phone and clogging up the wires.

"So, darlin', he's a retired investment banker," she says—only at first she's exaggerating her vowels so much that I think she's said he's a "retard investment banker"—"and his name is Harold Morgenthaler, and, darlin', he's just *the* most handsome man ah've ever seen in mah whole life, and just the sweetest thang you evuh saw. Besides all that, he's rich and he's got piles and piles of luscious white hair. Oh, yes, you are too, you big ole monkey man! You *are*! You're the richest thang since Donald Trump, darlin', and you know it. Ah swear, Maz, this has been the best two weeks of my life." She's making smooching noises, and I can hear people around her laughing.

"Two weeks?" I say, unable to help myself. "You've known him two weeks?"

"Now there you go! Okay, folks, here she goes," she says loudly. "Ah knew Maz would be the one who would need to point out that people aren't *supposed* to get married until they've known each other so long they're already bored." Then the wheedling voice starts, and I squeeze my eyes tight, but I can still see her: dyed black wig piled up in ringlets and her huge blue eyes, which she claims are violet, outlined in black, twinkling with imagined mischief and showmanship. It's Lucille's eyes that make you think it really is possible she's seeing into the future or the human heart, or wherever she gets all those messages from— intense, smoky, possibly they really are violet, like Liz Taylor's, like she always said. She also said, after her fifth marriage ended, "God, Maz, don't let me end up like Liz, marrying men all the goddamn time. When I get up to Liz, won't somebody just shoot me, please!"

She's probably forgotten that. She's saying in her matter-of-fact, don't-argue-with-Madame-Lucille voice: "Honey, now you just go wake up those younguns of yours an' git in the car and come on down here and be with us. I can't be havin' you up there in that cold old Connecticut when I'm down here havin' the time of my life. We've raised all the hell we can raise for one day, and now we're all just sittin' round the pool tryin' to decide what kinda weddin' we want to have, and whether or not we should wait any longer than this weekend to do it." She breaks out in a peal of laughter. "One man here says we're so goddamn old we shouldn't even buy green bananas anymore. So why the hell should we wait to get married?"

"Maybe so you know for sure he's not an axe murderer," I say, grateful that Dan isn't there.

"An axe murderer!" She explodes with laughter. "Now just who do you think you're talkin to? Darlin', I think I can tell a little bit more than *that* about people."

"I don't know. You've messed up *at least* five times before." I don't want to mention that she stuck it out with my own father for only the approximately twenty minutes it took for him to get her pregnant—and then he was gone for good.

She laughs in a mean way, and I hear her clicking her cigarette lighter. "Oh, *you*! You know as well as I do those were practice runs—sort of like *your* marriage to Lenny, sweetie. Harold's been married a few times himself, so he knows the value of a little, uh, practice."

Dan's still not back, so I say, in a low voice, "What happened to his other wives? Have you checked?"

"Good God in heaven," she says. "What's with you tonight? You know me bettah than that. I wouldn't do anything without the spirit guides. They've checked him out spiritually and psychically *and* emotionally, and they say he and I have just been waitin' to meet each other in this plane. We've actually known each other in every previous lifetime since we were in Atlantis, and they think we were medieval scribes in love with each other during the Middle Ages."

"Medieval scribes didn't fall in love. There wasn't the concept of romantic love until—"

"And then during, I don't know, in the eighteenth century or so, I was a lady of the court—we already knew that, of course, that's old news—and he was a duke who married me, over the objections of his family. That's how Irv put it, but Marvin thinks there's more to be said."

"Oh, please." She knows I can't stand it when she starts going on about the spirit guides, Irv and Marvin, whom she has always talked about as though they were my know-it-all uncles. They hover around her and tell her everything she needs to know. All my life they've been tattling on me to Lucille.

"Well, you *asked* me," she says. "But listen. I gotta tell you the best part, even though you'll laugh. Marv says that in our last life, Harold's exes were our *cats*."

There's a roar of laughter from the crowd, and she's away from the phone for a minute, meowing and making catfight noises.

"So *where* are you?" I say when she comes back.

"I told you, didn't I? I'm in a hotel in Palm Beach, by the pool. We've run out the young folks—they can't keep up with us—and so it's just me and Harold and all these people I've met here. I did some psychic readin's last night, honey, and got a whole bunch of people, all retired salt-of-the-earth types, who want to be friends. This is just the friendliest little community you ever saw—if you had good sense, you'd pack up those two little gals and move on down here. I showed your picture to the waiter, and he said you were 'bout the prettiest gal he'd seen. You could start over and get you some rich, good-lookin' man to take care of you! Hell, the waiter himself could do it, with the money we've been showerin' on him all night long."

Dan comes back, bringing with him the bottle of wine from the kitchen. He points to my empty glass and lifts his eyebrows, and I nod, so he pours some for both of us and sits down again on the floor. He pushes his hair back one more time and grins at me, and I look down at his socks and feel that little whiff of sex from him again. But—how to explain this?—the air feels changed, damaged, by Lucille.

"Can I call you back some other time?" I say to her.

"Hell, no! I'm *by the pool.* Didn't you hear me say that? Can't you just take a minute off from your very important life to listen to me? Besides that, the guides have some messages they told me to give you."

"No messages tonight." *God, please, no messages tonight.* "I'll call you tomorrow," I say. "Promise."

"Wait . . . message, message." She starts clicking her damn Bic lighter, and then she goes into her trance voice, like a robot on crack. I squeeze my eyes closed. I cannot tell you how much I hate this. "Okay, here it is. Wait for it . . . wait . . ." There is a long silence. Then she says, heavily, "Lenny is not coming back to you, sweetheart. What? *What?* Oh. Okay, I'll tell her. Honey, Marv and Irv are sayin' he's becoming quite a religious hotshot out there, and he's stayin' in Arizona."

"Santa Fe."

"Isn't Santa Fe in Arizona? Well, whatever. Marv and Irv haven't been on this plane in a long time. They forget where the cities are.

But—wait! What? There's more. He's really touchin' people's lives out there and not comin' back, but it's okay because he was never really right for you, so you should release him. He's gettin' it together on a spiritual plane that's far above what you can relate to."

"Oh, please," I say.

"You know, that's a thing about you, isn't it? You never seem to understand that some people aren't meant to live in *your* humdrum, ordinary—"

"I never said that . . ."

"But he's too large for marriage, sweetie. He needs to be out among the people."

I roll my eyes, forget for a moment that Dan is sitting right there next to me sipping his wine politely. "Look, Lucille, with all due respect, the spirit guides don't know anything about—"

"They know a shaman when they meet one, which is more than you do! They're sayin' he had a *callin'*, a callin' to go and live an unconventional life, touching people's lives—"

"Oh, for heaven's sake, Lucille! He touched their lives, all right. Touched their lives—and their bodies, too, particularly if they were young, willing girls. Maybe I'm crazy, but I don't think it's much of a calling if all you want is to go out and screw every attractive young woman you see. Now you tell the spirit guides thank you very much, but to butt out of my life, and they can keep their observations to themselves. Maybe they could turn their attention to something more pressing in the world, like solving the situation in the Mideast or something. They've got a few shamans out there that could stand having somebody think about them."

My eyes meet Dan's, and I feel the color spreading across my cheeks. He smiles and raises his eyebrows. *Shit, she got me again.*

She sniffs and starts again in her injured voice, pronouncing each word very precisely. "The spirit guides just wanted me to tell you that the universe will reward you for releasin' Lenny by sendin' somebody who's just perfect for you. Lenny never was what you needed, darlin'. Release him."

"He is *so* released. Now good-*bye*, Lucille."

She hesitates. I hear her lighter clicking. "Sweetie, there's one more thing they're *insistin'* that I tell you. Fix yourself up. I know that *pizzazz* doesn't come naturally to you—"

"Lucille, I do just fine," I say.

"You're not even wearing mascara most days, are you?"

I don't answer. I couldn't find my tube of mascara if my life depended on it.

"And, honey, would it kill you to exfoliate? And pluck your eyebrows and do somethin' with your hair? Men are like children, sweetie. They want a playmate. Somebody cute."

"Okay," I say, "bye!"

"And tell that darling little Hope that her Glamorous Grandmother, G.G., loves her and that I know that she and I share the sight. And I'm comin' to see her soon! *Tell* her."

"I am officially hanging up now. Good-bye." My teeth are gritted. *You and Hope do* not *share the sight. Hope is a regular girl, and you are screwed up beyond repair.* That's what I'd say if Dan wasn't there.

I have the receiver halfway to its cradle when I hear her shout, "Darlin'—SLEEP WITH HIM! You *need* it!"

# 2

"My mom," I say, miserably. I shrug.

"So I gathered."

I can't think of what to say. My face even feels a little overheated. He's watching me.

"So," I say. "What were we talking about? Sorry for the interruption, really. She's so tough to get off the phone. Just goes on and on about stuff."

He tilts his head, smiling. I can tell he's thinking, Did this woman's mother just tell her to sleep with me?

"Oh, I remember what we were talking about—the whole wheat thing!" I say brightly. I try for a sly grin. "Now, Dan, tell the truth here. Did your mother cook with whole wheat? Or did you discover its benefits in naturopathic school?"

"Mostly school," he says. "My mother wasn't really into nutrition that much." He sips his wine, won't stop looking at me. "How about yours—Lucille, you called her? Whole wheat or not?"

"Not so much," I say. I laugh a little. "She actually thought ketchup was a health food, I think. Vegetable, you know."

"Yeah," he says. He looks around the room. Our eyes meet, and we smile. Painfully. "Hey," he says. "I'm sorry for eavesdropping, but . . . were you talking about spirit guides?"

"Did I say anything about spirit guides?" I say. My voice is high and thin. "On the phone? Really?"

"I *thought* you did."

"My mother jokes around a lot. She's kind of a . . . character, actually." I look at my hands. "She talks like that. About spirit guides and stuff. She's a little—well, she's wacky. Listen, I'm sorry she called and interrupted things. With her wackiness."

He's smiling at me, so nicely that I want to burst into tears of embarrassment. And then I would like to go hunt her down and kill her.

"Oh," he says. "Well."

I lean over and pick up my wineglass so frantically that some of the wine sloshes out onto the rug. And then when I go to drink it, I start choking. Dan pats me on the back, and I think that if I can just keep choking for a while, something intelligent will occur to me, something to keep him from looking at me with this baffled look. But I can't think of anything, and after a while I've coughed all I can. My eyes are watering from the effort of it.

"Listen," he says in a very nice way. "I'm the one who's sorry. I'm embarrassing you. I shouldn't have asked about your conversation with her. Sorry."

"No!" I say. This is now worse. "It's just that—well, I'll tell you." This is it: the official time when I realize there is no point in pretending to be anything close to normal. He'd have found out anyway eventually; I'm obviously not fit for a romantic relationship. Give up, I think. So I say, "Look, it's weird. My mother's a fortune-teller, actually. She's, you know, well, she's a fortune-teller, and you know how they are—think they can just call you up any old time and butt into your life."

I'm fairly certain I see his eyes go rounder. "Really?" he says. "A fortune-teller? That's amazing. I never knew anybody who had a fortune-teller in the family."

"And now," I say—and here a hysterically pitched *ha* somehow escapes from my throat, and I can tell that I'm just going to have to go full-speed into hell with this story now—"well, now she's called to say she's getting married again for the *sixth time*, and telling me how I ought to live, as if anybody would want to listen to anything she has to say on the subject of relationships. Five husbands she's had! Five! Can you imagine?" *Run, Dan Briggs. Go get your coat and run out of here.*

He's running his fingers through his hair. "Wow," he says. "Did she—wear turbans and have a crystal ball and all that?"

"Sure she did," I tell him. "Whatever you picture about fortune-tellers, that's what we did."

"We?" he says. "So . . . you're a fortune-teller, too?"

"Me? *No!* Me? Absolutely not. God, no. But she worked in carnivals, you see, and during the summers we traveled all around the South in her trailer, and I was, you know, her assistant. It was my job to take the tickets and take the people into the tent, you know, and then she'd peer into the crystal ball and tell them whatever they wanted to know. Like, if they were going to be famous or were going to meet somebody soon—that's mostly what people want to know. How to find their one true love and all. . . ."

"Sounds like she *keeps* finding her one true love," he says and smiles.

"Oh, yeah." I laugh. "She's great at finding true love for herself," I say. Then I remember he probably heard her yelling at me to sleep with him, and feel myself blushing all the way to my hairline. For a moment, the silence that hangs in the air is almost unbearable, and then he clears his throat and says, "Wow. You've certainly had a much more interesting life than I have," which for some reason makes me feel just the way I used to feel when I'd be taking tickets at the tent, and all the regular, well-dressed kids would come by with their parents, and they'd want to have their fortunes told, and their wavy-haired, nicely groomed fathers would frown and say, "Oh, noooo, we're not going to waste our money on a stupid *fortune-teller.* That's all nonsense."

That's it. I am not going to sleep with Dan Briggs.

"I mean, the strangest thing that ever happened to me," he says, "was when a guy around the block said he saw a UFO one time, and it turned out to be a garbage can lid that had gotten stuck in a tree."

I aim for a smile, but I can feel it's a pitiful imitation. Nice story, garbage can lid in a tree. Very nice. I'd love it if that was the weirdest thing that had ever happened to me.

"Meanwhile," he says, "you were having quite a life. Quite an interesting life, from the sound of it."

"Oh, yeah, it was interesting all right, if by *interesting* you mean *dysfunctional.* Listen, are you done with that wineglass? It's really getting late, and I'm sure you have to get up as early as I do."

His face registers surprise. His wineglass is still half full, but he hands it to me slowly. I take it from him and head for the kitchen. I hope he will just get his coat and go, but of course, he doesn't. He unfortunately has good manners, so he follows me, and I can almost feel him trying to think of something polite to say, probably something appropriately doctorly and naturopathic that will make the parting go easier. I feel cold all the way down to my internal organs. It's time for me to go back and get under the blankets again and wait for the spring thaw of my soul. Obviously I have wandered out of hibernation too soon.

He clears his throat. "So what *was* it like, Maz? You traveled around during the summer, but what did you do the rest of the time?"

"Listen," I say. I put the wineglasses down in the sink very carefully and turn and face him. "Really, we don't have to go into this. I know you heard my mother on the phone. I know you heard her say I should sleep with you, and you're a very nice man and very polite, but if you want to just go home now, that would probably be the best thing. Obviously I can't really have any kind of normal thing, and anyway, everything is just too complicated."

I see him swallow. "You can't have a normal thing?" he says.

"No," I say. "Look at my situation. You see what's going on here with me. The husband, the kids, the fortune-telling mother. Divorce, probably. Custody stuff. Even the whole wheat. Look! Look in this cabinet." I fling open the one over the sink. "Do you see any whole wheat in here? No. And you know why? Because I don't *have* whole wheat. I cook with white flour and sugar and *Crisco,* Dan." He starts laughing. "No! *Really!* Listen to me. This is important. I spent most of my childhood rattling around in a trailer with a woman who taught me how to make gin and tonics and read a tarot card when I was five years old. I'm not who you think. You should just go, really."

"I don't want to go," he says quietly. But he's looking at the jumble of boxes in the cabinet as if he's mesmerized by the sight. Probably he's never even *seen* so many boxes of Kraft macaroni and cheese, except in a grocery store.

"No, listen. You should go anyway; it's not going to be like you think. I thought I could be normal for a bit, but that's not going to work. She did everything wrong you can do and not be brought up on charges. If we were doing that life today, the Department of Children and Families would be there so fast, it'd make your head swim. Why, if it wasn't for my grandmama taking me in and raising me whenever I needed a place to go, I'd probably be—well, I don't know what I'd be. I'd be a hell of a lot crazier than I am, though, that's what. As it is, I'm probably off the scale when it comes to being somebody who's, you know, right for anything normal. I don't even know what I'm talking about, but I just want to go to bed now and pull the covers up."

He is smiling at me. "Hey, I don't think you're crazy," he says. "And I mean, I'm not here for some kind of permanent, you know, *thing*, if you don't want to. I think you're—you're *interesting*. I like you. You don't have to be a certain normal with me, you know, whatever that is, which is a debatable thing anyhow." He takes a step toward me, but I back away from him, which turns out to be the luckiest thing that's happened all evening, because just then there's a noise in the doorway, and we both look over, and there stands my ten-year-old daughter, Hope, glowering at us. I feel Dan jump. And she does look truly bizarre: wearing Lenny's old Def Leppard T-shirt and his tiger-striped sweatpants that hang off her, with her pale blond hair sticking up like horns, from sleep. With her eyes narrowed and practically glittering, she looks a little poisonous, maybe like Patty McCormick from *The Bad Seed* after she's been thwarted once too often. She stands there, glaring from me to Dan and back again, all of her preteen indignation practically giving off noxious fumes.

Great, I think. Why don't we just fly Lenny in and my old high school boyfriend and my mother's five husbands? Do the whole evening up right! We could have Dan Briggs on his knees, begging to be released from here in no time.

"Hi, Hope," I say. "What are you doing up, honey?"

"Who's *this*?" she says, pointing to Dan, who lifts his hand and smiles and says, "Hello there, Hope," while she scowls at him.

"This," I say, and there is no good reason for me to feel suddenly like laughing, but I feel hysteria about to come over me in a wave, much like nausea. "This is Dr. Briggs, who is a friend of mine who has just moved to town. Dan, this is my daughter Hope."

"Hi," says Dan.

"I don't think he should be here," Hope says and glowers. "Does he know you're still married?"

"Of course he does. Now say hello."

"Well, did you tell him your husband is coming back?"

A little sound, almost an "eep," comes from Dan's direction. This, I think. Now this will be the last ultimate straw. Now he'll see that he has to get out of here, run for his life. If I look at his face, I know I'll dissolve in hysterical laughter, so I turn to her and say, "Now, Hope, that is not the way I expect you to behave when you come downstairs and find a friend of mine here, and whether I'm married or not has nothing to do with it. Do you hear me? Dan and I are friends. He's just moved to New Haven, and we were talking about what a nice place it is. Now did you need a drink of water or something?" That's it. Get the upper hand without resorting to yelling. Demonstrating model parenting despite sordid past.

"I do *not* want a drink of water," she says. "Daddy is coming back here, and this man should go."

"We'll talk about this later," I tell her. "But your daddy lives in Santa Fe now. He's told us he's staying there to build condos. You know that."

"He is *too* coming back," she says.

"No, darling, he's—"

"I just talked to Daddy on the telephone, and I told him that a man was here, and he says he's coming back home, and I came down to tell this *man* that he has to go home."

"Wait. You talked to your daddy? Tonight?" I say blankly.

"Yep. I called him up." She smirks at me and goes over to the table and slumps down in a chair.

I stare at her. "That's impossible. I've been on the phone nearly this whole time."

She sighs loudly. "I *know* that. I called him *after* you got off, and I told him all about what's going on, and he said he'd come back home."

"He did not," I say.

"Oh, yes, he did," she says.

"But you don't even have his phone number," I say, which I'm sure sounds a little inane under the circumstances, worrying about *that* little detail when Hope is clearly making a stand. But Lenny hardly ever calls the kids—or me either, for that matter. I have to force him to talk to them whenever I've called him, which now that I think of it, hasn't been for weeks. The last time I talked to him, we had one of our typical brief conversations: me saying he needed to send more money, and him saying he probably would, and adding that he didn't see as how he could come home in the foreseeable future, blah blah blah. It was his usual bit: Santa Fe is such a magic place, so much work to do there, plenty of what he calls "good people" and how they're all helping him "find himself."

Hope rolls her eyes. Did I somehow not know that other people could have phone conversations that I perhaps didn't know about? Didn't I know that he said to call him whenever she wanted? Huh? Did I know *nothing*?

Dan clears his throat. "Maz, maybe I really should call it a night."

"You should," Hope tells him. "And don't come back. She's married to a very nice man who was *devastated* when he heard she has a new boyfriend."

Now the laughter really does start to back up in my throat. "Hope," I say, and my voice is all wavery with the effort not to laugh out loud. "That is not true and you know it, and it is *not* the way to talk to my friends." I can't go on. My mouth is twitching.

Dan looks at me in disbelief. I can't look at him. He's the funniest part of all—I think of him showing up here tonight in all innocence, probably imagining he was going to sit around in a civilized way, maybe do a little experimental making out, but, oh no! Instead he finds himself surrounded by madness—first a serially married fortune-telling diva screaming that I should have sex with him, and now, this little pugilistic daughter, who looks as though she might go off at any moment and start in with a Lizzie Borden routine. It is taking all my will to keep from erupting into dangerous laughter.

They are both staring at me. This must mean those little yelping noises in the room are coming from me.

"Really," says Dan in a very, very calm voice. "Let's talk another time."

"She's still going to be married another time," says Hope.

I put my hand over my mouth as if I could trap the laugh, force it back down my throat.

Dan averts his eyes from me, looks worried. "Hope, it's been very nice meeting you, and I'm sorry that you feel bad that I was here, but I want to tell you that I am simply a friend of your mother's," he says. "I'm not her boyfriend."

"I don't know why she invited you," Hope says. "Look, just so you know, I do not want a new daddy. If she told you that we needed a new man around here . . ."

At this, Dan's eyebrows practically leap off the front of his face, and I collapse to the floor, laughing so hard now that I can't get breath. I hear him say, "Wow." In a moment, I fear, I will have lost all bladder control. It is only through the utmost effort of will that I am holding on. They both stand there and watch me in silence, but I can't even open my eyes wide enough to see their expressions. I laugh until I start choking. Dan comes over to me then, and lifts up my arms above my head, and Hope dashes right there, too, probably so she can make sure that while my hands are up, he won't try anything funny. The thought of this pushes me back to hysteria again.

"Stop it!" says Hope. "This is not one bit funny. Stop laughing!"

I get to my feet, wipe my eyes, hold onto the table. Dan gets one of the wineglasses and fills it with water and hands it to me. I drink it slowly.

"You okay now?" says Dan. I manage to nod.

"Okay, then listen, I'll let you two get back to your discussion, without an intruder here," he says, taking a deep breath. "It's late, anyway." One thing is for sure: we will never see him again.

"All right," I say. The mental image of him on his knees pleading to go for a moment threatens to send me back into gales of laughter, but I get control, manage to just snort a few times. "I'm sorry about all this," I say. My voice catches, and then, horrifyingly, tears start running down my face. None of us, particularly me, is sure if these are crying tears or laughing tears. "I'm so sorry."

"No, no, no," he says and looks at me, shakes his head. "It's fine. Just fine. A little adventure here, is all. We laughed, we cried. It was an evening's worth of emotion. Definitely got my money's worth."

Hope glares.

"Here, let me walk you to the door," I say. "Hope, go upstairs now and get back into bed. I'll be up in a minute."

"I'm staying right here," she says. She folds her arms.

"Go upstairs." My mouth is dry.

"No."

"Well," says Dan. "Gosh, Hope, it's been very nice to meet you." He extends his hand. She has the meanest frown on her face that I'm sure Dan has ever encountered, and she won't even acknowledge him. "I hope you work things out with your daddy."

"Hope," I say warningly. "Say good night to Dr. Briggs."

"Are you going to kiss him good-bye?" she says.

"Hope!"

"G'night," she says in a low voice. But she stands right there. I follow Dan out of the kitchen and into the living room. He gets his coat, which was folded over the back of the couch. Hope trails a few feet behind, watching closely. I have no doubt that if Dan should get within six feet of me, she'd be back on the telephone to Lenny.

"Again," I say. "I'm sorry."

"Nah, don't be. It's *fine*. We'll talk soon," he says. The cold whooshes in as soon as he opens the front door. For a moment we both look at each other, then he dashes off, underneath the glow of yellow light on the front porch, and then down the walk to his car, which is parked under the streetlight. I wait, but he doesn't wave as he drives by.

The air outside smells like iron, or more likely, snow. The old snow from two weeks ago is now brown and piled up against the curb, and our yard looks muddy and half-frozen. I should have brought in the garbage cans a few days ago. When was the collection day? Thursday? This whole yard looks run-down and scraggly, patches of gray grass and stark, bare trees. I've not been doing well at keeping house lately. Everything gets away from me so quickly. I hate having to remember it all. In the distance, a siren wails and a dog starts barking. I close the door and turn back wearily to Hope. Dan did not say, "I'll call you." He just said, "We'll talk soon." I haven't been in the dating world for a long time, but I think there's a big difference. Also, what was it he said about not looking at me in a permanent way—and then making sure that Hope knew that he wasn't my boyfriend? Oh, God, God, God. I have humiliated myself beyond belief. There's no question but that he's gone for good, and I don't blame him. I'd be gone for good from this, too, if I could.

I look at Hope, standing there looking defanged now, her arms like little wings folded up against her tiny, bony little chest. "So. Did you really call your daddy?" I ask her. "Really, really?"

"Yep."

"Come on, you didn't have time to call him. Why are you telling me this? What are you trying to do to me, anyway?"

"I didn't talk to him long," she says. She goes over and squats on the back of the couch, with her feet on the cushions, and then rolls off, until she's got her head on the floor and her butt on the cushions. Her voice has lost its edge. "He said he was busy, and we'd talk another time."

"So did he really say he was coming home, or did you make that up?"

She laughs. "I'm not telling you." She is so smug. I hate it that she thinks she has information, and that I have to ask the questions.

I go around turning off the lamps, picking lint off the carpet. "Come on upstairs, and let's get some sleep."

She follows me. "You don't believe me!"

I sigh. "It's just that I talked to him a while back, and he said he had no intention of coming home, that's all. It's a little hard to believe he's changed his plans so quickly without warning. That's not how people usually do things."

"Call him yourself if you don't believe me."

"I don't want to."

"You're mean to him."

"No, let's not go over this again. I was not and am not mean to him. We grew apart, and he went away. His choice."

"But you're the reason he won't come back. I know it." She flops down on my bed while I put on my nightgown, picking at a rough patch on her heel. "Can I sleep in your bed tonight?" she whines.

"No, Hope. Neither of us gets very good sleep when you sleep with me."

"But I'm scared in my room. I can't go to sleep in there."

"But your room is so wonderful and safe," I say. I look at her teary face, and reach over to hug her. She is the most maddening human being, and I'm always trying to hold her, as if somehow that can make things better, only it never does. She pulls away from me and starts to cry for real now, big loud gulping sobs. "Hope," I say. "It's all right. Stop crying."

I go into the bathroom and start brushing my teeth. My face looks pale, and some new lines seem to be starting up around my eyes, possibly just in the last three hours, I think. But still, for thirty-five, I don't look so bad. My body's all right, especially when it's fully clothed and you can't see all the little bulges and creases that I can still cram into jeans and turtlenecks. I heard a customer in the health food store say to Barry, my boss, the other day: "She's a great-looking gal, considering everything." I didn't know what he meant by "considering everything," but later Barry told me the guy knew what a flake Lenny was and the fact that I'd been married to him for twelve years and then he just packs up and leaves me with a full-time job and two kids to raise. I brush out my hair, which is blond and short and straight—but which will probably be gray by morning—and I turn off the light.

Hope is lying on my bed still, now with her feet on my pillow. She's still whimpering.

"Please get your dirty feet off my pillow," I say. "You know I can't stand that."

"Well, I can't stand to sleep in my own bed every night. It makes me sad about Daddy to be in there."

"All right, all right," I say. "You can sleep in my bed, but don't kick me."

"I won't kick if you won't snore." She dries her eyes and runs to her room to get her pillow, her blanket, and a freaky-looking witch doll that Lucille sent her when she was three. I put on my flannel night shirt, and she comes back and crawls into bed on Lenny's side. The radiator clangs and hisses as it shuts down for the night. We keep the thermostat at fifty-five at night, and the heater always thinks it's got to announce that its high-firing hours are done. The house settles into its usual nighttime creakiness. I have made friends with all of these noises over the past year.

She's still snuffling when I reach over and turn out the lamp.

"Hope, everything's fine," I say. "You don't have to cry." I pull her toward me, my large-sized child who suffers so much. Her hair smells like berry shampoo.

"I don't want you to have a man come here," she says after a long while.

"I know, sweetie, but you shouldn't be so rude. Dr. Briggs is a really nice person, and he didn't deserve the way you talked to him. I think you scared him."

She giggles in the darkness.

"That's funny?" I say.

"Yeah, it's funny. *You* were the one that scared him, with all that crazy laughing you did and then you started to cry," she says. "He looked like he was scared to death."

Hmm, I think. He did, didn't he?

After she falls asleep, I lie there, listening to her breathing, and to the radiator banging and, downstairs, the refrigerator motor cutting on and off, and I try to count up how many times I said "I'm sorry" to him in just this one evening. Too many. Even once is too many.

So much for my dating life.

# 3

Here's the thing about Lenny: he's a wonderfully handsome, charming *flake*. When he left last spring, he said he was going to Santa Fe to build condominiums with his friend Crocker because there was lots of money to be made there and he really didn't have anything cooking in New Haven. It was true; he didn't. He was halfheartedly building a deck on the back of our house for the landlord, which meant we could deduct something from the rent each month. He played keyboards at night with a couple of friends, and sometimes they made a few bucks playing at a bar in Fair Haven. And every now and then somebody would find some construction project they needed him for—but basically it was me, working at the Golden Granary baking whole wheat bread and carob muffins, making ends meet. He'd stay in Santa Fe for only two months, he said—long enough to get us back on our feet, pay off some bills, maybe replace the car—and then he'd be back for the summer. At least that's what he said.

But that wasn't really why.

The night before he left, we were supposed to go to the movies with some friends from day care—Liz Lawton, a single mother with two little kids, and Jolie Whiting, the teacher—but then I couldn't find a sitter. So Lenny went without me. Besides, I didn't want to go see *Independence Day* for the fourth time, despite how cute Jeff Goldblum looks in the ending scene. I was tired, as usual, from battling with Hope all day. And frankly I was a little bit pissed off at how Lenny was joyfully going around, packing up all his stuff, and acting as though he'd been sprung from a prison work camp. I mean, here he was supposedly going off to work very *hard*, and leaving his family all alone. Shouldn't he be just a little bit solemn and even contrite? Shouldn't he wipe that grin off his face?

He got home about midnight, about the time I was collapsed in bed, reading a magazine article on how to solve stress in your life by remembering to breathe deeply every hour or so. I was breathing very deeply and unstressfully when he came into our bedroom and sat down on the bed and took off his sneakers. He wouldn't look at me, I remember that. He just concentrated on his shoes as though they were the most absorbing pieces of matter on earth, untying them one by one and setting them aside, lining them up so the toes just matched. Then he stood up and turned away from me while he took off his jeans and T-shirt. He was already mostly bald—in his family, the men don't hold onto their hair, but they still have such vibrant, handsome faces that no one thinks much about their hair. Baldness kind of enhances their appearance, in fact, as though hair is merely a compensation for people who don't have compelling enough eyes to carry off a good look.

"Did you have a nice time?" I said. I was relaxed and even sort of tingly from all the deep breathing I'd been doing. Also, I was fairly sure he'd want to make love, it being his last night and all, so after some serious thought both while I was pissed off and then again when I was not so angry, I'd gone in and put in my diaphragm so at least I wouldn't have that extra step to do when the time came. It was his last night, after all. It felt important that things be symbolically good. I'd taken a hot bath and put on some plumeria-scented after-bath splash. A nice, loving send-off, with dynamite sex, despite the tensions we'd been living under for the past few months. "So!" I said. "Who did Liz manage to get for a sitter?"

"Oh. Uh, nobody," he said, folding up his jeans with his back still toward me. "Liz couldn't find anybody either. So Jolie and I just walked around and talked and stuff."

"You didn't even see the movie?" I got up on one elbow to see something. Yes, it was true. His jockey shorts were on wrong side out. The label—

"No. We didn't see the movie." An edge to the voice.

"Really," I said. I almost mentioned the jockey shorts—you know, as evidence for how distracted he was lately, and now he wasn't even paying attention to how his *guys* were clothed. (He loved to refer to his balls as his *guys*.) I thought I'd make a joke about that, but then he got up suddenly and went into the bathroom, closed the door, and stayed there for a long time. I lay in bed, trying to remember exactly how the article said deep breathing could help in this kind of situation—and by the time he came and crawled into bed next to me and turned off the light, my body was as taut as the high wire at the carnival, and my breath was light and fluttery at the very top of my chest. Very bad, as the magazine article would have pointed out.

"Lenny," I said in the darkness. He was as far as possible from me on the bed.

"What?"

Didn't he want—?

"What?"

"Well, you're going to be gone so long, so I thought we'd cuddle a bit and talk." I reached over and touched the small of his back.

"Maz, I'm tired."

It was spring, and the curtains at the window drifted lightly in a breeze that came up. Outside, I could hear the leaves rustling in the maple tree. I could barely breathe, but I turned toward him, bravely wrapped myself around him in the spoon position.

"Lenny, I do love you," I said. I felt as though I was outside my body.

He sighed. "I love you too, Maz, but I've got to get an early start."

I inched up farther on his pillow and kissed him on the neck. He didn't move. I gave him lots of little kisses all along his jawline, felt the muscles in his neck contract. And then—well, something happened in my head. I had floated up to the corner of the ceiling somehow, and now there was one of those *whoosh* moments, like when I was little and the Ferris wheel would just suddenly drop me, plunge me down toward the earth so fast my heart and lungs couldn't catch up. One minute I didn't know anything, and then I just *knew*, as though somehow the words had been typed up on the ceiling all along, and I was finally getting around to reading them.

That bastard had been fucking Jolie.

"Oh, my God," I said. I pulled away, felt my arms dragged down by a heaviness I didn't know they had.

"Oh, Maz, for God's sake, don't start this now."

"You *fucking* bastard."

"It's a little late for this, don't you think?"

I jumped out of bed and turned on the light, although at some level I knew I was acting madder than I really felt inside. Somewhere, deep down, as I told my friend Hannah the next day after he had gone, it was just the confirmation of knowledge that I realized I'd had for a long time.

Right, she said. It was the smoking gun, she said.

So we had the whole fight right then—because we had to, time running out and all. Because what if we didn't have the whole glorious fight, and he went off to Santa Fe, and I regretted not being given this one dramatic scene that I was owed? I yelled and slammed drawers and flung myself around the room, but the whole time I knew in some kind of creepy way that I was acting out of some historical outrage rather than anything generated right there in the present catastrophe. If I had done what I really felt like doing, I would have been sitting in the corner sucking my thumb. Instead, I had to fight, I had to be madder than I felt.

He sat on the side of the bed and tried to look guiltier than he felt.

At one point I yelled, "She's twenty-six years old, Lenny! How could you *do* this?"

He gave me such a *duh* kind of expression that we both started laughing. I didn't know you were allowed to laugh when your rotten husband was owning up to being unfaithful, but somehow it felt better than what we were pretending.

He reached into the bedside drawer and took out a joint and lit it. "She's not worth even half of you," he said. "Not on your worst day."

"Then why—?"

He shrugged. "Bored. The ADD thing. Can't hang on to good things. Don't play well with others. That old rules-are-made-to-be-broken problem."

"By the way, take that stuff with you when you go," I said. "I don't want the kids to find it." Then I said, calmly, "You know what I hate the worst, the very worst? That she takes care of the children, she's connected to all our friends. This is so embarrassing."

He just looked at me. "I know," he said. "I know that. I'm ending it. I'm leaving."

"But you're leaving *me*!"

"I'm really leaving her."

"Yeah, great. Just great. I get to be a single mom because you're breaking up with *her*."

"You'll be better off." He smoked the joint, smiled beatifically at me.

I was sitting on the floor with my head against the closet door. "I suppose everybody else knows about this," I said, and even I could hear the weariness in my voice.

"Nah. I don't think anyone knows."

"You're telling me none of our friends at day care know? Not even Liz?"

"We've been discreet. Anyway, nobody really cares. It's not that big a deal to most people."

At one point I thought that really all I wanted, all I really needed from this, was for him to just be *sorry,* to apologize. But he kept shrugging his shoulders. After a while, he just said, "You know how it's been." And then he said, "This is why I have to get out. It's getting too complicated, you know." Meanwhile, after ranting and raving all across the room, slamming doors and stomping around, I got up off the floor and sat down on the bed, feeling sad and ruined, and suddenly needing to review all the times I might have found out but didn't. I'd jump up and say, "Wait! That time in February when you said the truck broke down on the way back from a gig! You were really with Jolie, weren't you?" And he'd sigh and nod. I mean, he didn't even *lie* anymore. He'd been with Jolie for months, and it had all been going on right underneath everything else that was going on, and I fucking saw Jolie nearly every day—I did a day care turn with her, for God's sake—and all I could think of was that, despite what Lenny thought, no doubt every one of our friends knew, and right now they were probably thinking I wasn't much of a woman, not to keep him happy at home. That's what Lucille would say when she heard. *Lucille!* I put my face in my hands. Somewhere deep in my brain, I was thinking, Your husband is leaving—and these are the things that really bother you?

I'll give him this: he didn't come crawling over and try to tell lies. He didn't say all the things he'd said once before when he'd had a fling, a short fling, back when I was pregnant with Abbie—he just stood his ground, not groveling, meeting my eyes directly. I didn't even have the energy anymore to hate him for this, I just felt numb and cold all over. I didn't care if he went to Santa Fe, and I didn't care if I never saw him again. I could feel something switch off in my brain. There was almost an audible click, and I went under.

We didn't sleep, of course.

Around four, I said, "Were you going to tell me?"

"Tell you what?"

"That you were in love with Jolie?"

"I never said I was in love with Jolie."

"Were you going to tell me that you're not coming back from Santa Fe?"

"I haven't said that."

"But are you coming back?"

"I don't know."

"Well, *I* know. How is it that I know and you don't? You're not."

Around five-fifteen, I started shivering from the hugeness of what was befalling me—but it wasn't life without a husband. It was just the idea of single parenthood, figuring out how to tell Hope and Abbie, how to get a life going again. Never mind all the temporary stuff I was already being expected to deal with: getting the furnace fixed, shoveling the walk, getting the garbage cans hauled to the curb and back again. All that stuff of lightbulbs, creaky floors, radiator noises. The computer modem! The weird light switch to the hall light that sometimes needs to be taken apart—how on earth do you fix that? What if the basement floods again? Who has the Wet/Dry Vac we borrowed that time? This was going to be my life now *forever.* And who was going to love me? I couldn't think of that then. Only now I think of that.

And so it comes down to this, I thought then. Vacuum cleaners and light switches. But along with that feeling was a kind of exhilaration over the difficult drama of it all. I'll admit to that. I would be the heroine of my own life again, picking up the pieces, bravely going on. People would help me. Someday men might think I was attractive again, once my eyes weren't so swollen from crying.

Around six, he said we should make love, just for old time's sake—and reluctantly I let him touch me, let his hand reach over to my breast, slide lower down my belly. Sex had always been so good for us, and maybe I thought I could hurt him by making him remember that, all the times we'd been carried off by the sheer magnitude of feeling, those huge crescendos of orgasms. Did that stand for nothing? Could he just have that with everyone, even stupid Jolie?

But then I couldn't do it, and I cried, and then I slapped him because it suddenly mattered very much that *that very night* he had put his thing inside Jolie. He just lay there and let me hit him, without moving. That was a really weird feeling—that I might keep on hitting him and hitting him, building up to the kind of frenzy that leads women to finally kill men. But I was outside it all, at the same time, watching this other Maz having these intense reactions.

And then at six-thirty, he was gone. Two red taillights heading down Orange Street, toward I-95. Shivering, I called up Hannah, and she came over and we made tea and cried together, and Hannah said we should change around the furniture and take down all his stuff that I had never liked, purge the place. We carted his stuff down to the basement—all his nice wool sweaters I'd given him for Christmas presents, and his good down jacket, and his sheet music—and, as I hurled his stuff into a corner, I said a little prayer for extra mildew to come and get it all.

"You're praying to the god of mildew?" Hannah said. "That's good."

"Come, mildew, and take these sweaters and jackets!" we screamed together. Then I looked over at Hannah and thought, You are going to have to take care of me and nurse me back to some kind of feeling, because right now I don't have the slightest idea of how to run a life. I didn't say it out loud, but she seemed to understand that she had that role now. She made us more tea and gave me the explanation to tell the children when they woke up, and invited us to come over for dinner that night, which she said would be the worst night.

"After this, it will all get better, day by day," she said.

But I knew better. I knew I was deeply ill and lost, completely untethered, and that I was going to have to learn how to do everything all over again.

# 4

I would swear that five minutes later, the alarm goes off. I leap in midair, throw my left arm at the buzzing sound, and somehow manage to sweep the lamp, a glass of water, and the clock radio to the floor. There's a deafening crash, and I wait to see if I've died of electrocution. Grandmama always said you could die from water spilling on the electrical appliances, but it's possible she just said that to keep me from putting the radio on the side of the tub, the way Lucille liked to do.

The buzzing keeps going, from the floor. I sigh. Not dead.

"Stop that noise!" shouts Hope from the other side of the bed. "It's night!"

I haul myself out of the covers and turn off the alarm, and manage to put the lamp and clock back on the bedside table. It's not night. It's 5:25. Time to get up and go to work.

"Hope," I say. I turn on the light, and suddenly it's light enough to perform minor outpatient surgery in there. Hope pulls the pillow over her head, and who can blame her? I reach over and rub her shoulder. "Hope, honey, I'm going to go get in the shower, and when I come out, you have to get dressed. Okay? Hope. Do you hear me?"

Silence.

I kiss her neck. "When you hear the water turn off, I want you to go get your clothes on. All right? Will you do what I say?"

Longer and deeper silence.

"Hope."

"It's night."

"It's not night. I wish it was night. Come on, sweetie. I'll go first and then you."

"I hate my life."

I want to say, *I know. I kind of hate mine, too.* But I don't think you're allowed to say that to your children. You're supposed to protect them from realizing how excruciating things can get and that you have no control. Of course, I think, there were times when Lucille probably said that to me thirty or forty times a day when I was little, during those times when she got sick of telling fortunes or putting up with stupid carnival owners, and hanging out with bad men—everything her life consisted of back then. Maybe that's how I know not to say it to my own kids.

I give up on Hope, and go off to the shower, where just possibly I can wake myself up. Mornings have been hideous since Lenny left. When you're in charge, as I am, of baking all the breads for the store, you have to get to work no later than 6:15 if the loaves are going to get done in time. This wasn't so terrible when Lenny was still here; I'd wake up and slip out before anyone woke up, and he got the girls off to school and day care. But since he's been gone, I've had to wake them up early and take them with me. I've even fixed up a corner of the bakery kitchen—Barry, my boss, calls it a daughter nest—with quilts and toys and books, and they hang out there while I get the dough ready.

Sometimes Abbie falls back to sleep there, or else she cheerfully plays with the bread pans and a piece of dough I give her—but for Hope, who remembers family life as a rosy walk in the park and sees every change as more evidence that we're in dire straits—going to the bakery on the dark, cold mornings has been the equivalent of the Bataan Death March. Okay, so it's not ideal, but it's only four days a week—I have Fridays off for my day care turn and any errands I can't do during the week—and besides that, I can't see any other way. Anyway, as I've tried to explain to her, isn't there something sort of heroic and romantic about it: eating breakfast alone together in the warm bakery kitchen, next to the big black iron stove? We get yesterday's warmed-over rolls slathered with butter—and then, at 8:15, we walk outside and Hope catches her school bus right at the store's front door. We're practically the first people to be downtown each day—and isn't that exciting in itself, having the city to ourselves?

By the time she gets on the bus, the bread has almost come to its second rising, and as soon as Barry gets in at nine, I dash over to the co-op day care with Abbie and hurry right back to get the loaves in the oven.

Hey, it's far from perfect, but it's a life.

Most mornings, with almost full-tilt effort, I can just about get everybody out the door on time, but this morning, Hope is having none of it, and I start to feel that old familiar rise of panic in the back of my throat. When I get out of the shower, I find her curled into a little ball at the bottom of my bed, underneath the covers, so I try to tease her out, which sometimes works. "Come on, Hopey. I see you down there!" Putting on my bra and my black sweater and long denim skirt. "I see you hiding from me! Let's see how fast you can run to your room and get dressed."

"Stop treating me like a baby," she says.

She's right. I was using my coaxing-Abbie voice. I switch gears. "Then, if you don't want to be treated like a baby, get out of the covers and go get dressed," I tell her. I try to fluff my hair with my fingers. No time for the blow dryer this morning. "Come on. I'm going to get Abbie up. You have to move, darling."

Muffled, from under the blankets: "I hate my life. I told you that."

"I know you did, but there's nothing more we can do about it right now. We'll talk about how to fix your life when we come home tonight."

"There's no such thing as fixing lives," she says. She comes out from under the covers and studies me. "You know, you look a little bit fat in that sweater."

"I do?"

"Yes. You do." She flops down and puts her chin in her hand. "I think that man from last night probably won't be interested in you if you wear it."

I look in the mirror—can't help myself—and she shrieks, starts bouncing on the bed on her butt. "See? *See?* So he's not just a friend, is he? He *is* your boyfriend. I knew it. I knew it! I called it! I called it!"

"He isn't my boyfriend. Come on now. Please, honey. I need you to go get dressed—"

"Oh, but he is! Even though you're still married to Daddy, you have a boyfriend right now. I know it."

"Hope," I say. "Come on, *please.*"

"Don't tell me he's not. If he wasn't your boyfriend, why did he come over to see you, huh? Tell me *that.* And he came over at *night* when you thought we were sleeping."

"Look. He's a friend. He told you that. And he came at night because that's when he could get away from his work. Now come *on.*"

Hannah, who has three kids, once told me that she counted how many times she said "Come on" in the morning before school, and it was thirty-seven times. I told her that I easily say that in just the first ten minutes, to Hope alone. In fact, I say "Come on" so many times that I'm afraid one day I'll get stuck saying it, and won't be able to say anything else for the rest of the day, just a constant stream of "Come on"s until somebody slaps me silly. This may be the day. "Come on," I say once more.

I go across the hall into Abbie's room and stroke her silky blond hair, pulling her out of sleep. She turns over on her back, smiles, rubs her eyes, and lifts her arms up to be carried. She smells just like sleep, a mix of soap and oatmeal and maybe some melting crayons mixed in. She has to sleep with a deluxe box of sixty-four Crayola crayons, an umbrella, and a pink ruler on her pillow, she says. When I pick her up, she rests her baby head on my shoulder. We make our way over to the dresser, and while balancing her on my right hip, I manage to open the second drawer and look at the jumble of clothes inside.

Hope is standing at the door, her eyes filled up with tears. "You know that's not true. He was here because he didn't know you already have a husband—and he came here in the night because he didn't want to see me and Abbie!"

"Sweet honey Hopey," I say, and for a moment I feel as though my words are just flailing about helplessly in my head, and I have no idea what order to put them in so we can get her dressed and get out of the house. What if we have to stay here all morning long, debating my romantic status? And what if in the end I crack and say that *damn it, yes, I do want a boyfriend. I deserve a life!* What then would happen? She'd probably call the Child Abuse Hotline, and we'd probably have to get a team of psychotherapists over here immediately.

I shift Abbie in my arms. "Hope, honey, I am begging you to get ready for school right now. Here, Abbie, I'm going to put you down now, and I want you to go pee. Okay? Now, listen to me, Hope, and listen good. I promise you that I don't have a boyfriend, and I promise you that Dan Briggs did not come over here for any reason other than to talk about living in the city and opening up his practice. Now can we please move forward on this day before I get to work so late that the good people of New Haven don't have any bread to eat, and Barry fires me?"

"What's a practice?"

"A medical practice. He's a doctor." I pick out blue corduroy pants and a white sweatshirt with the Teletubbies on it for Abbie to wear. Blue socks—well, okay, a blue one and a white one. She doesn't care if they match. In fact, she considers it an amazing coincidence if her two socks match. I wonder if Dan feels that way about *his* socks, too. Or was that a mistake—those unmatched socks? A casualty of recently moving.

"Ohhhhh! So he's a *doctor*! Moving up in the world, I see."

"Okay, now you're making me mad. I'm going to count to ten. . . . One . . ."

She gets up and starts inching her way across the room.

"Two," I say. I go back to my room and put on lipstick and then rub it into my cheeks. The hurried woman's blush. It's now 5:58. "Girls! We have to leave in five minutes! Abbie! Are you done in the bathroom?"

"Yes, I'm done!" she calls back.

"Okay, sweetcakes, that's good. Now this morning let's just take you to the bakery in your p.j.s and bring your clothes along. You can get dressed there. Did you see your clothes that I picked out? On the bed?" I see my tube of mascara lying underneath my dresser and get it out and quickly put it on. It clumps on my eyelashes like smears of tar. No time to even it out.

There's a moment of quiet, and then Abbie's little voice pipes up, "I don't like these clothes. I'll get more ones."

"Honey, could today you just bring the ones I picked out for you? Please?"

"Well, okay," she says. "But I want to wear my pink slip, too. On the top of my clothes."

"Slips go underneath skirts and dresses, honey."

"But you can't *see* them underneath," she says. "I want to wear my slip on top. It's pretty that way."

"Abbie, I don't think—"

"Mommy, I *haf to*!"

Hope is still standing there, staring at me. "Mommy," she says, and I stop and look at her in the mirror.

"What?"

"Tell me the truth. He's really, really not your boyfriend?"

I sigh loudly. "No."

"And you don't have a boyfriend?"

"Hope, why are you doing this to me? Go get ready for school."

She stares at me so hard I feel myself almost flinching. "You do really look very fat in that sweater," she says. "It's almost too tight for you."

By the time the school bus has come for Hope, and I have dropped off Abbie at day care—wearing the pink slip over her corduroy pants and shirt *and* her winter coat—I think I have said "Come on" seventy-five more times, have promised that Dan is not my boyfriend at least ten more times, and the little pulse near my temples has become a major tension headache, possibly a brain tumor, and I am thinking I should probably just go right over to the hospital and schedule myself for an MRI so we can know sooner rather than later. Barry has left me a note that, in addition to the usual loaves of bread, he'd like to start the week off with some carrot-carob muffins and perhaps a celery-cilantro-curry soup for the lunch rush. "Everything starts with C!!!" he wrote. "It's a C day! Maybe we should think about having alphabet theme days. Try to come up with some D menus!"

I would like to go out and explain to him that, starting with C or not, none of those flavors actually *goes* together, but that would simply mean that every conversation I've had today has resulted in an argument, and I don't think I have the energy at this exact moment. So I get to work, shuddering to think about the D menu. What could it be— dandelions sautéed with dill and dates? Dehydrated doughnuts?

It's almost a relief to settle into the huge, old-fashioned industrial-sized kitchen, which now that I've been here over a year, still doesn't quite feel like home, but doesn't feel as intimidating as it once did, either. I hunt up all the ingredients, then stir them in the huge stainless steel mixing bowl while I sip herbal tea. All that mixing and blending of compliant, inert edible things impresses me, the way they gradually give up their lumps and agree to get along together. Since Lenny, I am in danger of seeing metaphors everywhere. The store is crazy busy this morning; I can hear Barry with his booming voice giving advice about vitamins and his new line of cosmetic supplements—and I turn on the Mozart CD, tie on my chef's apron, and settle at once into the familiar rhythm of kneading, pouring, and mixing.

At around eleven, my cell phone rings and it's—who else?— Lucille.

"I just realized somethin'," she says. "I have been proposed to by twenty-seven men. And that's not countin' the ones where a man has just said, 'Boy, if I were your husband . . .' I'm talkin' *serious* proposals, darlin'."

"Fantastic," I say. I look warily over at the bowl of dough that is oozing over the top of the rim. Time to smash it down.

"How many have you had?" she says. "Tell the truth."

"I'll get my accountants right on it, and get back to you at the end of the day."

She laughs. "Oh, *you*. Now I also didn't count the men whose fortunes I had just told, because I think they were mostly jokin' when they asked if I was the woman they were supposed to meet. You know?"

It's my turn to say something, but I'm busy now, fisting the wad of dough as hard as I can. It loses its puffiness all at once, retreats back to its real essence. I like to think I'm helping it. I tuck it in again, put the towel over it, and push it back on the counter.

"The guides have told me that Lenny was your only proposal. Can that be right?" she says.

"Actually," I say, "I don't know if the guides mentioned *this* to you or not, but I'm at work right now."

"That job isn't the right job for you anyhow," she says.

I sigh. "It pays the bills. And I gotta go."

"Wait! You can take a minute. They give you breaks. I just want to know what you think this mornin' about my news, now that you had a chance to sleep on it." She laughs and does her little clicking thing. "Did I tell you that he's the richest man who ever proposed?"

"Oops, know what? My battery is beeping. It's running low."

She sniffs. "You always say that. Can't you keep that thing charged?"

"Beep," I say. "I've got to hang up."

She starts talking faster now. "I don't even think you said congratulations. That's all I want, is a little bit of you bein' impressed. I did it! I've arrived!"

"Congratulations," I say.

"It doesn't mean anything if I have to prompt you."

"Beeeeeep," I say. And I click off the phone just as Barry comes barreling in with tomorrow's special orders for loaves of barley bread. Good, I think. This means I can spend the rest of the afternoon smashing dough. I'm no longer emotionally fit to deal with the counter crowd.

Outside, the temperature falls all day long. I hear customers talking about a twenty-degree drop as they come inside, stamping their feet on the wooden floor. Gusts keep slamming the back door to the kitchen, but I go and open it again and again, holding my face in the cool wind and looking up at the gray, threatening sky. At three-thirty, I sit down and have a cup of soup, and then I put this evening's loaves into the big black gas oven, including a spicy tomato and onion loaf that I've made to take to Hannah. Somewhere, I think I hear Dan Briggs's voice and smooth down my apron, thinking that at any moment he'll show up at the kitchen door. Perhaps he'll come in and sweep me up; we'll kiss. I'll start to tell him again that my life is too complicated, but he'll put his finger over my lips to quiet me, and then we'll hurry off to the pantry, fumbling with buttons and zippers, breathing heavy, our hearts slamming against each other as we rush to love.

But—not much of a surprise—he doesn't come back to the kitchen, and later Barry doesn't even mention that he was there. Maybe it was somebody else, after all.

# 5

I finish cleaning up the store by four-thirty and head over to Hannah's house, where Abbie and Hope go after day care and school. Hannah and Michael have three kids, a boy and two girls, and both of their daughters are the same ages as mine, so we've had this system ever since Lenny left: Hannah picks up Abbie from day care and Hope from the bus stop, and takes them home with her and feeds them afternoon snack. Lexie and Hope get started on their homework, and Abbie and Rachel play dress-ups, and then—the best part, the thing I live for lately—when I come in, Hannah and I sit for a while in her warm kitchen and drink a glass of wine and talk.

Today, I can't wait to get there. I love that moment when I walk inside, and the house smells just like it always does: a mixture of Hannah's oil paints and whatever's cooking on the stove, along with a lovely, musty wood-floor smell mixed with scented candles and patchouli.

Today when I come in, Lexie and Hope come racing down the front stairs into the dark, narrow front hall, still crammed with bicycles from the summer. Hope's still thinking about Dan's visit, I can tell just by the look she gives me when I come in—cloudy with a chance of tantrums, as Lenny used to say. She brushes past me, and wiggles away when I try to give her a kiss on the cheek.

"How'd your day go, Hope?" I ask, and she says in a singsong, "Terrible."

"How was the fractions test?" Once we'd gotten to the Golden

Granary this morning, she'd remembered that she had a test she hadn't studied for. There had been wailing and gnashing of teeth. And I had been late getting the muffins ready because I had to stop and test her on math. Then, when we were standing out in the cold waiting for the bus, tears started rolling down her face and she told me she has no friends.

"Everyone loves you," I told her, but she just gave me a sorrowful look that broke my heart down to its core. What could she be talking about?

Now she's glaring at me again. "How should I know how the test was? What do you think, that they just give them right back? Haven't you ever gone to school?"

I've opened my mouth and am about to say something in my own defense when Hannah comes out from the kitchen, smiling and drying her hands on a dishtowel. "Hey, Maz! Oh my God, what is that divine thing you're holding—bread? You wonderful thing, you! Hey, girls, why don't you grab some crackers and cheese and take them back upstairs while you do your homework? Maz and I are going to collapse and talk for a while."

"Oh, riiiight. You have to talk about that *man* who came over last night—the handsome *doctor*," says Hope, and Lexie just laughs and puts her hands on Hope's shoulders and gently chugs her to the kitchen, where they grab a handful of Ritz crackers, and then back down the hall and up the stairs. Hope manages not to meet my eyes, even when I reach over and stroke her arm.

"God, we need wine, and then you have to tell me everything," says Hannah as I settle into her white wicker rocker in the kitchen. "Don't leave out one little detail." She always says we need wine—I love that about her—except for the really bad days when she's been known to say, "God, we need Chivas Regal." She clears the mail, some catalogs, and a couple of kids' backpacks off the table and pours us red wine into two smudged glasses, which is another thing I love about her: she's far too distracted most days to care if the dishes get really clean, or if the clutter in her house stays at more than a passably manageable level. Abbie comes in from the living room and snuggles up next to me. She's still wearing the pink slip over her corduroy pants. She tells me that everybody at day care said she was beautiful, and they all wanted her slip for themselves.

I let her clamber up on my lap and bury my face in her neck, breathing in the paste-and-crayons smell of her. But then Rachel calls her away, and they scamper upstairs, hauling the cat with them. He's going to have to try on some baby clothes, Rachel tells me. I hear them giggling upstairs, and next to that, a low, rumbling sound. Hannah says that noise is Evan, her twelve-year-old son, riding a skateboard.

"In the house," I say. "Fascinating."

"It's winter, Maz," she says. "This is why we can't ever get the floors refinished—because how would people ever get ready for the spring skateboarding season?" She redoes her masses of strawberry blond curls that have come loose from a denim scrunchy—yanking them back and rewinding them into the piece of cloth. I'd give anything for that hair; mine is limp and faded blond and most days won't do anything I want, even hold a barrette. But Hannah hates her hair, because it's thick and opinionated, she says, and too wild to just hang free; she's always having to shove it into some kind of device. Today she's wearing a long maroon corduroy skirt and a dark green Dartmouth sweatshirt. And bunny slippers. I know that if you looked under the skirt, she'd have on leggings and another pair of long pants, too. Hannah is always cold in her drafty old farmhouse, always bundling herself up in more and more layers, which she sheds during the summer, like a butterfly coming out of its cocoon. In April, she says, people are always amazed to see that she doesn't weigh two hundred pounds.

"Well?" she says to me. "Spill. The suspense is killing me."

I take a deep breath. "You're going to be so disappointed, but the fact is that he hates me after all, and it's over."

She laughs.

"Go ahead and laugh," I say, "but he left my house so fast last night, he was practically a blur. There are skid marks on the kitchen floor. *And,* may I add, he did not even bother with the lie about how he was going to call me again. He just said, 'I hate you, and I hope that you will forget that I ever put my lips on yours, and let's try to go on with our lives and never cross paths again.'"

"No, he didn't."

"Well, I read between the lines. That's what he wanted to say."

"Ahh, what he *wanted* to say."

"He would have said it, if he could have found the power of speech," I tell her. "As it was, he was so aghast at the way I have to live my life that all he could think of was just to run to his car."

"No, I know that's not it. I am quite certain that he really, really likes you."

"Yeah, well, we'll see. The way we'll know that he really likes me is that he'll be sending over a social worker to get my whole family some therapy. Other than that, I'd say he's a goner."

She laughs. "Okay, that's it. You have to stay for dinner. I can't possibly do the amount of reconvincing you're going to need in just these short predinner hours." She stares inside the refrigerator. "We're having this leftover barbecued chicken from two nights ago, and I'll make my broccoli and garlic thingie, and I think there's enough of this rice dish to go around, too. Oh, and carrots and dip. And your bread."

"Hannah, you're always having to feed us!" I am fake-protesting. Really, I feel relieved. Not only do I not have to face my dark, cold house with its jumbled-up cabinets and leftovers from hell, but Hannah is going to do her best to reconvince me that Dan Briggs actually does care about me. She and I have already spent approximately one thousand hours dissecting and analyzing the three infamous kisses, as well as every inflection of his voice. That's how pathetic and boring my postmarried life has been: a man smiles at me in the health food store, takes me for a walk, and then—through some accident or miracle—puts his lips on mine, and Hannah and I can't stop talking about what it all might mean. Besides, she met him once at the Golden Granary, and she swears he adores me, just from some look she saw in his eye. That's Hannah for you.

"So what in the hell happened?" she says as she thrusts some carrots and a peeler toward me, so that I can get to work.

Amid the scraping of carrots, I tell her about my insane conversation with him, when we wasted valuable minutes of our lives discussing the benefits of various types of flour products, and how if anyone had told me that was going to be the best part of the evening, I would have gone in and banged my head against the sink or something.

"You're not going to tell me that the flour thing," she interrupts me, "was enough to run him off." She's arranging pieces of chicken on a roasting pan.

"No, no, that was just the practice trouble," I say, taking a deep breath. I tell her about the Madame Lucille call, the sixth husband lining up in the wings, the messages from Marv and Irv (Hannah insists we call them Moe and Schmoe), then the way I ended up blurting out the whole horrible story of my childhood on the road—and then even admitted that I hate whole wheat flour.

"This sounds good," she says. "Honest. Refreshing."

And so *then* I have to tell her about Hope getting up and scaring him off, and the call she may have made to Lenny, and how she's claiming Lenny's coming back—and oh yeah, then how Lucille says *she's* coming, too, because Hope needs her. Oh yeah, and then how I went hysterical and had to practically have CPR.

I'm exhausted when I finish.

"He's not gone," she pronounces at the end of all of it. "First of all, you really are a very normal person, and anyone would find it fascinating that you led this interesting life when you were a kid. You know what I did when I was a kid? I roller-skated to my friend Lisa's house, and we watched *My Mother the Car* episodes. The most exciting thing that ever happened to me was that I got to sell Girl Scout cookies once a year outside the grocery store, and a man in a beat-up Buick once tried to pick me up. Do you think that story would exactly keep a man riveted through a whole evening?"

"I don't know." I munch on a carrot. "The fact is, you're happily married, and I'm not, so obviously your story has won the jackpot."

Just then there's an awful crash upstairs and Hope and Lexie start screaming at Evan, who's evidently managed to break something, possibly all the windows in the upstairs rooms, from the sound of it—and Hannah ends up having to go up there to sort everything out. I hear them all yelling, Hannah's voice being the only one with the slightest bit of sanity to it. After a few minutes, I get up and put the pan of chicken in the oven and pour the bowl of rice into a saucepan, add some chicken stock to it and some scallions that I find in the vegetable drawer. Hannah is negotiating with everyone to be calm, pick up the broken stuff, and put the skateboard away for a while; Evan and Lexie are shouting at each other. I hate to say it, but it's nice to hear other people's kids having a meltdown. Especially *married* people's kids—people who have such a healthy and affectionate life together as Hannah and Michael do.

When Hannah comes back down, she's shaking her head. "Why people reproduce themselves, I do not know," she says. "You never think it's going to lead to this."

"What did it lead to this time?"

"Never mind." She shakes her head again and looks at me. "Now back to you. Where were we? Oh, yeah. Dan isn't going to pan out, according to you."

"It's for the best," I say, straightening myself up. "Really. Judging from the way Hope went all psycho on me last night, I'd say the last thing she's ready for is for me to hook up with somebody. I'm calling it quits."

"Oh, good, so you can be celibate for the rest of your life, to please Hope. An excellent plan."

"Well, I just can't see harming her anymore. She was really and truly upset. And you saw her today—she's a walking bruise. She can't handle anything. You should have seen us this morning. I thought we were going to have to call in the mental health authorities before we could even get out of the house."

"I know, I know." Hannah is thinking. "Where's the chicken?" she says suddenly, and I point to the oven. "Thanks," she says. She plops down in the chair and looks directly at me. "You know, I think we have to rethink this whole Hope thing."

"What do you mean? I believe it's too late to send her back."

"I mean, letting her call the shots. I've been giving this a lot of thought, and I think what's happening here is that Hope is confused about your marriage. I think she'll actually be better off when you are in a relationship with somebody—even if you're just having a secret fling that she doesn't know about." She sees my face and says, "No, really. That's probably why she's fantasizing that Lenny's coming home; she wants to know for herself what the boundaries are."

"Hmm," I say.

"So when you start acting for sure that you're done with Lenny, then she'll adapt."

"So I should pursue this poor Dan Briggs to the end of the earth," I say. "You know, now that I think of it, maybe it's *me* who isn't really ready."

"Sweetheart, I don't think I've ever seen anybody who needs a fling worse than you do right now. You may be clinically in need of male attention."

"I'm terrified."

"Of course you're terrified. But just think of this: you're going to fall in love again, and it's going to be the most wonderful thing for you— and for both your girls."

I know that she's probably right, but I also know that she's incredibly optimistic about love. How could she not be? What in the world has Hannah ever wanted that she couldn't have? For one thing, she's married to the world's nicest man, a guy who restores barns for a living during the day, for God's sake—*restores* old things instead of knocking them down—and then he comes home each night and helps their three kids with their homework and stares adoringly at Hannah's every move. He thinks her paintings are the most beautiful things ever created on the earth, and he finds everything she says to be full of insights and nuances—which, okay, everything she says *is* like that, but I've never seen a husband who keeps recognizing that. Call me jaded about marriage, but I frankly don't think it works all that well for most people.

I sigh and take another sip of wine. She puts on a Bonnie Raitt CD, which for a moment drowns out the babble of children upstairs. Sitting there basking in her family life, I feel somewhat like a poor kid with her nose pressed up against the window. I have never had this for myself, not as a child, not even once through my years of marriage to Lenny. Never felt as secure as I do now, just sitting here in her rocking chair looking at her rows of cookbooks, her bread box, her old chipped porcelain sink and blue gingham curtains, the blue pottery teacups hanging on hooks, the crocheted rug, the worn wood floor. How will I ever find this in my own life, I wonder.

Then Michael comes home, brushing snow off his overcoat, and the flavor changes, but we gladly make room for him. He stands at the countertop, rifling through the mail while he tells us about a barn in North Branford he loves, and she teases him about how barns get him all hot—and he says, "Excuse us, Maz," and kisses her passionately. "It's *not* barns," he says when he's finished kissing her.

I watch them. I can't help it. Their marriage is legendary in the day care. I overheard one of the other women saying to her once, "If you and Michael ever got divorced, the rest of us would have to get divorced, too, just in honor of the thing." Instead of looking pleased, though, Hannah had said quietly, "Oh, you have no idea what it's like being married to Mr. Perfection."

Then, just before all the dinner chaos starts up—we can hear Michael herding the kids upstairs and forcing them to wash their hands, which, from the sounds of it, is like a stint at the elephant cage of the zoo—she suddenly turns to me and says in a thoughtful voice, "You know, I've been thinking about what you said, and for some reason, I just have a feeling that Madame Lucille coming might be the very best thing for Hope. You know, a grandmother can be a wonderful influence."

*"What?"* I can't help laughing. I hadn't even been sure Hannah had heard the part about Lucille coming. "Are you crazy? Lucille is a narcissist with borderline personality disorder, and she uses people—"

"She used *you.* But you're her daughter, and that's the most difficult relationship there is. And maybe she's changed, anyhow. She's certainly flamboyant and exciting, and that might just give Hope a big charge right now when she's so sad."

"I don't know . . . I think Lucille is criminally weird. Did I tell you she called me at work today, just because she needed to remind me that I haven't had as many marriage proposals as she's had?"

"And *you*! Sweetie, you've got to snap out of this funk you're in," she says. "You need a fling so badly that you don't even *remember* what it's like. If you ask me, I think you ought to go home tonight and call up that Dan Briggs and beg him for another chance."

I laugh. "That's so easy for you to say," I tell her. "You'll still be married to Michael a hundred and forty-seven years from now."

"Oh, boy! Doesn't that make *me* the lucky one!" she says, and then, before I can figure out just what she means, all hell breaks loose. Hannah's family and my kids have arrived for that madness called dinner, and in the jumble of passing plates and cleaning up knocked-over milk glasses, Hope looks up and actually smiles at me. I blow her an experimental kiss, and my God, she blows it back.

# 6

*Two days later,* I'm heading over to the bank on my lunch hour when I see Dan Briggs heading down the sidewalk in my direction. My immediate instinct, which I manage to carry out with impeccable split-second timing, is to duck into the Starbucks and hope the yuppies will simply enfold me in their mob, hiding me from view. But wouldn't you know that Dan turns into the doorway, too, and despite my graceful effort to drop to the floor suddenly on the pretense of picking up a piece of lint on the carpet, he sees me. In fact, he nearly steps on me. This gives me a chance to be eye-level once again with his socks, which, I am pleased to see, still do not match. This time one is black and one is an argyle pattern with blues and maroons.

"Oh, hi," he says, as if nothing seems weird about my being crouched on the floor. I stand up. "Why, it's the fortune-teller's daughter. How are you?"

"Good," I say. "There was this *thing* on the carpet, and I thought people might trip on it." I hold up the piece of dangerous lint I've retrieved. He frowns at it.

"Then I go and almost trip on *you,*" he says. "Are you all right?"

"Oh, yes, fine. You didn't hurt me or anything."

We stand there. "Good," he says at last. "Well, that's good. So—how's life? Did Hope recover from her trauma the other night?"

"Oh, yes. Of course. Listen, I'm so sorry about that strange evening. The whole thing could not have been more stressful, could it? My crazy mother and the long phone call, and then Hope—"

"No, no," he says. "Don't apologize. Please. It's life. And—so"—he looks around, as though we have to be careful—"is your husband on his way back?"

"No," I say, shaking my head. "I don't think that was ever really an option. He's told me a million times he doesn't want to come back. Hope kind of imagines things sometimes. My friend who was a social worker says that kids do this when they don't know what the adults in their lives are really doing. They kind of make up scenarios, just to test the waters, you might say. And Hope is kind of an emotional kid, so it makes sense that . . ." I am aware that I'm babbling. People are crowding to get into the Starbucks, and we get pushed over to the corner, next to the sugars and straws and napkins and creamers. I stop talking. There's no place for Dan's arm except to lean it on the wall above my shoulder.

"Listen," he says. We're now practically pinned together against the wall by a sudden mob that is desperate for accessories for their coffees. "What do you say we get together again sometime? Maybe this time go out for dinner."

I close my eyes, and take a deep breath. *No. The answer has to be NO.* "Dan, really. You see what my life is like. I'd like to say that what happened the other night isn't the way I really live, but it's pretty much the way I really live."

"I know that, Maz. I figured that part out."

"I can't believe you even want to do this."

"Well, frankly, between your mother and your daughter, I'm scared to death, but you're the first person I've met who seems the least bit like someone who has a real life."

"Oh, it's real, all right."

"I can see that."

"If it scared you then, you'll probably be completely terrified when you see what else there is."

He laughs, a low, easy sound. And he says in a voice so low and sexy that I feel my knees just slightly buckling, "Unless it's a box of rattlesnakes, I think I can handle it."

"I have to go really, really slow," I say. "I'm not handling things so well."

"Glacially," he says. "My favorite speed."

There's this: what if I end up really, really liking him and we get together, and then Hope turns out to be a difficult teenager, and he comes to me one day five or six years from now and tells me that he can't see his way clear to raising her one more second, and that he's leaving? What then? What about that?

"I don't know," I say. I am wishing Starbucks pumped more oxygen into its sugar-and-cream corner.

"Can you . . . um, get a sitter or something? We could go out to dinner, if you wanted. Like civilized people. We could talk. Just talk."

"Look," I say. *Are you going to sail into my life and then decide it's so difficult, you can't stick around?* I clear my throat. "One thing. About the food thing. I've gotta know if you just eat health food. Because I need to tell you right now that I can't bear tempeh or anything like that."

Now he does laugh. "Ah, yes. The queen of white flour. Who would have guessed?"

"I'm a mole in a health food store."

He laughs. "I swear I never eat health food unless one of my patients might be watching. Is there a good Mexican place around here?"

And so, after a moment of fumbling with calendars and his Palm Pilot while people jostle us with their elbows, it's settled. I'll get a sitter, and we'll go to a Mexican restaurant on Saturday night. I walk back to the Golden Granary on rubbery legs. For the rest of the day, I'm on the verge of a nervous breakdown. Sounds keep startling me—I leap into the air when Siobhan starts the mixer, and nearly pass out when Barry brings a tray of dirty cups back to the dishwasher. But then I realize the scariest sound of all is my own heart just flopping around in my chest, hoping for something good to happen.

# 7

"Honey, does Lenny use that Viagra stuff?" Lucille is on the phone, several days later. I'm actually cooking supper for once, instant macaroni and cheese and frozen chicken nuggets, and listening to Hope and Abbie, who are in the living room having the sort of play-fight that is steadily escalating into violence. Soon I'm probably going to have to intervene, but not just yet.

"What did you say?" I prop the phone under my chin and stir like hell to make sure orange cheese powder gets on every sticky noodle.

"Lenny, honey. Pay attention. Does. He. Use. Viagra?"

"Now how should I know?"

"You *were* married to him."

"Why don't you call him up and ask him yourself? Or ask the spirit guides. Don't tell me Marvin and Irv aren't keeping their erection records up to date."

"Jesus Christ," she says. "You're certainly on a hair trigger."

"I just don't see why you need to know."

"Oh, Masden." The lighter starts its vigorous clicking. "When are you gonna start bein' nicer to me? Honey, I pray every day that you and I'll repair our relationship. When I was about your age, I really started to appreciate my mama, and . . ."

I take the chicken nuggets out of the oven. They are done to a mellow, toasty brown just like on the package—a triumph for me, who is usually so distracted that the damn things burn. "What," I ask her, "does Lenny using Viagra possibly have to do with you or me—or even more impossibly, what does it have to do with *your* mother?"

She talks fast. "Well, Harold, darlin', is havin' a little *problem* in that area, if you know what I mean, and even though he's very willin' to go on Viagra, he's also a little bit worried about the side effects. So I wanted to know if Lenny had any side effects."

In the living room, Hope has started to screech, "Because you're a baby, that's why!" And Abbie is saying, "I'm not a baby! I'm not a baby! I'm not a baby!"

"Of course," Lucille's saying, "as *I* explained, the side effects of him *not* bein' on Viagra could be pretty bad, too. I'm still a young woman, you know, and I . . ."

I slide four chicken nuggets onto each of our paper plates and dump a wad of perfectly evenly oranged macaroni on there, too. "Lenny, to *my* knowledge, never needed Viagra, Lucille. But you raise a good point, no pun intended, and I, for one, think it's high time we found out whether he's having good erections. I mean, what if the women of Santa Fe are being deprived of his full powers? I gotta tell you that has *really* been on my mind lately, in between trying to figure out if the goddamn macaroni is done and if the deck Lenny half-built before he left is going to stay on the back of the house or if it's going to fall apart during the snowstorms we keep having."

She slams down the phone.


"I think we should have a new rule," I tell Hope and Abbie at supper. I have a new calm voice, which I am very proud of. After Lucille hung up, I had lined up all the paper plates under the stove light to keep warm, and made myself take ten long, deep yoga-type breaths, the type any therapist would be pleased to declare restful and relaxing. Let the cheese clot and be cold, and the grease congeal on the nuggets. It is much more important to do restorative breathing when you think you can't talk without screaming.

"I think," I say slowly to the girls, "that we should try to do three nice things for each other every day. Because sometimes we forget that we're really each other's family and that we love each other very much."

"I do nice things for Hope, but she just calls me a baby," says Abbie.

She gives Hope a baleful look and shoves another huge spoonful of macaroni into her mouth.

"I do not. I only call you a baby when you're wrecking my stuff."

"Hope, I never wreck your stuff. You say I wreck it if I just look at it, and that's not fair. I get to look at anything in the whole house." Abbie always talks slowly, like somebody who's not going to get rattled no matter what.

"Well, whatever," I say. "What if we did nice things for each other, and then the bad parts that happen might not seem so bad?"

"I think three things is too many," says Hope. "It's not really *sensible* to do that many in one day. I might have to stay up too late to get them all done."

"But lots of things could count," I tell her. "Like if you say, 'Excuse me' when you sneeze, even that could be a nice thing."

"What if I sneezed, and I said, 'Excuse me, excuse me, excuse me,' would that count for the whole day?"

I allow myself a moment to wonder why I was so adamantly in favor of having children; couldn't someone have warned me? But then I smile at her across the table and allow myself another really deep breath. "We have to think of the spirit of the rule, not how to get them over with."

"I don't know," she says.

"Well, I'm going to tell you some nice things I already saw you do today," I tell her. "I noticed that when we got home from Hannah's today, you finished up your spelling without me even asking you to. And I also noticed that when Hannah asked Lexie to feed Bustercat, you were the one who opened up the can and found the cat fork."

She rolls her eyes. "They don't *have* a cat fork. They use the same fork for feeding the cat as they do for their own food. Which I think is very yucky, and I told Lexie they have to stop it."

"Ewww, that's so grossie!" says Abbie. "Cat food on the people forks?"

"I guess it really doesn't make any difference, as long as the fork gets washed," I say evenly.

"But cat food is so gross!" Hope says. "It's the grossest thing in the whole wide world! It's the stinkiest stuff there ever was!" Suddenly, without any warning, she turns herself to liquid and, in one flowing maneuver, manages to ooze herself off her chair onto the floor, head first. "It's like eating boogers!"

"Cats eat boogers!" says Abbie. "Boogers are yuck!"

"It's like poop!" Hope screams, laughing.

"Come on, Hope," I say. "Get back up on your chair and finish your supper."

"It's like poop and boogers and—and the kind of dog doo that sticks to your shoe!" she says. She lies on her back, stomping her feet on the ground, marching-style.

"And pee on your shoe, too!" says Abbie. But she's looking at me out of the corner of her eye, nervously, to see if I'm going to make them stop. I check—and yes, I *am* still a looser human being, so, smiling at Abbie, I sort of slide off my chair, too, and roll around with Hope on the floor, both of us yelping like dogs in heat. Abbie leaps on top of us, nearly puncturing one of my lungs with my own rib, and I grab her and roll around with her, too. We're all laughing and screaming.

"What about—what about vomit?" shouts Hope, breathless from laughter.

"And mucus!" I say.

"No, snot!" Hope yells. "Big old globs of stinky green snot from somebody who has had a cold since November."

"With worms in it." From Abbie. "Big fat green and black worms who have a bad cold."

"No, they are diarrhea. Worms with diarrhea."

I tickle them. Hope lies on her back, kicking her legs in the air, and I have to dodge them to keep from having my teeth knocked out, but I don't mind. I wrestle her around, making ferocious noises deep in my throat, and hold Abbie around the middle. We are one great big seething sea of laughing and growling, out-of-control laughing, and shouting out everything bad we can think of, although later I think you can't get much worse than green and black worm diarrhea. Too bad I couldn't have yelled the worst thing I was really thinking, which was, "Harold Whoever-He-Is taking Viagra!"

After a while, we just lie there on the floor, gasping for breath. Their bodies lie touching mine. I've forgotten how to make a home, but hey, at least I know how to shout wicked things that make kids laugh.

"Let's do it again!" says Abbie. "Let's fall off our chairs again."

"No, no, not again," I say.

"Okay, then tomorrow night! Every night! Let's make a rule that every night we have to fall off our chairs and tickle each other."

The telephone rings, and I get up. Abbie's holding onto my legs, and I have to pry her fingers off my ankles, so I can walk, and I'm laughing as I get to the phone. I'm actually hoping just the tiniest bit that it might be Dan Briggs. Today he had stopped into the Golden Granary, and I told him Hannah was planning to keep the kids on Saturday. I almost blurted out, "Can you believe this is my *first date* since Lenny left me?" But the more I thought about it, the more I thought that might be something he might throw back in my face months from now, when he's realized he can't stand being with me after all. Anyone might. I mean, why *hand* the guy one more weapon to use against me? He already has an arsenal, if he chooses to use it.

"Hello?" I say on the phone, a little breathlessly.

"I don't want to bother you. Would you please just put Hope on?" It's Lucille, speaking in a clipped voice.

"Hope?"

"Yes. There's somethin' I need to tell her. I'm not lookin' to bother you at all. I know you're an *extremely busy* person."

"You're not bothering me," I say. "Before I just failed to see why you were calling *me* to ask about—you know."

"I know. You made that very clear. Now I need to speak to Hope."

I want to say, "Whoa! What the hell for? You tell me first what you want to say to her!" But I don't. I just say, "Hope, your grandmother wishes to speak with you." And as she comes over to the phone, I shrug at her questioning look, and she says, "Hi, G.G. How are you?" She looks so grown up standing there, her eyes wide and uncertain. I touch her arm, but she pulls away from me, listening intently and smiling.

•    •    •

*Later,* as I'm tucking Hope into bed, I say, "So you and your grand-mother had a long talk. What did she want?"

"Oh, nothing."

"No, really. What did she want?"

"Um, she said I should keep it just between me and her."

My heart does a dull somersault. "I don't think she meant not to tell *me*," I say evenly. "She tells me everything herself already. She proba-bly meant just don't go calling the newspapers." I start picking up toys so that she can't read in my face how nervous I feel.

"Oh, *okay*," she says impatiently, but pleased at the same time. "I can tell you a tiny, tiny part of it. She was just telling me that she's sorry I can't be there when she gets married."

"Oh."

"And. You didn't tell me she was getting married."

"I guess I forgot."

"She said of *course* you forgot. She said she wasn't surprised."

"Well, I've had a lot on my mind," I say. *And it is the sixth time, after all. Not really big news.* "But I'm sorry, I should have told you."

"And she said she wants to come and see us, and that we can have the wedding all over again, and I can be the bridesmaid, and Abbie can be the flower girl."

"Oh, joy," I say. I pick up some stuffed animals and arrange them on her bookshelf with extra care. I even use my thumb to polish the but-tons of Mr. Huggins's eyes. He had once enjoyed Most Favored Bunny status. "You know, Hope, I think this is my favorite room in the whole house. I love the way we decorated it. We worked so hard on it, you and I, and we really did a great job." I realize I'm shamelessly trying to bring her back to me.

"I don't know."

"What? You don't like it?"

"Sometimes I don't. It makes me think about Daddy. Remember how he was the one who painted it?"

"I know. But you and I picked out the material and we sewed the curtains and bought the carpet and the comforter." *And planned the whole thing, and had to nag him to paint it, and he'd been drinking beer all day and wouldn't do it, and we had a big fight, and then finally at ten-thirty at night, he stomped in and did it and made a big mess. But why quibble? He did paint the room. Yes, he did.*

"But we're here," Hope says, "and can see each other every day. When I think about Daddy painting, all I have is the thought of him."

"I know." I sit down next to her on the bed, and feel such a rush of affection and sadness for her that I gather her up in my arms and bury my nose in her hair. To my surprise, she lets herself slump into me. After a minute, she says, "Do you think people can really see the future?"

I hold my breath. "You mean like Lucille?"

"Yeah. She says she just got a big reward from the police because she found a little boy who had got kidnapped. And the police put her on TV and now she's famous. She *knew* where the little boy was hidden, and she just went with the police and told them which house he was in."

"She's certainly something, isn't she?" I say. I pull Hope against me again, and lean back into the pillows, holding her head and stroking her temples.

"Can you see things like that?" she asks.

"No."

There's a long silence. I watch the snow falling outside, lit up by the streetlight. Hope feels so fragile and tentative in my arms that I don't even want to shift my breathing, for fear she'll pull away. How is it, I wonder, that some people can give off that effect—as though they're always just about to go off and leave you? Lenny and Lucille could do that, too: turn practically to mist while you thought you were holding on to them.

"G.G. says I'm like her," she says quietly after a long time.

"Why? Do you see the future, Hope?" Little prickles of something dance along the back of my neck.

"Maybe. I don't know." Her voice is soft.

I clear my throat. "You know, I'm not sure if Lucille *really* sees into the future. I know she says she does, but I think she just thinks hard about what people want to happen, and then some of it comes true, and some of it doesn't."

"But what about the little boy she found? How did she know that?"

"I don't know. There's a lot about it I don't really understand. But I'm glad I can't do it, because I think it's a hard way to live. Lucille wasn't very happy when she was growing up. She said nobody liked her."

"She told me about that," Hope says. "She said that's probably how it is for me, too."

"What do you mean?" My mouth suddenly feels dry. "You've got lots of friends."

"No, I don't. I told you that. I'm not one of the popular girls."

"Are you kidding? Everybody likes you. Anyway, tell me: who's the most popular girl in your class?"

"Tiffany Gilbert." She pulls away now and stretches out on the sunflower quilt and looks up at me. Her large dark eyes are fastened on mine, and she does look a bit like Lucille, kind of smoky-eyed and ready to flare up into a kind of intensity you'd later wish had just stayed buried.

"Listen," I say. "I'll bet if you asked Tiffany Gilbert if she's one of the popular girls, she'd say no. Nobody ever thinks other people really like them, especially when they're your age."

"Oh, no!" she says. "Tiffany Gilbert knows she's popular. She, like, hangs around with a bunch of cool girls, and they, like, write stuff on their hands."

"What do they write on their hands?"

"Oh, phone numbers and each other's locker combinations. Just stuff."

"Still. Even though she writes on her hands instead of paper, I'll bet she's not as sure about being popular as you think she is."

She doesn't even smile at my feeble joke. "I don't have *any* friends except Lexie, and she only likes me because her mom makes her."

"No, she doesn't. Nobody ever likes anybody just because their mom makes them. Lexie and you have been friends since you were two years old, when we joined day care. You guys play together every day."

"You're not there at school. You don't see what it's like for me." Her voice is getting shrill. "This year when Lexie's on a different team, I have to eat lunch all by myself because nobody wants to eat with me."

I bite my lip, picturing her there alone. "Well, why don't you just go sit at the table with some other girls?"

She groans. "Mo-*om*. You can't do that in fifth grade."

"The teachers won't let you?"

She rolls her eyes. "The *girls* will make you leave. Some girls are mean. Have you ever thought of that? Did you ever really even *go* to school?"

"Well, find a girl who isn't mean. Surely somebody else is sitting by herself, too. Go up and sit with her and tell her your name, and maybe you'll make a new friend."

She looks down and starts picking at the threads of her comforter. "G.G. says girls probably don't like me because they know I know stuff about them."

"*What* is she talking about? What stuff do you know about them?" God, I never should have let her talk to Hope without my being on the other line. Better yet, I should never have told Lucille I was having children, or lived in New Haven, or owned a telephone. I bet she's not psychic enough that she ever would have been able to find me.

"I know they're mean." She speaks barely above a whisper.

"You know, honey, we need a little reality check here. The truth is that sometimes girls are mean without even thinking about it. Especially in fifth grade. Kids don't realize that they're hurting each other's feelings."

"How can you say that when you don't even know these girls?" She flings herself back against her pillow. "G.G. knows. She said she could see these girls as clear as day."

"Hope, G.G. can't see them! She doesn't know. I swear to you, she has no idea!" My hackles are full out, and I have to work to keep myself from sounding too intense.

She studies the ceiling for a long time, thinking. Finally she says, "Then why do *you* think girls don't like me?"

I feel myself ready to launch into the but-they-*do*-like-you speech again, but then I get an idea. "I know what!" I leap up off the bed. Take it easy, I think. But I can't help myself. "Sweetie, I've got the best idea! Let's plan a really fun day together, with some friends of yours. We'll invite whoever you want. What would you like to do? Want to go to the movies? Or ice-skating? Whatever you want, we'll do."

She's quiet a long while, frowning. I'm sure she's about to say no. But then she says, grouchily, "Can it be a sleepover?"

"Really, a sleepover? Sure! Now who do you want to invite?" I'm thinking crepe paper streamers, homemade pizza, ice cream sundaes that the girls could decorate themselves—maybe a jewelry-making project after supper, and videos! Or Twister! Pictionary!

"I don't know. Maybe nobody will want to come."

"They'll come."

"Tiffany Gilbert might say no." She picks at her comforter. "But if she said yes, then probably Danielle and Amelia would come."

"Okay. We'll plan the whole thing out during the week so that it's just the way you want it. You'll see, it'll go well." I lean over and kiss her good night, and she hugs me back limply. "I'm excited about this, poopsie. Now you get some sleep."

I'm all the way out in the hall when I hear her say, "G.G.'s gonna think this is the dumbest idea she ever heard about."

"G.G.," I tell her, "doesn't have the slightest notion of what a good idea is. She wouldn't know a good idea if it came up and smacked her on the face." Which is exactly what I want to do.

# 8

*I go downstairs* and suddenly I'm so mad that I can barely think what to do. I clean the kitchen, scrubbing off the stove every last little morsel of stuck-on cheese. I even clean the shelves of the refrigerator and the area behind the sink that always gets so scummy because the faucet leaks a little. Then, when I can't think of one more thing to clean without screaming, I dial Lucille's number.

It rings three times, and then a man answers in a voice that sounds rich and flowing, like dark chocolate.

"Oh," I say. "Is this . . . Harold?"

"Yessss."

"Oh, so nice to talk to you. This is Maz, Lucille's daughter. I guess congratulations are in order."

"Well, Maz, thank you there; that's very nice of you," he says.

*Oh, no, no, no. It's nice of you.* I should make a little nice conversation. Have the two of them set the date?

"Week after next," he says very formally, but there's a rich little chuckle in his voice that makes me like him and feel simultaneously sorry for him. "Week after next, the little lady and I will belong to each other."

"Well," I say. "I certainly wish you all the best." *No reason that number six won't be the one that sticks, right?* "Is, um, the little lady there?"

He laughs and says he's looking forward to meeting me when they come up in a few weeks, and I manage to say something that sounds plausibly as though I'm looking forward to it, too, although I'm thinking, Help! A few weeks?! Then he puts Lucille on, and I say, in a completely ferocious tone, "What in the *hell* did you say to Hope?"

"What are you *talkin'* about?" she says.

"You obviously know what I'm talking about. She said you're telling her that she's psychic, and that's why nobody likes her. . . ."

Lucille's lighter is clicking, but her voice is calm. "Honey, honey, I didn't say nobody *likes* her. I simply said that she has a gift, like my gift, and that I understand what she's goin' through."

"You've told her that she can see all the mean things that people are thinking, and I won't have it."

"Now just a minute. I didn't say people think mean things. You're gettin' everythin' all wrong. Put her on the phone, darlin'."

"I am not putting her on the phone. You're filling up her head with all this drama, with this . . . fortune-telling crap, and it pushes her away from everything and everybody that she needs to get along with right now. Don't you see what you do when you meddle like this? I can't believe that somebody who claims to be able to read human hearts can't see how taking one little child and making her feel like she alone can be singled out for some cockamamie *gift*, as you call it, makes her unable to get along with *anybody else*. . . . She's *not* a fortune-teller. She's *not*."

"Sweetie, why is this so bad? I'm makin' her feel like somebody understands her. I think you've lost your mind. I'm *shocked*. Harold, honey, would you hand me my drink, dahlin'? Right there on the table."

"You're shocked that I don't want you filling my daughter's head with all this stuff, making her think she can't get along with her friends because she's too *special* for ordinary people to understand? *That* shocks you?"

"I just don't see what's wrong with lettin' Hope know that when she has troubles, there are other ways, dahlin', of solvin' things. That she's somebody special and that she has a wonderful, wonderful gift. I would have given anythin' at all if somebody could have reached out to me when I was a child the way I'm reachin' out to her." Click, click, click. "Honey, I'll be ready to go in just a minute. Maz's flyin' off the handle at me. I've gotta get my dose of abuse."

"You're putting the whole idea into her head. Hope isn't psychic. And furthermore, she's *my* kid, and I believe it's written somewhere that I get to say how I want her raised."

At this, she chuckles. "My goodness, you just don't like the idea of *anybody* havin' a gift you don't have, do you? Never have, probably never will. But, sweetie, she *is* psychic—and besides that, she's drawn to that world, whether you like it or not. And I'm her grandmother, whether you like that or not, either. I don't want to get you all hot and bothered, but, sweetie, I really do think you're overreactin'."

"Look. You don't know Hope. And you certainly don't know her social situation here. The last thing she needs is to feel herself set apart from all her friends—"

"Dahlin', let me ask you a question."

"—her friends, that she *needs* to get along with, because this is an age that's very, very social, and they all *have* to go to each other's sleep-over parties and birthday parties, or else they get—"

"One question."

"And Hope already thinks she's *not* part of things, plus the fact that Lenny has left us, and I'm sure she must think she's somehow responsible for *that*."

"A question, Maz."

*"What?"*

"Honey, are you gittin' any?"

"Any what?" I say, before I can think. She takes a moment to laugh uproariously before she says, "Uh-huh. I thought so! No nookie for a long, long time. No monkey bizness! Now what happened to that young man from the other night?" she goes on. "He seemed like such a good possibility. Sweetie, for God's sake, don't tell me you already blew it. I told you if you'd fix yourself up a little, do somethin' with that hair—I'll bet it's all stringy and static-y with the winter dryness. And you need to exfoliate! I can tell that from here. Honey, hang up the phone and go take a nice hot oil bath, and use the loofah, and give yourself a facial and you'll feel so much better. Then tomorrow you can see about gittin' yourself somethin' goin'."

I may hate her. I really, really might hate her.

# 9

When I hang up the telephone, my head is throbbing so hard, I think my eyes must be boinging in and out of their sockets, as though they were connected to me only by rubber bands. I try a few deep, cleansing breaths. Nothing. You can't scrub Lucille out of your brain using only air.

I go outside onto the deck. Maybe out here the combination of wind and darkness can clear my head. The thermometer reads thirty-eight degrees, and that doesn't take into account the stiff breeze coming off the river. The evergreen trees silhouetted against the streetlight make sharp, flickering, clawlike shadows on the boards of the deck. I shiver and wait to feel calm. Maybe I should call up Hannah, tell her what's happened. But that's ridiculous. Hannah would give me the little speech about how great it's going to be for Hope when she has a grandmother in her life, and how glorious the day will be when I start my little fling with Dan Briggs. She doesn't have the faintest idea what Lucille is capable of. I haven't even told her the worst of it, about Robbie Martindale.

Robbie Martindale was my boyfriend my senior year of high school. I'd just come back to Starke, Florida, back to my grandparents' house in the parsonage after a summer traveling with Lucille. It was a shock to be back in my other life—back where Big Daddy, my grandfather, thundered his sermons every Sunday, and Grandmama ran the clothing drives and kept the town in line. As much as I loved going off to tell fortunes with Lucille in those days, I had usually loved coming back, too, getting to be a child again, in a regular house with meals and homework and chores.

But this summer had been more harrowing than most. This was the year Lucille had stopped treating me like a kid and more like a best friend. Not that she'd ever been maternal, but now she and I were partners, she said. We would get all dolled up each night and go into whatever town we were staying in. She had me wear some of her clothes, which I remember feeling a little uneasy about, but with Lucille, it was so much more trouble to oppose her than it was to meet her expectations. She'd throw push-up black lace bras and slinky red dresses in my direction. I wore tons of eye makeup and bright red lipstick, and together we sculpted my hair into structures that required a half can of hairspray to hold them. Sometimes I'd look into the mirror and feel as though I were playing dress-up.

"You've got to wear that dress with some *conviction*, honey," she said to me once. "No wonder the men always look at me and never look at you. You look like a lost soul in that getup."

Naturally, we met men wherever we went. Lucille flirted with everyone, even the ones I knew she really disliked and who would never be her type. She needed to be the Most Special Person Anyone Had Ever Met. Had to be. I remember a hugely overweight businessman with a round, doughy face—and the way she kept leaning over and pinching his cheek and calling him Slick Willie. He kept calling her Little Miss in a voice that could have been featured in a medical training film about emphysema. He was so fat he'd groaned each time the waitress would come over with another drink, and he'd have to lean over and strain to get to his wallet. There was a huge wad of bills inside of it, and he'd peel off one of the big ones each time. Twenties and fifties seemed to fly out of his billfold, accompanied each time by moans and groans. In the restroom later, I said to her, "Why are you *doing* this? He's so disgusting!" And she gave me a blank look, as if she couldn't quite imagine what I was talking about. "I'm just bein' friendly," she said, injured. "That man has a lonely, lonely life. If we can make him feel just a little bit bettah about himself, darlin', where's the harm?"

Later, she left with him, and I drove her car and spent the night in the trailer by myself. As weird as it was to be there by myself—it was such a rickety old thing and was so connected to her it seemed almost like being alone in her body—still, it was better than the times when I was younger when I'd have to go along with her when she'd leave someplace with a new man. Then I'd be told to wait in the car with the doors locked and the windows rolled up while she followed him into a motel, or sometimes into a darkened suburban house. I'd wait hours for her sometimes, trying to sleep, watching the doorway for some sign of her coming out. When she finally did, she'd be all disheveled and grouchy for a few hours, until she got some sleep. I'd have to tiptoe around the trailer and try not to make any noise until it was time for her to go to work again. She never thought I minded. She said these were our adventures.

This year, though, she wasn't calling them adventures. She said it had been hilarious, she wished I could have seen: the fat guy had been a lousy lay and besides that was perverted. He'd wanted her to put baby powder all over him and then spank him before putting him in a specially made diaper, she said, laughing.

"Please," I said. It was about ninety-five degrees, and I had a splitting headache. If I had to think about that man's bottom, I was sure I'd faint.

"Darlin', don't you think that's the funniest thang? Where's your sense of humor? Me and that five hundred–pound asshole and a whole bottle of baby powdah? Sweetie, I don't think I even put any baby powdah on *you,* and I sure as hell wasn't gonna put any on *him.* I don't care what kind of money he had."

By the time I got back to Starke that year—four days after my senior year had started, because she refused to drive me home and I had to catch a Greyhound to get there—I was numb. Culture shock, probably. Posttraumatic stress syndrome, they'd call it today. I scrubbed my face on the bus, took down my hair, and tried to arrange it into something Grandmama wouldn't shriek over. It looked silly in a ponytail now, so I pulled it back into a bun. But Grandmama was in the hospital with pneumonia when I got home. She wouldn't have noticed if I'd come home with my hair shaved off. In fact, she'd been sick for a few weeks, and wasn't ever really strong again after that, although she held on for about another year. I was lost. I went back to school listlessly, not really expecting to have a good time. The return was like coming back to darkness, I wrote in my journal. *This town has nothing for me. I don't know where I belong or who I am anymore.*

And then came Robbie Martindale. When he transferred into my English class, I didn't pay any attention to him at all. I was off men. Maybe I was still stunned to find out that a woman might be asked to diaper them right up into old age. Just how many of them were truly bizarre? As I looked around me, it seemed plausible that just about everyone was.

But Robbie, who had transferred in from out of town, was definitely not bizarre and didn't seem to have even any strange tendencies. I was a cheerleader that year, even though I hadn't attended any of the practices over the summer. It was the late seventies, and there was a shortage of girls who were willing to put on the maroon-and-cream–colored uniforms and jump around every Friday night at the football games. I did it because I didn't care what I did and my guidance counselor said extracurricular activities would help me look "well rounded" on college applications, and I badly wanted to go away to college.

Robbie and I got assigned to run the math team together, which was something I could safely get into. When I wasn't practicing with the squad, we worked in the afternoons, doing math drills and studying together. I liked how he listened to me, and how he didn't seem weird. We hung out at the Dairy Queen and drove around town, talking. He wasn't handsome, although he had longish blond hair and blue eyes, and he laughed a lot. There was something too big about his mouth and jaw, an intense look in his eyes that kept him from being really good-looking. He had the look of somebody who's too intelligent, but I liked how you could tell him things and he just got them. He thought it was amazing that I was a cheerleader. Once, to startle him, I told him how I'd spent the summer wearing skin-tight leopard-skin dresses and dangling earrings and watching my mother pick up men at bars, and he didn't even leave then.

We kissed a little, almost experimentally, but that part didn't really take off, at least not at first. I liked that about him, that he wasn't one of those guys only "out for one thing." He seemed perfectly happy to sit with me in the booth at the Woolworth's, in the back, talking about life and all the other kids, and of course the math team. He was so blessedly and wonderfully sane. His mother loved me, too. Lois Martindale taught me to bake pound cake and chocolate fudge. Sometimes she and I sat out in the sun together in our bathing suits in the grass of her backyard, drinking Cokes and talking, smearing ourselves with baby oil and iodine as we worked on our tans. She was such a regular mom, with her bobbed brown hair and friendly eyes. I loved the way I was always welcome there, an unquestioned member of the family. I could walk in and out anytime I chose, fix myself a piece of pie and grab a Coke, and go watch television with the rest of them.

I told myself I was saving sex. Not from any purity on my part, or reticence. I just didn't want things to change between Robbie and me. I didn't have that high an opinion of what sex could do for a relationship anyway. When he'd try to do anything more than kiss me, I'd pull away after a minute or two and tell him not yet. He was understanding about it, just because that's the way he was, but it made me feel terrible. I felt guilty sometimes that I wasn't going to have sex with him, and I couldn't really explain why. I mean, I wanted to; I often thought about him in that way, and I always knew it would happen someday—but it was never *just right*. I didn't know why. Once I almost talked to his mother about it, but then at the last second, realized with surprise that she wasn't the right one. We were talking about her son, after all.

In March, my grandmother got so sick that it looked as though she might die. Lucille came home unexpectedly. I don't know how they got her to come home, but she breezed in, acting even more outrageous than usual. I made sure to keep busy while she was there, guarding everything about my *other* life from her prying and contempt. But she got wind of Robbie. I should have known she'd sniff out love.

I had told him all about her, of course. But there was no preparing him for the real full-strength Lucille, and that's what was playing that March. She was restless. I'd seen that look in her eyes before, the way she seemed to be always scanning the landscape for the Next Thing. She'd spend the morning visiting Grandmama in the hospital and by the time I got home from school late in the afternoons, she and Big

Daddy would be sitting, drinking bourbon, on the porch. He'd nearly be in a stupor by then, and Lucille, always lounging around in halter tops and shorts or else minidresses that barely covered her ass, would urge me to invite Robbie over for supper.

"Sorry, he can't come. He's busy," I'd always say. "He's the captain of the math team, you know, and when he's not off solving quadratic equations, he's at the dermatologist's trying to get some new medication for his chronic acne problem. And when he's not there, well, then, he's trying to find some remedy for BO. You know how it is."

I thought I was so damn smart, keeping him separate from her. Robbie got hired to deliver liquor from the Beeline Liquor Store. I got a job at the Dairy Queen so I didn't have to be home too much and didn't have to talk to Lucille. Robbie came by the DQ each night to pick me up, and we'd sit outside in his parked car, talking and making out a little.

"Why don't we just go ahead and do it?" he said one night. "I want you so much. It's not like we don't love each other."

"Not yet. Soon," I said. That was the first time I'd let him in on the idea that we were even someday going to. I had it all planned out: we'd do it near the end of senior year, then we'd go away to college together, get married right after graduation, and then have three kids, spaced two years apart. I'd quit my job to take care of them and Robbie would support us—and then, when the youngest one was six, I'd go back to work full-time. I didn't know where we'd live, but somewhere probably far away. Maybe his parents would move away with us; it'd be nice having his mom next door. I knew that as soon as I let him in on the plan, he'd be in full agreement. That's just how agreeable and easy he was. It was as though my plan would automatically be his plan, too.

A week after that conversation, Robbie called and said he had a late delivery that night and wouldn't be around, so I drove my own car to the Dairy Queen and stayed late helping Crystal close up. When I got home, the house was all dark. Big Daddy wasn't even on the porch; he was snoring in the living room in front of the television set; I could hear him even from the porch. I didn't want to go in. There was a tiny light on in Lucille's trailer. She'd driven it down with her for this visit rather than leave it in South Carolina, where she was running a kind of fortune-telling salon for bored housewives. I figured I'd go over and ask her how Grandmama had been that morning.

I knocked at the door of the trailer and then let myself in. She never locked the door. At first—I'll never forget this—she laughed when she saw me there. She was sitting up in bed, the sheet pulled up to her chin, with a funny expression on her face. She was the only one I saw in the dimness, but something about the way she said, "Oh, *Maz*" set all my senses crazy, like little Mexican jumping beans she'd brought me once from the carnival in Texas. And I could feel my eyes straining harder to focus in the darkness, and yes—oops, there was someone with her, and I was backing away, about to say, "Oh, sorry," but then the picture sprang into my brain, all illuminated in perfect detail, and it was—but it couldn't be, but it was—Robbie. Sitting next to her, holding the sheet up to cover himself—to hide his nakedness from me—*me,* his girlfriend. There were just his eyes and that big round O of a mouth showing over the top of the sheet. The air went out of me. I felt everything go dark, as though all the empty spaces in my head were filling up with little black squares, all closing in until the whole picture was going to crash in on me in another moment. I must have turned and stumbled out of the trailer, and she was saying over the roar of blood in my ears, "Now, darlin', don't go makin' a federal case out of this; this was just us havin' a little mischief, it didn't mean anythin', you know how I am," and Robbie was silent, silent. Who knew what he could have been thinking? And she with that sly, guilty smile, but triumphant, saying, "Oh, let her go. We didn't even *do* anythin'! She'll come to her senses soon."

I didn't speak to her again until my sophomore year in college. Not one word. It takes a lot of willpower to do that, and that's one of the ways I know that I am very strong when I need to be. She would try to get me to talk any way she could think of, but I was stony, silent. The Sphinx.

In my sophomore year, she sent some chocolate-flavored underpants and a note that said, "He and I were so sorry, Maz. Haven't your grandparents taught you about forgiveness?" And that's when I called her on the phone and told her in the steadiest voice I could manage that my grandparents couldn't conceive of the kind of forgiveness it would take to include *her*. She said she'd keep trying in case I changed my mind.

And, you know, I eventually did. A therapist told me it was taking too much of my valuable energy to stay mad forever, and the truth was, I got to miss her. She was somebody who loved me after all even though the way she loved me was crazy and not at all what people usually mean when they talk about a mother's love. And with Grandmama and Big Daddy gone by then, the number of people who loved me was dwindling. She was my *family*. Little by little, I could bring myself to talk to her. I was going with Lenny by then, who was a musician in a rock band, sexy and dangerous as hell. One day senior year—the day he asked me if I would, you know, sort of be *committed* (that was the way he worded it, since it was the early eighties, and where we were, people didn't say the word *marriage* so easily), we sat down together for coffee, and I told him about Lucille. Then I told him the story of Robbie, and I said she was a snake in the grass. I said, "If you so much as look at her in a sexy way, I'll rip your lungs out and you'll never sing in a band again." And he didn't. She came to our wedding in a demure blue chiffon dress with little mirrors sewn all over it, and I said to her, "Too bad they're not pointed so you can see *yourself* in them," and she said, "Oh, get over it, will you? It's been years!"

She wanted to come to visit when Hope was born, but I had postpartum depression, stretch marks, and a stomach that refused to go flat again, and besides that, Hope cried all the time just from the frustration of trying to live on earth and learn to burp and poop at regular intervals, and Lenny kept saying we needed to start having sex again because he was horny as hell. So I said no to her, but she showed up anyway one afternoon, carrying a suitcase filled with baby clothes she'd obviously bought at a secondhand store. I stood up for the whole duration of her visit, and after she left that night, I threw all those ratty clothes away.

When Abbie came along, six years later, we were living in New Haven, and I felt a little stronger, so I said she could come. She was in fine spirits then, dating a new man who had promised to take her to

Europe, and when she visited, she pronounced everything wonderful about our lives: what a great husband I had, a terrific little house in New Haven—how clever of me to leave the South!—and wasn't Hope just the most special darling in the whole world, and of course Abbie would grow up to be just great, too. She said great like "gright." She was grighting on my nerves.

We never mentioned Robbie. I had heard from Mrs. Martindale that he had married somebody from out of town and was living in Pennsylvania. "What a shame you two broke up," his mother said. "I'll never understand what could have happened."

I kept an eye on Lucille and Lenny, almost instinctively. I was tired, but I made sure to eat dinner downstairs with the two of them every night, and to observe every bit of eye contact between them. If they went into a room, I went in there, too. It was exhausting, and when she got in her trailer and drove back to wherever it was she was scamming people that year, I felt a relief that was almost physical. I went to bed and slept for a week, holding Abbie and Hope and my whole life tight around me.

That was back when I still thought you could just reject the past and have it disappear into the night, riding off in a trailer, gone for good.

# 10

*As if life* isn't weird enough, I realize on Saturday morning that there are three reasons why dating Dan Briggs is a mistake of possibly epic proportions.

1. Hannah can't keep my kids after all, because she's remembered that she has to attend her parents' forty-fifth anniversary party in Waterbury.

2. Dan, when hearing about this, *doesn't* wisely say we should cancel and agree never to see each other again; instead, he cheerfully tells me he really likes kids, and he's fine with getting to know them better. The man has obviously come unhinged from reality. Was he not standing in my kitchen a week ago and hearing my daughter screech at him? Somehow I hear myself numbly agreeing to taking them along.

3. When I tell Hope and Abbie that we're all three going out to dinner with Dan, Hope threatens to march into the Department of Children and Families and have my parental rights revoked. Okay, so she doesn't say that. She means it, though. She cries and pouts and tells me that I'm violating my marriage vows. I end up having to take Hannah's advice and explain that, in fact, Lenny and I *aren't* getting back together again. I have to give the entire Modern No-Guilt Divorce Speech, which of course is always more convincing when delivered by both parents together—but what choice do I have?

Later I realize it would have been just so *great* if I hadn't had to give that speech on the very day I was going out with a new man and taking them along. That's all. We sit on the living room pillows, sipping tea from the good china cups, and very carefully, I explain that sometimes grown-ups stop loving each other, and it's nobody's fault, but mommies and daddies come to realize that to have a happy life, they have to live apart. We all know the words of the Modern No-Guilt Divorce Speech by heart, even if we've never had to actually deliver it; it's practically endemic to our culture. I feel as though I've thought it through hundreds of times, and yet, sitting here now, the sun streaming in through the dusty windows on a Saturday morning, I feel unutterably sad saying these worn and meant-to-be-comforting words. I emphasize the part about how we both love them so very much, and that they'll have chances to see Lenny during their school vacations and at holiday times, which I devoutly hope is true. I say that he's decided after being in Santa Fe for a while that that's where he wants to settle, and that we have our lives here, so we're staying in New Haven.

Then Hope says, flatly, "Well, like it or not, he's coming back."

"He's not," I tell her softly. I try to reach over and touch her, but she pulls away. "That's just you wishing things could be the same. Which is fine to wish for. I know you do. But things are going to stay the way they are for now."

"You don't know," says Hope.

"Are you having love with the other guy?" asks Abbie quietly.

Hope scowls and says, "*Yes!* Yes! She *is!*" And I say, "No. Dan and I are just friends. And just like when you have a friend, you like to spend time with her, that's the way it is for Dan and me. It's good for grown-ups to get to see other grown-ups sometimes."

"You mean *kiss* other grown-ups," says Hope. "What you *really* mean is that you want to kiss men."

"Hopey, don't be mean," says Abbie.

"I'm not the one that's mean," says Hope. "Daddy won't come back because Mommy was mean to *him*."

"That is so not true," I say to her. She's lying upside down with her legs on the couch and her head on the floor, not looking at me. "I wasn't mean to Daddy. I loved Daddy very much, and I wanted our marriage to work."

"Yeah, but you were always trying to get him to work harder and to go get a job," she says. "You yelled at him. A lot."

"But don't you think Daddy should have worked to help support us?"

"I think you were too mean. That's why he had to go away."

"That really isn't it, sweetie. Things that happen between people in a marriage are a lot more complicated than that. I wish I could explain the whole thing to you in a way you could understand, but I can't, I'm afraid."

"I think if you called Daddy and told him you'd be nice, he'd be so glad to come back and live with you again," she says. "If you could make him believe you, which I don't know why he would. You never change."

*Dan arrives* at about six, not knowing that he's reentering the pit of vipers, poor guy. I feel momentarily sorry for him, but I feel so much worse for myself that I can't waste a lot of sympathy on what he's going to go through here. A woman who had her wits about her would have called him earlier in the day and said it wasn't a good night after all. I think there's probably a rule that the very day you tell the kids the marriage is over *isn't* a day to go out on a date with them along.

But I didn't have the energy to make the telephone call. Instead I spent the day listlessly cleaning house, swiping at dust kitties under beds, vacuuming the rugs and washing the mirrors, doing stuff I haven't done in months, in the hopes that it would make me feel more in control. Instead, I just felt a cold, dark dread, like there was a hand wrapped around my aorta that every now and then gave it an icy squeeze.

Hope stayed in her room most of the day, doing a project, she said, and not wanting to be disturbed. Periodically I'd hear her go downstairs to the basement. Who could tell what she was up to? I almost went in a few times to see if she wanted to talk, but I knew she'd just push me away.

Anyhow, promptly at six, Dan bops into this whole miserable drama, looking great and smelling fantastic, like somebody who's recently taken all his vitamins and gotten his full component of sleep, and is ready for whatever the situation asks of him. Each breath he takes seems to flood him with oxygen, as though he's about to run a road race instead of date a mentally unbalanced woman with two kids. He's wearing khaki pants and a blue knit shirt that makes his eyes look like they're neon, lit from behind. And boat shoes. I love men in boat shoes. No socks. Seeing him makes me so scared that I'm nearly catatonic. I want to crawl under the couch and lie there in the fetal position until he gets the hint and goes away.

He brings the children a bag of something—bribes, I think, what a clever idea. Or perhaps he was smart enough to bring a pair of stun guns. But no. It's just kids' vitamins, which he makes the mistake of handing to Hope. She looks into the bag and says, "Is this candy?" And when he patiently starts explaining about how they are vitamins to help your body grow strong, she sighs and closes the bag and looks over at me. "Oh, it's drugs," she says. "Great."

"Say thank you," I tell her. "Dr. Briggs was very nice to bring those to you." I hate my tone of voice.

"Thank you for the drugs," she says dully.

"Well," he says and laughs. "I wouldn't characterize vitamins as *drugs* exactly. . . ."

I give her one of my meaningful looks and have her take the vitamins to the kitchen and put them away, so that I can start in on being effusively grateful for them. *Oh, thank you sooo much, Dan. What a wonderful idea—vitamins for the children! And don't you know, we were just saying to each other a couple of days ago that it would be so very wonderful if we ever remembered to get some. . . .*

"Let's leave, shall we?" I say happily, idiotically happily. "Everybody all set?"

Hope is back from the kitchen. "I want to sit down in the living room first," she says.

"You do?" I say. "But why?"

"Yes," she says, prissily. "To chat."

Dan shrugs, grins a little, to say this is fine with him, *anything* is fine with him—and so we move in there, and that's when I realize, with a sinking heart, just what she's been up to. She's turned the place into an entire shrine to Lenny and our marriage. There's our wedding picture, of course, in the central spot—the photo with me in a hippie-style white peasant dress and a big straw hat, smiling up at Lenny in his purple poet shirt and his long black beard. Then, grouped around that are the birth pictures, the ones I thought for sure we'd decided were *private:* me, sweaty, bare breasted, so exhausted from labor that my eyes are practically rolled up in the back of my head, but smilingly cradling a scrawny, crying newborn. And then all the sentimental occasions: the family picnics, Christmases past with Lenny grinning into the camera, Lenny kissing me once on the beach. She's even brought out her own childish drawings from day care, with *Daddy I Love You* scrawled in red crayon. And there's a specially created banner across the fireplace, saying, *My daddy will come home soon.*

Dan is smiling. I have to hand it to the guy: he is game. "Oh, is this a picture of your daddy?" he asks. "Let me see. Wow! He's a handsome guy, isn't he?" It's as though he's read a textbook on how to date a woman with kids. I'm a wreck, of course. I hadn't looked at these pictures in a long time, and to have them displayed so lovingly and sentimentally actually makes me feel like weeping.

Our family life, all that Hope and Abbie remember.


*When we get* to the restaurant, a Mexican family-style place called La Tolteca, the hostess says there's a long wait, so we stand in the vestibule with about four thousand other people, all of whom seem to have a multitude of squirmy kids. It's as though the place hands out kids. I keep bonking my head on a piñata that's swinging from the ceiling. Salsa music crackles from a loudspeaker. Dan tells corny jokes for a while, and then, when only I am laughing, he must decide what the hell and switches to polite, generic conversation. Date conversation. Hope interrupts him to say that her daddy knows how to build things—does

Dan? He does not, but boy, he sure admires people who can do that. Abbie wanders over to the window of the restaurant, and to my shock, sticks out her tongue and starts licking the glass in long, languid strokes.

I disengage myself from listening to Dan tell me about the new apartment he's considering moving into in Westville and fly over to Abbie. "Why are you doing that? We don't lick windows!"

"I was pretending it was ice cream," she says, stepping back, stricken.

"Say, maybe we can go out for ice cream afterward," says Dan, right behind us. "It seems a shame to have to lick windows." He smiles and whispers to me, "Maybe she's not getting enough Windex in her diet." I can imagine him on the telephone to his real friends later tonight. *First I had to look at every photograph from her first marriage, and then we get to a restaurant, and her kid starts licking the window. Plus, I took them probably $45 of perfectly good children's vitamins, and the kids didn't even say thanks. One of them acted like I'd handed her a bag of crack cocaine that she didn't want.*

Dinner seems to take hours. Clearly we've entered the third circle of Hell. Once we get a table, the service is slow, the bowl of hot sauce mysteriously tips over, and the tortilla chips aren't salty enough for Hope, so she pours about half a pound of salt on them. I see Dan frown just the merest amount, about three of his eyebrow hairs dipping southward, but he's quick to recover his smiling mask. *And the stuff they eat!* he'll say to the friends.

I order a Dos Equis and try not to clutch it too desperately when the waitress finally brings it over. "So tell me more about the apartment," I say, concentrating on making my voice sound interested. "Does it have a nice porch?"

He looks puzzled. Had anybody said anything about a porch? "It's, uh, not got a porch, really, but three back steps," he says.

"Oh?" I say. Next I'll be inquiring as to whether the steps have a nice railing. To stop myself, I take a big gulp of my beer. Abbie says, "My daddy builds decks!"

Hope says loudly, "Now I remember why we never come here any-more. Look at the way they pile food up on the plates. I hate that. All the food is touching all the other food!" She's pointing to the plates at other people's tables. "It's *disgusting*!"

"It's fine," I say to her. "That's the way people eat Mexican food."

"Well, I like to put it in different bowls. Could you see if they would put it in different bowls for me?" She says this just as the waitress glides up, smiling, with our plates. Hope stands up to see if her plate has mushed-together food, and knocks the waitress's hand, and a plate wobbles and almost—almost, but not quite—falls on Dan. He jumps up. I think now surely we'll see him explode, but he gathers himself together effortlessly, and even, while he's standing, helps the waitress hand out the plates. Still smiling, even. He gets an A+. I'm feeling sweat trickling down underneath my clothes.

"This is a hazardous job you've got," he tells the waitress, smiling. Good, I think. Go off and marry her. Find out when she gets off work. You'll have a much easier time of it.

Hope becomes adamant about wanting her food in separate con-tainers, and the waitress agrees to this, still smiling in a strained kind of way, and comes back with a stack of little plates, and I transfer all the foods over to them, making sure that each strand of cheese and each grain of rice ends up where it belongs and doesn't get contaminated by any other kind of food. Abbie says to Dan, "Did you see my daddy's new deck? My daddy built a deck all by himself."

"No, no, I didn't," he says, smiling back at her so hard his eyes squint. "But I sure would like to."

He holds up his beer in a toast to me once we get all this taken care of and everyone is eating. I think I see beads of sweat forming at his hairline. We try to talk about nice, dinner-table kinds of things—the site of his new office, the weather, vacations we've each taken to places where they served Mexican food—but, fascinating though all this is, the kids interrupt us each time we manage two consecutive words. After five bites, Abbie twitches and writhes in her seat and then leans down and, with her little tongue darting out like a lizard's, licks the table.

"No!" I say, too loudly and suddenly. "Abbie! You've got to stop doing that!"

She draws back, scared, and then starts wailing—hard, wracking sobs with tears that seem to spurt, cartoon-style, from her blue eyes. I hold her, and she leans against me, knocking my plate into Dan's water glass, which spills into the hot sauce. We're all almost finished anyway. He calls for the check, and Hope tells the waitress, "My food was *inedible*!"

The waitress shrugs at Dan, and he smiles back. I just hope she doesn't openly give him her telephone number while I'm there. My teeth have that raw spinach feel again.

"Anybody still feel like ice cream?" says Dan when we get into the car. He sounds a little more weary than before. The clock on the dashboard says it's only seven-thirty. Hope belches loudly and has to be reminded to say "Excuse me," and then she and Abbie go into a giggling fit. This leads to some fairly rough slap-fighting in the backseat, which I try to ignore as long as possible. I'm struggling to concentrate on a story Dan is trying to tell about his aunt who lived in South America for a time, God knows when. I can't imagine why he's trying to tell this story *now*, or what could be the point of it. I keep nodding and saying, "Oh, wow," but finally I do have to turn around and make everybody stop hitting each other, which makes them collapse in another round of giggles. I remember then that my plan is to be looser, and I actually smile at Dan helplessly and shrug.

"I think the silliness is often what's the hardest," I tell him.

"Really," he says. I realize that from his point of view, there must be so much that's hard that it would be impossible to pinpoint any one thing. Just then his beeper goes off, and after a short call on his cell phone, he says, "Well, sad to say this evening has to come to an abrupt end. I've got a patient."

It's possible, I think, that he had worked out a secret signal with a friend: *I'll drive past your house and flick the lights, and you call my beeper and say there's an emergency.* What kind of naturopathic emergencies come up, anyhow? Somebody drop one of their vitamins down the drain?

I'm in the process of thanking him for the lovely evening and accepting his apologies for having to leave us so soon, when Abbie says, "Wait a minute, Mommy, wait a minute! That thing you said today. I don't understand why Daddy can't come be here if he still loves us. Why can't he come back home and be my daddy again?"

Hope says, "I *told* you. He is coming back."


*Later I'm soaking* in the bathtub and considering having a good cry when the telephone rings. I hate for the phone to ring when I'm in the tub, especially if I'm going to be crying soon, because I never can figure out whether to just let the machine pick it up and risk missing The One Person Who Might Be Able to Solve Everything or if I should jump out and drip water all the way down the hall to my bedroom, only to discover that a telemarketer wants to discuss some aluminum siding.

It's probably Lucille, I think. She wants to tell me that Lenny is now the biggest, most honorable holy asshole ever in the Western world, and that he now practically *owns* spirituality, and that new laws are being considered requiring all of us to bow down to him. I carry my dripping self to my bedroom and pick it up anyway.

"Hi, Maz." It's Dan.

"No, no. Please don't."

"Don't what? What are you talking about?"

I close my eyes. Why the hell does he have to *call* me when even he can surely see that this is doomed, not going to happen? We're not even together. Can't he just go off and pretend none of this ever happened?

"*You* know," I say. "Don't talk to me about tonight."

"Why?" he says. He laughs a little bit. "I had a good time. I'm just sorry I had to run off like that."

"Yeah. I bet."

"Maz! Come on. It was interesting."

"You use the word 'interesting' in some strange contexts. Do you know that?"

"Do you have any idea how boring other people are? You don't, do you?"

I am silent.

"I was going to ask you if I could come over. If you thought that would be okay."

"I thought tonight was hideous," I say to him. "The kids were ridiculous, and I was tense, and while we were at the restaurant, I kept thinking how the waitress would make such a nice girlfriend for you."

"The *waitress*!"

"Yes. She was very attractive, and she obviously thought you were incredibly gallant and patient. You should call her."

He laughs. "I'm not calling her," he says. "Listen, your kids are great. They're so *honest*."

"Really, Dan, please don't do this. They were awful, and if you don't agree they were awful, then you're just asking too little of life. It was *painful*."

"No!" he says, and then, as if he might need more convincing himself, "*No!* Maz, listen. They're very, very cute, and they don't know me from Adam. It's natural they're going to be a little wary. And Hope is very protective of you, as she should be."

"A little wary?" I say. Licking windows and knocking over plates, making a *shrine* to their father—why wasn't he freaking out over these things? That stuff is Not Okay. He should be running away as fast as he can.

"Well," he says. And stops. He doesn't seem to have an answer to that. So I help him.

"Listen, Dan," I say. And then I go into my second prepared, canned speech of the day: "You're such a nice guy and all, but I think it's just too soon for me to have anything to do with a real . . . human being, you know? This isn't going to work, I'm too raw, they're too impossible, we're all messed up here, we'd just drive you crazy, and then the day would come . . . please. . . ."

"Really, Maz, it's okay," he says. "I know all about this. My aunt and uncle were divorced, my cousins went through this—"

"No," I say. "It's too hard."

He laughs again. "So what if it's hard?" he says. "That's what life *is*. Did anybody ever tell us it was always going to be easy all the time?"

"Dan," I say. I swallow. How to explain this? "Listen, here's the truth of it. You're too together, and I don't want to be the one who's screwed up and has a weird life, while you get to be the one who's so magnanimous and willing to overlook every little weird thing that happens. It gets weird here. It gets really, really weird."

"That's all *right*," he says. "I know. I can take it."

"No," I say. "I don't want your sympathy and your pity while I try to hold everything together. You're a great guy and all that, but I can't even try to date until my kids have adjusted a little more. They can't even accept the vitamins you gave them without acting like the world has come to an end. You see where we are?"

He's quiet.

"I have to wait. I want to go lie down in a dark hole somewhere and wait for the next few reels of my life to pass," I say. "Maybe we could have that kind of scene where the calendar pages are flipping off—three years, five years. *Then* call me."

"What if I come over right now?" he says. "Right now. We'll talk. We'll throw the vitamins in the trash can. . . ."

"Five years," I say. "Maybe three if we find a good therapist."

When I hang up, I go over and stand by the window and watch needles of rain fall in the beam of the streetlight. The radiator huffs and rumbles, and there's a blast of heat next to my foot. But it's such fake heat, I think—just a dry blast of manufactured, spoiled air, nothing like the real warmth that I'd feel if the sun were shining in the window.

He's probably everything I need, and everything I want—but it's the damnedest thing: I can't reach deep enough to know. I'm frozen so far down that the sun could shine on me for a month and not start to thaw me.

# II

*Friday morning* is my usual day care turn, but Hannah, who is the scheduler these days, calls me on Wednesday night and asks if I can switch to the Thursday morning turn instead of my usual Friday shift. All the parents in the co-op are required to work four hours a week, taking care of the children.

"But I like to do my turn with you," I tell her. It's the high point of my week.

"So I'll switch my turn, too," she says. "It's just that Jonathan, who has the Thursday morning turn, has a job interview at ten, and he was going to get Melanie to do his turn, but then she couldn't because she has to take her mother to the surgeon—but both of them can do the Friday morning turn, so it would be easier—"

"Okay, *okay*. I'll switch. I'll get Siobhan to do the muffins, and I'll do the bread in advance."

"If it's trouble . . ."

Of course it's trouble. But it's more trouble to argue with Hannah and to figure out how we can get Jonathan to a job interview without disrupting even more people's lives. I sigh and twist the phone cord around my fingers.

"There's one other tiny little thing," she says.

"What?"

"You know that means we'll have to work with Jolie."

"Oh, God." I haven't had to work a turn with Jolie, who is the one paid staff member, since Lenny left. It's in her contract that she gets Friday off each week—so that day, Hannah explained to me, is the one traditionally reserved for the person whose spouse Jolie is currently sleeping with. Ha ha ha. We are *so* hilarious and free thinking at this day care.

Still, I've seen Jolie, of course, many times during the last year, and we've been polite to each other at the evening day care meetings and at pickups and drop-offs. I have been exceedingly cool and never once let her know that *I* know she was sleeping with Lenny, because I didn't want to give her the satisfaction of thinking of me as the aggrieved wife. A little leftover training from Lucille: *Never let the Other Woman see you jealous.* Also—and this may be the real reason—I was terrified that if I ever let on, the subject would find its way onto the agenda of a day care meeting some evening. I know most people probably would have left a day care center if they found out the teacher was boinking their own dear spouse, but I just couldn't bring myself to drop out. It's weird, I know, but all my friends in New Haven are in that day care—and besides that, I couldn't see disrupting Abbie's life just because her parents were screwed up. But work with Jolie? That was a different problem altogether.

"Hannah, I don't think I can do it," I say. "I hate it that she thinks she put one over on me."

"I know," she says mournfully. Then she says, "Well, look, it's only one turn, four little hours. And I'll work it out so that she stays as far away from you as possible. She can do the tricycles, and we'll do the diapers and the snack. And if she starts saying she's put one over on you, I'll take her out back and rough her up."

I'd forgotten a thing about Jolie, which is the way she seems to float through the day care center, with her long flowy skirts billowing out around her as she pads along in little black silk slippers, her long dark hair pulled back in a braid down her back. She has enormous green eyes and an unconscious elegance to her that goes away abruptly as soon as she opens her mouth and you realize that she speaks Valley Girl. Men don't seem to find this a huge drawback. I have seen guys meet her for the first time—married fathers with toddlers on their backs and their nice-looking, bouncy wives right beside them—and they have to sit down and get their hearts restarted after simply being introduced. Lucille would have said I was insane to ever let Lenny go to the movies with her unchaperoned.

"Maz!" Jolie says when I come in for my day care turn, stamping the snow off my clunky boots. She's just hanging up the telephone by the door, and she turns in a pirouette and holds her arms wide. "I haven't seen you in like *ages!* How *are* you?"

"Hi," I say. I hope she knows this is my dangerous, leave-me-the-hell-alone voice. I had been practicing my low growl all the way over in the car. There are about six parents standing right inside the entrance to the day care, all talking at once, helping their array of kids take off wet jackets, many of which land on the floor—so after saying hi to her and so I can keep from making eye contact, I get busy picking up coats and making sure Abbie puts her boots in her cubby. I say hi to Liz and Melanie and Sarah, give little David a hug. But then there's Jolie again, right in my line of sight, smiling one of those huge smiles that shows about eight rows of perfect white teeth, and she says, "So, Mazzie, tell me: what do you hear from Lenny lately?" The place seems to fall silent all of a sudden, and I feel the color leave my face. This is a direct violation of the Wife/Other Woman Code of Ethics. "Rule No. 3: The Other Woman must never purposefully bring up the husband's name in casual conversation with the wife, or ex-wife, as the case may be." Next to me, Sarah makes a snorting sound and hurries over to the cubbies to put away her daughter Jezebel's things.

Jolie keeps smiling at me, and then, even worse, she reaches over to me and starts adjusting my purple scarf with her long, white fingers. She's standing so close to me I can see every teeny tiny pore of her perfectly flawless skin, and the flecks of saliva on her gleaming, even teeth.

I wonder if it would be totally inappropriate if I smacked her hand away, if we'd have to have a day care meeting about *that*.

"Don't," I say quietly, "touch me."

There's so much commotion that she doesn't hear me. I wonder for a moment if I really said it aloud. She's finished with my scarf, so now she leans in to me even closer, if such a thing is possible, and says, "Isn't it just the biggest surprise ever that he's coming home? Were you, like, *stunned*?"

Well, I am now, like, stunned. My God, so it's true that he's coming. Hope wasn't making this up. But why isn't he telling me? Did he expect that the news would just trickle down somehow, and that it would all be fine with me? Does he think he can just get away with this? Is he just planning to show up, the prodigal husband, and start interfering in my life again?

She's watching my face, so I compose my features as best I can.

"It's just great," I say. "Just splendid! I think that's the only word for it, don't you?"

She smiles again, smugly, and floats off somewhere to help kids settle in. Her silver bracelets are jingling. My ears are ringing.

The morning day care chaos is well under way, and I get swept up into it, grateful. People are suddenly everywhere, writing their children's names on the blackboard so that later we can make sure we haven't lost anyone, scribbling in little instructions about antibiotics for lingering ear infections, potty directions ("Always call it poop. Someone last week said 'doody' to him and we don't like that."), and giving the time they intend to pick up their kids. I am already getting a headache. A Jolie headache.

And then, good God, she floats back over to me, fat little Hallie riding on her hip. "I mean, I was thinking he was there like for good, and then he calls and says he's like really seriously thinking of coming back," she is saying. She says the first syllable of seriously like the word "sir." *Siriously.* "I mean, I'm all weirded out. Aren't you?"

"Totally weirded out," I say.

"I can imagine!" she says. Then she cocks her head prettily and holds up one finger. "I hear a cell phone coming from your bag, Maz. Oooh, maybe it's Lenny? We've conjured him up!"

I stare at her. There are too many people trying to conjure things up all around me, and if she somehow has gotten Lenny to call, I don't know what to think. But it's not him. It's Lucille.

"Not Lenny?" says Jolie, and she makes a little pout as she floats away.

I take the phone and walk outside into the freezing cold. "What?" I say to Lucille. "I'm doing my day care turn, and I can't talk."

"So when *are* you ever able to talk?" she says. "Every time I call you, there's always somethin' that keeps you from talkin'. I feel like I've always got to apologize just for takin' up some of your precious, precious time. It's like I don't even have a daughter."

"Oh, please," I say. I am still furious with her. "Just tell me what you want. I've got fifteen kids I'm in charge of at the moment."

"Still not gettin' any nookie, I see," she says drily. "Those men in Connecticut must be made of weak stuff, is all I can say. I've gotta come up there and show them what that thing they have is *for*."

"What thing?" I say without thinking, and then she really roars with laughter.

"Good God, none of you Northerners knows a *damn* thing, do you?" she says. "Maz, one question: how *did* you get those kids? Any memory of that whole bizness?"

"Uh oh, cell phone battery's low again," I say.

"Oh, come off it. I just want to ask you somethin'. Don't be fakin' those beeps again at me. Now pay attention and think on this a minute. Is it horrible of me to get married again in my pink dress, and do I have to go get a new one?"

"What?"

"I've got this pretty pink thing that I wore when I married Art, and it still fits, and it's the nicest thing I've got—but it just seems tacky to wear it to the altar again, you know. Of course ole Harold won't know the difference, but what if he ever sees the pictures of me and Art? Do you think he'd think this was cynical of me?"

"How do I know what he'll think? Why don't you ask him?"

"That's not somethin' you can exactly ask."

"Just go get a new dress," I say. "New man, new dress. One dress per wedding. That's the rule."

"Good," she says. "I knew you'd know the etiquette. You Yankees know about all the rules."

When I go back inside, Jolie waves and smiles at me. "I've been thinking. One of us has to call Lenny soon and start making plans with him," she says. "You want to, or should I?"

I go look for Hannah, who's back in the art room with a small group of kids mixing finger paints. Hannah can't resist the art projects, and she's already got purple finger paint above her eyebrows, like a big bruise.

"Hannah, she's making me crazy," I say.

"I figured she might. Stay in here with me."

"She's still *talking* to him! Did you know that?"

"To who?"

"To Lenny, for God's sake!"

"Well. I thought maybe she was, but I didn't really know. Besides that, who cares? We are so over Lenny."

"But you didn't tell me?"

"What's the use? What could any of us do about it? And we don't care anymore who Lenny talks to. Remember that. We don't care."

"I know that, but that's not really the point, is it? Jeez, Hannah! He's told *her* that he's coming home. He's told everybody in the freaking world except me."

"Well, he hasn't told me."

"Okay, so he hasn't told you and me."

"Maybe he wants to surprise you."

"God. I didn't believe Hope. I still can't believe it." I sit down in one of the tiny wooden chairs and put my head down on the table. "When am I supposed to find out about all this? When does he think he'll give *me* the news? And does he think he's staying? Or is this just a little vacation to stir things up?"

She hands little Bradley a piece of shiny white paper and guides his plump baby hand into the blue fingerpaint. He grins up at her. "Like this," she says. "Just smoosh it all over the paper. That's right." She looks over at me. "Get a grip, Maz. It's going to be okay, even if he docs come. It's called closure, honey. He'll see that you're settled in a life without him, and he'll get in the truck and go back to Santa Fe, after a suitable amount of whining, and that will be that."

"He hasn't told me because he's probably coming just to see Jolie," I tell her. "To rub my nose in it one more time. How can I possibly start getting a life if I always have to be reminded that he wanted Jolie instead of me?"

"He's not coming to see Jolie. I guarantee that. She's a lightweight compared to how he feels about you. He's coming to see if he can screw things up for you. You haven't been squawking about him being gone, and he needs to find out why. *That's* why he's coming. And if you let him—well, you just won't, that's all." Then she sees my face and says in a careful, measured voice, "You know, I think you should give Dan Briggs a call. This time I'll keep the kids for sure and you can go out on a real date."

"Dan Briggs is no longer a possibility. I told you that. I told him it wasn't going to work, and deep down, I think he was relieved."

"Yeah, you told me. But I wasn't convinced, and I'm still not. I think you should give him another chance."

"You're too optimistic about men," I tell her. "Married way too long to have a real clue."

"Probably," she says in a weird voice. She looks out the window.

"Hannah, I'm kidding."

"Well, but I . . ." She looks at me funny, shrugs, starts to say something else, but then Bradley leans over and knocks the bottle of blue finger paint over on its side, and Hannah gets some paper towels and starts mopping it up. Outside the window, I can see snow softly falling on the swing set. It's almost the end of March, but we cannot seem to figure out how to stop having winter. I wonder if it's possible that somehow my internal emotions are directing the weather.

After a few minutes, Hannah says, "Well, maybe Lucille can figure this whole thing out. Isn't she supposed to be arriving, too?"

I throw my head down on the table. "God. Do you think if I drank the finger paints I could maybe put myself out my misery?"

"I'm pretty sure they're nontoxic."

That's my life: the chemicals are safe and only the people are toxic.

After a snack of apples and peanut butter, Jolie is loading the red and blue plastic plates on the cart, when she gives me a sly smile. I brace myself for the worst—perhaps she's now going to tell me that she and Lenny are getting married while he's here—but no. She says, "I know this isn't really, like, kosher, but my boyfriend is going to come hang out here for a little while this morning. He's, like, really interested in kids, and I told him that he could come and, like, read them a story or something. He's thinking of going to school to get to be a teacher. So he could come and see if this is, like, the career for him."

I stare at her. I am still hung up on the word "boyfriend."

"That's nice," says Hannah quickly, with the authority vested in her as the scheduler. "We can use all the help we can get." We often have Yale volunteers come in to read stories or to rock the smaller ones to sleep at naptime.

"A boyfriend," I say. "Have you been seeing him a long time?" I ask sweetly, and Hannah slides her eyes over at me.

"Well, yeah," says Jolie. "For, like, about a year."

*Since Lenny left. How nice.* "That's great," I tell her. "I'm happy for you."

"Yeah," says Jolie uncertainly.

"Because it's important and good to have somebody, you know, somebody to come home to—"

Hannah steers me over to the diaper area. "Do you want diapers, or do you want to take the big kids to the potty?" she says. Then she whispers, "Don't do this to yourself. She is not worth it. Not one millimeter of her is worth this."

I pick diapers because I just love the way the babies kick their fat little thighs on the changing table, and how you can hold onto their dimply arms for a moment and feel as though you've come upon some big ripe peaches, right there in the wintertime. Of course, there is the smell of the shit, which *is* bad, but it's worth it if you get to snuggle the baby after the changing part is all done. Plus, if you lean over and shake your head and let your hair tickle their bellies, they giggle.

I am in an ecstasy of shaking and giggling with little Ryan, and I am thinking that this is so much better than baking bread or handling oven mitts and that my life would be perfect if I could just play with babies all day without Jolie around, when I look up to see that Jolie has come over to the changing table, and is standing there, gazing off into space, looking as though she's about to say something.

"What?" I say.

"Oh, I don't know." She laughs. "I was just wondering something."

I don't ask her what. I try to get Ryan to laugh again; maybe he can drown her out, and I won't have to hear this. But no one can laugh that loud. She leans way over into my ear and says, "I shouldn't say this, I know, but I was just kinda wondering where Lenny thinks he's gonna stay whenever it is that he gets here from Santa Fe—your house or mine?"

# 12

*It's a rule of life*, I've found, that unless you're Lenny, who had a special talent in this regard, you hardly ever fall in love on an ordinary day care turn. Certainly you don't if you're already in a foul mood, which I most definitely am, on account of Jolie and my whole rotten life and all. Oh, sure, you can swoon sometimes from the smell of the children's sweet-smelling hair or the feel of a pudgy hand reaching up to grab yours—and sometimes I've even found myself feeling moved by the idea that sex brought all these babies into the world. But look up across the dirty diapers and the spilled orange juice and feel your heart dislocate itself inside your chest from beating so hard? Not so much.

But today, after Jolie has gone downstairs *without* my having to punch her out, I'm helping David and Curtis and Cameron make a tower in the block corner. And I hear a man laughing over by the door, and when I look up, there's a guy I've never seen before, taking off a blue puffy coat. Then he leans down and picks up Jezebel, a one-year-old who seems to have a thing for men, and I hear him asking her, "So where's Jolie?" Since Jezebel can't talk yet, I unfold myself and walk over to him. After all, he could be a kidnapper come to steal our kids; I can't leave Jezebel to handle him. She'd just go off with him, happily. "I'm Maz," I say. "I'm not sure where Jolie's got to. I think she might be downstairs dancing with some kids." Actually, Hannah had shooed her downstairs, thinking I really might deck her.

"I'm Josh," he says. He has the most startlingly blue eyes, and dark hair that is so glossy that it looks as if each individual curl was put through a polisher. He *shines*. Jolie's boyfriend. Of course he would shine. "I came to hang out. Glad to meet you."

Hannah and I get him established in the reading corner with a few kids who want to hear *Mike Mulligan and His Steam Shovel,* which is always a favorite. I keep an eye on him because, after all, we don't really know him, only Jolie does and she might not be thinking straight. But he reads well, with a booming voice when he's Mike Mulligan and with a silly voice when he's going through the drill about Mike Mulligan's qualifications. Even the children in the block corner suddenly say they're sick of blocks and drift over to the reading corner, which is a big comfy mattress covered with an Indian bedspread. Josh is stretched out on it, and kids are cuddled in every nook and cranny of him. Hannah comes over and we start picking up the blocks.

"He seems to be doing *fine*," she whispers. "Maybe we could get him to sign up for a regular turn."

"He's gorgeous," I say.

"Well, that too," she says. "Easy on the eyes."

He finishes up *Mike Mulligan* and then four other books, including the real test, *Fox in Socks,* which most adults in the day care (me included) refuse to read on the grounds that all the tongue-twisters make our mouths hurt. By the time he's done, it's lunchtime, and we all troop downstairs to the church kitchen for tuna fish sandwiches on whole wheat bread, carrot sticks, and milk. Josh jumps right in, cutting sandwiches in crustless triangles, doling out the plastic dishes, and negotiating who gets the red plates and who gets the blue ones. He pours milk and pretends to draw with carrot sticks. Okay, he does some weird stuff, too. He gets a little bit too antic and starts pretending to hide carrot sticks on top of kids' heads, in their hair, and then letting them eat them. Once I look up and am shocked to see he's got carrot sticks stuck in both nostrils, and I can't bear to see if he decides to eat those, too. The kids are hysterical. I feel myself frowning a little, but neither Hannah nor Jolie seems to notice.

Jolie keeps sidling up to him and smiling at him, running her hands along his arms or touching him with her perfect, pointed toe, and I think what a cute couple they make. At one point she feeds him a part of her sandwich, the way brides feed bridegrooms a piece of wedding cake, which makes all the kids laugh hard and then start trying to cram sandwiches into each other's mouths as well. We have to rush around and put a stop to it before fistfights break out.

I get the job of washing the lunch dishes just so I won't have to hang near Jolie. While Hannah, Josh, and Jolie take the kids to the bathroom and then let them run around in the Running Area, I drag the cart to the huge church kitchen and load the dishwasher. I'm nearly done when Josh comes in. He's sweaty and has taken off his red sweater and is wearing a Def Leppard T-shirt. It's just like the one that belonged to Lenny, that Hope now wears to bed. Maybe Jolie has a thing for Def Leppard fans, I think.

"Whew," he says. "This has got to be the most fun job in the whole world. But, God, I need a Coke or something."

"I think there might be one in the back of the fridge," I say. "Although generally people here are kind of strict about kids seeing us drink Cokes."

He looks surprised.

"Caffeine, sugar, carbonation, world domination by an American industrial complex," I say. "I mean, *I* don't mind. I love the stuff myself. Drink up."

He rummages around and finds a can near the back and puts it on his forehead to cool off.

"I hear you want to be a teacher," I say.

"Yeah. To do this every day would be heaven."

"I know."

"So why don't you?"

"I don't know. I guess because when I joined, Jolie already had the job."

"You could work at a different day care, then," he says. "I thought you were sensational with that block structure. Like prime architect material." I suddenly realize he's flirting with me.

"Sensational, huh? You should see what I can do with Play-Doh. It's naps I can't do. Of course, I never could get my own kids to sleep either, so there you go."

"Maybe you're just so much fun that they don't want to miss a minute of you."

I laugh. "That must be it."

"So what *do* you do?" he says after a moment. *"Are* you an architect?"

"I'm a baker. In a health food store."

"Do you like doing that?"

"Well. Usually it's okay. You get to tell the ingredients what to do instead of them bossing you around. You put the dough in a bowl, put a cloth on it, and it rests. No arguing. And at the end of the day, you can eat what you made."

He makes a face. "Yeah, but it's *health food.* Isn't it all that whole wheat, hard brown stuff that is supposed to be so good for you?" He holds up the can of Coke, as if he's going to propose a toast. "I'm more of a Wonder bread and Coke man, myself."

I laugh. "Yeah. That's the downside. Of course, it keeps me from wanting to eat everything I bake."

He is looking at me. "Your daughter is Abbie? She's certainly a cute one."

I wipe off the countertops. "Yeah, they're all cute. That's the good part of day care. That, and the fact that you get to smell them."

"God, I know! Don't they smell *wonderful?* It's like, how did we lose that smell?"

I like him. He's wiping his face off on his T-shirt, and I can see that his jeans are down low, riding on sharp hipbones. I like hipbones in a man. From the top of his jeans I can see some blue plaid boxer shorts. Usually I'm more suspicious of men as good-looking as he is. But he's leaning against the big silver refrigerator, and there's something so open and almost vulnerable about his face when he's talking about kids. But he's Jolie's, I remind myself. Plus, he's about twenty-seven or twenty-eight. Then I have to give myself a little talking-to about how I'm not looking for anything *from* him; I'm just appreciating him. And when

I look up, he's smiling at me so sweetly, so . . . *appreciatively*. I don't have to do anything else but just be there with him looking at me, don't have to run around making him feel good, don't have to impress him with any excellent moral development, or courage, or my ultimate coolness. I'm just standing there in my jeans with a black turtleneck and my hair all roughed up from playing with kids. I'm a mess.

"So, you always work on Thursday mornings?" he says. "I'm thinking of making this a regular thing."

"Oh. Actually no. I'm Friday mornings usually. I was just filling in for somebody today."

"Friday morning," he says and thinks. "Well, then, that's when I'll come."

"If you come then, though, you won't be working with Jolie," I say. "That's her time off."

"Oh, I don't care about that," he says. "In fact, that might be better."

I don't want to ask him what he means. I hang the dishrag on the hook, turn off the lights, and we walk upstairs together. I'm aware of his body near mine all the way up to the second floor. At one point his hip brushes against my hand, and he says, "Oops, sorry," and he smiles at me, that kind of bad boy smile that I've always liked. *Stop it,* I say to myself.

"Does, uh, Abbie's dad do turns here, too?" he says.

"Well," I say slowly, "he did, and he would again if he weren't in Santa Fe. He left last year to go build condos, and he hasn't come back yet."

"Oh." He frowns slightly, and I wonder if he's heard about Lenny from Jolie.

"We have another kid, too. Hope, who's ten."

"Really! Santa Fe, huh?"

"Yep. Building condos, he says."

"When *is* he coming back?"

"Well, now," I say, "that's a good question. Other people tell me he's planning a visit soon, but to tell you the truth, if he's coming at all and that's a big *if, I* think he's coming here just to end the marriage and go right back. That's sort of what I'm expecting."

He reaches over then and squeezes my hand, but then holds onto it. "I'm sorry," he says. "That must be kinda rough."

I shrug, take my hand back. "Well," I say, "it's been a weird year. But I'm over it now." We've gotten to the door of the day care and can hear the kids and the afternoon turn-doers arriving, all sorting out what's next. It's one o'clock, so some kids go down for naps while others get to go to the story corner and have a rest. I can hear Hannah calling Rachel to put on her socks. "You can't be barefooted in day care," she is saying.

Josh laughs a little. "You can't be barefooted in day care?" he says softly. And then he just kind of leans over and brushes his lips against my forehead, just as smoothly and simply as anything. And then his lips kind of move down, bump into my nose, and I must tilt my head, startled, because suddenly he's kissing me on the lips. Just a brief kiss—no tongue, nothing sexy about it—but still. Deep, warm, cushiony lips.

Okay, so look. I know the difference here. I can tell he's obviously one of those who hugs and kisses people easily. I mean, just the way he came into the day care and ten seconds later, had scooped up little Jezebel, and ten minutes after *that,* had the whole day care cuddled against him. He's just one of those *physical* people. I manage to squash down an impulse to reach up and run my finger along the outline of his lips, and he smiles at me as if he can see just what I was thinking. I push the door open quickly and we are immediately delivered into the chaos of the Changing of the Turn-doers. Robert, just arriving for his afternoon turn, is sorting out the nappers from the story-hearers. Jolie is getting her coat on, and she looks over expectantly at Josh and me. "Wanna go for lunch?" she calls to him, and he runs his fingers through all that magnificent curly hair and says something about having a paper to work on. Hannah's rummaging for her car keys. I kiss Abbie good-bye, and she scampers over to the story area. Josh smiles at me, touches my hand.

"I'll see you next week," he says in a low voice. And then I swear he winks at me. I can't help enjoying Jolie's confusion.

*Oh, Jolie, did something disturb you about the way Josh just looked at me? Oh, my goodness gracious! Did you somehow get the impression that you get every man? Is that the way things are supposed to work?*

Then I slide my exceedingly-mature-and-hardly-bitter-at-all self into my coat and wave good-bye to the kids and go out the door. Hannah comes out ten seconds later and rushes to catch up with me. The sky is hard, the color of a bruise. I can see her breath, hanging in the air like a thought balloon.

"What in the world was all that about?" she says. She's breathing hard. "You've got five seconds to tell me everything!"

I walk fast with my head down, smiling so hard my cheeks hurt. "Don't make me tell you. I'm trying to be a grown-up."

"Come on." She grabs my hands, laughing.

"Really. It was nothing. Nothing at all. Practically nothing."

"If you tell me your secret, I'll tell you mine."

"You don't have a secret." We get to the cars, parked at the curbside. I want to get into mine and sit there, hunched over the steering wheel, hugging myself, sorting myself out, getting under some control. Hannah watches me, head tilted.

"Josh was cute," she says experimentally. "And I do, too, have a secret."

I look at the trees. "I guess so. He's too young, but he's cute."

She laughs. "I was so hoping you were downstairs necking with him. Were you?"

"Hannah, please, please stop. I'm barely holding together as it is."

"It was just interesting, that's all. Jolie kept asking me where the two of you were. I think she was really freaked out."

I lean against the hood of the car. "I should go. Quick. Before he comes out."

"Wouldn't that be something," she says, "*you* taking Jolie's boy-friend away from her? Now that would be such a hoot, I think we'd have to throw a party just to watch the whole thing play out. And he's adorable. This could be a lot of fun."

"It's nothing," I say. Then I look at her smiling eyes and say, "He did sort of kiss me."

"*Really?* No. Get out of town. He did not kiss you."

"He did. We were talking in the kitchen, and then we came upstairs, and I was telling him about Lenny, and first he squeezed my hand, and then he leaned over and kissed me."

"Like a *kiss* kiss?"

"Well. No. Not exactly. It was on the forehead, and then his lips sort of slid down and he kissed me on the mouth."

"On the mouth? Jesus."

"I think it was just a sympathy kiss. He's a little impulsive, I think."

"God, yes, impulsive. But still! A mouth kiss. Wow. While you were doing the dishes, he had kids jumping off his shoulders onto the mattress."

"He might be a little crazy. Did you see how he put carrots in his nose?"

She nods. "Still," she says, "crazy might be fun. Temporarily. You and Josh making Jolie crazy."

"It's not going to happen," I say. We're silent a moment. I look at her face, which is drawn all of a sudden. She looks like she might cry. "Hey. What's going on with you?"

"I've been debating whether to talk to you about this."

"Is there anything you can't talk to me about?" I say. "Aren't the two of us required by law to tell each other everything?"

"Well," she says.

"So what is it?"

She's silent for a moment more, bites her lip, looks up at the bare branches of the trees, and then she says, "Well, I haven't wanted to say anything about this, but the truth is that I . . . well, I have a little crush on somebody." I can't help it; I feel my heart slide down into my stomach. Michael's face hovers for a moment in the air between us.

"A crush on somebody?" I say, trying to make sure I keep smiling. "On whom?"

"You're thinking about Michael," she says to me. "Stop thinking Michael for a minute."

"Okay." Deep breath. "So who do you have a crush on?"

"On the guy at the arts workshop."

I must look blank because she says, "Remember when I took the oil painting course? The teacher was this guy, Zeke, who's *wonderful*. And a few weeks ago, I ran into him, and we had coffee, and, oh, Maz, I've been *wanting* to talk to you about it, but we always have about a million children around us, and"—she stops and hugs herself—"but, Maz, he's so cute, and he's so nice, and now we've been meeting for coffee and talking on the phone a lot—and I think I could really be falling in infatuation with him."

"Not love?" I keep myself smiling so steadily that my cheekbones are hurting.

"Well, I'm holding it at infatuation."

"But he can't be more wonderful than Michael," I say and then I'm sorry, because her face gets dark.

"Can't somebody have somebody wonderful and also a little crazy fantasy life?" she says. "That's the trouble with you—you don't know the difference."

I try to look as though maybe I do know the difference. "I mean, I know you're not going to *act* on this. I'm sorry I said that," I tell her quickly. "But isn't it a little bit . . . dangerous?"

She slams her hand against the hood of the car. "Listen, *life* is dangerous!" she says. "Didn't anybody ever tell you that? The whole enterprise is just the most dangerous, heart-rending thing there is. But we can't stop having our feelings, just because of that."

I touch the spot on my forehead where Josh kissed me. It still feels warm. Then Hannah flings herself at me, and she's hugging me ferociously. "Oh, Mazzie, it's going to be fine, just fine! I feel so alive right now, and I've been so . . . I don't know . . . bogged down and in a rut. I mean, this guy loves my *paintings*."

I can't help thinking, Michael loves your paintings, too.

She's watching me think that. "Yeah, yeah, Michael says he does, but he doesn't know anything about art. Zeke knows, and he loves my paintings. And we talk about stuff that Michael doesn't know anything about—art and paintings and all these crazy political ideas that I never talk to anybody about. I've missed feeling this way so much. Don't get all gloomy about this."

"I won't," I tell her. "But please be careful, will you?" I feel a bad taste in my mouth. I can't help thinking that she looks like Lucille used to look, back when she was trying to justify leaving one guy for another, newer, streamlined version. But surely Hannah isn't really going to leave Michael. She can't.

"You are sooo getting gloomy," she says. She puts her hands on my shoulders. "Listen to me. You've got such uptight issues about the whole man-woman thing. It's left over from your childhood. Don't get so anxious, baby. I'm *fine*."

She may be right. I try for a more authentic, reassuring smile. This is *Hannah*, not Lucille.

"Anyway," she says, "you're the one with the possibilities, making out in the day care, you know. Next thing I know, you two will be searching for a crib you can fit into."

I'm so glad she can't see how just the thought makes me shiver.

# 13

I *admit it.* I got my weird ideas of love at an early age. Most people have to wait at least until puberty before they figure out how bizarre the whole man-woman game can be, but when you live part-time on the road with an itinerant fortune-teller like Madame Lucille, well, you can pretty much get the gist of things early.

Summer after summer, she and I drove together through the South in her Buick convertible with the top down, the rusty orange and white trailer bumping along behind us, going from one carnival and country fair to the other. I remember mostly the endless flat, yellow fields dotted with pine trees, a dome of midnight blue sky overhead, and clouds so big and cottony, you could see any picture you wanted in them—and Lucille clutching the steering wheel, with a cigarette dangling out of her mouth and a bottle of ice-cold Co-Cola jammed between her thighs, while she talked nonstop, keeping me enthralled or bringing me to tears with the Amazing Story of Her Life.

I had my favorite Lucille stories, of course, and she'd tell these over and over again: the one about her next-door neighbor who'd been struck by lightning and had had his yellow hard hat *fused* onto his head so hard that his eyeballs turned the color of a canary; the woman who'd had a nervous breakdown and started foaming at the mouth in the supermarket when she was overcharged three cents; the old man with cancer who'd actually had a conversation with an angel in line at the post office. But best were the uncensored tales she told of what had happened in her own life—starting with discovering she was psychic when she was four years old and realized she saw things nobody else knew about. She'd had to make her own way because nobody, not even her own family, had ever really believed in her. There were also the stories of unscrupulous men, out for Only One Thing, who had taken advantage of her again and again. "Beautiful women have to be so careful around men all the goddamn time," she'd told me. "Now you—you're just cute, so you might not have to worry about this—but when you have real beauty, believe me, it's like a curse. You have to watch out every second."

And she was beautiful. God, just to be able to ride beside her in the car and look at her was almost enough joy for me: her smooth, creamy skin, dark blue eyes, and blond ponytail. She looked like the Barbie doll that I kept clutched in my lap the whole time, except there was no confusing *her* life with the blandness of Barbie's. Barbie, after all, had only Ken with his sculpted crest of hair and his benign little lump at the crotch. My mother had a whole stable of men who came, stayed a while, and then went—grunting, hairy, sweaty men who made a lot of noise in the night in her bed, and left little black whiskers in the trailer's tiny sink. They had real penises, too; I'd seen them sometimes, white flesh dangling from a nest of murky darkness, but only for a second, before they were quickly covered up. Sometimes a guy would forget and Lucille would bark out, "E*xcuse* me. I have a *kid*!"

I found the men mostly amusing, and curious, nothing like my grandfather, Big Daddy, who was rather meek except when he was preaching. These men shook the trailer whenever they walked, or moved. They had deep, booming laughs and funny smells. One of them could crush beer cans with his bare hands; another one liked to do card tricks, and one was always pulling a quarter out from behind my ear and laughing at me for not knowing it was there. But just as I'd get used to one, there'd be some inevitable problem, and then Lucille would have to go back to being alone—and that always set off the signal that meant that it was time for me to go back to living with my grandparents.

The carnivals and fairs were a blur to me, at least when I think back on them now: the hot, dusty fields, cotton candy, melting ice cream, and greasy fried dough, the shrieks of the dirty country kids, spinning around on the rides and screaming. I went on the rides as much as I wanted to, so I had nothing but contempt for kids who acted as though a roller coaster or Ferris wheel was the end-all of human existence. This was my world, after all: sticky and dirty and filled with twirling machines and bright lights.

Lucille would sit in a cramped little tent with her turban and crystal ball while customers lined up for their fortunes, and I took their tickets. I'd watch their faces when they came out. They were always smiling or else looking puzzled. I'd hear them say things like, "She said the number five is going to be very important in my life," or "She says I'm going to work hard but then come into a big inheritance." It was the same everywhere we went. After closing time, our trailer was filled with carnival workers, smoking and laughing loud and sitting in each other's laps while they drank beers and cussed and hollered. I loved soaking up all their diatribes, their jokes, the gossip they told about each other, as well as the sad stories that got told late when the beer was nearly gone. The women all seemed to me to be skinny and tired, with lots of makeup, teased-up hair, and a tough way of talking. Not Lucille, though. She was the queen of them all, and I knew the men thought so, too, because they always wanted to sleep in our trailer with her, even if she didn't really know them very well. She'd always say, "*Hell,* no! I've got a *kid* here, whaddaya think?" But then some nights when a guy would say that, the carny people would suddenly say I could go on the rides after hours, long after everything was supposed to be closed down. Just me. My favorite rides were the Tilt-A-Whirl and the Scrambler, and anything that flung me around in circles. By the time I got back to the trailer, somebody would say, "Oh, your mama's already gone to sleep, honey—why dontcha just come bunk with me tonight?" I'd get kind of a sick feeling then, knowing she'd wanted to have sex with that guy all along. Seeing those whip-around rides still makes me queasy, and even just catching a glimpse of an ordinary parking-lot carnival from the highway can make me feel cold for hours.

Lucille didn't keep anything from me. She'd sleep with a guy, and then the next day, we'd discuss whether or not he might be The One. We both were devout believers that there was one perfect guy somewhere, and we had to find him. We made lists of a new prospect's good characteristics: he's fun, he likes to dance, he believes in the spirit world, he doesn't hate the idea of a kid being around, he's good in bed. And the bad ones: he thinks women should cook every night and not tell people's fortunes, he looks at other women, he drinks too much beer, he's got a prison record, he shot a guy in Memphis. I had a thing for men with twinkly eyes and who called me a nickname, like Kiddo; I noticed that she liked them best when they had good cars and a sarcastic sense of humor.

The first one I got to vote on was Pete the Fireman, who I gave the thumbs-up to when I was four, and he repaid me by giving me a little gold wedding ring at the ceremony. He even took me to the firehouse and let me ride on the truck. I called him Daddy, which he said was okay since I didn't really have a daddy. Of course, I had one, because you can't get born without a daddy, as I explained to Pete—but I just didn't know him because Lucille and he didn't get married. Somebody else had got him first, I said. Otherwise, he'd be here for sure.

Pete the Fireman laughed and hugged me when I told him that, but he didn't stick around anyway. After a while, he and Lucille were yelling at each other all the time. She said he was immature and refused to be a man, and then she and I hitched up the trailer one night while he was at work, and we left him a note and got out of there. I was seven at the time, and I kept asking her if we'd see him again—maybe we were just going off to tell fortunes again—but she said no, I should forget all about Pete and also try not to get involved with a man like him when I got bigger, because even though he looked like a man and talked like a man, he wasn't a real man in bed. I spent years trying to figure out how somebody could be a man out of bed, but that in bed he turned into something else. But what?

Even though I missed Pete the Fireman a lot, I had to admit that things were better than ever with Lucille once he was out of the picture. I got to sleep next to her in the bed in the trailer, and when I'd wake up in the morning, there she'd be, with her pink satin sleep mask pulled over her eyes. She had beautiful teeth, shiny with moisture, and her mouth would be slightly open while she slept. I'd lie as still as I could in the morning and listen to her even, gentle breathing. When she woke up, she'd often reach over and snuggle with me and call me her sugar bear and honey bunny and tell me how much she loved me. Her breath would be bad from cigarettes and sleep, and her voice thick, but I didn't care.

After I'd been with her a while, the day would always come when Lucille would look up and say it was time to "break up the team." This meant I had to go back to live with my grandparents. I'd know then, with a heavy lump in the pit of my stomach, that she'd gotten sick of being a mother again. Sometimes she'd just get depressed, no matter how much fun we were having and how little trouble I was being. A few times I came into the trailer and discovered that she wouldn't get out of bed, wouldn't tell fortunes. She said the whole world could go to hell for all she cared. She'd taken pills, and she said she was going somewhere better. Even as a little kid, I knew what to do—how to call the ambulance and make sure she got to the hospital. Then I had to go be with Grandmama and Big Daddy again, back in Starke. Sometimes, after she'd had a "little vacation in the nut ward," as she put it, she'd show up there, too, and live for a while in their spare room. Once she tried to get kind of a salon going, telling fortunes to her old school friends in the evenings, and working at the Rexall drugstore in the daytime. But nothing like that could work for long. Even I could see Lucille didn't belong in Starke. She'd be there with us, but it was like she was always getting ready to leave, moony and restless, pacing through the house late at night and sleeping away half the day. She got on Grandmama's nerves.

I told her lots of times that I needed her to get a good daddy for me so that I could live with her all the time, but she said husbands were strange, not really the same as people's daddies, and that they all had their own little insanities. "You just have to figure out if you can put up with whatever particular brand of craziness he's got, and *then* you can figure out if you can have a kid around at the same time," she said. "I'm workin' on it, though. I know we'll find him somewhere. We're gonna get us The One, baby, and then we'll be together all the time."

I hated leaving her, but the truth was, I liked my life in Starke with my grandparents, too. In Starke, I was important, being the preacher's granddaughter. Grandmama Esther, who was fat and so pink that she looked as though she'd been steamed, ran all the missions projects and spent most of her time directing clothes drives and cooking meals for the poor. They lived in the parsonage, on a quiet road with sidewalks and picket fences. I was a different girl in Starke, my grandparents' girl, studying hard, playing ball with my friends in the road, dressing up on Sunday mornings. I actually forgot about Lucille for long stretches at a time. I got caught up being a regular kid: listening to Big Daddy thundering in the pulpit on Sundays and helping Grandmama fry chicken on weekend afternoons. I did well in school, spent the night with my best friend Dixie, and was careful not to step on cracks that might break my mama's back—though a lot of times I'd be surprised to realize it was Grandmama's back I was thinking of, and not Lucille's.

It's just that on some nights there, drifting off to sleep in my feather bed, hearing Big Daddy reading the Bible or the church people laughing on the porch, I'd think about creamy, drifty Lucille, out there wandering somewhere in the world, letting men sleep with her in the trailer, and living on Co-Cola and banana-mayonnaise sandwiches—and I'd feel myself thinking I had to find some way to save her.

When I was ten years old, just the age Hope is now, Lucille let me in on two big secrets about her life, and everything for us changed after that.

Number one was that she already *knew* who The One was—you know, the one we'd both been looking for. She had met him when she was sixteen, and his name was Jackson Angus. She said that name with the same reverence I mostly heard when people said, "Our God the Father." It was a name that she let roll around on her tongue. He had loved her, too; they had had a great romance, which she still loved to tell the details of, and then he had got away from her. But she was going to find him, she said. She looked in bars and at carnivals, in the next car at stoplights, at the man pumping her gas in the filling station. She said, smiling real big, that we would someday hook up with him again.

"Why," I once asked her, "do you keep marrying these *other* guys and letting them sleep with you, when you know they're not The One?" She just laughed and said she had to do *something* while she waited. She wasn't dead, you know.

But it was the second truth that practically knocked me over, made me know we were into something badly serious. She and Jackson Angus, back when she was still just a kid, had made a baby together— a little girl she had named Cassandra—and even though he had gone away before that baby was born and had never even known about her, he was going to someday be so glad to hear that he was a daddy.

I had to have this fully explained to me—how it was you could make a baby with somebody and they wouldn't know. And how you could have a baby and then just not have it with you anymore. Was she someday going to just show up and Lucille would be *her* mother, too?

Yes oh yes, and it would be wonderful when it happened. Lucille's eyes practically shot off sparks when she talked about the great day when Jackson Angus and Cassandra and I would be all together again, a very special family. She'd seen Cassandra for only a few minutes after the birth, before they'd whisked her away and given her to some other family—but in those few moments, Lucille had known that Cassandra was her soul mate.

"I had this impulse to just grab her and run out of that hospital," she said to me, "but you couldn't do that then. They'd made me sign the papers already. I just gave up my little Cassandra, and that is my greatest sorrow. She's your big sister, honey, and wherever she is, I can just feel how much she loves us and wants us to find her."

The stories about Cassandra and Jackson Angus were fascinating, but they made my stomach hurt so bad that I would have given anything to go back to some of her old favorite stories instead, like the story of the man whose hard hat had stuck to his head after the lightning bolt. Cassandra was an unknown quantity—always called a "little angel"— but whenever the stories turned to Jackson Angus, you could feel a kind of dangerous electricity in the air, like a thunderstorm was just about to hit and your hair was standing on end.

He was a drifter type, who drove a red Mercury and wore tight jeans and had that kind of slicked-down hair with a big Woody Woodpecker kind of crest in the front, and to hear her tell it, nobody could look at him without falling madly in love with him. And he was edgy—Jesus Christ, he had the hard-to-get game down to a science. Lucille met him when he got hired by Big Daddy to do some work around the parsonage, and it was while he dangled from ladders, flexing his muscles and smoking his cigarettes down to the butt, that Lucille realized he was somebody she had to have. He had a cruel smile, and a jaw that jutted out and for some reason made her weak. Years later, you say to her, "What was really so sexy about Jackson Angus?" and she'll rhapsodize for forty-five minutes about that jaw. I have told her that it's never been the jaw that's driven me mad for a man. More the eyes—or even the butt. She says that's because I'm too conventional, that it's the jaw that holds all the danger and cruelty. Eyes and butts are easy to win over, she says, but it's the jaw you have to watch out for.

Lucille was proud to tell me she didn't have friends in high school, mainly because she was always telling them stuff about themselves they didn't really want anybody to know. In a town where everybody either played football, marched in the band, or was a cheerleader, Lucille and her tarot cards enjoyed a kind of outlaw status. She pranced around in fishnet stockings and skirts with slits in them, and she carried—God help us—a cigarette holder. She hung out with misfits, those alienated kids who were too misshapen or unhygienic or klutzy to fit in with the athletic-worshiping crowd—some pimply girl named Priscilla Pummeland, and a couple of others whose names Lucille didn't tell me. I think Grandmama and Big Daddy were probably just holding their breath, praying that Lucille would grow up and get the hell out of Starke before she brought down the whole town somehow.

It didn't take Jackson Angus long to figure out what was what with her, so he steadily ignored her while she flounced around him. And then one night, she told me, after getting no attention from him, she just got up in the middle of the night and snuck out of the house and walked through the woods to the garage where he lived and gave herself to him. Just like a movie, the most romantic movie ever, she said. At first he told her no. Oh, he tried hard to resist her because he knew how *golden* she was, what a present she was, and he didn't want to take her gift away from her. But she kept after him, she said proudly—and always, at this point in the story, she would become so dreamy and far away, it was as though she never thought for a minute who she was telling all this to. The important thing—the real thing, she said—was that she had triumphed over him, that she had worked to get him and then had won him. Nothing could beat that.

For nearly a year, that was their pattern: she'd sneak out a few times a week and take food from Esther's kitchen and go have sex with Jackson. She thought up deliciously wicked ways to entice him each time, brought him sexy stories and games and costumes. He never once encouraged her, and in fact, quite a few times she'd get there and he'd meet her at the half-cracked door and declare that he was finished with "screwing children," as he put it, and he'd make her go back home. He'd get scared about her daddy, him being the preacher and all, that was the way she saw it. But mostly, she told me, she was able to get what she wanted from him. He could not resist her, because she had so much heat about her. And he loved her wild, inventive stories. After sex, she would tell him tales about the rest of the misfits at the high school, particularly the overweight Priscilla Pummeland, whom everyone called The Pump. He loved those stories of everyday high school life, the cruelties, the catastrophes. One day she told him that The Pump had fallen on her back in the hallway and couldn't get up, and she lay there with her legs waving in the air, and everybody who walked by looked up her dress and discovered she wasn't wearing underpants. It wasn't true, but she still remembers how he threw back his head and laughed so hard, she thought he was going to choke. He'd say to her, "Tell me again about that Priscilla."

After months of sneaking out and having the best sex she could imagine, she says that trouble came to find them. Trouble, she told me, always comes just when you're the happiest and expecting it the least. And anyway, she'd been a fool, not making Jackson Angus use *precautions*. She just didn't ever want anything to come between them, nothing like a rubber—and where was she going to get birth control pills, with her mama on the board of every clinic in town? She just pushed the whole idea out of her mind, she says, didn't give it one second's thought that anything bad could happen. And who knows? Maybe, she said, in her psychic fortune-telling wisdom back then, maybe it was the right thing that she hadn't taken precautions. It was meant to be. One night, getting dressed to meet him, in a cheerleader outfit she'd stolen from the girls' locker room and which he found very sexy, she discovered she couldn't even button the thing up. She tried to think of the last time she'd been visited by her "friend" (that's what she always called her period, smiling coyly at me at the whole time), and damned if she couldn't remember. She sat down on the bed and stared at the calendar and then at her belly, which was sticking out like some kind of coconut—and she said to herself, "Goddamn if I'm not pregnant." Those were the very words she used: "Goddamn if I'm not pregnant."

No wonder, she thought then, no wonder she hadn't been feeling so alone lately. For weeks now, she'd been holding Jackson's baby inside her. She'd never be by herself again. A lot of girls might have thought this was a bad thing, she told me. But, after the initial five seconds of shock wore off, she said, she was thrilled—amazed and delighted! She couldn't wait to tell him this great momentous news. Their lives were changing, she was getting the hell out of Starke. Oh, she was sure he'd want to get married right away—they'd leave Starke together, raise their amazing child, and her life would be settled at last. No more arguing with Big Daddy and Esther; no more sulking around the house, wondering how she was ever going to get out. This was Big. This was her ticket. She couldn't wait to see the look on Jackson's face. He would *know* this was meant to tie them together forever.

When she got to his garage, though—well, it was one of his tight-ass nights. He didn't want to have sex. He didn't even want to talk. He said the cheerleading outfit made her look like a fucking tart, and he told her she had to forget all about him and never come back again. Ha! Like that was even possible. But she was used to this kind of tiresome treatment of his, the way he was always running hot and cold. That was just the way Jackson Angus was. This was the part of his personality that she was going to cure by loving him enough and finally helping him find the life he was meant to lead, not just being a handyman for people. She didn't even flinch or beg him this time. Filled with resolve, she left him the basket of fried chicken and cole slaw she'd brought for them and sashayed herself back home, where she spent the rest of the night dreaming about where they'd live once the baby came. She worked it all out: they should go to a city, a place where nobody knew them, and Jackson Angus could get work in some kind of building industry, and she could raise the baby and run a salon with lots of interesting people. They'd have young, hip friends, and everyone would admire their baby and tell Lucille how brilliant and beautiful she was.

Then the next day all hell broke loose.

Lucille woke up to hear a house full of people, all talking loud and stamping around downstairs. The phone was ringing off the hook, and even from her bedroom upstairs, she could feel the vibe of something gone very wrong. When she went downstairs, she found out that Priscilla Pummeland was missing, and, just like she was somebody important to anybody, the whole town had gathered at Lucille's house to organize a search for her. Priscilla had last been seen walking down the creek road the day before, and her father—an alcoholic who always seemed to be in tears—couldn't remember if she'd come home the night before or not. Lucille, in the thick of her daydream about her new life, really couldn't have cared less. The house was crammed with a bunch of busybodies, all running around like they were detectives or something, reporting in from their searches. Lucille's mother kept calling herself Command Central. She whipped up casseroles and muffins for the searchers, and everybody just kept shaking their heads and speculating and wringing their hands over how sad the whole thing was. Really, Lucille couldn't believe it—all this for a stupid girl like Priscilla, who didn't have even one lick of sense. And now she'd run off somewhere. A *tragedy*. Lucille wanted nothing more than to get away from them.

She put up with it as long as she could and then she stomped upstairs to take a nap and dream about her new life. Frankly, she was disturbed that nobody ever came to *her* and asked her opinion on where The Pump might be. She was the town's psychic, after all; hadn't she proven that again and again? Besides that, she was mad at The Pump. Lately Priscilla had gotten even fatter and more pimply and disgusting, if possible, and now that Lucille had this thing going with Jackson Angus, they had nothing to talk about anymore.

When Lucille woke up a few hours later, she says she knew immediately, all through her body, that her life had curdled around her. She stood and stared at herself in the bathroom mirror, her face luminous as the moon. Something was very wrong. At first she thought she'd lost the baby, she felt that alone. Downstairs, she could hear people coming in and talking about the futility of the search. She says, in inimitable Lucille fashion, that she knew just what she had to do.

Even though her hands felt clammy and her stomach turned over again and again, she walked downstairs, past all the useless searchers, out the door, and down the street, out to the edge of town, way past Jackson's garage. Even now she'll tell you she remembers everything about that walk—the oppressive heat and humidity, the feel of her footfalls that seemed to shake her bones clear through, and the way a breeze came up in the darkness and caught at her hair. She remembers the rumble of a train from far away, and the way everything felt still and unnatural, as if the world itself were holding its breath, waiting until she made her discovery. She didn't look around, not even when she cut across an empty lot where people threw out their old tires and bedsprings, over by the creek where the Spanish moss hung down like unkempt gray beards covering everything. When she came to the stump of an oak tree, she looked around and there he was, just as she knew he'd be: a newborn baby, still with flecks of blood and white cheesy stuff on his face. But he was alive; he was wrapped tightly in a newspaper and making little mewing noises. He turned his head toward her when she picked him up. She saw his tiny unfocused eyes, wrapped her own long fingers around his curled-up little fists. She was surprised by the weight of him as she carried him back to Jackson's, at how he moved underneath the newspaper and how he kept turning his face to her body, searching for food or comfort from her. She could barely stand to hold him. Twice she stopped to vomit in the weeds.

Of course Jackson Angus was gone from the garage. The landlady, a woman in her thirties who always wore a red bandanna and smiled knowingly at Lucille whenever she saw her there late at night, answered her loud yelling at the garage door and said, "Honey, don't even bother. Jackson paid off all the rent he owed, packed up his stuff, and I don't expect that either one of us is gonna see him again." Lucille nodded at her, as if in a dream. The woman said, "I'm so sorry, honey. That kind of man—omigod, is that a baby?" But Lucille held up her hand to silence her. "I'm not asking for you being sorry," she said. She felt like the whole top of her head was coming off right then, it was so filled up with the horrible truth.

When Lucille got back to her house, still carrying the baby, who was howling by then, she went into the kitchen, still cluttered with people drinking coffee and eating cake and shaking their heads and ruminating about everything. Everybody stopped when she came in. Forks were in midair. Voices came to a halt. She handed the baby over to Esther, still kicking about in his stupid newspaper blanket. Very calmly, she said that if anyone wanted to find Priscilla, they'd better hurry. Priscilla, she said, had had a baby in the woods, and now she was in Gainesville with Jackson Angus, sitting in a diner just outside of town, but Jackson would be leaving without Priscilla soon after, and then Priscilla would probably go, too, on the money Jackson Angus would be handing over.

"Jackson *Angus*? That handyman?" said one of the searchers, and the men gave each other strange looks, but after a long silence, Esther said, "I don't know why, but Lord knows she's probably right." And so everybody got in their cars and when they came back, they had Priscilla with them. There had been no sign of Jackson Angus, they said, just Priscilla sitting at a table in the diner, as Lucille had said, drinking black coffee and staring straight ahead. She had a little pink overnight bag sitting next to her in the booth, the hard cardboard kind with a tiny mirror in the lid.

I've always hated this next part of the story, which only occasionally gets told—usually late at night, when Lucille has been drinking and crying. How she took Priscilla up to her bedroom, saying she'd help her get cleaned up, and then how she made Priscilla tell all the details, giving her chocolate and belts of whiskey, until she had the whole story out of her: that Jackson tracked her down, would come around the factory where Priscilla worked after school and offer to drive her home, how they'd go out the lake road to a place he knew where they wouldn't be disturbed. Lucille slapped her across the face, and said to her, "He was *mine,* you stupid cow! You took my man away from me, and now look at how you've ruined everything!" Priscilla stared back at her without emotion, as if this were just one more odd thing to take in about the day.

Priscilla was sent away somewhere, and the baby went to a foundling home where he would certainly be adopted right away. Of course Lucille had to leave town, too. You couldn't be pregnant and just hang around Starke, while people watched your stomach grow and talked about you. Not if you were the pastor's daughter, particularly, and especially not if there was no boyfriend to be hustled into marrying you. She went to live with Big Daddy's sister, Noraleen, in Georgia, while she waited for her due date. Years later, she says that what she hates the most about the whole ordeal is that she never got to tell Jackson Angus she was pregnant, to see the amazed surprise on his face. He would have wanted to know, would have wanted to make things good for them. Once the Priscilla incident was behind him (Lucille calls this his "little unintended mistake"), he could have straightened himself out and been a good husband. Jackson Angus was the one true man for her, and she will forever search for him.

"The point of this story," she says, and I think she really believes this, "is that you have to seize love wherever you find it. I should have told him that night that there was a baby. I should have listened to my heart in the first place."

Why, I've often wondered, was it Jackson Angus that obsessed her—why him, and not any of the other men who waltzed in and out of her life, doing equally unspeakable things? After all this time, I think I know the answer. She simply can't stand the idea that she didn't see what was happening. Jackson Angus might have faded to just a distant memory, a blip on the screen, except that he committed the ultimate sin: not just betraying her by fucking her friend, but doing it right around her, without her psychic radar picking up the motion. Even at sixteen, she was already becoming Madame Lucille—and if she craves him still, it's merely because she's determined to get another chance to make the whole story come out the way she planned it in the first place. She wants to be right.

"If you had married Jackson Angus, then I would have never been born," I pointed out to her once when I was a teenager.

She was quiet at this, thinking of the other baby, I know, who still *would* have been born, who would have stayed hers, probably could have been taught to read the tarot cards or the tea leaves. Her and Jackson's child—now *that* is a person worth holding onto. Sometimes I'd hear her crying at night—and I'd turn away, heartsick, knowing she was crying for that other baby. Those two times I came into the trailer to find her lying on the floor with an empty bottle of pills lying next to her, she told me that the grief of losing little Cassandra—of never getting to show her off to Jackson—sometimes made her want to die.

After Cassandra's birth, Lucille stayed with her aunt Noraleen—Big Daddy was not in favor of bringing her back to town, subjecting her to what people would say—and when she was eighteen, she married an auto mechanic named Mike McCord, the son of one of her aunt's friends, and they lived with his parents for several years. Then a traveling stage show came to town, and Lucille fell in love with an actor in the company, right while he was on stage doing a love scene at the matinee. She went to his dressing room afterward to get his autograph, and something about the way he looked at her set off a spark within her that lit up those old, choked-off areas in her heart.

He was my father. But unfortunately, he was already married and couldn't stick around to meet me.

# 14

*I don't think* about Josh all week, and he doesn't come to do a turn the next Friday because we haven't had the official day care parents' meeting for the group to approve his joining up. This is fine with me because I'm busy getting ready for what I'm secretly calling the Get-Everybody-to-Like-Hope Party, which is the following Saturday.

I'm excited while it's still an idea—but then fifteen minutes into the party, I cannot think of why this ever seemed like something that would work. I must have been out of my mind. Not only have I sent Abbie away to Hannah's house for the night, but here's what I have bought for the occasion: crepe paper streamers, embroidery floss and muslin squares (in case we need a fun project late at night), two packages of hot dogs, buns, ketchup, a special kind of chips that are loaded into cans because Hope says those are the cool kind, a chocolate cake from the grocery store (she says my chocolate cakes are too rich and gooey, and I don't even argue with her), balloons, popcorn, Cokes in cans, hot chocolate mix, marshmallows, three cans of whipped cream, special scented candles, two rented videos, a book of ghost stories, three decks of cards, a Disney Trivial Pursuit game, fourteen colors of nail polish, a new vinyl tablecloth with a flannel backing, plastic silverware, and tickets to the ice-skating rink for five little girls.

Okay. It is the tiniest bit possible that I am trying too hard. I am imagining how, on Monday morning, her friends will say, "Wow, Hope, your mom is so *cool*," and Hope won't think anymore that I was mean to Lenny. Which I was not anyway, but it's no good having her think everything is all my fault.

Being the coolest of the moms, though, is a lot harder than I thought. "Oh, yuck! Is this a birthday party?" says one snotty kid as she walks in and sees the streamers and the balloons. "Because you should have told me. I didn't buy a present."

"No, no," I say quickly. "It's a—a Just Because Party."

Everybody, even Hannah's sweet daughter Lexie, looks at me as though a piece of furniture has somehow acquired human speech, and then they all turn back to one another and get down to the business of comparing shoes, friendship bracelets, hair ornaments, and nail polish colors. Tiffany Gilbert seems to win every contest. She keeps tossing her long wavy hair that's obviously been permed and probably streaked as well. What kind of mother would let a ten-year-old highlight her hair? Besides Lucille, I mean, who started putting Light 'n Bright on my hair when I was probably about three months old. I think she spent her rent money to make sure my hair had the proper amount of sparkly blond in it.

"How about some potato chips?" I say brightly, but no one answers.

I try again, in the approximate voice of a Dallas Cowboys cheer-leader. "We could eat something *before* we go to the skating rink, or we could buy snacks there!"

Tiffany says, answering somebody's question about something: "Oh, my mom got these in New York. I forget the name of the store. Besides, you can't get them anymore anyhow."

"Girls," I say. "Is anybody hungry?"

A kid who I think is named Danielle says, "Oh, my mom saw those in Boston, but, get this, she didn't think they were cool enough for me."

There is much admiring laughter. I look over at Hope, who looks out of place and slightly miserable. I know the feeling.

"Chips? Popcorn?" I say. "Cokes?"

But I have been rendered invisible, so I go into the kitchen and open the *Better Homes and Gardens* magazine and read about redwood planters. I'm in a full fantasy about how nice they'd look on the deck in the summertime, if by chance we *have* a deck in the summertime, when the telephone rings. It's Lucille.

"What are you doing on the phone? Aren't you supposed to be getting married right now?" I ask her.

"Oh, honey, the weddin's in another few hours. But, darlin', I just don't know what to think." Her voice catches. "Last night I dreamed about Jackson Angus, and now this mornin' I look at ole Harold, and sweetie, he just looks to me like some old man. I don't know what to do."

"Jeez, Lucille. You dream about your old boyfriend and so now you're not going to marry Harold?"

"I didn't say that. I just said he's an old, old man."

"Jackson Angus is an old man now, too."

"I guess you're right." I hear her clicking. Sniffling and clicking. "So you think I ought to go through with it? This is the right thing?"

"You're asking *me*?" I say. "I've never even met the man."

"I should go through with it, I reckon," she says. "He's nice to me, and he does have plenty of money." She laughs. "Now aren't I just the most horrible thing? That's just the kind of remark that gets me in trouble with you, 'cause you take everythin' I say so seriously. Listen, just forget I called. It's just that sometimes, I don't know, I start thinkin' about Jackson and little Cassandra and what might have been, and I think my whole life is just one big waste." She gives out a little melodramatic sob.

Just then the girls come trooping in and Hope says to me in a voice I don't recognize, "So are we going to the ice-skating rink or not?" She has her hand on her hip and her eyes seem heavy-lidded and dull. Her school self.

"Lucille, I've gotta go. I've got a kitchen full of kids wanting to go ice-skating. Listen, marry the guy and live it up. You deserve it."

"What I *deserve* is my rightful family," she says, sniffling. "That's what I deserve."

*What I deserve* is the Mother's Medal of Honor, I think later. The skating-rink deal at first seems like a fiasco. Hope whines when she can't rent skates that are just the right color, and by the time she finally accepts her fate and gets herself laced up and out on the ice, everybody else is gliding around, skating arm in arm. I see her stumble out there and pick her way around the side for a time, relearning how to do it. My heart starts cranking up its old familiar ache.

I buy a large cup of coffee from the snack bar and drag myself over to the benches where I can see the skaters more clearly. By now Hope has managed to get herself hooked up with her friends, but she still has a strained expression on her face. I don't think they really listen to her when she talks, and that makes me feel bad. But perhaps I'm just over-relating. When we get back home, I'll cook some hot dogs on the gas grill on the half-made deck, and then maybe I'll get out the embroidery floss and the muslin squares and we can all do a sewing project together. Or maybe we'll watch the videos or read ghost stories by the fire. I'll be a constant presence, Hope's protector. And if any of those sniveling little girls gives her a hard time, I'll take them in a separate room and tell them a ghost story that will curl their little highlighted hairs, and then I'll say, "And if you're ever mean to my daughter again, *this* will just be a pleasant memory compared to what happens to you *then*!"

"Omigod! Maz!" I hear just behind me, and when I turn around, there's Jolie. And behind her, Josh. Jolie is giving me her huge sharky smile. "What in the world are you doing here?" She peers out across the ice with her hand shielding her eyes. "Oh, look, there's Hope. Now where's Abbie?"

"She's staying with Rachel today," I say. I look up and smile at Josh, who's looking down at me and grinning.

"Isn't this, like, amazing? I was just saying to Josh that you can't go anywhere in New Haven without running into somebody you know, and, like, here you are! Are you skating? Or are you just like *the mom*, watching everybody's stuff?" When she says the word "mom," she does a little ironic curtsy, sort of like something Mary Tyler Moore would have done when she was talking to Mr. Grant. Really too, too cute for words. Lenny would *die* from this. "Well, I guess *somebody's* got to do it!" she says. "That's why I don't have kids. Too selfish for all that watching-after stuff, once I get off work, that is. I want to be, like, the one having the fun." She sits down and starts taking off her black leather boots and yanking on her skates.

Josh sits down on the other side of me. He spreads his hands across his knees. He's wearing brown corduroy pants and a black sweater. He is devastating. "I don't really skate," he says, smiling at me as though we're old friends. "Jolie's making me do this."

"It's time he, like, took some risks," she pronounces. "I told him, like, wear snow pants, but he claims he doesn't have any. Really," she says, leaning toward me conspiratorially, "he just thinks they're, like, too uncool. He's such an adolescent."

I can't take this, so I say I've got to make a phone call, and then I go stand by the door and try to think of somebody to call. Hannah's off taking the kids shopping. I suppose I could try calling Lenny again. I've tried him several times over the past few days, just waiting to say to him, "What the hell is going on? Are you coming home or not?" But I've been relieved each time when the phone has just rung and rung with no answer. The truth is I haven't decided yet if I really do want to know. Maybe, as long as I don't think about it, it won't be real. But then I shake myself out of that thinking. Hannah's right: I am so over Lenny, and I might as well find out what he's up to. It's stupid to keep my head in the sand. So slowly, as if in a dream, I tap in my calling card numbers and then his telephone number. While it rings, I look back over at the benches. Jolie and Josh are gone. She's on the ice, skating backward, and he's leaning on the fence, watching her. Then slowly he turns back and looks at me and holds up two fingers, the peace sign.

"Hello?" says a woman's voice after the third ring. She sounds breathless, like she ran there to pick up the phone. Or maybe she was just in the middle of the greatest orgasm of her life, but something made her pick up the phone anyhow.

I can't make myself say anything, even though I feel like I'm honestly trying to make sounds. My throat is so dry that all that comes out is a nearly inaudible squeak. I mean, who in the whole United States wasn't aware that Lenny was probably living with another woman—but somehow, having her answer the telephone, and in *that* breathless voice, I'm just caught up short, that's all.

"Hello?" she says again, this time with more impatience in her voice. I try to hear if there's any background noise; maybe I'll hear Lenny say, "Oh, give *me* the phone," or maybe I'll hear something that lets me know this is a wrong number. I strain, but there's nothing. "*Hello?*" she says one more time, and then she says, "Oh, fuck this," and hangs up.

I click off too and go get another cup of coffee, and when I come back to the bench, Josh turns and walks over to me. Behind him, I can see Jolie gliding with one leg extended into the air.

"I'm, um, really glad to see you again," he says. He leans against the wall near where I'm about to sit. "I think I worked it out with . . . Hannah, is it? . . . to be on the same turn with you. Isn't that great?"

"That's nice," I say.

He sits down next to me. "Say, how do you feel about motorcycles?"

"Hate 'em."

He laughs. "Would you like a little ride with me on mine? It's safe."

"No," I say. "I'm here watching about four million little girls." I tilt my head over to the ice, where the girls are all locked elbow-to-elbow sailing across the ice. Even Hope has lost her sour expression, and I have a moment of silent gratitude.

"Jolie'll watch them for you. Look, she's with them anyway."

It's true. Jolie has linked up with them, skating backward while they skate forward, and they are all giving her amazed looks, except for Tiffany, who probably could skate backward the day she came home from the hospital right after birth. She looks bored and tosses her head, forgetting that her hair is caught up in a stupid purple hat with a tassle on the top.

"Come on," he says after a moment. "You only live once."

"I know that. I just don't want it to end yet," I say.

"It won't end! Come on anyway. Wind in your hair, motor right under your legs, and, hey, not even any bugs in your teeth since it's March. A once-in-a-lifetime offer."

I look back at the girls.

"*Please*," he says. "You'll be happy you did it."

"Not for very long? I am giving a party."

"Jolie will handle the party. But no, not for very long."

So I go off with him. First, of course, I shout to Jolie that I'll be right back and could she watch the girls for me? She looks at them, counts heads, and then nods back. "I'll only be a minute!" I yell. Josh flashes her some bit of sign language. She looks confused but nods her head up and down. No one else seems to notice we're leaving.

He gives me Jolie's white helmet and I put it on. I feel like a creature from the space program, especially when he doesn't put one on at all. "I hate the way they feel, but you strike me as the safety-conscious type," he says. The motor makes a kind of loud, rumbling, burbling sound, and I climb on behind him. There's a place for my feet, but nowhere for my hands except around the middle of Josh. I have to say, it feels good to tuck myself up against him like that, to feel how warm and solid he is. The cold air stings my lips and cheeks, so I bury my face in his back. I can feel the bones of his spine and ribs, even through his coat, and underneath me the motor thrumming away, a kind of comforting low bass sound that vibrates my whole body. He takes off slowly, and we go down street after street, leaning into turns. Sometimes he talks to me above the motor. He says, "This is my favorite hill. Look over there!" And once he turns his head back and yells, "Isn't this the best feeling in the world? Next to sex, I mean."

I have to say, it is nice. But nothing like the little ripple of something I felt just hearing him say the word "sex."

He calls back to me, "Let's go up East Rock and look at the city."

"I don't know!" I shout. "We might need to get back!" My voice seems to blow back behind me instead of landing anywhere near him.

"Just for a minute!" he says.

"Won't Jolie mind?" I yell, although actually I don't much care if she minds or not. Let her mind. I'm more concerned about Hope.

"Nah!" he says. "Jolie's cool about this stuff."

When we get up to the top of East Rock, the view is really breathtaking. Lenny and I used to bring the kids up here a long time ago and have picnics near the statue. One time, he and Hope rolled down the hill into the meadow, end over end, and were so dizzy at the bottom that they had to go to bed for the rest of the day.

"What are you thinking about?" Josh says as we hop off the bike, so

I tell him about rolling down the hill, and he looks at me a long moment and says, "Man, that must be tough, breaking up. I'd be insane."

"It is possible that I am," I say as I shove my hands down into my pockets. The sky is getting cloudy. It must be about four o'clock, I think, and the wind is picking up. Josh leans over the bike, and then turns on the radio. "We need music in the world!" he hollers, and turns and smiles at me and holds out his hands. "In the Mood" is playing, and he turns it up loud and pulls me to him, and we start dancing around on the gravel, just tentatively at first but then picking up speed. My legs and arms can barely remember how to move in a dancelike way. But he knows how to twirl and dip and all that stuff, and soon I'm laughing hard as he spins me back and forth. He's got a silly expression on his face, happy like a child gets happy. Look at this, I think. I'm standing on the top of East Rock—if I squint through the trees, I can see my kitchen window from here—and I'm dancing with this guy I just met, and I'm laughing, hard, and as a bonus, it's pissing off Jolie to no end, no matter what *he* thinks. At the last note of the song, he grips my waist suddenly and dips me all the way down to the ground, and when he pulls me back up, his face is so close to mine that I lose my breath. And that's when he puts his mouth over mine, and kisses me so gently and tenderly that I'm certain I'm going to pass out as soon as he releases me. It is a kiss that is absolutely perfect.

He doesn't let me go. He says, "God, I've been wanting to do that." And then he starts kissing me again.

I'm quite certain that when we get back to the skating rink, the place will be locked up, with Jolie and all five little girls standing outside in the freezing cold, glaring at us as we come up on the bike. I'm almost shivering with guilt. This will be a story that Hope will be able to tell to therapists years from now, just the way I tell stories about Lucille's irresponsible behavior when I was a kid.

Even worse, I'm positive I must have little kiss trails all over my face and mouth and hair. And my body has turned languid, as though I'm drugged. When Josh and I started kissing up there on the hill, we didn't stop for a while. We just sat down on the rocks, with the beautiful view in front of us, and kissed until I lost track of time. I was beginning to see that there are good reasons for driving in automobiles instead of motorcycles: not everybody who's around gets to watch you kissing.

But when we get back to the rink, hell has not broken loose. The kids are drinking hot chocolate and sitting on the benches, still in their skates. Jolie is still out on the ice, sailing around like Katarina Witt, and the guy behind the counter is still admitting people to the rink. Hope looks happy, although her face clouds over just a tad when she sees me walk up with Josh. It's the old *who's this* look she gave me the other night with Dan Briggs.

"Say, who's ready to go out on the ice and teach me how to skate?" says Josh, swinging his arms back and forth and grinning at the girls. I see them size him up silently, and then because he's gorgeous and because he's not so old, and because they *are* females, I can see the little calculator in Tiffany's head registering him a good score. Out of the sizing-up silence, she is the first to say, "I'll teach you how to skate!" And then, what do you know, they *all* want to teach him how to skate. Hot chocolate cups are abandoned, skates are retied, and Josh puts on a pair of black hockey skates that it turned out he had brought along and that were tucked underneath the bench. The five little girls all help him lace them and tie them, and then all of them trundle onto the ice, Hope in the middle of them, smiling. She actually looks relaxed. I try to catch her eye, but she doesn't look in my direction.

Josh, of course, can already skate beautifully, and he glides along, pretending to stumble, grabbing onto this one and that one. They all laugh and shriek and show him their skating maneuvers. I hear them, "Can you do *this*, Josh? Look at me do *this*!" I get a fresh cup of coffee, although by now my heart is hammering so hard that I fear the caffeine is going to cause me to start break-dancing and singing Broadway show tunes right there in the rink. Jolie skates around and around in lazy circles, not looking at Josh or the girls.

I don't care what she does. I sit there and think about kissing.

• • •

*There's of course* no excuse for this, but when the rink closes an hour later, the girls run over and say that Josh is coming home with us, that he wants us all to get a pizza together, and I say okay.

To my credit, I do try to protest. "But we're having burgers and hot dogs," I say lamely, but the chorus of voices outnumbers mine. "No, pizza! Pizza! Pizza!"

Josh shrugs at me, his eyes crinkly and smiling. "I've just got to run Jolie home—her sister's coming over tonight—and then I could come back?" he says. He lifts his eyebrow at me. I'm so weak I'm not sure I can stand it, but I don't seem to be able to say no, either. Part of me is thinking, *What if I lose control and start having wild sex with him right there in the house?*

*I won't. Of course I won't.*

But what will stop me?

*Fear will stop me.*

That's right. Fear. It has ruled me so far in everything else in life. Surely just because I rode a motorcycle today to the top of East Rock while I was supposed to be giving a party for my daughter, and then made out with a *kid* eleven years younger than me, who just happened to be the boyfriend of my husband's lover—surely *that* won't change anything. I've still got all my fears intact. That's why my heart is beating so hard.

As I'm getting the girls to put on their coats, Josh whispers to me, "Is this really all right with you?"

I see Tiffany looking at us out of the corner of her eye. Then she smiles at me, a big toothy smile. Apparently I'm now cool. In my new coolness, I smile back at her. "Sure," I say to Josh. What the hell?

# 15

*Later,* I am cleaning up the kitchen when the girl named Danielle comes in and leans on the counter and watches me. "Josh knows how to have a lot of fun," she says. "Do you think you'll get married to him?"

I am folding up the empty pizza boxes and pouring more glasses of orange soda. Soon I will cut slices of the chocolate cake. Josh, in the living room, has made a roaring fire, and everyone is roasting marshmallows on wire coat hangers.

"I don't imagine so," I say. I walk three large boxes over to the garbage can and try to stuff them in.

"Why not? Isn't he nice?"

"Sure, he's nice. But it takes a little more than that." *Don't ask me what. I don't right now remember.*

"My mother," she says, "just got married to a guy who has three kids, and we have three kids in our family—and my new stepmother, who got married last year to my dad, also has three kids."

I want to say, *My God! Are you planning to file neglect charges?* Instead, I manage: "Wow. That must be a lot of kids to keep track of for you."

She regards me seriously. "That's why I think you might want to marry Josh or somebody like him," she says. "I don't think he has any kids, does he?"

"Nope."

"You can always tell."

"Really? You can?"

"People without kids do stuff like roast marshmallows in the fireplace in the house," she says solemnly. She eyes me curiously. "You wouldn't have let us do that, would you?"

"Probably not," I say.

She shrugs and says, "I'd advise marrying him as soon as he asks you."

*I am thinking* that the rest of the party could not be better.

Danielle and I take the glasses of orange soda into the living room. Somebody has turned off the lights. They're all kneeling next to the fireplace, leaning in, poking their coat hangers into the flames. I put the tray on the table and watch them.

"This one's too gooey inside," says Amelia. "Anyone want it?"

"Oooh, look what you made me do! Mine got in the flames because you pushed me!"

"I did not push you." It's Hope.

"Did."

"Did not."

"It's another one for Josh," says Lexie. "He likes the burned ones."

"Yum," he says, and turns to smile at me. "I'm getting my full daily requirement for charcoal tonight." He gulps down the blackest marshmallow I've ever seen in my life, and then says to them, "I know! Let's tell ghost stories!"

There's a chorus of *yeahs* and *oh cools,* and I feel like The Official Mom on the Premises again, worried that the stories are going to get too scary, and that I'll be dealing with someone's mother pretty soon, apologizing because her daughter is dreaming of headless gnomes or something. But Josh is the hit, and I hate to say it, but we're all sort of mesmerized by him. He could say we were going to play fireman and jump out of the upstairs window, and I probably would just have to go right along, leaping out the window into his arms. He gets us all to sit in a circle on the floor, all snuggled up against each other. I sit across the circle from Josh, in between Danielle and Lexie. It's nice here. I can see how the firelight glints on his curls, and how bright his eyes look even in the semidarkness. Hope, sitting next to him, smiles at me. I give her a questioning thumbs-up, and she answers back shyly with her own thumb in the air.

I can barely even listen to the ghost stories, I'm so happy sitting there just hugging my knees and watching the expectant, animated faces of the kids. When it's my turn, I tell a lame little story about a guy who thinks he hears a noise, and he keeps moving closer and closer. I speak in a whisper that gets lower and lower, and when everybody's leaning in, I shout, "Boo!" and they all jump.

Josh tells the famous one about the guy who meets a girl at a dance, and he gives her his sweater and then drives her home to her old farmhouse. She forgets to give him the sweater back, so he drives back later to get it, only to be told by her sad father that the girl died a year before. He tells it well, dropping his voice mysteriously. And he gets up and picks his way along the circle, touching each girl on the shoulder when he's describing the old farmhouse and the guy's fear about going back there. When he gets to me, he's at the part about the guy finding his sweater hanging from the gravestone in the cemetery. He sits down next to me, and says, "Brrrrrr!" and hugs me to him.

The fire is nearly gone out by this time, and we all sit in the dark for a few moments. Then I say, "Well, girls, I think it's time for bed."

"*Bed?*" they say incredulously, almost in unison.

"Bed," I say. "It's already almost midnight. Why don't you all go upstairs and brush your teeth and get into your p.j.s and then we'll set up the sleeping bags down here?"

"Not bed!" says Hope. "No one goes to bed this early at a sleepover!" Like she knows.

"I think we should go outside for a moonlight walk!" says Tiffany.

"Yeah!"

"Yeah! Let's go for a walk!"

"No," I say. "It's cold and it's too dark."

Josh clears his throat, and I'm terrified of what he's going to say. Yes to the moonlight walk, perhaps, complete with a picnic down on the high school track? Or—I know!—individual motorcycle rides to the top of East Rock where we'll see if we can camp all night and watch the sun come up. He seems capable of just about anything. But then he says, "Maz, how about if they watch a video until they fall asleep?"

I'm so relieved I start to nod my head.

"Not so fast," he whispers in my ear. "Pretend you need to be convinced."

"Weeellll," I say. "On second thought, all of you have to get up early tomorrow. I think just brushing your teeth and going to sleep is the better idea."

"No! No!"

"*Please* can we watch a video? Just one?"

"Please, please, please!"

They jump up and down around me. Josh is smiling into his hand.

"Well," I say. "Okay. But just one, and you have to promise to go to sleep while it's on. All right?"

They scamper off upstairs, yelling, "Yay! Yay!"

"How do you know this stuff?" I say to him once they're gone.

"Camp counselor. Four summers."

"Ah," I say, suddenly feeling shy around him, my fingertips tingling, so I get busy opening the sleeping bags and setting them out in the middle of the room, just so I don't have to look at him. He takes *The Sound of Music* video and snaps it in the VCR, and then starts fluffing pillows and spreading out bags, too. Then he goes over to the stairs and calls up, "Okay, everybody, last one in the bag has to sing 'Climb Every Mountain' along with Julie Andrews!"

It takes approximately forever to get everybody all tucked in, to rearrange the sleeping bags four times so the right people are next to the *other* right people. Hope, I notice, gets a plum spot right between Tiffany and Danielle. She snuggles down and looks happy. I know better than to lean down and kiss her, so I walk through the middle of the room between the bags, blowing kisses to everybody, which they pretend to catch. When I look around, Josh has gone to the kitchen.

I check the fire embers one last time, click off the light, and go to the kitchen, too. My heart is beating so loudly I'm surprised it doesn't drown out the movie. I close the door to the kitchen.

He's standing by the counter, holding up a square of white muslin and the blue embroidery floss, and smiling at me. "What's this?"

"Oh, nothing much. A piece of material and some thread."

"Was this by chance for the party?"

"In case we needed it."

"What do you do with it?"

"We were going to scw."

"You were going to have them *sew*, at a slumber party?" His smile is huge.

"Well . . ."

He comes over and wraps his arms around me and pulls me over to him. He smells smoky and sexy and a bit like a marshmallow. "Maz, you are so *cute* I almost can't believe it!" He kisses me on the forehead and on the tip of my nose. I can feel my knees start to buckle just slightly. "I just love picturing you and those five little girls all bending over your sewing together."

"You don't think it would have worked?"

"Maybe for twenty or thirty seconds," he says. He is gazing at my face, smiling. Then he says, "Oh, God, Maz," and starts kissing me on the mouth so hard, it's as though we'll never bring ourselves to stop. We're leaning against the kitchen counter and practically gasping when we come up for air. I reach up and touch all that silky hair, his warm, rough cheeks, anything I can reach. Then his hands are moving against me everywhere—and I'm losing it. I have one fleeting worry that one of the girls will come charging in, and then another lesser fear that we're possibly making out in the middle of the chocolate cake, but then both those thoughts disappear, along with what's left of my rational self.

"Come on," he whispers, and he reaches over and opens the door to the deck. "Out here."

So we sort of crab-walk ourselves outside, not detaching from each other. It's sharply cold, of course, and mostly dark. My house is on the corner, so there's a tiny street that runs just ten feet from the deck, usually deserted at night. And there's a stand of evergreen trees blocking the one streetlight from beaming right down on us. I can smell the hard gray smell of the river. We move away from the glass door, over against the wall of the house—but there are still hard piles of leftover snow everywhere and boards leaning everywhere, no place to stretch out, so we back ourselves up against the house. I am leaning, trembling, against the rough shingles, and he is over me, pulling up my sweater, kissing me, saying my name over and over. Oh, God. His hands are so warm and strong, moving across my body, and, Jesus, under his shirt his whole body is warm and strong, and I can't get enough of him. It's like I want to be able to crawl inside his whole person, live in him.

He comes up from kissing my breasts and says, out of breath, "Maybe we should get in your car." His fingers are in the waistband of my sweatpants, tugging them down.

"No," I say. I can just barely form words. "My car keys are in the living room."

"Well, then, the motorcycle?" he whispers. "I could bring it up on the deck—"

I laugh, and he takes his hands away and then puts his fingers in my mouth so I won't be loud, and then I lick his fingers and suck on them—long, brown, warm, marshmallow-flavored fingers—and he closes his eyes, and somehow the rest of our clothing just kind of gets pushed aside or falls away, whatever needs to happen. He's pushing against me, and it's as if my whole body is leaping up to meet him, all the cells crying out to be there, too. I wrap one leg around his legs. And somewhere deep I'm thinking, Jesus Christ, I'm having a quickie on my deck in the middle of goddamned winter! Then everything else is falling away; nothing else exists except him and me. He grips onto me to hold me up, and I have to hide my face in his shoulder to keep from screaming out. I don't know how long we've been there when I feel his body shudder against mine. We slump down. I really think we might fall onto the snow, or perhaps crash into the window, and I'm not sure I care about that either.

But we don't fall down.

He kisses my face over and over, tiny little kisses on my eyelids, cheekbones, nose, lips. I open my eyes and see his face suddenly illuminated.

Could it be that making love has literally caused the earth to light up? But no. He's pulling back and whispering, "Who's that? There's a truck pulling up."

I move slightly from underneath him and peek around his shoulder. He's right: there is a truck that has just pulled up next to the house, its headlights shining on parts of us, the sticking-up boards of the deck, and through the branches of the evergreen trees. I automatically reach down to pull up my sweatpants, which I'm only wearing one leg of. The other is stuck around my foot somewhere. The engine cuts out. We are quiet. I yank at the leg of my pants, which is turned inside out. I'm scrambling, breathless.

I hear a muffled male voice call out: "Hey, Maz? Is that you?" The truck door slams, there are footsteps on the sidewalk. I can make out a man's form coming around the front of the truck. And then the form takes more shape, becomes dark against the brightness of the sky, and I can see that it's Lenny.

"Maz?" he says. "I'm baaack!"

# 16

When I can find my voice again, I whisper, "Oh, my God, it's Lenny." I try to untangle my foot from the sweatpants waistband.

"Who's Lenny?" Josh whispers back.

"My husband."

"Are you shitting me? Your *husband* has come back?" As though he's in a French farce, Josh is grabbing wildly for anything, everything, to cover himself up. I'd probably be laughing if I weren't out of my mind with stark, naked fear. We're both yanking and zipping and fastening—and Lenny's opening the gate, still saying from the darkness, "Hey, Maz! Maz? Is that you?" And then he stops and squints, holding his hand up over his eyes, and says, "Ohhhh!"

I know I must have the proverbial deer-in-the-headlights look. Everything shifts down to incredibly slow motion, frame by frame. I mean to gather my wits and say, "Lenny, what in the hell are you doing here?" but I just stand there, with those words and probably a lot of others crammed in my throat. Josh is looking at me as though I should be able to change the reels of this movie and put things back where they were.

"Whoa! What the fuck *is* this? Maz, are you all right?" Lenny yells, and then, without any grace whatsoever, he charges up the three steps to the deck and, before I can even move or see what's about to happen, he pulls back his fist and pops Josh one right across the jaw, and Josh goes sprawling down off the deck into the spines of the forsythia bush, landing on his back.

Then we all start yelling. Lenny, standing over Josh, is shouting,

"What do you think you're doing to her? She happens to be my *wife*!" I'm screaming at Lenny to get away from him, and Josh, moaning and yelling, is getting up out of the bushes, holding onto his jaw, and looking stunned as hell.

"Lenny, damn you, get away from him!" I yell. "Look what you've done." I reach over the deck and help pull Josh up, not at all sure that I'm not going to just tumble over the side, too. Lenny, wearing all black leather and looking skinny and mean and every bit the part of a dangerous criminally insane lunatic, is waving his arms in the air and sputtering words that don't make any sense to me at that moment—words like "rape" and "attack" and "save your life."

"Are you drunk?" I hiss at him. "What in the world do you mean coming up here and acting like such a horse's ass? What are you doing here anyway?"

"No, no, no!" he says. "You tell me who *this* is!" and I say, "He's a friend of mi—" when the deck floodlights come on. I'm relieved to see that Josh and I are both dressed—even if a little disheveled—and some little girl is screaming, "Mrs. Lombard? Mrs. Lombard? *Mrs. Lombard, please*!"

"See what you've done?" I say to Lenny. "You're scaring everybody to death!"

"And who's *that*?" he says. "Exactly what is going on here?"

I open the back door, and Tiffany Gilbert, of all people, queen of the fifth grade, holder of my daughter's reputation, comes tumbling out of the door, holding her hands over her face and sobbing in loud, heaving noises, as though she expects the Academy Awards committee to be scoring her performance. Following her is a host of silent, solemn little girls, all staring. Hope isn't among them. She's probably dialing 911.

I take a moment, swallow hard. "Everything's okay," I say to them. "We're all just a little worked up, but everybody's okay. This is Hope's dad."

"DADD-DEEEEE!" comes the banshee wail from Hope.

"I'm not okay," sobs Tiffany. "I'm v-ve-very up-upset. Hope was telling our fortunes, and she told me I'm going to *die* in a car accident!"

I'm at a loss. Hope has sped past me and has landed on Lenny, who is twirling her around in a circle. Josh is watching me, looking slightly puffy around the jawline but still quite game, like somebody who has landed in a ridiculous situation but now is willing to make the best of it somehow, whatever that may ask of him. He leans down, puts his arm across Tiffany's shoulder, and tells her that that's crazy, nobody can see the future, least of all when people are going to *die*. Hope, he says, was playing a party game. That's all. Nothing to worry about.

"It's just a game, right, Hope?" he says. But Hope is oblivious to all of us out there shivering on the deck. She's now scaled Lenny's body as though he were a piece of playground equipment, and the two of them are doing a thing they've done since she was a baby, where they put their foreheads together and chant, "Abba dabba abba dabba" over and over until you just want to karate-chop them to get it to stop.

"I *told* you he was coming home!" is all she'll say to me, once they finally do wind down. As to the question about what she said to Tiffany Gilbert, all she'll say is, "I didn't say *when,* you idiot! Everybody's gonna die, you know, and maybe this is a hundred years from now! Did you ever think of *that?*"


*When I was* a little girl, I remember seeing a *Twilight Zone* episode in which people were given a camera that, instead of photographing what was happening right then, showed them what would be taking place ten minutes into the future.

All I can think is that ten minutes ago—no, even as recently as seven minutes ago—I was feeling an incredible glow from having sex for the first time in one whole year; I was being held and kissed and nibbled on. I was feeling a pleasing mix of guilt and sexiness and, yes, a little revenge thrown in. And now, just minutes later, my husband is standing glowering in front of me, my lover has just had to haul himself out of the bushes, Hope's party is ruined because she's predicting the deaths of the guests, *and* I realize I have chocolate cake all over my backside.

That's of course when the phone rings. And it's Lucille, who starts right in with, "Darlin', I just wanted to tell you that I did it! I married him. And when the judge said, 'Do you take this man . . .' and all that jazz, I just said, 'I reckon.' Turns out you can say whatever you please. You don't have to say 'I do.'"

"Lucille," I say wearily. "Do you know that it's after midnight?"

"So what, honey? You sure as hell weren't sleepin'," she says. "Hallelujah, honey!"

# 17

"*Let me make sure* I've got this straight," says Hannah the next morning. We've gone to Marjolaine's pastry shop on State Street for a cup of coffee while our clothes are on the wash cycle in the laundromat around the corner. She takes a sip of coffee out of a blue china cup, leans back in her chair, and smiles at me. "So let's see. You're schtupping Jolie's lover outside on your deck, and from out of nowhere, fresh from Santa Fe, Cowboy Lenny sprints up over the deck and slugs the guy."

I laugh. "Yep. Knocks him in the shrubbery."

"And meanwhile, little girls *inside* your house have all gone ape-shit because Hope has decided how they're all going to die, and is telling them just how that's going to happen." She shakes her head. "God*damn,* woman. When you have an evening, you really have an evening."

"*And,*" I say, "while I'm trying to help Josh out of the bushes, and make sure that Lenny doesn't clobber him again, all the while making sure the little girls aren't all freaked out over the assault and battery that's just taken place, the phone rings, and it's Lucille wanting to tell me all about her wedding. Lucille!"

"So other than all *that,* how was the party?" she says.

"Oh, I don't know. Other than that," I say, "it also turns out I sat in the chocolate cake while Josh and I were making out in the kitchen—so while all the little party monsters are crying, and Josh is trying to comfort them, and Lenny is finding an ice pack for Josh's jaw, I'm off in the bathroom trying to wash chocolate off my ass."

She laughs and so do I. But then, when the laughter dies away, I sit and stir my Earl Grey tea slowly, watching the pattern the spoon makes on the surface. The truth is, I'm so wired I could fall over. I may be, in fact, *clinically* rattled. My degree of rattlement could be measured with instruments. I can't remember ever feeling this way, as though little hamsters are running around inside my brain, chewing on the synapses. It's possible that I wouldn't be able to recognize my own life even if it came up and introduced itself to me.

There was no question but that I had to get out of the house this morning and talk to Hannah about all of this. It was all I could do not to call her at two in the morning to discuss the whole thing, sit down and unpack the situation right there, get her moment-to-moment input. After a year of numbing nothingness, how could I be having an adventure so juicy and dramatic without Hannah to help me analyze it and figure out what it all means for me?

So this morning, I got up early and left Hope and Abbie with Lenny and told him I was going to the laundromat. He gave me a funny look, as though now he doesn't know what to think of me. I have to say, he's trying to be on his best behavior, but he's a little taken aback at this new me, the me that has a lover. Last night after everything died down, he said he honestly thought Josh was some rapist, out violating me on the deck—and that my life needed saving. "If I had known you were just getting some action, I would have driven around the block a couple more times," he said.

Yeah, right.

I tell Hannah that, but she doesn't laugh this time. She is tearing up sugar packets and not looking at me, which is what she does when she's percolating something. Her hair is pulled back into a bun but with curls straggling out and falling into her eyes. I can't quite read her expression, but that may be because I'm so psycho. For a moment, I try to lean back into the silence between us, and let myself feel that any minute now she'll tell me in her inimitable Hannah style just what it is that I must do, and that it will be exactly the right thing.

I close my eyes and what comes up is Josh's hands sliding down my body.

"So do you have a plan yet?" she says slowly.

A plan? A *plan*?

"Yeah. A plan. For getting rid of Lenny."

"I don't even know if he's planning to stay."

"And don't you think that might be something you need to find out, ASAP?" She's not smiling.

"Well, sure. I'd *like* to know," I say. "But we didn't get that far yet."

"If you ask me, that should have been Question Number One, right at the door last night," she says. She sits back and studies me until I feel uncomfortable under that determined gaze.

"Right at the door last night," I repeat. "Hmm. Would that have been *after* we pulled Josh out of the bushes and before we tried to convince the little girls that Hope can't see the future? Or maybe it would have been better while I was on the phone with my crazy mother. There wasn't a whole lot of time, you know. I didn't exactly have the luxury of advance planning."

Then she says, "Maz, for God's sake, what do you *want* to happen here? That's what you've got to ask yourself first, then it doesn't matter when you do it. What do *you* want?" Hannah always thinks people know what they want. This way of looking at life astonishes me.

"Well," I say. I take a sip of my tea. She is watching my face. "Well, I know it probably sounds horrible, but so far I just want to magically have Lenny go away again, and then I want to find a nice, soft bed—preferably one with feathers and down comforters and lots of pillows with satin pillowcases—and then I want to get into it with Josh, and let the whole world just disappear." I stretch out and laugh, the luxurious laugh of the recently well fucked.

"With *Josh*," she says flatly.

"Yeah."

"Maz!" She's looking at me in disbelief.

"Why not? He's wonderful," I say, but I'm getting kind of a hollow feeling in the pit of my stomach, as if I got up to the big board, gave the wrong answer, and will now lose everything. "Anyway, you asked me what I wanted. I know that it's not—"

"He's a *kid*," she says. "And, not that it means anything to you right at the moment, but he *is* Jolie's boyfriend. They go out together. They sleep together. Surely even *you* find that a little sickening."

"Even me?" I say. The truth is, I couldn't care less, but it sounds too flaky to say that out loud.

She stacks a pile of sugar wrappers carefully. "So did he say he's going to stop seeing her?"

I look at her in confusion. "No. Of course not. We didn't get to that kind of conversation. Listen! You're not getting this, somehow. Things were happening fast—"

"So you really want a relationship with a guy who's not going to be exclusive?"

"Hannah! Wait a minute. Didn't we—you and I—just a few days ago have a conversation in which you yourself said how much fun it would be if I started seeing Jolie's boyfriend? You know, fun revenge and all that?"

"Yeah, but, Maz, I didn't think you were going to go right out and sleep with him the next week. I was seeing it more as a theoretical little fling, you know. A fantasy."

"Well." I sit back and watch her as she energetically starts shredding a napkin. Marjolaine's may not realize how close it is coming to being turned into rubble. At this rate, and with her level of anger, she'll get through the stack of napkins in no time and be up tearing apart the upholstery and then the bricks. "Neither did I," I say to her, and I sound like a petulant thirteen-year-old, even to my own ears. I shift gears, lower my voice, and try to get her to look at me. "You know what happened. The opportunity just sort of came up all of a sudden. Remember that part? We rode up to East Rock Park on his motorcycle?"

"You told me the whole bit, believe me. You kissed up there where everybody could see you, blah blah blah, and now . . ."

"Blah, blah blah?" I say. "Wait just a minute. This is my *life* we're talking about. Not blah blah blah. A guy takes me up to the top of East Rock and kisses me madly, when I haven't been kissed since my rotten scummy husband left—"

"Correction," she says. "You've been kissed by Dan Briggs, who is a much more appropriate and grown-up partner for you."

*Oh, yeah. Dan.* I stop short. That was different.

"Dan is . . . well, sane and mellow," I say to her. "He's settled. You know?"

"Settled is good," she says. "There's nothing particularly wrong with settled, is there? And last time I checked, sane and mellow were also two fairly decent personal attributes."

"Yeah, but, Hannah, he's so together that he makes me feel like I'm always going to be the one with all the complications, all the screwups. You know what I mean?"

She's shaking her head, now shredding the petals of a carnation from the centerpiece. Next: the chair cushions.

"No, really, Han. Hear me out. Josh is so different. He just looks at me like I'm *fine* the way I am. Dan looks at me, and, I don't know, I feel kind of horrified at the way my life is going. Like, I should always be in control. I'm tired of being in control. And I'm tired of being, you know, the *wife who got left*. Don't you see it? I want to be the bad one for a change. Everybody's had a turn to be bad but me."

There. It's out. I want to be bad. A guy made out with me in public, and then made love to me on my deck while my daughter and her friends were watching a movie two rooms away—and now this is the way I want my life to go. I sit back in my chair, let the seconds tick between us, think that maybe Hannah could look better if she didn't wear Michael's sweatshirt out in public. Does she know there are rips in the armpits?

"You've lost your mind, sweetie," she says at last. "I can understand that you're tired of everybody around you acting like a child while you have to be the good adult, but no matter how addled you are at the moment, surely even you can see that the last thing you need is to be kissing Jolie's boyfriend on the top of East Rock and then letting him fuck you on the deck. And you certainly don't need to continue with him. I mean, get real. Think about what you're signing on for."

"God! You make it sound so cheap. Can't we just enjoy it for a little while, for five more minutes? Can we just bask in it for five tiny minutes?"

She laughs at this, thank God. She says okay, five more minutes. The old Hannah is still in there somewhere. Then she lies and says, "Look, I think it's great, I really do. You needed a fling in the worst way, and you got one. Okay, end of that chapter. Move on."

"I don't think my five minutes of basking are up. Not by a long shot."

At first I think she'll laugh again and that somehow things will settle back down. We'll be Maz and Hannah, best-friends-from-day-care-and-on-the-same-wavelength again. She'll still say these mean things about how crazy I am, but it will be all fuzzy with the way she loves me so much and knows what I've been through. She'll say, "Well, god-*damn,* girl, Josh is just about the cutest thing there ever was, and of course you're crazy about him!" and we'll go on and have the rest of our coffee and then walk down to the laundromat and fling the clothes into the dryer and stand around, whispering and speculating about the other customers the way we always do, and I'll go home strengthened and put out of my wobbly misery again.

But she doesn't. She starts to say something, and then shakes her head, and then starts again, and this time she says it, as if she's blurting this out, "I mean, what if the kids came out there while you were doing it? What if Hope had come thundering out the door and had seen you with Josh?"

I know by the way my hairline freezes at the mention of his name that I perhaps have got it bad for him. I want her to say it again. *I* want to say it again. When I can find a voice that doesn't just insist on saying, "Josh Josh Josh Josh," I manage to say, "What happened was bad enough. I don't see why we have to go imagining other horrible scenarios. Besides, it was romantic passion. Remember that part? Getting swept up in the moment? Aren't people supposed to get a few of those in their lives? Something to remember when they're sitting in the nursing home at eighty-five, knitting sweaters?"

"I don't see it," she says. "I'm sorry because I know I'm not reacting the way you want me to, but I just think there's something horribly irresponsible and, yes, even a little bit self-destructive in what you're doing, and I can't sit here and laugh at it with you, as much as you want me to. It's wrong on so many levels that it actually takes my breath away. Josh is not going to be a good thing for you, he's not going to break up with Jolie for you, and in the meantime, you've now got *Lenny* thinking he can just barge in and take over your life once again—"

"Nobody told Lenny he could barge in and take over."

"Yeah, but he's staying there, isn't he? Isn't he? And when does he plan to go back?"

"What was I supposed to do? It's his *house,* Hannah. And he arrived at midnight, so where else was he going to go?"

She sighs. "Maz, that's his problem, not yours. Don't you get it? You're not responsible for where he stays, you don't have to provide a place for him. It's confusing for everyone when you let him do stuff like that. I bet you anything that Hope is now all fired up again, sure that everything's going to work out all hunky-dory."

"Hope is thrilled that he's back," I say miserably. "There was no way I could send him off with the way she was carrying on."

Hannah looks at me. "So it's better to wait and make it more painful later? I'm sorry, Maz. You've got to do the tough things here, take charge and get a plan together. This is not the time to be sitting around giggling about how you couldn't find your pants while you were fucking Jolie's boyfriend on the deck. The stakes are just a little too high for that, don't you think? I'm not sure you have that kind of time."

I feel as though I've been slapped. But then I get mad. Here's what I want to know: how is it that some people get that kind of confidence, to just tell other people what they should do in their lives, and point out all the stupid ways they're going wrong? Did Hannah get all this personal authority from her degree in social work? Maybe on her diploma it says, "Degree in Knowing Everything, Always, for All Time." All my goddamned life people have been telling me what I'm supposed to do, starting with Lucille, who acted as though she had the whole goddamned Unseen World of Spirit Guides lined up on her side. And then Lenny—ordering me around and acting as though he shouldn't have to work and making me earn all the money. And now Hannah, so smug in her perfect little marriage and doling out advice to all the rest of us poor slobs who weren't as lucky as to marry Michael. Meanwhile she's got some infatuation going with somebody else, and acting like that, too, is just her perfect right.

It's too much.

When I can trust myself to speak again, I say, "Look. You do not have to worry about *me*. There's no way I'm letting things get out of hand with either Lenny or Josh. I am the one in control of things. Me."

She shakes her head. "Honey, you're not even in control of yourself," she says.

"Look, just stop it," I tell her. "I had a fling, like we talked about, and now you're making it sound like I'm responsible for the end of civilization as we know it. Like Josh and I were parading through the house naked or something, like we were one step away from calling in barnyard animals and a video crew."

"Well," she says. "I've got to be honest with you. I'm frankly worried. Because, unlike the rest of us who were raised by regular mothers, you don't seem to know the difference between what's a little fling and what's going to end up being self-destructive."

"Speaking of self-destructive," I say—and wish, oh, how I wish I could stop myself—"*I'm* not the one who's got a supposedly perfect husband and a supposedly perfect marriage and yet falling into infatuation with some art teacher guy."

She turns to me, almost in slow motion, and suddenly, shockingly, I realize that Hannah is madder than I've ever seen her. "Look," she says, and she stands up so quickly the table shakes. She leans down to me and practically bares her teeth. For a moment, I wonder if she's intending to bite me. "I have never once claimed to have a perfect marriage and a perfect husband. I have a very *flawed* marriage, like everybody else, and I make the best of it while all around me people romanticize it. And if in my life I find someone who makes me see things in a whole new way, who makes me *smile,* who *appreciates* me for some qualities that no one else brings *out* in me, then that's just fucking tough if it happens to inconvenience *you* and your little idea of who I am. But at least I'm going into life without some stupid idea that I'm entitled to this because of how I was raised, or what my silly, ridiculous mother did to me years ago! At least I'm being *honest* about what it all means and not blaming some stupid fortune-telling babble."

"Well, congratulations to you!" I say and raise my cup high. But then, half accidentally and half on purpose, I let it wobble, and the rest of the lukewarm tea spills on the table and splashes on my sweater. I don't know why I thought that would make Hannah laugh, but when she looks at me with such a look of frozen contempt, I know we're in serious trouble, and that nothing is going to be easy to sort out anymore.

When I go home, dragging my laundry bag, I feel as though my heart is loping behind me, about a half-block down the street, not quite willing to follow me all the way to my house. And as soon as I turn the corner, my spirit sinks even further when I see Lenny sitting on the front steps, talking on his cell phone, while Hope and Abbie, wearing their flannel nightgowns outside in the chilly morning, spill over into cartwheels in front of him. What kind of father lets his children outside in their nightgowns? Worse, Hope goes over and stands behind Lenny and covers his eyes and tries to grab his cell phone away. *"Daddy!"* Her voice zings its way across the Sunday morning stillness. Then she leans down into his face, and he grabs for her and pulls her onto his lap and pretends to be devouring her. Abbie is jumping up and down and windmilling her arms, and even from the corner, I can hear her shrieks. They're so happy, I think with a dullness that resounds through me. *Shit. They're happy. What does Hannah know about anything?*

I stand there, watching. I will go over to them and send the children inside to put on clothes. And then I will turn to Lenny and say, "Why are you here? And when are you getting the hell back to Santa Fe?" And when he gives me whatever cockamamie, stupid, manipulative answer that he's cooked up inside his head, I will be firm and tell him that he's to leave immediately.

But then I do nothing of the kind.

I sit down next to him on the steps. In the morning light, I can see that he's much skinnier than he used to be, and he could hardly afford to lose even one more ounce of anything. And he's balder, if possible, and his face has a lined, leathery look to it, like he's been out in the sun, squinting without sunglasses, the whole year. He's also wearing some little pouch around his neck, on a rawhide string. Part of his shamanism thing, no doubt. I don't want to ask.

Hope comes over and butts him with her head right in the ribs, and then Abbie gets on Lenny's shoulders, and even though I tell the two of them three separate times to go put on regular clothes, they're laughing so hard with Lenny that my voice might as well be part of the wind. He keeps sneaking little sly looks over my way and being flirtatious, and that does make me mad, that he might be thinking he can just do as he pleases. After a while, he pats them both on the butt and says that the first one to get her clothes on will get to fix him a bologna sandwich for lunch.

They go, shrieking and punching each other, into the house.

"We don't have any bologna," I say when they're gone. I'm sitting on the step with my hands clasped between my knees.

"Oh, that's right. I forgot," he says, and kind of leans his body far enough over so that he knocks into me. Playfully. "You're a big time health food store nut now. One of the granola people."

"Hardly that. It's just everyone knows that the nitrites in the bologna cause cancer and—"

"Easy, easy," he says. He's laughing at me. He gives my elbow a little poke and says, "Hey, cheer up. You sure look sour for a woman whose life is crawling with men."

I don't say anything, just stare up at the trees, wondering if they'll ever get any leaf buds.

"That little boy from last night called," he says. "How old is he anyway, fourteen or so?"

I hold my silence.

"I've always thought the penalties for statutory rape were too severe anyway."

"Lenny, please . . ."

"Oh, and then another one called while you were gone." Long pause. I don't ask. "Dan somebody. I told him to get the fuck away from you and not to ever darken this door again, what did he think we were running, some kind of brothel or something?"

"Ha, ha. Very funny."

"I told him the last guy who called on you got his jaw dislocated in the forsythia bush." He leans over and socks me in the arm. "No, I didn't."

We are silent. A car glides slowly down the street, with a guy who's obviously checking for an address. He keeps glancing down at something on the seat and then peering out the window of his Buick, squinting at the numbers on the houses.

"Jeez, is this *another* one? Am I holding you up from an 'appointment'?" He stands up, cups his hands around his mouth and calls out, "Sorry, sir. She's quitting the business. Her husband's returned!"

"Lenny," I hiss at him.

He laughs and sits back down. The Buick rolls away.

"Lenny," I say. "What did you come home for?"

"Well, now, let's see. When I left here, I do believe I said I was coming back in two months, and I want to apologize for being a little tardy—" He sees my shocked face and laughs, pretends to fall off the porch in amazement. "Wow! Holy fucking cow! That got a rise out of you, didn't it? My God. You really don't even *want* me to come back, do you? That's it, isn't it? All those phone calls when I first went away . . . all that, 'Oh, Lenny, why did you have to go?' stuff. That's over now, isn't it?"

I study a piece of mud on my boots.

"Well," he says, "I think it's grand that you feel that way. Just grand. Years of marriage, but now I can put away all my guilt and just live my life."

"Good, you do that," I say. "So . . . is that what you drove all the way out here to say? Without even bothering, by the way, to tell me you were coming?"

"Oh, now. Don't give me that. I did tell Hope I was coming."

"And Jolie."

He studies my face. "Okay, fair enough. *And* Jolie. For Christ sake, still with the Jolie bit, huh? You have guys panting after you all over the yard, and still you're jealous of Jolie. Isn't that something?"

"Lenny, what did you come back here for? This is not fair to anybody, least of all Hope, who deserves to know what's going on with her life."

"I wanted to move back!" he says, and after a long pause, laughs out loud. "Sorry, just wanted to see that expression on your face again," he says. "It's so fun, the way you react to the idea of me moving back in with you. You turn kind of purple, and your eyes bug out, and your hair stands on end. . . ."

"Will you stop this and answer the question?"

He tries to look solemn and serious, like somebody who's just gotten in trouble with the teacher and now is trying to be good. He's so clownish, thinks he's cute this way. I want to haul off and slug him.

"Okay, Mrs. Lombard. Here's the answer to your question, if you must know. I am opening a big-deal spiritual center out there in the desert—nothing you would think was cool or anything, so I don't even want to go into it with you because of the way you sneer at all things that have the slightest tinge of—oh, I don't know—call it shamanism, for lack of a better word. So I concede the point to you that this is all hogwash and bullshit, but the fact is, I'm opening this Hogwash and Bullshit Center and I'm going to be the spiritual leader of it, and so I came back here to see if anybody we know might want to, you know, help me out with a nice investment."

"Lenny—"

He puts up his hand to stop me. "Ah, ah, ah! I concede the point, Madame Lombard. The center *is* the Hogwash and Bullshit Center, so right there we can't argue about the merits of doing such a thing. Let's just say I've been *called* to it by some very reliable and spiritual people, and I'm doing it, so don't even try to make me feel bad about it."

"I'm not trying to make you feel bad about it," I say. "I couldn't care less about it. I just want to know when you're going to collect money from all our friends and get back to it, because in the meantime, I don't think I want you staying here."

"Oh, but I have to stay here," he says.

"As a matter of actual fact, you don't."

"Oh, but I do. For one thing, I have promised the landlord once and for all that I would finish that deck, and for another thing, there is just the little matter of that I pay the rent on this place, and two of my very dearest children live here, not to mention my lawfully wedded wife, even though she is abusing her vows in a disgraceful way, having sexual intercourse with strangers on the above-mentioned deck." He leans over and leers. "Just think how much more comfortable your arrangements will be once I get the deck finished. You and your young stud can christen it together. Think of that, and it'll be easier to bear."

I should throw him the hell out. I should stand up right now and say *no, no, no, a thousand times no,* or stomp off somewhere in a whirling tantrum. My limbs feel weighted down. *Now,* I say to myself. *Tell him now that he can't stay.*

Hope yells from the front window that she's going to make him a bologna sandwich, because she got dressed first.

*Tell him now.* Instead what I hear myself saying is, "How long is this all going to take?"

"That's more like it," he says and knocks his knee into mine playfully.

# 18

*Here's a news flash*: life goes on, thrives even, despite all indicators pointing to that being completely impossible. Here I am, mentally prepared to have a ringside seat at the spectacle of my life falling completely apart, and instead I find that things are actually better than they have been. Better? Am I allowed to admit that? Hannah, if she were speaking to me, would say I have lost my mind, that I am living in denial, things simply can't be good, and are surely about to fall apart in some hideous fashion I haven't recognized yet. But the fact is—and you'll have to trust me on this, I have examined my situation relentlessly, searching for flaws—we are all Okay.

Oh, sure, there are *some* problems. It's weird, for one thing, not having Hannah to talk to. She moved herself off our day care turn (the advantage to being the scheduler is that you can put yourself anywhere you please) and had Michael tell me it was absolutely not because of anything having to do with me, that it was simply because the time for her art class had been changed, and she found it more convenient to do the Monday morning turn instead. Yeah, right. Her *art class*, huh? Now clearly *that* was a cry for help. Her art class was where she had to do with whatever his name was, that wicked art teacher, Michael's rival. I tell you, I almost wanted to take Michael aside, shake him by the shoulders, and warn him that Hannah was flirting with disaster. Worse than disaster—marital ruin, even. But I simply smiled at him, thinking, You poor, poor guy, and murmured something about time and priorities changing.

So anyway, with Hannah no longer on my day care turn—and now, as it turns out, with Lenny home, we have no need for the children to go over to Hannah's house after school anyway—so there's just a Great Wall of Silence coming from there. I can feel it when I pass her street sign, even. A great, brooding pool of silence hovering at the corner.

I've also noticed that now that I no longer hang out with her after work, I am no longer drinking a glass of wine every afternoon and examining my life. You'd think this could be a big loss, but contrary to what they tell us in the popular press, the unexamined life has lots to recommend it. For one thing, you're not always asking yourself if there isn't something you could be doing *right now* to make yourself feel better. And since that usually only makes you feel further like a first-class screwup, you feel terrific when you avoid the topic altogether and just get busy cooking dinner, or making the bed, or heading off to your job, and the days pass rather well, actually.

I think it's possible to go on for quite a while this way, and that's exactly my plan.

Lenny, who must be operating on the same system, hasn't really made up his mind yet what he's doing—or if he has, he's doing damn little to implement it. He's settled himself in the living room, spreading out all his belongings all over the place so that all of us have to step over them. Every few days or so, I kick them over to the corner, and they stay there for a few hours until they start creeping their way back into the walkway again.

So the living room has become his. He sleeps on the couch with only the occasional whine that he should be allowed to sleep in our bedroom again, since he is, as he points out, the one who pays the rent here, and we are lawfully married. I just give him one of my looks, and he pipes right down, though.

Sometimes in the middle of the night, I wake up to hear him yelling into the phone, at somebody apparently named Kimmie, who seems to be the latest unfortunate woman to need something from Lenny. It's impossible to tell what, but I can guess. He's always drawing out her name like: "Kiiiiimmmmmmmmmmmmmiieeeeeeeeeeee" and pleading with her to let him find himself, give him the space he needs to work out his confusion. From these conversations I have gleaned the following things: he intends to go back to Santa Fe, he is not having good luck raising all the money he wished, and he is a desperately married man whose wife and children need him for emotional support right now, so he doesn't know when he'll be able to do what she wants of him.

I roll over and go back to sleep.

I go to work every day, and I suppose he spends the day trying to shake down people for money for his Hogwash and Bullshit Center. He calls people at night, wheeling and dealing—and then, when he perceives that the three of us are listening to him, suddenly he'll stop, glance at his watch, pull out that ridiculous bag of herbs he wears around his neck, close his eyes, and start chanting some tuneless, wordless thing.

I have developed an amazing capacity for ignoring Lenny.

Especially now that I'm having a full-blown affair with Josh. Yes, I have joined that Great American Institution of Love Affair Havers, a club I never even knew I wanted to join. Yet here I am, an official member, sneaking off at every opportunity to make love with Josh. Now, if Hannah and I were speaking, and if she were at all rational, we could have some interesting analysis of whether what Josh and I have is technically an Affair, when my marriage isn't actually intact, and he's not married at all. But, this is the way I look at it—and believe me, I think about this nearly all the time—if it feels like mad, delicious cheating, then it's definitely an affair. And I think Hannah would agree with me, if she would only think about it.

I've fallen into a pattern lately of going to his apartment on my lunch hour whenever I can. He lives near the university, in a properly seedy, second-floor student apartment, with properly seedy roommates called Bleu and Storrow, who seem to be perpetually at home—never once are they in class in the middle of the day—drinking beer in the living room. I see them as props in my little drama, sent over from Central Casting to add a college-y character to the place. Josh, disheveled, smiling, usually shirtless and barefooted, meets me at the front door and leads me past them and their beer bottles and what seems to be all the laundry in the Western hemisphere, back into his bedroom. I say hi to them in sign language, but I'm always relieved that I don't have to get into a real conversation. It's too loud in there for the normal brain to even form coherent thoughts. They keep the music at a level that rattles the windows and makes the walls thump with the bass notes, like the whole place is going to vibrate apart. This is fine with me, since it fits with what's happening to me, too.

Josh's room is furnished with an old mattress charmingly flung on the floor, some fabulous plastic milk crates packed with sweaters and T-shirts, an Oriental rug that hasn't been washed since the Ming Dynasty, and a stereo system that, quite unnecessarily, is also on and bellowing out music. He has posters on the wall of brooding, dangerous-looking rock musicians—there's somebody named Beck I never heard of, and a few nostalgic posters, he once told me, of the Beastie Boys and the Clash. I can barely breathe, seeing his clothing all tumbled into the crates that way, seeing the rock stars he thinks are good. How is it that looking at a pile of sweaters can make me more sexually moved than I have ever been before? And that by the time I am looking down at his hipbones, coming into view as he slides out of his jeans—well, then it's all I can do not to come crashing down on top of him, in some kind of sexual swoon.

Within ten seconds of his closing his door each time, I am lying naked on the mattress on the floor next to him, my hands submerged in his curly, shiny hair, and I am making unearthly animal noises. And just the thought of what we are about to do—again—has made me quite out of my mind. All else falls away.

Later, driving back to the Golden Granary to my normal place among the soups and the herbs, I quite simply cannot believe this is me, and that these events all strung together were meant to catapult into my life this way. Surely, I think, they were meant for somebody else and just landed on me by mistake. Someday soon, the authorities will show up at the front door and say there's been a wrong delivery, that all these orgasms were addressed to someone on the next block. Poof—it will be as though they never happened.

Josh whispered to me once that Jolie is "not thrilled" with this arrangement, and I perhaps had a triple orgasm right at that moment. I may have short-circuited something in my brain. That's how good life is.

"They cheated on us," he said, cupping his hands around my ear so he could be heard over the multiple stereo systems in the apartment. "But, know something? We ended up getting the better part of the deal. I mean, just look at you! You're beautiful. That ape Lenny was an idiot to ever let you get away from him." Has anything nicer ever been said to anyone? I thought the "ape" touch was sheer genius. And after that remark, I glowed for days.

So now my head is crammed all day with thoughts of Josh, each little brain synapse happy to go back over and over the last time we made love, the way he looked at me and touched me. *Where* he touched me. What he said, when that could be heard at all. And how young he is. That, too. How, when he's lying on top of me looking down into my eyes, it's all I can do not to pass out. Do other people know about this kind of thing? Is this what is going on in the hearts and minds and bodies of all the people I pass on the street, or serve soup to in the Golden Granary? Or am I the only one who knows about the True Purpose and Meaning of Sex? If I were speaking to Hannah, perhaps I would ask her.


"So *what is it* with you lately?" says Barry one day when I'm putting away the flour and getting ready to go home. He sticks his pencil behind his ear and rubs his bald head. "You seem different."

I smile at him shyly. So he's noticed! It must be true what they say about good sex. When you're getting it good, your whole appearance changes. You become radiant, secure. Your hair gleams, your teeth sparkle.

"Well . . ." I say. I'm ready to go into a boss-worthy explanation of how lovely my life is suddenly, when he says, "I don't mean to be nosy or anything, but is something wrong at home? You seem distracted and kind of distant."

I feel myself blanch. "Really?"

"Yeah, and I've gotta tell you, it's beginning to show a little bit in your work."

"My work's *fine*," I say.

"Well, I don't know. There's just something. It's like you're not really here. You take those long lunch breaks now, and when you come back, you're sort of spacey. And then when I wanted you to help me think up menus to go along with all the letters in the alphabet—A Day and B Day and all that, you just didn't even *try* to get into it. That's not like you."

"Okay. I'll think up menus to go along with the alphabet."

"But I want you to *want* to!"

*Barry,* I want to say, *you can make me do it, but you can't make me want to.* I look at his kind face and change my mind, though. He's really been so great and understanding about everything all jumbled up in my life, letting me bring the kids into the Daughter Nest every day before Lenny got back, even giving me those long lunch hours without blinking an eye. And I can't afford to lose this job.

I turn and give him a bright smile. "No, no, I do want to! Tomorrow can be B Day, and I'll sit down right now and think what we can make."

"Blueberry muffins," he says. "Baked brie."

"Bread." *Bozo Barry.*

"Are you going to let Daddy stay?" Hope asks me this a few days later while I'm driving her to the dentist.

"Well," I say, and try to get in the left lane to turn onto Humphrey Street, but some guy in a yellow SUV won't let me in. He honks loudly, and I say something not altogether nice about his grandmother and his parentage. I say to her, "Did you see what that guy did? He sees that I'm trying to get in the left lane, and would it kill him to just let me get in front of him?"

There's a silence. "Are you?" she says at last.

"Am I what? I can't believe that at *rush hour*, somebody wouldn't try to be courteous just so traffic could keep moving. Now I'm blocking two lanes—"

"Are you going to let Daddy stay with us?" She's standing up in the backseat, leaning over, practically in my face.

"He *is* staying there," I say. "I don't think it's a matter of *letting* him. He just is. And you need to get back in your seat belt."

"But it's not the same as it was," she says.

"No, I suppose it isn't the same. That's not my fault. Sit back down. Please."

"You don't let him sleep in his old bed with you. You make him sleep on the couch."

"Hope, I don't *make* him do anything," I say, and just then, finally I am able to maneuver my way into the other lane just as the light turns red. My hind end—or rather the hind end of the car—is sticking into the other lane of traffic, which is annoying the hell out of the other drivers. I turn and look at her. "Honey, it is way more complicated than it seems to you. Marriage is one of those things that both people decide about—and your daddy and I are both making decisions. It's not all up to me."

"He wants to sleep in the bed upstairs with you. I know he does. If you'd just say yes." She sits back and looks out the window. "At least you got rid of those other men," she says. "That was a start."


*One Saturday,* when I'm out with Hope buying her a new backpack, I run into Dan. Run smack into him, in fact.

We're in Kohl's, and as usual, I've been given the slip by Hope, who has practically run from the parking lot to the backpack section of the store, hoping to not be seen with me. I don't even know where the backpack section is—would it be with purses, or with school supplies?— and so I'm hurrying through the men's sweater section, wondering if kidnappers really do steal children out of department stores and if I should be more worried about her or just enjoy this brief respite of silence, when I turn the corner and collide right into something large, brown, and furry.

It's one of Dan's nubbly sweaters, with Dan in it, although it takes me a while to sort that out. At first I just think I've slammed into a big breathing brown animal. But then he laughs, and says, "Maz? Oh, my God. It *is* you. Hi!"

I take two steps backward and look up at him, only right then my left eye starts tearing up, and I realize two things: the first is that this is Dan who's laughing and talking to me, and the second is that one of his sweater nubbles seems to have punctured my eyeball.

"How are you?" he says.

"Dan!" I say. "My goodness, I'm so sorry. I wasn't looking where I was going, and now—well, now, my eye is all weird."

"Ohhh, what's the matter?" he says and puts his face right up to mine.

"Something in my eye," I say and I put my purse down on the floor so I can rub my eye more thoroughly, rub it completely out of my body if necessary, but he says, "No, no, don't rub it—that's the worst thing you can do," and then he's got a hold of my eyelid and just does some little naturopathic-doctorish maneuver to it, flips it over onto itself, and peers into my eye so hard I think that he's probably examining my brains.

"Aha!" he says, and reaches into my eye. "Got it."

It was, as I had feared, fluff from his sweater, and after we get it established that his sweater is actually a weapon and could be used in combat, he just stands there smiling at me. Then we hear, "Dan!" from some singingly female voice, and he gets almost a guilty look on his face and looks down the aisle of men's sweaters. It's then that I see her: a young woman standing a whole row down from us, holding a pile of sweaters. She has one of those perfect black pageboys and big brown eyes and the kind of neat, tailored clothes you see in magazines, and she's waving and saying, "Dan, how about a blue one? To go with your eyes?"

"Just a sec," he calls down. I think, Hmm, just a sec. The way you'd say it to somebody you were currently involved with, an easy casual oh-honey-I'm-home kind of voice. But he's looking down at me, his eyes sort of smiling and embarrassed the way they were that night when he was at my house and Lucille called. That bad night. *So what that he's got somebody else now? I've got Josh. So there.*

"So, how are things?" he says in a low voice, and I try to stand up straight and look impressively put together, which is not that possible because my eye is still streaming, and also I had spent the afternoon at home with Hope and Abbie, who were playing a game called Throw All Toys in the Middle of the Living Room Floor to Impress Daddy, and it had been dawning on me slowly over the course of the day that I was not totally suited for putting up with Lenny, you know, *indefinitely.*

"You look wonderful," says Dan. Then he leans over and says, "So . . . your husband came back after all." Which is when I remember that he had called once and left a message for me with Lenny, a message I never returned.

I nod, shrug, make some kind of strangling noise in my throat in an attempt to convey how little Lenny means to me.

"And it's working out okay? You're all right?" he says, and I nod again, and then shake my head no, to cover all the bases as clearly as possible.

"And I've gotta know. The fortune-telling mama. Did she get married after all?"

I smile at him. "Yeah. Yeah, she did. I'm surprised you remember all that."

"Are you kidding? I've been dying to find out."

And then the woman, sensing there is territory to be defended, comes tramping over holding two sweaters for him to look at, and she gives me one of those woman-to-woman proprietary smiles, and he introduces us, only I immediately forget her name, and I shake her hand, and then I say I have to go.

I wish for one tiny second that I could go and call Hannah and we could figure out what Dan's look meant and why I care when I am really so very satisfied and happy with Josh.


"In Santa Fe, you don't go to real schools," I hear Hope saying to Abbie while they are both in the bathtub.

"What do you go to?" asks Abbie.

"You go to a place, like somebody's house, and you sit in a circle on their living room floor, and then you talk about fun stuff," she says. "And then you go for a hike outside and cook food in the fireplace, and then you might go swimming in the hot springs and talk about other stuff. You don't have any tests and nobody ever gets mad at you."

"I like that," says Abbie.

I'm about to go in and explain that even in the perfect world of Santa Fe, children do have to go to school, when the phone rings and it's Lucille. She can't believe, she tells me, how much fun it is to be happily married for the first time in her life.

"You have *got* to get yourself fixed up and get yourself a good husband," she says. "Honey, when you get it right, you just won't believe how good it can be! Now tell me one thing. I talked to the guides tonight, and they both told me that you are in the market for a husband in a *big way.* So I thought I'd call you and see if you need me to do any spells or anything for you. . . ."

"No," I say. "I do not."

"Would you just try to be open-minded for a change?" she says. "Darlin', I can help you. I do know quite a bit about love and romance at my age, and with all my experience, you know."

"No spells," I say.

"Well, then," she says. "At least do something to look pretty, will you? I'm rich now, so I'll send you some money to buy yourself some sexy lingerie or something. Get your hair done. I bet you look tired and worn out."

*Actually,* I want to say, *I've got all the sexy lingerie I can stand right now. And if I look tired, it's because I'm having too much sex. And just by the way, those guides seem to be slipping a little if they haven't picked up on this. So there.*

"Okay, then," she says, when I continue to refuse to have spells done in my honor, "would you put that sweet little Hope on the phone? At least she appreciates me."

And since Hope is at that moment walking past me, all wrapped up in towels and looking clean and adorable, I hand her the telephone and go downstairs to finish making dinner.

Without even thinking about what a stupid thing to do that might be.

One evening after I get home from work, Lenny follows me into the kitchen and pops open a beer, then leans on the counter, watching me make dinner. "You're good people, you know that?" he says. He smacks his lips, as if I'm something he'd like to pop into his mouth. "You've come through that uptight phase that you had, and now you're just giving off an aura that really draws people in. Your energy is really clean now. That must feel good, that even after two kids, and putting up with me, you've still got it." He's moving over closer to me, his eyes looking filmy.

"Lenny. Stop." *Shake the salt into the water. Put the shaker down. Turn on the burner. Don't make eye contact with him.*

I go to the kitchen door and call into the living room: "Hope, Abbie, I want the two of you to go upstairs and get into the bathtub together while Daddy and I cook supper. And tonight you can turn on the shower radio while you bathe." I don't know how this is going to go, and I do not want them to hear any of our conversation.

They argue, of course. They fuss. Since the other day when it was perfectly fine to take a bath together, now Hope has decided she doesn't want Abbie to see her naked. Abbie says that Hope never lets her sit in the front of the tub and besides that, she splashes. Patiently, like some kind of saintly mother, I sort out all their arguments and make them go anyway. In a brilliant stroke of parenting genius, I end up promising them each a dollar if they will do what I say. I am ready to go as high as promising a pony.

Then I go back to Lenny, who's dreamily leaning on his elbow and drinking his beer.

"I never expected in a million years to come home and have to hit a guy on the deck. You know, I really, really thought—"

"I know, Lenny. Let's not go into it again."

There's a beat of silence, and his voice changes, drops lower. "I gotta say, it really turns me on that you're not so hung up on this monogamy stuff anymore."

"Oh, does it?" I say. Then, because I have to, I say, "You know, that is so not the point of anything. I do believe in monogamy very strongly. It's just that—" I look up. He's smiling at me. I stop talking, go back to unwrapping the pork chops.

He takes a big slug of his beer and forms his words carefully. "Well, given that you're more easy-going—shall we say, for lack of a better word—about monogamy, given that, do you ever think about maybe coming out to Santa Fe?"

"Nope, not even once. Were there any calls today while I was gone?"

"Any of your men, you mean?"

"I mean, were there any calls?"

"Hope and Abbie want to go. I've been talking to them about the school out there—"

"I know you have, and I wish you'd stop it. There's no point in getting them worked up about it. Were there any calls?"

"Calls, calls. Oh, yeah, speaking of schools. Hope's teacher called. She wants you to come in tomorrow for a conference."

The hairs stand at attention on the back of my neck. "A conference? Why does she want a conference? It's not report card time yet."

"Yeah, well, that's what she said. She said some things have come up, and she needed to talk to you. She said I should come, too. She wants to talk to us together." He puts the beer bottle down harder than necessary. I startle. "Listen, Maz. Maybe it's time for us to get out of here. Together this time."

"*What* things have come up? Teachers don't just call home and schedule conferences unless there's a big problem. What did her voice sound like?" I'm talking low so Hope can't hear, although I know that with her antenna, she can probably hear every single word and nuance, even above the tub water running and the radio on.

"Christ, I don't know what her voice sounded like. She said it was a conference. Got it? She wants us both there. She wants to talk to us. About Hope." He drains his beer and gets another one from the refrigerator. "If we get out of here tonight, we'll never have to know. We can just be gone, start over again, free as anything."

I don't answer. I line the broiler pan with aluminum foil and put the pork chops on it. Pork chops, potatoes. We should have a vegetable. And Hope's teacher would not just call for anything. "Do you want carrots or frozen corn?" I say.

"Did you hear one thing I'm saying? I'm asking you to come out to Santa Fe."

She would call only if it was something bad. Something truly bad. "First things first. Carrots or corn?"

"It's beautiful there, and you could be a baker in the new center."

"Carrots, then."

"Christ, I don't care! I don't care what fucking vegetable we have, and I don't care about some dumb-ass teacher's evaluation of Hope right now. I want to know if you want to come to Santa Fe, if we should give the landlord notice and move the rest of this damn furniture out there, buy ourselves a coffee table, and figure out our lives again."

"No. We shouldn't."

"Listen to me. The kids need a dad in their lives, and even if we just lived near each other, surely that would be better for them than me being two thousand miles away."

"Where does it say that you get to move two thousand miles away, and then come back demanding that the rest of us follow you? If you cared about being close to them in the first place, you would have stuck around."

"I was making our lives better by going. I was going to earn money!"

"Yeah, well, you did improve things for us, but mainly through not coming back."

"I'm asking you one more time if you want to come."

"Um. Do I want to come? Uh, let's see. No."

He sighs and looks at the blackness at the window. "How can I convince you that it's great there? Lots better than here. Not uptight like New England. The people are cool and a little bit wacky, but in a good way. There's lots to do. The kids would grow up happy there. . . ." He's waving his arms around in a vague way. "People *understand* what life is supposed to be about. It's, like, paradise there."

"Oooh, and I could meet Kimmie," I say, unable to help myself.

He looks a little surprised, I'm happy to see. He thinks he lives in a soundproof universe when he's yelling into his cell phone at night, I suppose. "Listen," he says. "Kimmie's a kid I got kind of tangled up with, and it's over. She's moving out while I'm here. I left because things were getting too weird with her, and I'm not ready for all that shit she's trying to pull. She wants a baby, she wants me to promise all kinds of things."

"Oh, I see. You left *here* because it was getting too weird with Jolie, and now you're leaving Santa Fe because it's too weird with Kimmie. But it's complicated because you really do want to live *there,* and so now you're trying to get me and the kids to come out there with you and scare Kimmie off, at least temporarily. But you don't want to be married to me anymore. You just want to keep all your options open."

"Anything wrong with open options?" he says. "You got people, I got people."

"No," I say. "That's not the way it's going to be."

He watches me get the forks out of the silverware drawer. Then he says, "Doesn't it ever bother you that Josh fucks Jolie, too? How come that's okay for him but wasn't okay for me?"

Then he puts his beer bottle down on the counter and leaves. I hear the front door slam as hard as it can without breaking all the windows.

At the table, Hope sits, her face closed to me. "Where did he go?" she says.

"Actually, he didn't say," I tell her. "He just left."

"He left," she repeats, dully. "Oh, I get it. You made him mad again, and he's gone."

# 19

Hope's teacher, Felicia Morris, explains first off that she has been teaching only since *September,* so she has not had a lot of *experience* with all *situations* that might come *up.* She is wearing a blue corduroy jumper with a neat white blouse, and her long blond hair is tied back with red yarn. She is so nice and smiles so hard that she looks as though she is about to cry when she talks. And God, she is so concerned about Hope that before I've been in the classroom five minutes, all my hackles are standing straight up. Lenny's not helping, either. He's taken on an air of studied sincerity and calm, drifting through the room, praising all the bright-colored bulletin boards and asking questions concerning the latest educational theories about children's art. Like he cares. I just want to hear the bad news, agree to her idea for a solution, and get the hell out of there.

But of course we don't start there. Miss Morris says in a sweet voice, "First I just want to tell you how much *fun* it is being Hope's teacher. She's so . . . so *creative* and dramatic and interesting."

I know that, in Teacher Speak, all those are really bad things. They probably mean that Hope won't do her spelling, incites the other children to riot, and always has a smart answer for why her homework didn't get done. I put my head in my hands.

Miss Morris is silent, and when I look up, she and Lenny are both looking at me. I smile weakly. "Go on," I say.

She stacks her papers very carefully without looking at us. "But some things have come up that I and the other teachers feel could be a cause, not for alarm, certainly, but for concern. Maybe not even *concern,* but just for consideration. That's it. We need to *consider* some things, and I thought that you, Mrs. Lombard, might want to come in and hear about our concerns—well, not our concerns, but our . . ."

"Considerations," I say. Lenny pokes me under the table. She purses her lips and I think she really might cry.

"So what's going on?" says Lenny, looking bored. He's wearing his Violent Femmes T-shirt just for good measure, an insurance policy against any chance of us being seen as normal parents.

"Well," she says softly, leaning forward. Her long blond hair touches the table top. "Hope is saying some rather upsetting things to the other children. Sometimes."

"What things?" I say.

"Well, she has set up . . . kind of a business . . . on the playground at recess and then again at lunch and again at free time, and then sometimes after school. . . ."

"A business?" The specter of lunch money extortion projects rises up in my head. But I know what's coming. It's worse.

"She's telling people's fortunes. Selling them, actually." The air in the room goes flat.

"So?" says Lenny. "What the hell?"

I kick him lightly under the table. I think we should save the swear words for when we all know one another better.

From the look of things, Miss Morris thinks so, too. Possibly she has never heard the word "hell" in that context. She draws back a little. "Well, first of all, we don't like the children to take money from the other children, and then we're . . . uh, concerned . . . about the content of some of these messages. So there are really two issues here that are causing some . . ."

"Consideration," I supply.

". . . consideration, thank you," she says. "Consideration among the other teachers and staff members and myself. I don't know if you're aware of this, but Hope *says* she's a psychic and is getting secret messages from spirit guides, and she's giving everybody predictions about the future."

"Look, her grandmother makes a good living doing that," says Lenny. "Some people do have that talent, you know."

"Yes, I'm quite sure that it's a respectable occupation—"

"Actually, not so much respectable as lucrative," he says. I poke him under the table. Again. "I myself am employed as a shaman, in case you were wondering."

Her eyes widen two whole clicks. My ears take up a buzzing sound.

"Lenny, please, this is not about you," I say.

"Now shamanism isn't like fortune-telling, it's true," he says. "But just to show you that Hope perhaps has the genes for this sort of mystical thing. I don't think it's something the school system should be squashing—that's all I'm saying."

"Could you please can it?" I say.

"Mr. Lombard, that may well be, and I don't wish to get into an argument with you about mysticism, but we here at the school can't really support this kind of activity, especially when it's causing lots of anxiety and consternation among the other students. I mean, children this age are very gullible, and some of them are quite, uh, concerned."

"So they're not just *considering,* they've moved into being *concerned,*" says Lenny.

"I beg your pardon?" she says.

"The other children. You said the teachers and you were *considering,* but now you've said the children are *concerned,* so I was just wondering if that meant the children have moved up a notch in their worriedness. You know, from where you stand."

She is staring at him, uncomprehending. I imagine she's wishing there was an alarm button underneath the desk that she could slide her foot over and summon the authorities.

"Nothing," he tells her. "Forget it." He reclines in the chair, stretching out to his full length. She and I are treated to a full display of the Violent Femmes and his hairy belly. His fringed belly button, a disgusting outie, is actually showing. She blinks but then goes back to hard, sad smiling. He says, "So tell me, has anyone—anyone at all—moved yet from *concerned* to *alarmed?*"

She looks at him with hatred in her eyes. I didn't think that would be possible after just ten minutes. My hat is off to her. "Well, children were crying just yesterday," she says. Her voice has risen a few octaves, and there's a slight twitch at the corner of her creamy mouth. *Easy, sweetheart,* I'd like to tell her. *It only gets worse if he sees you weakening.* She plows on: "I think Hope told one little girl that her parents were getting a divorce, and then she told a little boy that he would never get a good job. It's been problematic on the playground."

"Very problematic, I can see that," he says solemnly. "How *do* you cope with such daily traumas and battles? You should really apply for extra pay. These conditions you work under are abhorrent."

She bristles and tamps her sheaf of papers into line. "It's more serious than you think, Mr. Lombard. I think some of their parents are possibly going to want to talk to you, if the school doesn't do anything about this. One mother is threatening to speak about the problem at the PTA meeting next month, if we don't come up with a plan. There's even been some talk of harassment charges."

"Oh, for God's sake!" He slams the front legs of the chair down on the floor.

"We take these kinds of discipline problems very seriously now, Mr. Lombard. The school environment must be a safe place for every student. There's no room for this kind of treatment of the other students. We have a zero tolerance policy now concerning violence and such, and I would just like to say that, while this isn't violence, it certainly is not sanctioned and comes under the purview of some pretty serious concerns."

"Listen, I'll talk to Hope," I say quickly. "It's been kind of a hard time for her lately. Her father and I are split up, and I think she's reacting to that by trying to get some kind of control over her life. Which I don't think fortune-telling really does, but you can't tell a ten-year-old that. In fact, you can't tell them much, really now, can you?" I'm babbling. "Also, as my soon-to-be-ex-husband says"—and I nod toward Lenny—"her grandmother is a fortune-teller, and I think she's encouraging her to tell fortunes, which I don't approve of. I've spoken to her, but I'll talk to her again. Don't worry."

"Well," says Miss Morris, "perhaps a warning in this case will be enough. We've told Hope this is inappropriate, but to tell you the truth, I don't think she has a lot of respect these days for anything that school officials have to say to her. She's become a little . . . defiant. Particularly in the last few weeks."

Since the party, of course. "Tell me," I say miserably. I lean forward, trying to show by my body language that Lenny should be excluded from now on. *It's just you and me, Miss Morris.* "Does she have any friends?"

Lenny snorts. "She could have all the friends she wants!" he says. "It wouldn't matter in this oppressive environment. Obviously."

Miss Morris looks surprised. "Well, I don't really keep track of who she eats lunch with, if that's what you mean. I mean, I've got so many of them to watch at once. And it is a very catty age among girls, with lots of changes on a day-to-day basis—fluidity, you know, in the social scene."

"Don't I know it." I say to Miss Morris. I attempt a big smile. "But I'll work with Hope. Don't worry. I'll make sure this doesn't keep happening." I stand up. "Tell me, though. Does she still sit next to Lexie Mundy in class?" If Hannah's daughter is still in the picture, then I think I won't have to feel too bad.

Miss Morris looks relieved. "Well . . . things seem to have cooled between them perhaps a little. I don't think Lexie really approves of the fortune-telling business, you know."

"This is just bullshit, plain and simple," says Lenny, getting up. I send him a murderous look, and say, "Good-bye, Miss Morris. Thank you for your concern."

"Consideration," he says. "She's not concerned *yet*."

"Actually," she says, "I am now."

On the way home, he yells at me for being nice to the teacher, whom he calls many horrible names, all having to do with her stupidity as it relates to her sexuality and probable preferences for livestock over virile heterosexual men, like himself, no doubt. Then, not satisfied to stop there, he starts in on the whole bureaucratic military-industrial complex, the Board of Education, the system of town government, the universities in this country that would confer a degree on someone as stupid and pig-headed as Miss Morris, and he finishes up with a finely tuned but gratuitous diatribe on Lucille, who doesn't know her ass from a hole in the ground. Eventually he winds down and stares out the car window.

"Well, I hope you see that you've pretty much *got* to come to Santa Fe now," he says finally. "This wouldn't happen there, you know. Not a chance in hell. They don't make children conform to every little thing. They *care."*

"Lenny, I'm tired of you ranting and raving. Just please stop." It's rush hour traffic, and we're barely moving down Whalley Avenue in the gathering darkness. The kids are at Hannah's, and I'm thinking how I'll have to face her, and what *that* will be like: strained and formal, or perhaps worse? My stomach has seemed to have lost its moorings in the abdominal cavity and is now taking applications for another place to hook up, perhaps somewhere near the heart-and-lungs region, from the feel of things. I'm not sure, but I think I may have forgotten to eat lunch at the Golden Granary before I left for the teacher conference, so maybe it's just that my stomach has gone in search of some other internal organ that it can eat.

Also, this might not be the time to think of this, but I have had no sex today, even though it was one of my regular days to go meet Josh. Barry was going to a Chamber of Commerce meeting and wouldn't notice if I took a little extra time, so I was going to have all the time in the world—perhaps even ten extra minutes. I feel my shoulder muscles tighten. What's with me, mulling over my own sexual frustration instead of what to do about Hope? I try to straighten up, put my meaningless sexual relationship out of my mind and be a good mother.

"We've got to get her out of this environment," says Lenny. "It'll be the best thing for her. For her sake."

"No."

"I didn't like that crack about *soon-to-be-ex*-husband either," he says.

"You are *so* soon-to-be-ex," I tell him. "You are like seconds from being ex. If I thought there was a lawyer's office still open on this street right now, believe me, I'd file the papers this minute."

And that's when I press down on the clutch, and my foot goes all the way to the floor, and the car slides helplessly to a stop in rush hour. Damn it, damn it, damn it.

"What the hell are you doing? You idiot! Are you trying to get us killed or something? Is this one of those suicide/homicide pacts without my permission? Push down on the clutch!"

"Lenny," I say very calmly. "The car is breaking down, in addition to everything else."

As we wait for the AAA guy to come and tow the car to the mechanic, while Lenny chants something with his little bag of herbs, stopping to yell at me every few minutes, I can't help counting on my fingers a little list of everything that's going wrong.

Hope is a full-blown maniac psychic now, who may end up expelled.

Lenny is not going to go home until he solves the unsolvable Kimmie problem.

Hannah may, in fact, hate me.

I am afraid I may actually be addicted to having sex with Josh, even though I have nothing to say to him.

My car now needs a new clutch. At least a clutch, and no doubt when they get it into the shop, they'll also discover it needs motor mounts, tappets, spark plugs, an accelerator pedal renovation, windshield wiper blades, and a radio antenna. And more things that only they can come up with.

*And*—now I have to go to my left hand—I need a rental car.

Also, I have no idea how to turn Lenny into an ex-husband, but I've got to figure it out soon.

I need a new job. Barry is still thinking I don't care about work, all because I couldn't think of anything for H Day. I made jalapeño muffins, but he said that was cheating, it wasn't enough that it *sounded* like *H*. It had to actually start with *H*. What the hell kind of muffins did he want me to make on H Day, I asked him—hydrogenated vegetable oil muffins?

Also—the cell phone battery is dead, so I can't call Hannah to tell her I'm going to be late coming to get the kids.

And it's now pouring.

Two hands' worth of trouble.

*But there's more,* because once the universe gets going thinking up complications for your situations, it doesn't like to stop until it's covered all bases, left you a whimpering, quivering mass of protoplasm in the wreckage of your life.

When, an hour later, I stop at home with the rental car, to let Lenny off before going on to Hannah's house, there's a huge motor home parked on the street behind Lenny's truck, right in the spot where I would be parking the rental car, if nothing was taking up the spot.

We sit in silence and gape at its monstrous size. Then, like a bad movie, it dawns on me what this is. This monstrosity has words on it, visible in their goldenosity, visible even through the steady sheets of rain. They say quite plainly: "Madame Lucille, Fortune-Teller to the Stars" on the side in gold-plate script.

"Shit," I say. And then, because that seems so inadequate: "Shit, shit, shit, *shit.*"

"That's for sure," Lenny says. We both sit and look at it. The vast picture windows of the motor home are all dark, but our house—*my* house—including the deck, is lit up like Christmas.

"She got in," I say softly. "How in the world did she get in?"

"She can do anything."

"But the door *was* locked, wasn't it?"

"Do you think there's any oxygen in this car?" he asks me. "I mean, like any molecules of O-two whatsoever?"

"No."

"How *did* she get in?"

"She has ways. Maybe we could get her for breaking and entering."

"That's it. Have her arrested first thing. That'll buy us a little more time."

"Do you think?" I say. I don't think I have feeling anymore in any of my limbs. "Well, let's go." I can't believe I'm actually feeling somewhat fond of Lenny, as the least of about six or seven evils. We run up to the door together, and when we get there, I remember why. There's something I should have said to him long ago. "Wait," I say. "I just want to thank you for not ever sleeping with Lucille. Did I ever thank you for that?"

"You can thank me by leaving New Haven and moving to Santa Fe."

"No."

"You're crazy. You're going to see that you're crazy," he says and puts his key into the lock.

# 20

*Madame Lucille* is holding court in the middle of the living room when we go in. The house is ablaze with light, and she's perched on the edge of the armchair in a purple jumpsuit and matching turban, something Elvis might have admired in his Las Vegas years. She's waving her arms in the air and talking a mile a minute, huge chunky gold jewelry catching the light.

My heart stops beating for a moment when I see her. And an actual lump, approximately the size of North Dakota, forms in my throat.

"Well, for heaven's sake!" she says. "Look at what the cat dragged in! Oh, darlin', just look at you! And is this—*Lenny? All the way from Santa Fe?* I heard a rumor you were here, too, sweetheart. Darlin', come over here and give me a hug! No, you, Masden! Get ovah here, my big ole baby!" She stands up, and it's then I really take in that crowded around her, sitting on the floor, are Hope and Abbie—and, my God, Hannah, too. And Hannah's daughters, Lexie and Rachel. Lucille wades through them, as they tip sideways to let her go through. Everybody's looking at me, and then I'm in Lucille's grip, and she hasn't stopped talking for one second, not even to draw a breath. She smells like Jean Nate spray cologne and grilled onions, and this close, practically mashed up against her neck, I see that her skin is pink with caked-up bits of powder. Clumps of the stuff are stuck in all the little lines and crevices on her cheeks and on her neck, with two big red puddles of rouge on her cheeks. God, she looks old, like somebody's retired show poodle, all done up. Old and painted up all wrong. Her eyelashes are fat with mascara, with a thick black line drawn haphazardly across the crepey lids, and her lipstick is a shade of fluorescent lavender never found in nature. I close my eyes, disturbed by my own meanness, and give in to being squashed into her massive bosom. This is Mom, after all. I almost can feel my eyes and nose stinging with tears.

"... well, aren't you just the cutest thang," she is saying, "I can't believe my eyes, seein' you again. That color is so gright on you, sweetie pie. You're so smart to wear those pinks with your blond, blond hair. It makes you look younger, you know, and at your age, that's somethin' we gotta think about. I was sayin' to Harold just as we were drivin' up, isn't this the cutest little house you ever saw in your whole *life,* and it's just like Maz to find the cutest house in New Haven, where, let's face it, darlin', there aren't many cute little houses. . . . Come here, sweetie, and tell me all about how you are! These little gals of yours just got so *big* and beautiful! They're like princesses you read about in a book. Can you *believe* we're finally here?" *Believe she's finally here? Did I even really know she was coming? And doesn't anyone in this family know that you should alert others when you're planning to show up for a long-term visit?*

Then she's off, ignoring the princesses, set on telling the history of the trip— when they started, what they ate along the way, where they stopped, everything people *said* in various locations, and how it feels to be here, and by God, it just *feels* wonderful and terrific and oh so gright. She has her lighter out, although she's not smoking, and she's click-ing away.

I look around at everyone. Hannah is grinning, and Hope's mouth is absolutely hanging wide open; I've never seen her eyes this round. Full-strength Lucille, in the flesh, *is* amazing, a force of nature. Perhaps I'd never truly been able to communicate that to all these people in my life, judging from how stunned they look. Abbie and Rachel are hold-ing onto each other's hands and jumping up and down, as though they can't contain the energy coursing through their own bodies. Lucille hasn't been around in ages; Abbie's too young to even remember her, and Hope probably has only vague impressions. Lenny is leaning against the wall, arms folded, smiling in his usual ironic, sardonic way. Hannah and I make eye contact, and she widens her eyes at me, which would have made me laugh, if I had had any control whatsoever of my facial expressions. She mouths, "She's *wonderful*!"

"Yeah," I mouth back.

Here's the thing about Lucille that I always forget in between times: it's not just that she's talking all the time, which of course she is, but you can get used to someone yammering away and finally tune them out in self-defense, or else, out of desperation for the sound of your own voice, you learn to conduct your own conversations around them. But with Lucille, it's the intensity that does you in. You can't quite ever get away from her. While she's talking, it's as though she's got you engaged in some kind of Primal Mind Meld. It's not just eye contact—no, no, it's more that her eyes burn into your very soul while she talks. Your neck gets stiff from being pinned down by her magnetic force. She's like a scientist, and you're the little bug she has pinned to the giant piece of black paper, and it's no good squirming to get away, because she's got you.

After a minute or two—well, who really knows how long? You can't tell time under these circumstances—I become aware that the blender is on in the kitchen, and then a man's voice calls, "Honey! Honey? Do you want the Morgenthaler Special or somethin' else?" She stops talking. My God. She just stops. The silence is like air rushing through the room.

Then Harold Morgenthaler—at least I assume that's who this is, although one can never be sure with Lucille; she might have met another man since the time she married Harold—comes out of the kitchen to the living room doorway, holding the blender pitcher, and then there's a flurry of introductions all around. He's a dignified, heavyset man with white hair and bright pink skin and a floppy, wide mustache that hides his mouth. Frankly, he looks like the guy on the Monopoly game. I go over, smiling, and shake his hand, and he jerks forward, almost as though he's surprised at himself, wraps me in a hug, blender and all, and says he's so glad to meet me, and what a nice house I have, and it's so nice to be here. In the background, Lucille is telling all of us about the dinner she *thought* about cooking for us as she rode

down the road this morning—Roast duck? A turkey? Filet mignon?—
but then Harold said to her, "Heck, honey, let's just take 'em all out for
dinner," and so we're to pick the place where we most want to go but
never get to because it's too expensive. Hannah and her family are to
come too, *no excuses*—but Hannah explains that Michael and Evan
have gone off on a father-son bonding, barn fact-finding expedition.
Lucille stops, hearing this, and stares at her.

"Well, what the hell, then? Just you and those little gals! The sky's
the limit tonight, baby!" she says. "Tomorrow we may all be eatin'
peanut butter and ketchup sandwiches, but tonight we're livin' it up!
That's the way we do things, ain't it, Maz? We feast together when we
can, and then we go through the dry times, too. The good an' the bad.
The lean an' the fat." She pulls Hope over to her, in what amounts to a
headlock. "Your old G.G. is gonna take care of you, baby girl, you'll see.
I've got a lot of time to make up for because I've been so busy out solvin'
the world's problems, and helpin' the police catch the bad guys, but now
I'm ready to devote myself to my family. Because if you don't have family around you, what have you got? That's what ole Harold has taught
me, bless his heart."

As we're putting on our coats to go to the restaurant, she pulls me
aside and hugs me. I think she's about to tell me again how much it
means to see us, but instead she says, "Isn't this purple getup just the
livin *end*? We've got to get you one of these jumpsuits, honey. They're
just the best things goin'. The only disadvantage is when you've got to
tinkle, you have to take the whole damn thing off, but that's a small
price to pay. Yessirree, a small price to pay to look this terrific!"

We have been at the restaurant only ten minutes when Lucille has
identified the waitress as somebody who's destined to become a great
novelist. She pulls this fact out of the air, and by the waitress's startled
reaction I can see that it just might actually be one of her fondest hopes.
Hannah looks perplexed, but I whisper to her that this is what Lucille
always does. She *is* the great Madame Lucille.

"What's your name, sweetie?" Lucille says, and we all turn and look at the waitress, who blushes. Her name is Kaarina, and she's got beautiful brown eyes, and yes, she is working on a novel, as a matter of fact. And, wouldn't you know, it turns out that Lenny painted her house a couple of years ago, and hey, what fun, they even went out for a few beers together one night when he finished up late. He looks completely embarrassed, and gets up and kisses Kaarina on both cheeks, and explains to us all how Kaarina's bedroom has a boa constrictor in it, and he had to paint *around* this huge cage while this six-foot long *reptile* stared at him, unblinking, for hours. Lucille, laughing, says that if she'd known about this little association, she'd have tried some of her long-distance magic to get that boa constrictor loose so it could have scared old Lenny right back home.

"That wasn't the *only* snake in that bedroom," she says, and we all laugh. "And no doubt my daughter was waitin' at home for you with two little babies."

"A *beer,* Lucille! It was just a beer!" says Lenny, laughing helplessly. "Christ, don't piss off a witch! But, say, Kaarina, what time you get off tonight?" Then, when everyone's laughing again, he looks around at all of us and says, "Nah, I'm just kidding! But, hey, you still got that snake in the bedroom?"

I sneak a glance at Hope, but she's smiling and looking right at Lucille, with something like awe on her face.

Harold orders an expensive bottle of wine and encourages everybody to order whatever they choose from the menu. But he does it quietly, not as though he's determined to impress all of us. One of Lucille's husbands—I can't think which one—used to take out a gold money clip and peel off hundred-dollar bills while he made smacking noises. This is not Harold. I like him, I realize with some surprise. He's not like any of the other husbands, or even the intermediaries that didn't get the actual marriage license. He has a slow, kind way of talking, and liquid brown eyes that look like bing cherries sunk into pink folds of skin. I like the way he periodically reaches over and squeezes Lucille's hand or touches her shoulder. She makes a big show of snuggling up next to him and smooching around his head, launching into Amazing

Stories about how they met, or Harold's miserable past life without her, or some other such thing. Sometimes they tell together the wonderful, fabulous stories of their wedding and the salt-of-the-earth types down in Florida who instantly saw them as soul mates and helped them get married.

"Harold doesn't realize that it's always been like that for me, hasn't it, Maz? He says, why are people constantly comin' up to you and tellin' you such unbelievable stories? And I say, honey, I don't know, but people are just magnetized to me sometimes, and you never know what it was that brought them to me. I used to think it was the guides, workin' for me out in the universe, gettin' the right things and people to come into my life, but who knows? It's just the way it's always been! I woulda thought that everybody had the same experience with other people, but nope, I hear folks say they go their whole lives without makin' these connections. So I guess it just must be me!"

Hannah, sitting to my right, leans over and says, "She's hysterically funny. You never told me she was funny."

"Weeellll," I say, "she has her moments." I'm surprised to see that I'm having a wonderful time. It's like being a child again—those exciting nights in the trailer with Lucille and all her friends, the liquor flowing, the laughter ringing off the walls, and Lucille at the center of it, glittery and glowing as though there's an invisible spotlight shining from within her.

I eat prime rib, which I never order, and I even get it rare. It's like cutting into a slice of butter. And a baked potato, piled high with butter *and* sour cream. All rules are gone tonight. Salad with chunks of bleu cheese and glass after glass of merlot. Mama is at the head of the table, and I feel, in a deep way, as though I have been given permission to eat whatever I want, to say and do anything out of the usual. I'm not the adult tonight. Mama Lucille says it's okay. She's even smiling at me. Mama's not crazy. And she can't send me back to my grandparents anymore.

After two glasses of wine, I feel as though I'm in some kind of Impressionist painting, blurry with the beauty all around me. I sit and watch all the faces: Harold and Lucille, mellow and smiling; Hannah, laughing easily and sending me little messages with her eyes; Lenny, grinning and asking interested questions of everybody, even chatting with Hannah, whom he's always disliked with a passion. He helps Hope pull apart her lobster, both of them making faces and scooting the lobster claws around the plate until Hope thinks up the great idea to waggle them at Abbie, who delights them by shrieking. Butter drips all over the white tablecloth, but none of us says enough is enough. There's no reason for any of us to stop. We eat and eat and laugh and drink wine. Harold teaches the bartender how to make a Morgenthaler Special, and then we all get slices of death-by-chocolate cake, piled high with whipped cream. The kids want ice cream as well, and of course, that's fine, too. Lucille leans back and tells stories. Miracles and cures, police stories, near-death experiences. She and Harold together back in Atlantis. Harold's former wives once being her *cats*. Later, near closing time, Kaarina and the owner, Henry, come over and sit down at our table. The place is nearly empty. Abbie has snuggled up in my lap and gone to sleep. Hannah is holding onto Rachel. She leans over and whispers to me that she saw Dan Briggs at the Golden Granary the other day when I wasn't working, and that he had a million questions about me.

I frown. "Oh, him. He's got somebody else. Did he tell you that?"

"Really? He acted like he couldn't get enough of hearing about *you*," she says.

"Well, then, we should have invited him along," I whisper to her. "That would have cured him for sure." But the vision of Dan Briggs forms in a little thought balloon over my head, smiling at me. I feel a tug.

"Also," she whispers, "I've got to tell you something. Zeke and I are over. We've decided not to get together anymore." I look at her closely and she bites her lip. "Believe it or not, it wasn't that painful. I mean, it was the right time. Are you still . . . with Josh?"

I nod at her, biting my lip, and she leans over to whisper something, but then Lucille says there can't be secrets at the table, especially with her there. "Besides that, I know what you're talkin' about! Your young men! Maz, darlin', you should have invited your young man to come along with us tonight! Why didn't you, sweetheart?"

"Maybe because he had to study for a junior high science exam," says Lenny. "Do you *know* about this guy, Lucille? He's all of about thirteen years old!"

"And just how old is your little chickie in Santa Fe?" she asks, and I choke on my sip of wine, which makes everyone think I'm choking because what she said was so funny. Hannah's laughing, too, and beating me on the back. And then Lucille gives us all her predictions: Hannah will fall in love again, a renewed relationship with her husband—"a glorious reconnecting!"—and oh, yes, they'll have another baby. (Hannah pretends to fall on the floor, gasping, at this.) Lenny will go back to Santa Fe and found himself a spiritual center and stop fucking around (she actually says "fucking around") with teenyboppers, and he'll attract artists and writers and spiritual guides from all over the world. Kaarina will write her novel. Henry will lose this restaurant but open another one in Boston.

And I—here she raises her eyes to bore into mine—I have some trouble ahead. But if I just open my eyes, I might realize there's love out there for me as well. "Sorry, kid," she says. "Nothin' comes easy for you, does it? But that's what the guides say."

It's just lucky I don't believe in anything she says.

# 21

"Hope, you have to stop telling fortunes at school," I say. It's now a couple of days later, and it occurs to me that I should have brought this up right away after the teacher conference. But I forgot. Who can think anymore, with all that's going on since Lucille and Harold arrived?

"I know it's fun to be eccentric and all," I say, "but your teacher says you're scaring the other kids."

"They like me to tell their fortunes," she tells me. She's sitting at the dining room table doing her homework, and she doesn't even look up at me when she says it.

"Tell them you can't. You can't go around telling people scary things."

Now she looks up and sticks her chin out. "But what if they want to be scared? Did you ever think of that? People go to scary movies, you know, because they like to get all scared and stuff."

"That's true," I say. "But I would like it very much if you weren't the one scaring them. Miss Morris says that some of the parents want to go to the PTA and the principal and get you to stop."

"Miss Morris is a dweeb."

"Hope," I say. "I am asking you right now to stop telling fortunes at school."

"G.G. says I am very talented."

"Listen," I say and sit down next to her and touch her arm. "You *are* very talented, and you're very smart, and you've got a lot of things to be thankful for. But if you make everyone mad at you, then you won't have friends left, and that's not good."

"I don't care if they're mad at me." She sticks her chin out.

"Yes, you do," I say. "You know you really don't want everyone to not like you. No one feels that way."

"I do."

"Hope."

"Stop talking to me like that! Anyway, nobody's mad at me. They're always asking me to tell their fortunes! They come and ask me everything every single day. You don't know because you're not there!"

"But then they tell their parents, and their parents get very upset. The principal is about to get involved, and the PTA. This is not good. I don't want to have to go down to a meeting with the principal and have to hear bad things about you."

"Then tell her you can't come."

"Hope. Stop it. And stop telling fortunes at school. I mean it. I don't want to talk about this again."

She slumps down in the chair and folds her arms.

"Will you stop? Please?"

"Okay," she says. "But can I tell your fortune?"

"All right," I say. "If you promise to stop telling the fortunes of kids at school, you can tell me my fortune all the time."

"Give me your hand," she says. She takes it and closes her eyes. I study her serious face, the frown around her eyes, how angelic she looks just now, how scary she really is.

"You are going to get back together with Daddy," she says slowly. "You are going to let him be famous and go to Santa Fe, and you will go too and you will not have any boyfriends."


*Life is so strange,* I tell Hannah a week or so later. "Who would have guessed that things could be smooth with both Lenny *and* Lucille right here on the premises?"

Despite all my misgivings, I have to admit that we've settled into some kind of domestic rhythm that works. Even Lenny, who's usually buzzing about in some possibly over-the-line-into-psychosis plane of existence, chanting and muttering over his little herb sack around his neck and then growling about my love life, seems to have lost his usual edge. There has been no more mention of me packing up the house and following him to Santa Fe to be the baker in his little fiefdom. And judging from some rather loud telephone conversations, I gather that he's seeing Jolie again, which makes me exquisitely and irrationally happy. If Jolie is with Lenny, I figure, then she's not with Josh. I know that shouldn't matter since Josh and I aren't *serious* (besides the fact that we have nothing in common, we couldn't possibly even have the conversation it would require to convert our relationship to serious, since the words would have to be shouted out). But still, just knowing at any given moment that Josh is not with Jolie brings me a foolish kind of happiness.

And Harold—he's a wonderful, big teddy bear of a man, always smiling and padding around the house, being helpful. I love his voice, so rich and deep it practically rolls around us, like a ball of chocolate melting in boiling water. He seems to adore Lucille and to be in constant amazement at how fortunate he is to have found a family to care for. He's fixed the maddening drip of the hot water faucet in the bathtub, and changed some of the lightbulbs in the living room to soft pink ones. He tacked down the life-threatening piece of carpeting that always tries to trip people as they come in the front door, and rearranged the tools in the shed so that they make some kind of sense. Plus, he and Lenny work together on the deck nearly every afternoon, Lenny doing all the carrying and Harold doing the measuring. And every morning, Harold comes over from the motor home and makes a big pot of hazelnut coffee, and Lucille, right behind him in her bright yellow bathrobe, scrambles eggs before the kids go off to school and day care. The two of them are functioning like real, bona fide grandparents—the kind in books who read stories to the kids, straighten up the newspapers and magazines, and even dust the furniture with some bergamot-flavored oil they found in Tennessee.

I have to say, the house looks and smells spectacular. When I come home in the late afternoon, there's always something cooking: sometimes a roasting chicken, or pork chops simmering in brown gravy, or Cornish game hens stuffed and golden brown in their own little pans.

Lucille makes pound cake and chocolate fudge with the children. We eat mashed potatoes from scratch—I didn't even know she *knew* potatoes came in a form other than little flakes in a cardboard box, I tell Hannah. All these surprises!

And speaking of surprises, the other day, I'd come home from work and found Hannah, of all people, sitting on the kitchen stool while Lucille cooked dinner. Lucille was telling Hannah her theory about how your period will never ever start if you're already wearing a preemptive tampon. It was such a typical Lucille crazy conversation, and Hannah was laughing hard, saying it explained so many things about her life.

"I think that may be how I ended up pregnant three times!" she was saying. "I'd put on that damn tampon thinking my period was going to start—and then it never would."

"Of *course* it's how you got pregnant," Lucille is saying. "That whole idea about the male having sperm and all that gooey stuff makin' *children*—it's completely without scientific basis. Maybe at one time that's how babies got started, but in the modern day, everybody knows that babies come from premature tampon insertion."

"I think you should publish this," says Hannah. They both break down in laughter, and then look at me standing in the doorway. I'd almost had to shake my head in disbelief at the sight of them—Hannah and *Lucille,* the two theory queens, laughing together. Having something in common.

It sounds silly and implausible, I know, but I almost see Lucille with new eyes now. Could it be she's been tamed? She seems so comfortable in her own life, and while not exactly settled down into a kind of motherliness that most people would be able to relate to, she's charming and eccentric and generous. Quirky rather than psychopathic. It's true, she does constantly say things to me like, "Do you really *like* your hair that way? Don't you want to borrow one of my wigs?" And "Wouldn't you look less tired if you put on some blue eye shadow?" And I do have to remember to compliment her outfits and tell her that her hair looks gorgeous or she gets huffy—but, I think, who deep down doesn't need that kind of attention? She's just more up-front about it than most folks.

Even the nighttime routine has gotten easier. Lucille and Harold sleep in the motor home at night, and usually either Hope or Abbie joins them there. Most nights it's Hope, who is actually blooming under Lucille's attention. I often find them, heads together, scraping carrots for stew or talking quietly together about something. If there is any little molecule of doubt buzzing around my head—and let's face it, there always is *something*—it's just this: maybe I should find out what it is they are talking about. Lucille, although she shows no signs of it right now, *is* a card-carrying sociopath, and she's getting awfully close to my vulnerable daughter. But how to find out without making a fuss? And, hey, at least I'm not finding voodoo dolls around the house. They haven't gone into the black arts just yet.

"So has Hope agreed to quit telling fortunes at school?" Hannah asks me one day. We're talking on the telephone, which is so much easier than being together in person. Not only has my schedule these days made it impossible to go back to spending an hour in her rocking chair after work, but frankly, there's still just the tiniest, ever-present crackle of tension between us. I suspect it comes from the fact that she knows I'm still seeing Josh, and her disapproval is right there below the surface, just waiting for me to say his name. That's when the lecture she's biting back will come springing out at me, like one of those stuffed snakes coiled up into a can.

Apparently, I tell her, Hope *has* stopped telling fortunes—or at least doesn't seem to be getting caught at it anymore, since a whole week has passed with no more complaints.

"Excellent," says Hannah. "See? She does care what people think of her."

"Well, she spends a lot of time with Lucille in the motor home, and I'm hoping that gives her enough wacky stuff to do so that she's not having to do it at school anymore," I say. "You know, once you have your quota of wacky, maybe you don't have to parade around on the school ground."

"Interesting theory," says Hannah. "The wack quotient."

Later that night I go over to Lucille's motor home just to maybe pop in on them and see what they're doing, see if exorcists are going to have to be called in at some point. When I get there, Lucille is sitting on the bed, talking on the telephone, and Hope is wearing Lucille's purple turban and marching around the motor home claiming that different objects are actually her friends. I can't tell if she's kidding, so it seems best to act as though she is.

"This steering wheel," she says to me, grandly. "It may look like a regular steering wheel, just huger than most, but it is really an antenna to the spirit world. It talks to me!"

"What does it say?" I ask her.

She thinks for a moment. "It says, Drive me to Santa Fe."

Hey, I'm sure this is fine. Just a little more wackiness from Lucille. Nothing at all to worry about.

# 22

*I come home* from the Golden Granary one evening a few days later to find Lenny in the kitchen, leaning on the counter, while Lucille is making dinner. It's late April by now, and the sun is shining in patchwork patterns through the kitchen windows. I'm about to mention the miraculous fact of it still being light out—light! springtime! flowers!—but something stops me. I realize that they've stopped talking when I come in. Lucille is chopping onions and frying them in garlicky oil. It smells divine, I tell her.

"Honey, we were just talkin' about the school system," she says after a moment of silence during which we all stare at the sizzling onions as though the secret of life will be revealed there. "Lenny here was just tellin' me about the trouble with Hope's teacher. You didn't tell me that kind of thing was goin' on."

Oh, great. I give him a scary look behind her back. "I don't really think it was that big a deal," I say. "Besides which, we had a meeting, I talked to Hope, and it's all been taken care of."

"On the contrary," he says, and I see that his lips are in a thin line, "it has *not* been taken care of, in the true sense. I see this as a civil rights issue. The school had no right to say those things to her, and *you*, of all people, as her mother, should be incensed about it."

Ah, I think. So today we are bringing out the high horses and prancing around on them for Lucille's sake. How very charming. Why couldn't somebody have phoned me at work and warned me of this?

I sigh loudly. "Listen, Lenny. The schools have a right not to want kids upsetting the other kids. If one kid is going to start getting everybody all weirded out by predicting people's *deaths,* then, yes, I think the school should say knock it off." I grab a fried onion that fell onto the stovetop, and Lucille smiles at me and offers me a few more from the spatula.

"It's a repressive, paranoid school, Maz," says Lenny. "Hope wasn't doing anything that was upsetting *anybody.* She and I have talked about it, and now I understand the situation. One pain-in-the-ass little girl who's jealous of Hope—somebody named *Tiffany*—ran home and told her parents that Hope was scaring everybody. She was just mad because Hope is best friends with somebody who used to be *her* friend. It's politics. And the school takes it seriously, like it's a goddamned cult or something."

"Listen, kids are just always going through those kinds of fights," I say. "Fifth-grade girls are always mad at each other on account of their hormones are raging all over the place. I don't think we can blame the school for that."

I take a mouthful of onions and wait. I just know that Lucille, with her ingrown hatred of anything organized, will jump right in and assist Lenny. Instead, she says, "It's a god-awful age. And what are the schools goin' to do, anyway? I guess they have a right to be paranoid, because of the shootin's from the last few years."

"Right," I say.

"Of course, it's too *bad* they have to be that way," she says. "When I think of all the talent we waste by lettin' children spend six or seven hours a day in such a conformist atmosphere. . . ."

"Exactly," says Lenny, and his eyes, I swear, start shooting sparks. "Kids shouldn't have to be in that atmosphere. Listen to me, Maz. I'm friends with some people in Santa Fe who are doing a wonderful job of homeschooling their kids. That's what Hope needs. Those kids are getting the message that they're beautiful and calm and *respected* for who they really are."

I give him one of my famous meaningful stares, the kind that can singe his eyebrows. "And you, I suppose, have time and the patience and qualifications to run a school here so that your daughter never has to worry about being misunderstood by the outside world?"

"I may not be able to run one *here,* but I sure as hell—"

"Not to mention making sure that she gets the social skills she needs from school every single day, learning just what it is that you can and can't say to people on the playground, and—"

"*Social skills?*" he yells. "Did you say *social skills?* Because, excuse me if I'm from another planet or something, but I think the only social skills she's getting are to be the same as everybody else and not make any waves. Don't be yourself! That's the *social skills* they know at that school."

I just know Lucille is going to jump in now and declare that Lenny's right. I'm all tensed up for it, ready to argue more. I am just now unpacking my full ammunition for a full-out fight, if that's going to turn out to be necessary. I am all set to wave the banner of how my daughter will be raised in the Real World with Real People, so help me God. But then a strange thing happens. A kind of calm takes over the room, as though some kind of make-nice gas is being filtered through the heater vents. Lucille merely smiles at us both, and somehow the air changes. Huh! We're not going to fight. "Now, Lenny," she says, "you know Maz's got a good point. If we're not goin' to overthrow the whole system, then maybe we just have to figure out how to work with it. And Hope will be fine. We all know that."

To my surprise, he grins at her. And the whole thing is dropped—just like that. The Air Force bombers that were just a moment ago circling up near the ceiling, ready to drop their neutron bombs on our heads, quietly fly in formation back to their hangars. And a discussion that would have turned into a major emotional slugfest just dissipates into thin air, like in some unrealistic fantasy.

Lenny actually smiles and starts getting out forks and knives to set the table. He even touches my arm—and not with a knifepoint—as he passes by me, and Lucille winks at me before she turns back to the stove, humming under her breath. After a short moment, my stomach unclenches itself, my blood pressure goes back to the acceptable range, and I start to breathe normally again.

Right then Harold comes in from the deck with a pile of newspapers he's planning to recycle, and Abbie's scampering along next to him, talking a mile a minute.

Harold's face is lit up when he sees us all together. "Guess what!" he says. "Abbie wants to call me Grandpa." She hangs back shyly, sucking her thumb and smiling around it.

"Maybe you can be Glamorous Grandpa, to match me," says Lucille. She kisses him on the cheek. "Or, if you want initials, you can be G.G.H. Glamorous Grandmother's Husband. How's that?"

He rubs his nose in her black hair. "I think Grandpa suits me better."

I can't help but wonder if I stumbled onto the set of *The Waltons* or something. In a moment, John-Boy will call out, "Good night, Maz."

*Later that night,* regular life reasserts itself, and something kind of bad happens. Suzanne Gilbert, Tiffany Gilbert's mother, someone I've never talked to or wanted to talk to, calls me on the phone. Since I hold her personally responsible for allowing ten-year-old girls to highlight their hair, get body piercings, and toss their hair dismissively at everything not currently *cool*, I am shocked to hear that she seems to have a problem with *me*. Right away, she sets the tone for the conversation by speaking in a clipped, long-suffering voice and starting every sentence with, "Mrs. Lombard, are you aware that . . . ?" It's a little like listening to reruns of the Watergate hearings.

Am I *aware* that *my daughter* is still telling fortunes at school? And am I *aware* that some of the parents are now so upset that they've gone to the principal? And am I *aware* that some people are so furious they want to go to the Board of Education, the highest authority in the land, and have my daughter expelled from school if nothing can be done to control this behavior?

Not her, though. Suzanne Gilbert wants me to know that, despite the horrors she and her family have suffered at the hands of my daughter, *she* is the sole voice of rationality, howling in the wilderness for calm and sanity. But not for much longer. She is weary of being the only one with the finger in the dike.

After drawing myself up to my full height and mustering all the authority that I can call upon, here's the only thing I can think of to say: "Hope told me this isn't going on anymore, that she's stopped doing this."

There's a silence, while Suzanne Gilbert takes in this piece of news. Then she snaps, "Well, she hasn't stopped. Not a bit. Mrs. Lombard, are you not aware of the séance?"

"The . . . séance?"

I can hear her mentally working out whether she likes me enough to tell me the details. "All right," she says finally. She lowers her voice. "I didn't think you knew, although the others told me that your *mother* is some kind of medium, and that this is probably what goes on in your house every day." She laughs shortly.

"No, no, really, I've never even been to a séance," I say. "I wouldn't know what that's all about. Just what I've seen in the movies, you know, what we all probably know about séances—all that woo-woo stuff." I laugh, a sound that hyenas would recognize.

"Well, *is* your mother a medium?"

I want to say, *No, my mother is definitely an extra-large,* but Suzanne Gilbert doesn't sound as though she's much in the mood for humor. Probably fire would shoot out at me from the telephone receiver. So I say carefully, aware that this is probably going to go into a file somewhere and that it had better be carefully put, "Um, well, my mother is certainly unusual. She's told fortunes in the past, you know, just for fun at carnivals and stuff. And she works with police departments to find missing people, I believe—but I don't recall that she's ever talked to dead people." *Just Marvin and Irv, but surely they don't count since they technically don't exist.*

She considers this. Then in a low voice, she says, "Well. All right then. Since you don't know, I'll tell you. Your daughter held what amounted to a séance the other day before school, and she told everybody she was in contact with my mother, Tiffany's grandmother, who died last year."

I try to picture what a séance in a playground might look like. Doesn't your average séance need tables with cloths, and candlelight, and dim shadows? How did Hope manage this? And how has this kid got everyone convinced that she's contacting dead people in the schoolyard?

"Now, call me stupid or something, but I think that's bad enough, Mrs. Lombard. Right there I've gotta problem with it. You know? But then your daughter just goes on and somehow thinks up *the* most hurtful, terrible things to say. She went on and on about how Tiffany had never loved her grandmother, and that her grandmother is right now up in heaven, angry with Tiffany and planning to strike her dead." She waits. I hear what sounds like a drag on a cigarette. "So anyhow, all this has just made our home life a nightmare. Tiffany's not sleeping at night, and she tells me that she said some bad things to her grandmother right before she died, and now she thinks—she really believes this, because of your daughter telling her it's true—that she's going to get killed somehow and have to face her grandmother in heaven."

"Oh," I say. It is tempting to ask her what in the world she thinks heaven could be like, if up there people are all supposed to be plotting revenge. But perhaps we don't need to go into that.

She starts to sniffle. "It's been the worst time. My mother and Tiffany had a big fight because Tiffany wanted to get her navel pierced, and my mother said she had to wait until at least sixth grade for something like that—so then Tiff wanted a tattoo, and my mother, who was really very conservative although very, very well-meaning, said no. So they yelled and yelled at each other. I finally had to turn off the TV set and go in and tell them to knock it off. And then what do you think happened?"

I can't imagine what to say. Suzanne Gilbert evidently mistakes my silence for stunned grief instead of what it really is—shock that a person should wait until the ripe old age of eleven before getting her navel pierced. She says in a low voice, "That's right, Mrs. Lombard. The next day we get up, and find my mother has died in the night. Of a heart attack. Or a broken heart, is more like it. And your daughter makes that into a tragedy every single day."

I now hear the hoofbeats in my head. "I'll talk to her," I manage.

"Well. I didn't think you knew," says Suzanne Gilbert. "And, Mrs. Lombard—may I call you by your first name?"

"Of course. Please call me Maz."

"Call you what?"

"Maz."

"Why would I call you Mass?"

"No. Maz. It's my name. Maz."

"Well. I've got to tell you, *Math,* that I'm not even the parent who's the most upset. Apparently, there's another little girl in the class, and your daughter told *her* that her darling one-year-old baby brother is going to grow up and shoot people."

A sound, something between a nose whistle and a whimper, escapes from me.

"And I think there are others besides. Your daughter is certainly having herself a time. By the way, and forgive me for prying into your personal affairs, but did I hear that you and her father are getting divorced, and that both of you are, uh, involved with other people now?"

"It's . . . complicated," I say.

"Because it's none of my business, of course, but I'm thinking maybe she needs a shrink or something."

"Hmphshf."

"You've gotta get some help for that child. It's not natural, what she's doing and saying, you know. This is, like, antisocial behavior of the highest order. She may even be a psychopathic maniac or something."

After I hang up, I trudge over to Lucille's trailer again, where this time I find them having a routine run-of-the-mill grandmother/grand-daughter bonding experience, except that now they are both wearing purple turbans and are playing with the Ouija board. I actually feel a moment's relief that they're not doing rituals using the entrails of small animals, psychopathic maniac style. I mean, say what you will about a Ouija board, they do sell them in regular department stores, and many otherwise normally well-adjusted children play with them at parties. As much as I would rather they were painting their faces to look slutty, using all the rouge and eyeliner they can find, at least it must be said that Ouija boards are still legal in all fifty states.

I stand and watch them for a moment, wondering why it is that I am suddenly creeped out at the sight of their two heads bent together over the board and the identical looks of concentration on their faces.

At last Lucille says, "There! You see? You *were* right!" And they sit up, smiling at each other, and then Lucille's eyes swing over to me and she says, easily, calmly, "Why, hello there, my big ole baby. I was just teachin' little Hope here how you can get in touch with *real* spirits. Until she finds her own Irv and Marvin, she's got to shop around a bit."

"Well, that's certainly nice. So you're shopping for spirits with the Ouija board?" I say. I try to make this sound as though they've gone on the internet looking for Barbie doll outfits.

"She's got such an aptitude for this stuff, did you know that?" says Lucille. She leans over and squeezes Hope's knee. I move and sit down next to Hope on the padded bench by the table. Her smooth little baby hands are poised on the Ouija board pointer, as if at any moment she's going to start channeling Beelzebub or something.

Lucille's face suddenly changes. "Uh oh. Somethin's wrong. I feel it. What is it?"

"Well," I say. "It's kind of between Hope and me. I think she should come home and have a talk with me."

They exchange looks.

"It's those girls at school again," says Lucille.

"Jeez, maybe you really are psychic," I say and swallow hard. "But, actually this is something that I think Hope and I are going to have to work out on our own."

"I know the whole situation," says Lucille. "And I can help here. After all, sweetheart, no offense meant, but I am the only one in this room who has some experience with these kinds of jams. Remember, sweetie, when I was tellin' all those women in Starke who their husbands were seein' on the side, and I turned out to be right, of course, but no one really wanted to hear about it? Remember that?"

"Not really," I say. "And that's not what we're really talking about here." I turn to Hope. "Come on back to the house now. It's time for bed."

"I did not do anything bad," says Hope. "You believe everybody else before you believe me."

"I didn't even say what it is yet," I say. "And it's not a matter of me believing you or not believing you. I want to know what's going on.

Tiffany Gilbert's mother was just on the telephone, and she was practically crying because of how upset Tiffany is over stuff you've said."

"I didn't say anything to that cow! I don't even talk to her anymore." Hope's eyes have turned opaque. "She just tells lies to everybody, and it's all because Amelia wants to sit with me at lunch and not with her. She's just jealous, and now she's got everybody mad at me, and now even you're going to take her side."

"Hey, I'm just trying to fi—"

Lucille shakes her head at me and then reaches over and puts her hand on top of Hope's. "Hope, are you tellin' girls things in the playground?" she asks softly.

"No! I don't even talk to Tiffany Gilbert anymore!"

Again, I start to say something, and am waved off by Lucille. "Honey, listen to me. I've had to put up with people like this my whole life. It's not worth it to say things that are going to upset 'em even if you feel like you're seein' the real truth for them. You just can't do it."

"I don't do it," says Hope.

"Please don't lie to me about this," I say.

"You always believe everybody else but me!"

"No, no," I say. "I believe you. Honey, I do believe you if you say it's true." I reach out and pat her shoulder. "Tell me again that it's true." I pull her close to me and stroke her hair, still damp from her shower. She gives in to my hug and leans against me. After a moment, she whispers, "It is true, Mommy. I promise."

Lucille smiles at us. "Listen, baby, I know what you're up against with girls like this. They ask you to tell 'em stuff, and then you do, and they make it out like you're the bad guy. They get all mad at you. Use you when they want to, and then get mad when it all doesn't work out like they wanted. It's just part of life when you are psychic, sweetie—"

I make a sound, something like, "Achhh—" by which I mean to indicate that we are not calling Hope a *psychic* at this stage in her life, and not pretending that she's following in her insane grandmother's footsteps. I believe this "achhh" sums that up nicely. Lucille, in fact, gets it and shushes me down once again.

"So you gotta promise both me and your mama that you won't tell fortunes anymore at school."

"Okay," says Hope.

"Now you promise me that?"

"Okay, I promise."

"Psychics' honor?"

"Okay."

They do some weird little thing then, with their fingertips, tapping each other's and then their own, and then swiping their cheeks and lips. It's all I can do to watch this display of whatever it is, some kind of witches' camaraderie or something. I can't think anymore about it tonight. Hope has promised not to tell any more fortunes. Lucille has made her promise, and Lucille seems to be the one with the clout lately.

"It's over," she says. "What's done is done, and Hope will make amends. Won't you, Hope dahlin'? No more talkin' to that Tiffany Gilbert about her ole grandmother. And then, why, if I have to go to that school myself, I'll make sure these people stop givin' you a hard time."

"Okay," says Hope and smiles at both of us.

And for a moment I sit and look at them and think that Lucille has stepped in to help just in time. *Maybe,* I think, and not for the first time since she's arrived, maybe she's learned at last how to be a mom. I feel tears stinging my eyes and have to look away.

# 23

"*Maz*. Are you really sleeping, or are you faking?"

I come awake immediately and look at the clock. It is 3:24.

"Hunnnh?"

"Are you fake-sleeping? You are, aren't you?" It's Lenny, and he's getting into bed next to me, shoving me over so he has enough room. His toes are like ice on my legs. I can barely make out his face in the darkness, but it seems to me he's smiling. "Come on, give me some room."

"Lenny! I thought we went over this, and decided that you—"

"I know, I know. But I want to talk to you, and there's always so many goddamned people around, we never have any privacy any-more."

"Privacy?" I manage to haul myself over to the side of the bed, and tuck the covers up around me. "Listen, just don't touch me. Stay on that side."

"In your dreams I touch you," he says. "You wish."

"What are you doing here?"

"What? In this bed, back in New Haven, or on the planet earth at all? I wish I knew. I can't sleep." He pats the covers around him and fluffs his pillow. "So. I was wondering. What would you say the top five good moments in our marriage were?"

"Lenny. I was sleeping. I have to go to work in the morning."

"Top five, that's all I ask. Don't have any? Okay, here are mine. First of all, the day we met, when you came to audition for that rock band I was advertising, only there wasn't really a rock band, and it turned out you didn't know how to sing, either. That was the day I figured you were a fraud, too, and that we could hook up."

"I wanted to be a singer," I point out. "I thought I could learn."

"Still very fraudulent to claim you already were," he says. "Anyway, moving on, then there's our wedding day. Major major stonedness on my part, for which I apologize. But what I do remember is how you looked like you had some kind of gold aura around you—you just kept moving through the crowd and smiling, and you looked like, I don't know, queen of the sun or something. And then, of course, that night when we were getting it on. First time as husband and wife. Heavy."

"So then is that number two and number three?"

"I don't know," he says. "Maybe. But I thought of more. D'you remember the day we went to the Village in New York, and I was scoring some dope from that guy McLean, and we were standing in the elevator and singing along to some Beatles tune that was in our heads, and then we started making out in the elevator and pretty soon you're taking off your clothes, and we're—"

"No," I say.

"Come on, you remember. And we had to keep pressing the buttons so the elevator would just keep going up and up, and not stop?"

"No. Lenny, that wasn't me."

"It had to be you! It was summer, remember? That's the only way we got away with it because there wasn't all that much clothing to take off—?" He stops talking and I feel him shake his head. "Okay. Forget it."

"It wasn't me, was it?"

He laughs. "No."

"Get that. One of the top five things from our marriage, and it wasn't even me. You were doing it with somebody else."

He laughs again and threads his fingers through mine. His voice is husky in the darkness. "I haven't been so good at marriage. It's not one of my talents."

"No."

"I think I'm ADD or something."

"Something, certainly."

"So how many women do you think I've cheated on you with?"

"Oh, I don't know. I kept myself in denial pretty much of the time."

"Only two or three, not a million like you probably think," he says. He turns and puts his face right up close to mine. I can see his eyes shining in the light from the street. I feel almost numb, looking into them. "I really tried not to hurt you. I didn't want things to go this way. I just want you to know that. I just get itchy and bored. Can't stay focused on what I'm supposed to be doing."

"Thank you for telling me that."

"I did love you. And the kids. I love the kids."

"I know that."

"I just can't do the whole marriage and family thing," he says. "I'd be a good uncle maybe. When I came back here, I thought that this time I really might be able to stick it out. I wanted to tell you that I was here to stay again, but then you had somebody else—several guys, maybe, it looks like—and so I just waited and pretended I was getting money for my center. But these last few weeks, with Lucille and Harold here . . . I don't know. I just can't do it."

"So when are you going back?" I say.

"Oh, I dunno. You know how I hate planning. That's why you didn't know I was coming. One day I just got up and said, 'Today's the day. I'm going to New Haven.' That'll be the way it is when I go back, too."

"This time will you be the one to tell the girls?" I say. "They blame me when you leave. They think I push you out."

"Okay," he says. Then he thinks about it and says, "Maybe."

"No," I tell him. "You have to."

"Okay. Sure. I'll think of something."

"And so what about the center?" I say. "Are you really a shaman or whatever you say you are?"

He laughs softly. "Nah. I'm just me. Same as I ever was. People— well, they believe stuff about me. I don't know why really. If I say I'm a rock musician, people come to hear me do stupid stuff on the guitar and clap for me, and if I say I'm a builder, they give me these jobs building condos. I fake it. And so this year I just somehow got hooked up with some people who seemed a little bit lost, and I'd tell 'em stuff, and—I don't know. One thing led to another, and now there's this whole center I'm supposed to do."

"You don't have to, you know."

"What else is there?" he says. "I'm sick of doing construction. I don't have any other talent other than making people believe my bullshit. That's not much to go on, when you stop and think about it."

"How about a real job? You know, going back to school and learning to do something useful and then doing it?"

He laughs. "Maz! Who are you talking to?"

"You could learn to be an electrician or a plumber. . . ."

"Maz, who do you think I am? I'm the King of Bullshit is who I am. I can't go sit down and be an electrician. I'd electrocute somebody, be responsible for their whole house going up in flames. Baby, I can't *care*."

*Can't care.* So there you have it. I lie there in the dark, and after a minute he says, "So, do you think we could fuck?"

"Mmm, tempting," I say. "But absolutely not."

'Two days later, I'm saying to Lucille, "I can't believe it's springtime here! Would you come out here on the deck and just *look* at all these daffodils and tulips in bloom!"

It's a little after eight, and Hope has already left for the school bus, promising once again that she will say *nothing* about anybody's dead grandparents, the future of their baby brothers, or anything else that isn't absolutely obvious to anyone else's line of vision. Even Lucille has reminded her once again, gently, that it's not worth it to waste your gifts telling people stuff that they don't want to hear, particularly when it comes to their dead relatives, and Hope has agreed.

Upstairs, Abbie's getting herself dressed for day care. She's kicked me out of the room, probably because she's decided to wear something unreasonable—like last week, when she wanted to wear her bathing suit and a floor-length sundress because it had gotten to be almost sixty degrees. I know that soon I'll have to go up and assess the value of an early-morning Discussion on Appropriate Clothing, but right now I just feel like being with Lucille.

She comes out onto the deck, holding both our mugs of coffee and hands me mine. "This weather must just feel amazin' to you, after such a long winter," she says. "I swear, I don't see how you do it! Or *why* you do it, frankly, when you could live anywhere you want to."

"I do really like it here," I say. "All my friends, and the day care, and my job. I get tired of winter, but I like the change of seasons."

"I reckon," she says.

"You know, it's really been nice having you here," I say suddenly. "I didn't realize how miserable I really was all this year—all that Lenny business, and the kids adjusting. It's been hard, and now everything just seems to be falling into place."

"Well, honey," she says, smiling at me, "I just knew it would be a good thing for all of us. You just needed a little boost. We all do from time to time." She reaches over and pats me on the arm.

"I guess that's true," I say. "You've been so great, doing all that cooking and just being here for the kids. This place has felt like a home again to me. I feel like I have my strength back." I almost want to curl up around her and put my head on her yellow chenille shoulder. I pull two deck chairs up to the white plastic table. "Let's sit here and eat our breakfast," I say. I wonder if I'll tell her about Josh.

"Oh, I should go see how Harold's doin'," she says. "He wasn't feelin' too well last night so I just snuck out this mornin' and let him sleep."

"Oh dear, what's wrong?"

"I think it's just some heartburn," she says. "He's got a couple things goin' on, healthwise—nothin' real serious, but he could use the rest."

"He's really a terrific man," I say. "I still can't believe you found him. He was definitely worth waiting for."

She doesn't say anything, but she does go sit down in one of the deck chairs and turns her face upward to the sun. I love her like this, before she's put on all that makeup and her wig with all those ridiculous ringlets everywhere. Her natural hair is almost thoroughly gray and wispy and soft around her face.

"Don't look at me, darlin'," she says, eyes closed. "I know I must look like hell with my face and hair not on."

"You look beautiful," I say, stretching out and wrapping my hands around the warm mug. "I like you this way."

"You're lookin' pretty damn good yourself," she says without opening her eyes. "I think that young guy you're seein' must be doin' you a world of good."

"Oh, Josh," I say, pleased. I stretch out my legs and flex my toes. "God, he's wonderful."

"Got Lenny sure hot and bothered, and that's worth somethin'," she says.

I laugh. "*Lenny*," I say. "He's not exactly pining away for me. We've talked it all through, and agreed now that the marriage is really over. Sad, but necessary." *I don't want to talk about Lenny. Ask me more about Josh. Let me tell you what it's like to feel so sexy all the time.*

"Well," she says, and smiles at me. "You look like the cat who ate the canary. All satisfied and strong. You must be gettin' some good action."

"Omigod," I say. "You can't imagine. He's just so sexy. It's so—so wicked. You know? I mean, he's way too young for me, and it's not going to last, even I know that, but there's something just delicious and sexy about being with a guy like this. Do you know what I mean?"

"Do *I* know what you mean, darlin'? Who do you think you're talkin' to? I built my life around that kind of lovin'," she says. "Those are the days, Maz, that'll get you through old age. That kind of sex. It carries you."

"Carries you," I say, appreciatively. "Yes, it does. That's exactly what this is like. Like I'm being carried. I feel as though I'm slightly not really me anymore. Weird."

She reaches over and squeezes my hand. "Oh, you're you. Just enhanced."

*Enhanced. That's right.*

We sit in silence for a little while. I hear Abbie turn on the television set in the living room. Cartoons. I should go in and make sure she ate all her scrambled eggs and is wearing actual prescribed clothing, but it's too nice out here for the time being. I feel like I've missed a whole bunch of mothering, and I have only this time to catch up on it.

"So you and Harold—you're doing fine?" I say after a while.

"Eh. It's a marriage," she says, without opening her eyes. "You know how that is. Give and take."

I laugh. "But some marriages are better than others. How's this one rate?"

At this, she opens her eyes and looks squarely at me. That Charles Manson magnetic stare. I feel prickles on the back of my neck.

"Maz, you did know, didn't you, that Lenny knows Jackson?"

"Jackson who?" Though I know.

Her eyes have locked onto mine. "You know. *Jackson Angus.* My Jackson. My old boyfriend from Starke. The one who broke my heart way back when."

"I thought he died," I say. My mouth, I realize, has gone a little dry.

"Hell no, he didn't die. He shoulda died, after what he did to all of us there, but no, he's still goin' strong."

"Well, but . . . how in the world would Lenny know him? And how do you *know* that Lenny really knows him?"

"He says he met him in Santa Fe at some builders' meetin'. You know, Santa Fe does attract a lot of different types of people, and I can see Jackson Angus driftin' around and endin' up in a place like that."

"Well, but so what, right? I mean, that's an amazing coincidence, Lenny *knowing* him, but . . ."

". . . But nothin'," she says. She leans forward and takes a long drink of her coffee.

Whew. I smile at her. *Nothing. She said nothing.*

She puts down her cup hard on the table and swings her eyes back to mine. They've gone black, with a couple of shooting sparks, just for good measure. To put the fear of God in me. "I've just got to see him, is all," she says. "Unfinished business."

My neck starts to hurt. After a moment, I say, softly, "What unfinished business?"

"Maz, come on, get real. We had a *child* together. A child he never knew about. Cassandra is *his*, sweetie. I think I owe it to him, to tell him, don't you?" Her voice is flat and hard. She's leaning forward now, those eyes burning into mine. I hear my own heartbeat, taste something metallic in the back of my throat. Oh, my God, we're back to Cassandra again. The ghost child who would have known just how to handle Lucille, who would have made life so perfect. And now here she is again, materializing on the deck, like something shimmering just off to the side. Shit.

"Oh, *please*," I say. "Lots of people have children that they never know about—that's what adoption *is*, you give up a child and other people raise that kid, and you don't see it anymore. And for guys especially, they just don't even know the kid ever existed. How's that going to have any meaning to Jackson from all those years ago? What's he supposed to do with that information? Why bring all that up to him now?" I'm talking too sharply. My breath feels high in my chest. "Anyway, how do you know for sure it's even him? I think there might be a couple of guys named Jackson Angus in the world, you know."

"Maz, think of who you're talkin' to. I mean, who *am* I? Madame Lucille could have found him years ago if I'd really wanted to, if I'd been ready. The point is—and Lenny sees this, even if you don't, he's so *evolved*—there's a time and a place for these situations to culminate. It's not our job to know why or when things happen. I just know that now I'm ready." She sits up straight and drinks her coffee. I see a look on her face that I recognize from when I was a little girl.

"What are you going to do?" *Don't tell me you're going there, please. Please. I don't want to know. Don't go looking for Jackson anymore.*

"Of course I'm going to Santa Fe," she says. "I *have* to check this out."

"But what about Harold?"

"He'll be fine about it. Harold and I aren't constrained by the binds that make up most marriages. When you're older and you get married, you get some unexpected benefits. He understands I have to get what I need. He calls me his little free spirit."

"So then he's going with you?"

"Well," she says. "No. Of course he's not comin' with me," she says. She looks at me hard. "That's where you could do me just the biggest favor of all. Harold, I think, should stay with you. It's just not fair to subject him to a search like that, I don't think. And who knows what's goin' to happen? It could be pretty rigorous, and I'm not sure Harold's up to it. I'm pretty sure Jackson and I are gonna go off lookin' for Cassandra once we get back together. That's most likely what he's going to want, knowin' him."

"*Knowing him?* What the hell are you talking about? You don't know him! He was a fling, a mistake, when you were sixteen years old. He's not going to want to go off looking for some grown woman who's supposedly his child."

"You are not the expert on either my life or Jackson Angus's life."

"Apparently you aren't either."

We stare at each other. *Oh my God, she really is crazy. She really is truly, truly insane. And I have been trusting her. I have been trusting her with my children, my household, my life. . . .*

"So," she says, "Lenny and I will take the motor home and go to Santa Fe. And you and Harold can stay here and play house and take care of—of everythin'."

"You're going back to Santa Fe with *Lenny?*" In the pine trees surrounding the deck, a squirrel suddenly starts screeching.

"Don't get so upset," she says, as though it was me making all that noise in the tree, and, who knows, maybe it was. I certainly feel like it. "This is somethin' I've got to do, and Lenny understands that, bless his heart."

"Don't get *upset?* I'm in shock," I say. She's done it again. She's fucking done it again—come crashing into my life and changed everything around to suit herself. I can't believe it. "Why would you go with Lenny? Don't you *see* what that would do? You're leaving Harold and me and the children and *everything* to go off with Lenny?"

She smiles at me. "You and the children could come too. Lenny certainly wants you to, and we might all benefit from livin' out there."

"Wait a minute. Is *that* what you see as the solution—that I follow my soon-to-be-ex-husband across the country and try to make a separate life for myself so far from everything that means anything to me? You really think I'm supposed to start all over again, just living in Lenny's little orbit, for his convenience?"

"I just don't see why you have to see things that way. Lenny and I are talkin' about gettin' together and openin' that spiritual center out there, and you could be a part of that. You'd have your own thing. You'd—"

"Bake bread for the shamans? Is that what I'd do?" Then I start talking fast. "Listen to me. I've talked to Lenny about that center, and he told me right straight out that he's a fraud. He calls it the Hogwash and Bullshit Center, did you know *that*? He doesn't know the first damn thing about being a shaman or a spiritual leader. He's a *con man*. He'll take your money—"

"I think I know Lenny. I'm quite an accomplished psychic, in case you were wonderin' what I've been doing all these years."

"He's told me he's a fraud!"

"Lenny," she says, "has certain *talents*. And Maz, you live in such a limited, uptight little world that I just have to feel sorry for you. One thing you never need to worry about is whether Lenny's goin' to be okay. He's got charm and charisma, and believe me, that takes a person a lot further than you might think. People believe in him, and he'll start believin' in himself. Trust me. It happened to me."

She's staring at me. Then she says in a quiet voice, "As for you, if you want to come, it'd be entirely up to you what you did out there. Your choice, darlin'." She drinks a slug of coffee, which gives her the opportunity to look away. Then she resettles herself on the chair, purses her lips, and primps at her hair, all these old familiar gestures. Her freckled arm shows as the sleeve of the bathrobe falls back. "Anyhow, you say this as though I'm goin' off to *marry* Lenny or somethin', Maz. Get a grip on yourself, honey, and don't get so jealous. I'm mainly goin' to find Jackson Angus and Cassandra and to see some spiritual people out there, and if it's as wonderful as Lenny says it is, then, hell, I'll help him with his center. Why not? I'm always up for a new adventure."

"Oh, God."

"Don't overreact to everythin'," she says. "You act like everybody is doin' things just to get at you. You know, Lenny said you wouldn't take this well at all, but I said, no, she's come a long way. She'll be fine. I guess I was wrong."

I laugh. "You're wrong about everything," I tell her. "You've always been wrong. And you're going to tear this family apart over and over again."

"You give me *way* too much power," she says. "How is it that *I* git saddled with tearing the family apart?"

"You're going off to follow Lenny—now how's that going to be for Hope and Abbie? If you don't care anything about Harold, at least you could think of Hope, who you profess to love!"

"Bring 'em along," she says. "No one's sayin' you should stay here."

"How can you *do* this to Harold? Does it matter to you that he *loves* you, that he trusts you? Just the way he looks at you—and you're going off, looking for some dream you had when you were sixteen years old?"

Her eyes by now are reptilian, and she stands up. "Yes. Yes, I am. And I'll tell you why. I'm just somebody who's searchin' for the right path, and whenever I see where that leads me, why, that's where I have to go. I always have. My whole life. That's what I'm all about, darlin'. What you see is what you git with me." She holds out her palms, face up, and her face, squinting in the sun, aims for a smile but then turns into a grimace. I feel giddy and flushed all of a sudden, like I just might burst out laughing.

"I can't believe this. You're actually serious!"

"Serious as a heart attack," she says and goes into the house. And that may have been the most prophetic thing she's ever said.

# 24

And then, wouldn't you know, nothing happens.

Yep, that's right. Nothing happens.

I am tensed, waiting for their departure. But nothing changes. We all stay the same, in our places, Lucille cheerily cooking dinners most nights, Lenny hanging out working on the deck with Harold. Hope is still loud and shrill and now wears a turban at dinner, but I've talked to the three most concerned parents about her little extracurricular séances, and they promise not to file charges against her if she will promise to stop. One father even tells me he thought the whole thing was rather overblown. "These are just children," he says. "They are quite creative at thinking up ways to torment each other and us." I wanted to jump through the phone and hug him. And then Hope brings home a report card that has okay grades, and the teacher has written, "Social skills improving. Making some effort to get along with others."

In other good news, Jolie has broken off with Josh for good, and tells him that I, Maz Lombard, am the reason. Me! I feel as though I have finally achieved true status in the world. A woman has left a man because he's seeing me. I know this is a wicked sentiment on my part, and that I should be ashamed of myself for taking it so happily. But I'm not ashamed one bit. I'm just not. Also, and this is strictly a side benefit, Lenny told me that she threw some kind of hissy fit with him when she discovered that he was really home because he was running away from somebody named Kimmie, and so now, as far as I know, Jolie is home with her cats and her knitting every night, without the benefit of the company of any of the males we've been sharing.

Even so, the sun continues to come up each morning and set each evening. And still nothing is said about the trip to Santa Fe.

One morning in the shower, I have a fantastic, wonderful, glorious idea. Maybe, it is just slightly possible, I think, that my yelling at Lucille changed her mind, made her realize Harold had value to her. That has to be the explanation. She's acting just the same as always—smiling, telling stories, letting him nuzzle her at the dinner table. Once I even asked Lenny if he knew about Lucille's plan to go back with him, and he groaned and rolled his eyes. I took that as a *Yes, but I'm not buying it.*


*A week later,* I'm at Josh's apartment, all back to normal. I am lying on his mattress, in my usual addled, sex-besotted state, and I say to him, conversationally, "Hey, do you remember Tiffany Gilbert?"

The roommates, for some reason, are not at home, and so the apartment has only one stereo going. A person can actually talk. Two people who have been having sex together for weeks could, if they wished, engage in something resembling a conversation.

Outside his window the dogwood tree is in magnificent bloom, and I feel so languid and heavy it's as though I'm drunk. The only thing that would make this moment more perfect is if he were lying beside me. I would like it, say, if his hand were tracing my nipple the way it was a few minutes ago. But he's standing across the room, naked, fiddling with things on the top of the dresser. Still, from here, I have a nice view of his rounded, dimpled butt. I smile, thinking of myself thinking that, and then I stretch out on the mattress, admiring for a moment the way my leg arches so gracefully when I stick it straight out.

He hasn't answered.

"So," I say, "do you remember her . . . from the party? She was the one who seemed to have all the control? She was really cute, and they all wanted to be like her?"

"Yeah," he says. "I remember her."

"*Well,*" I say. "You are *not* going to believe this huge problem we're having with her. It turns out Hope has been telling fortunes at school—you knew that, right?—and even though we've all tried to get her to stop, the other day apparently she did a *séance,* and I guess she told Tiffany some god-awful things about her dead grandmother! Her mom called me up, *fit to be tied.*"

I wait for him to say something funny and sympathetic. I'm expecting maybe a humorous imitation of Tiffany or her mom. We could do a whole routine together, a nice postcoital comedy riff on all the weirdness around us. He likes Hope, after all. And he certainly knows how crazy kids are. He was *at* that insane party, after all.

"Maz," he says and turns around. His voice is strange. His *expression* is strange. I sit up then and look to see what he's been so busy doing at the dresser. Apparently he's simply been stacking quarters. A man gets out of bed after his usual sexual romp with a woman and has a burning desire to stack his quarters in a pile?

"What?" I say. "What is it?" My heart starts pounding, like a little kid who knows she's about to get a shot. Or maybe she knows her mother is about to tell her that some guy who was going to stick around for a really long time has turned out to be yet another temporary guy after all.

"Maz," he says, "I can't."

"You can't . . . what?"

"This. This just isn't working for me," he says. He walks back across the room to the bed. His penis is bobbing endearingly next to his thigh. *Not endearingly. Don't think in those terms. He's telling you this is over.*

He's got an apologetic smile on his face, as though he expects a lousy scene and is prepared to be very rational and kind throughout. It's a guidance counselor smile, I think. *Sorry you didn't get into the college you'd hoped. Sorry things aren't going the way we had all believed they would, but really, my dear . . .*

"Fine," I say, feeling a smile freeze on my face. "Of course. I was sort of thinking that, too."

He reaches for me. He probably knows I'm lying, it's so clear that I was never thinking that, not for one tiny second. I turn away from him, pull the sheet up over my breasts and start looking around on the floor next to the mattress for my clothes.

"Maz," he says.

The room has gone blurry. I can't see to find my pants.

"Come on, please," he says. "Let's talk about it."

"Talk about it?" I say. "What is there to talk about? It's fine. *I'm* fine." My underpants are not on the floor, and so I start rummaging around in the sheets, but damn it, they're not there, either. And he will not stop looking at me. He's dripping with pity and sorrow and all this mushy-confused stuff—all this poor-Maz-I've-hurt-her-so-desperately senti-ment just pooling in the corners of his mouth. He's pathetic, is what he is.

"Okay," I say. "You want to talk about it? Let's talk about it. Here we have just had the most astonishing love-making—it *was* fantastic, and you cannot tell me you were lying there the whole time planning the demise of this relationship while we were doing it—and then you just get done, stack your coins into piles, and that's it? You suddenly know that it's over?"

"I wasn't stacking my coins because . . ."

I thrash around in the sheets. *Where did my clothes get to?* "Don't men know, don't *you* know—that this, *this*—is right here, one of the reasons women hate them, the fact that they can cut off so completely?"

He hangs his head, looks down.

"What," I say, "are you going to hand me a bunch of quarters in a moment and say, 'Here's for your trouble'?"

He sits down heavily on the other side of the mattress and I can feel him watching me, although I can't look at him. I finally locate my under-pants shoved down in the bottom of the covers—they're my best ones, all creamy silk and lace, bought with him in mind—and I just hope he'll have the decency to turn away while I put them on. Is he too young to know you're not supposed to watch people naked when you've just told them the whole thing is over? Naked is for people who love each other.

"Don't," he says. He reaches over and touches my arm.

"No, *you* don't!" I say and pull my arm away from him. "Look. I'm really okay with this. In fact, I'm just fine. It's not like this was a per-manent arrangement or anything. It's just that I've got to get back to work. I don't have time to sit here while we beat our breasts and cry all afternoon. *You've* got that kind of time, obviously, but I don't."

"Maz—"

"And would you *please* stop looking at me? Just go. Go in the other room. You've told me. Okay. Now leave me alone."

"Baby, you're hurt," he says. "We should talk some more."

It's that "baby" that almost does me in. But I clamp my feelings down *hard.* I can see myself doing it, floating up somewhere near the ceiling, watching with a kind of detached, dazed interest while the rest of me pulls on underwear and khakis, bra, black turtleneck shirt, cotton cardigan. One of my socks is also lost in the covers, and takes some doing to liberate. I concentrate hard on having my hands not shake, on not letting my eyes fill with tears. I command my heart to stop beating hard and my breathing to even out.

"Look, I thought we both knew what this was all about," he says. "You were getting back at your husband, and I was happy to cheat on Jolie. We were doing . . . mischief."

"You think this was just mischief?" I say.

"Yes . . . I mean, no. It was fun." He sees my face. "It was more than fun. That doesn't sound right. It was . . . beautiful. But, I mean, Christ, we're ages apart! Look at you, you're an accomplished baker and a great mom, and everyone loves you. And I'm just some grad student who has no idea what he's doing. I ride *motorcycles,* for God's sake, when I can't think of anything else to do. You . . . you *do* things. You're a real grown-up."

I would like to tell him how this time with him has gotten me through every rotten, confusing little detail of life lately, how much it's meant to me knowing I could go and crawl up next to him in his bed, to be held there, how I would have kept on going this way for ages, never wanting anything more. But I keep getting dressed, the moment passes, and I'm aware that even the one stereo has stopped playing music, as though there had been only enough sound to last for the duration of the affair, and now it has stopped. I can hear the branches of the dogwood tree scratching against the window: *Maz, get out of there. Leave with your dignity if you can. Just go.*

When I get everything together, I turn to Josh and force myself to smile. The smile takes a little more work than all the rest of my efforts. It's tough, I can see, to keep the ends of it from wobbling. He leaps up off the mattress and goes to hug me, but I extend my hand and say, "Really. Don't worry about any of this. It was great, just great, but you're right, we both know the time has come. It was just sex. Nothing more."

He walks me to the door. He's saying some things. "Blah, blah . . . don't mean to hurt you . . . blah blah . . . some of the best sex . . . really great person . . . just so many complications . . ."

"It's Jolie, isn't it?" I say, and he gets this stupid look on his face.

"Well, it's not right, sleeping with two people," he says. He's leaning against the door jamb.

I stare at him.

"And you—Maz," he says, "you're living with your husband again, and she told me you're probably going to go back to him. I don't know what's happening with me and Jolie . . . I just figured it's time for a change. Might as well be exclusive with her, you know . . . see where things lead. . . . She says it's not right, two women sharing a guy."

By the time we get down the front steps of his apartment building, I'm so furious that I turn around and slap him as hard as I can across the face. "Fuck you," I say. I'm stunned at how much my hand hurts. I cross the street to my car, my eyes blinded with tears.

He calls after me mournfully, "I deserved that, I know," and that makes me so much madder that for a moment I consider going back and hitting him once again. No sense overdoing it, though. Then it would start to look like it really, *really* mattered to me, and that's the thing I can't afford.

# 25

I pull into the parking lot at work and can instantly see that I'm not going in there. I can't. If I tried to go back to work just now, I'd find myself smashing the little bottles of spices and hurling the bread dough at the customers. Not good. So I pull out of the lot—okay, so I peel out of the lot—then turn left onto Whitney Avenue, and just *go*. I'm speeding, I know, in between the traffic lights. At each light, I skid to a stop, seeing just how sudden I can make it. I imagine that pedestrians are worried for their safety, and I'd like to shout out the window, "You *should* be worried! Run from me! Be afraid. Very afraid." God, I don't know what to do. Maybe I should go to the movies. Or get on the highway and just . . . leave home. If Lenny and Lucille are going to pack up and go to fucking Santa Fe without caring what damage they're leaving behind, then surely I, Maz Lombard, can get away with not going back to work on a sunny, sad, horrific April afternoon. And maybe not go home tonight, either. Make 'em worry.

I start thinking it all through. Josh'll probably call at some point today, just to make sure I'm all right—and Lenny will tell him, "Gee, Josh, she didn't come home today. We were sort of wondering where she was, too." Everybody will turn to Lucille and ask her to be Madame Lucille and get out her crystal ball or whatever the hell she thinks works to find people these days—"Can't you even find your own daughter?" they'll all say, and of course she *can't*. She'll have to admit she's a big fat fraud who just used that fortune-teller bit to hook men, and my oh my, she did hook a lot of them. I mean, it worked just perfectly, and now she's got a terrific one, and yet, god*damn* if she doesn't have to go back and *rehook* the one stupid guy in the whole world who somehow managed to get away, back when she was sixteen years old. God! The damage that one breakup has done to so many people's lives—it's staggering. Maybe she'll admit she was a fraud all along, and then Harold Morgenthaler won't want her anymore, and then she'll have to focus her attention on getting *him* to stay, and she'll need to postpone going to get that idiot Jackson Angus one more time. And Cassandra. Stupid Cassandra who managed to get raised by somebody else. I wonder if that child ever knew how lucky she is. I wonder if she even exists, or if she's just some story meant to torture the rest of us. Wouldn't *that* be something?

I swipe at some tears and get on the highway heading east. I'll drive until I don't want to go anymore. That's what I'll do. Maybe I'll stop in Rhode Island—maybe the coastal wilderness of Maine. Or—I know— Nova Scotia. Who in God's name knows? I have my checkbook, some credit cards, and, um, seven-fifty in cash. I fumble through my purse, one-handed. Also there's an ATM card and I think there's probably five hundred dollars in the account. I'll buy a bathing suit and wait here for summer, and then stay in a motel, walk on the beach—or, hey, set up a small bakery in a fishing village and live on smoked fish that I trade wheat bread for. Maybe there will actually be people in the world who don't intend to betray me—or who at least don't *immediately* intend to.

The children. What about the children? I should drive back and pick them up from school and day care and take them with me. Except that I can see this just might be a crying day. It wouldn't do to pick them up and then spend the day crying in front of them. Well, fine. Later today, I'll call and arrange a drop-off point. I'll tell Lenny and Lucille that they are *not* to argue with my wishes, that the children and I are going to be citizens of somewhere else now. Just give me the children and go away quietly, off to your stupid Santa Fe to track down Jackson Fucking Angus and that stupid, stupid Cassandra. *She* can maybe be the daughter and wife you both wished me to be. Better yet, take Jolie back with you, too. She's obviously suffering so over having to cope with Josh liking *me*. Take her! She'll love Santa Fe. It'll be good for her. She can chase out the new chick—

what's her name? Oh yeah, Kimmie—in case Kimmie hasn't vacated Lenny's house yet. Maybe between Cassandra and Jolie and Kimmie, everybody can figure out the right way for Lenny and Lucille to be happy. God*damn* these people!

I get out the cell phone and call Barry to tell him I'm not coming back today. Josh and Lenny and Lucille may not deserve any explanation, but Barry certainly does. I can't have him sitting there worrying about me all afternoon. I push the button, and the cell phone doesn't come on. The battery is dead. *Again.* Why do I carry this thing, if I never can remember to keep it charged up? Good God in heaven. You try to engineer a perfectly reasonable running away from your life, and then you can't even call people to give your regrets.

I pull into the McDonald's just off the interstate, park in between a couple of SUVs, and enter its white tile interior. It's like some kind of postmodern horror movie set, maybe a slaughterhouse scene, with all this white tile and bright lights. And voices seem to bounce off the walls. Naturally, the place is filled with screaming children. There are sodden French fries squashed onto the floor, and a well-dressed woman standing by the rest room door is whining at a man, "But if we don't eat here, it's going to be *hours*!" I realize that I haven't eaten either—I gave up my lunch hour to be with Josh—but, really, what is she thinking? Who could eat in this place? It's hell in here. The smell of the grease is making my stomach turn over. Every few seconds machines behind the counter give out a series of high-pitched beeps—they're screeching that the fries are done, this soda cup is full, the hamburgers are well-done enough to keep people from dying of E. coli—but the workers just numbly keep going through the motions of whatever they were doing, not even reacting to the beeps. You could go insane in here and no one would know the difference.

I find the bank of phones and punch in the number to the Golden Granary. Barry answers, and when he hears it's me, his voice becomes so soft and concerned that for a moment I can't speak.

"Maz, honey, is everything okay?" he says.

"I-I can't come back today," I say, just barely keeping myself from sobbing. "There's a whole bunch of stuff—"

Then he says something I can't figure out. He says, "Oh, is it the school thing?"

For a fleeting second I think of asking him what he's talking about, but then, so quickly it's almost unconscious, I decide that I'm willing to sign on with any excuse he'll hand me. It would really be great if I didn't have to start telling him that my twentysomething lover has just decided not to have anything to do with me anymore. Why go into all that? How is a person supposed to have a public demeanor when everybody knows everything sordid that's happening?

"Yeah," I say. The school thing. Yeah.

"Take as much time as you need," he says.

I'm so relieved when I hang up the phone that I go stand in line behind the well-dressed, whiny woman, and, when it's my turn, I order large fries and a Coke, to go. The acne-scarred teenager behind the counter brings it to me and wants money. "Oh, I forgot, could you throw in a quarter pounder with cheese?" I ask him.

"Why, *sure!*" he says and smiles at me, as though it was so clever of me to remember that hamburger in time. I have to fight back tears again. *Don't be nice to me. Just put the hamburger in the bag and don't be nice about it.*

I decide to sit there in the McDonald's torture chamber rather than go to the car. I don't need this horrible food smell stinking up the car while I'm running away. It won't do to make myself sick, after all. I gobble down the burger—it tastes good in spite of itself—and eat the fries by the handful. I should call Hannah and see if she'll make sure the kids are all right. Of course Lenny and Lucille will be there when they get home from school, but I'm mad at them and not going to let them know where I am. At least if Hannah knows, then I won't have to worry that the kids will be scared. I don't want *them* to have to suffer for this. I just need time away. That's all. Time to think. Can't think clearly if I feel guilty at the same time.

I get up and make my way over to the phones again and tap in Hannah's number. She answers on the third ring.

"Listen," I tell her. "Don't get worried or anything, but I've got to get out of here for a little while. I just ate a big hamburger, and now I'm going to get in the car and ride until I'm sick of riding, and I'd like it if you could tell the kids that I'm fine. Maybe make sure Lucille and Lenny feed them dinner. See that Hope does her homework. You know." I lean my head against the cool metal wall. My face feels hot. I'm wondering why I put that in about the hamburger. Those are just the kind of details that are not necessary for people to know. Just say the thing: *I'm not going home for a while. Please make sure the kids are okay for me. Will you do it or won't you?*

"Are you all right?" she says.

"Josh broke up with me," I tell her. My voice catches. "I went to his apartment today, and we made love, and then he said it wasn't working anymore—which, if you say right now that you *knew* it wasn't going to work out, then I'll never speak to you again."

"I wasn't going to say that," she says quietly. "I'm sorry it happened."

"Well," I say. "Well, thank you."

"Why don't you just come over here instead? We'll sit and have tea and talk about how awful men are. . . ."

I look through the glass doors at the cars glistening in the sunlight of the parking lot. I want to *go.* "I can't," I say. "I need to go somewhere different. Also, it's not just men. It's that everything's just hitting me all at once—this whole Lucille-Lenny thing has been hard—you know about that, I guess."

"I don't know anything."

"You haven't talked to your best friend Lucille lately?"

"Maz, that's not fair. I've just been trying to be nice to her. What's going on?"

"She and Lenny are taking the motor home and going off to Santa Fe."

"What? . . . Together?"

I tell her about Lucille's crazy plan.

"She does live for herself," says Hannah slowly.

I stop talking. She does live for herself. Boy, that's the statement of the year. Oh, yes, she does.

"So you've really got to go somewhere?"

"I think so. Yes. I do."

"And where are you going?"

"Rhode Island," I say. That's right. Rhode Island. "I'm going to walk on the beach and stay in a motel. . . ."

"Well, good for you," she says, but without emotion in her voice. "And I'm sorry about Josh. When are Lenny and Lucille leaving?"

"I don't really know. They don't talk about it around me. We just ignore it."

"Good idea," she says.

"So will you just make sure the kids know I'm fine? You don't have to tell Lenny and Lucille anything. I don't care what they think. Let 'em think I died or something."

"Okay," she says. "I'll go over right after school. Don't worry. Do you have your cell phone?"

"The battery died," I say.

"Maz," she says. "It's all going to be okay, you know. I wish you'd come here instead."

The recording comes on then and tells me my three minutes are up and that I'll have to put in more money if I want to continue this, but guess what. I don't.

# 26

It takes only a couple of hours to get to the beach in Misquamicut, just across the border into Rhode Island, which isn't nearly long enough to be satisfying. I think for a moment about driving on to the Cape, or even up toward Maine. But the truth is, I'm tired when I get there, and my stomach hurts. That hamburger feels as though it's sitting, intact, right at the waistband of my khaki pants. I reach down and unbutton them underneath my sweater. Maybe I should just get out and walk around on the beach for a little while, and then I'll find a place to stay, and maybe take a nap. The sun is shining—it's only about four o'clock when I turn the corner onto Atlantic Avenue—and for a while, I just ride along, looking at all the schlocky motels and bars, and then it hits me that all of them are boarded up and that I'm going to have trouble finding a place to stay.

Running away isn't as easy as a person might think. I park the car in an abandoned parking lot, among weeds and chunks of asphalt and broken bottles and cans, and get out, lugging my shoulder bag. This is just the kind of day when it would be so easy to forget keys and wallets and stuff like that. I have to hold it together, be responsible for all my possessions. Can't be losing things and having to call home for help.

The ocean air, when it hits my face, is suddenly so cool and bracing and salty that I almost gasp. It reminds me of a summer Lucille and I spent living in our trailer at the beach, right after her breakup with Pete the Fireman. That may have been our best time together, those few months after he left. Even though I liked him so much, she was suddenly mine, all mine. After he left, she started saying that I was her very best friend. I was, she said, a very, very important thing: a *confidante*. That meant I had to promise to keep everything we talked about secret. And that was the summer—I remember it now—that she started talking about real adult stuff with me. She told me about men and sex and all the details of how people really do it. She said my grandparents wouldn't like it that we were having this little talk, that they probably didn't even know what sex was; they saw it as just some horrible thing that had to happen to people so they could get children. But Lucille knew that sex was fun, lots of fun. When I asked her what it felt like, she said it was like eating the best-tasting ice cream in the whole world, and being tickled and scratching an itchy mosquito bite, and, maybe I looked doubtful because she added that it was also like hearing that you could stay up all night and watch movies.

"I don't like being tickled," I'd said to her, and I remember that moment because she laughed so hard. She said I would like it a lot. Everyone did.

But best of all, she said, sex had lots of different names, some of them more disgusting than others, but that her favorite was *screwing*.

"Screwing says it all," she said. "Did you ever hear anybody say, 'Oh, I really got screwed on the price of that dress' or anything like that? They're talking about something else, like getting robbed. And sometimes, when things aren't so good, that's how sex seems too. You give and you give, and then you've been *screwed*."

I thought about this for a long time. "Did you get screwed with Pete?" I asked.

"Nah," she said. "He'd probably say that I screwed *him*. But, darlin', I couldn't stay there. He wasn't a real man. He had a serious problem with sex, you see. It's called premature ejaculation, which I'll tell you about another time. God, my mother would kill me if she'd even heard that I said those words in front of you!"

"Tell me now," I said. I sat up straight so I'd seem older to her.

"Well, a man needs to last a long time," she said. "At screwin'. And Pete could go maybe ten or fifteen seconds. I mean, guys in *high school* can do better than that. He was always havin' to cry and apologize afterwards. Sometimes sex was so bad that I threw up right afterward."

I leaned over then and patted her on the back. Why was sex supposed to be so much fun if it made you sometimes throw up? And all that bit about mosquito bites and tickling—it didn't sound so appealing. I nodded, though, and told her I understood. "I'm your best friend," I said. "We don't need Pete."

"Oh, you're a darlin', darlin' gal!" she said and hugged me. "What a great life we have together, just you and me! We don't need any stupid *men*."

I was stunned at the end of that summer when she said I had to go back to my grandparents' house. Of course it was because she had met someone new. At the end of the summer she'd gotten restless and started leaving me with people so she could go out to the bars at night. She forgot she said we could live at the beach all through the winter, and I could go to school there. Once we'd even driven out to see the elementary school—a low, pink brick building that looked nice enough. I knew I would like it there. I was in third grade that fall, and I would have been glad to change schools, since in Starke, I was going to have Miss Arthurson that year, and I'd heard her yelling all the way from the second-grade classroom. Plus, I wanted to stay with Lucille. We were having so much fun, staying up late and talking about sex. She let me parade around in her clothes, and even though there wasn't much fortune-telling business going on that summer, she had plenty of money. Pete the Fireman had to pay her, she told me. A man who pretended to be good and then wasn't had to pay. It was just the way life worked. A man might not like it, but men had so many advantages that it didn't matter if occasionally they had to do stuff they didn't think was really fair. "The world is mostly stacked against women," she said. "But every now and then, men get what's comin' to them, and women land on top. It's a *glorious* day when that happens, you'll see."

I walk down to the beach, picking my way through the parking lot and across the sand. There are still old paper cups half-buried in the sand, the detritus of last summer. I nearly trip over the bent-up aluminum frame of a chair, poking up in the soft wheat-colored sand.

Now why do I look down and see all the ugliness that's around, when anyone else would be looking at the sky that's the color of robin's eggs, such a delicate, springtime blue, with little high wispy clouds? It all looks foreign to me. I pull my sweater tighter around me against the wind. One time when I was little, I called them "whiskey clouds" to Lucille, and I remember how she threw her head back and laughed. Laughed so hard you could see the dark of her fillings embedded deep in her smile, and the cords of her long, pretty neck standing out as her head tilted far back. She scared me sometimes when she laughed like that, with such a deep, hollow sound—a real "Ha ha ha" sound, crowded with cigarette smoke and booze, just the slightest bit out of control. Later I heard her telling somebody about it on the telephone. "God*damn,*" she said. "What kind of horrible influence am I on this sweet little child, that she even sees booze in the clouds?" No, no, I wanted to tell her. That's not what I see. It was much later that I learned that with Lucille, everything is for the punch line. There's no going back and correcting a misimpression. Everything is just for the joke.

Ohhhh, I see the kind of day this is turning into. It's going to be one of those Review Your Whole Life days, sitting in the wet sand and staring out at the ocean and thinking of every bad thing Lucille ever did to me. Shall we tackle Robbie next? Go back over the look on his face when I found him in bed with her? The way he tried to explain it all away by telling me later, "Maz, I *swear* she tricked me into it!" Tricked him! Of course I hated him for saying that. How could she trick him out of his clothes? Tell him she was going to tailor them for him, and then jump on him and drag him to bed? He'd had tears in his eyes. "Maz, you know better than anyone how she is," he said. "She's practically evil."

God, no. No, no, no. I'm not going to do this. I've done this all my life. I get up and start walking down the beach. Seagulls swoop down, crying and calling. I stand and watch two of them fighting over a piece of crab—the first one obviously the dominant seagull on the beach (we'll call her Lucille) and the other just trying for a little pinch of something, just something to have for herself, just enough to sustain life perhaps. But no. Lucille the Seagull runs and attacks, with loud screeches. I plop down on the sand. Maybe the secondary seagull will find something else to eat. Maybe she'll turn and start pecking the Lucille Seagull to pieces. She'll say, "This is *mine*! I found *this*!"

God, this has got to stop. The thing is, I thought I was over all this angst about Lucille. I'd escaped from her orbit years ago, moved up north where she claims she could never live because people are too stuffy and conservative to go for her brand of fortune-telling, too rigid and reserved to appreciate the true force of her "gifts"—and I get married and make a home, practicing every day to make it different from anything I'd ever known. Every moment of my life I'm aware that I'm creating something that I don't know the meaning of, finding my way in the dark toward something I can believe in and respect just for myself. Something real.

That makes me think of Josh and all the hours of silent sex we had. It was meaningless, I know that, nothing but sensation—no substance to it, no whatever it is you're supposed to feel. No *resonance*. He was a kid, that's all, and it had to end. But I wouldn't have ended it. I never end anything except . . . well, except Dan. I did send him away. My one self-directed ending, the guy who said life was never supposed to be easy, that you had to give things time. Good riddance to *that*. I had wanted something way more instant than that.

Tears spring into my eyes, and then my whole body gives itself up to the crying.

I get up and start running on the beach. My bag bangs against my hip, my sneakers make a plopping noise on the wet, hard sand. At first I run awkwardly, feeling the constraints of my pants and sweater rubbing against my skin. The light slants over the water, the little frothy bits of foam play at the edge of the beach, almost coming up close to my shoes, and then receding, as if they'd thought better of it after all. But I keep running, my lungs filling to the point of bursting. I kind of like the sound of my own gasping while I run. The blood beats in my ears and in my head. I'd love to shed everything as I go—bag and sweater and long pants—to just luxuriate in long, even strides. But I know I have to hold on. Just hold on and run.

Way down the beach is a man with a black dog. They're playing Frisbee, with the disk heading outward in long, slow arcs that make the dog leap into the air, like a ballet dog pirouetting and landing, joyfully, on his feet each time. I run toward them in huge, breathless footfalls, as though everything depends on my getting to them, as though they've been waiting for me.

You see, the thing is this: I thought you were allowed to simply walk away from people in your life, people who had shown themselves to be against you. And that having been abandoned by Lucille over and over again, I could just declare that she wasn't really my mother anymore. I could play like she was dead, like she meant nothing. I could move north, marry some guy, have a couple of babies, put up wallpaper and learn to bake bread, and work turns in a day care. I didn't know that trailer, those stinging tears, those five husbands, were all locked some-how into me—and that Lucille could so easily come back, and that we'd go through the same old shitty stuff all over again. Once more, with feeling. Once more, with *husbands*.

And this is what I see now, as I'm hurtling myself down the beach, windmilling my arms and taking huge deep draughts of ocean air into my lungs: I'm going to have to figure myself out all over again. Goddamn if I don't have to do the whole thing one more time.

"Shit! Shit! Shit! *Shit*!" I scream. Scream and run, for as long as I can keep it up. I'm aware that the wind is blowing hard, and that the sky is a color so light blue it seems almost as if it could crack open to a deeper blue beneath. The water, out of the corner of my eye, is the color of steel, hard and bright and cold, and flecks of white foam wash up like clumps of soapsuds. I feel as though I can outrun my skin, as if every-thing could simply fall away—all that misplaced trust, that stupid dumb-animal willingness to believe. I have ignored everything that is obvious in my life for as long as I could. I run toward the man and his dog, and I don't know why.

When I almost can't breathe anymore, suddenly my body seems to shift into another gear, and I feel as if I could go on indefinitely. Ah, the famous second wind. Or maybe it's because, as Lucille would say, I'm at last doing the thing I'm supposed to be doing, running toward the one person in the universe who has the power to help me. Maybe this man, with his arm outstretched, the Frisbee just leaving his fingertips, will turn toward me when I come nearer. Maybe he'll say, "Oh, I've been waiting for you to get here," and I'll tell him I was running away and then I'll explain about Lenny and Lucille and Josh—and even Hannah—but I won't have to tell him everything, because he'll already understand. He'll put his arms around me and he'll listen. He'll know what I mean. We'll build a fire on the beach and talk all night. Someday I'll be telling my grandchildren, "And you know, if I hadn't gone to Rhode Island that day . . . and who knows what it was that made me get in the car and just *go?* But there he was, waiting for me, and the rest, as they say, is history." And I'll beam at him, by then gray and stooped over but still smiling at me, remembering this first day.

But when I get to the place where the man is, he's packed up. I see him roll up a blanket that was on the ground and put on his jacket. He gathers the Frisbee and whistles for the dog, and together they troop up the hill, the dog leaping ahead and the man trudging along behind, rocking from side to side as he walks. When I get closer, I see he has a pickup truck, and I stop running and watch as he and the dog get in. He does not turn and see me at the last possible second. His face does not break into a knowing smile. He does not call my name. I hear the truck motor turn over, see a puff of smoke, and, of course, he pulls away.

I stand there for a moment, my arms at my sides, my breathing struggling to become normal again. God, it's so stupid the way I see my life, see all my existence as if there's some magic out there waiting just for me. Maybe that's what comes from being raised by a fortune-teller: even if you don't buy into the seeing-into-the-future stuff, you always cling to the idea that something will step out of the shadows one day and save you. A stranger will suddenly slow down, back his truck up into the parking space, get out, look at you, kiss you—and your story will get rewritten right at that moment. The man at the red light will turn, and he will be the love you always knew you'd find, not the creep you married by mistake.

I walk back down the beach to my car. It's not so far, really. I thought I had run miles, but it was not so much. It's getting dark now, though, and colder, and my legs and shoulders feel tired and weighed down. The anger seems to have drained out of me. What the hell am I doing here? At home, they're probably fixing dinner now. Lucille, in her typical late-afternoon whirlwind state, will be talking a mile a minute and asking Lenny to set the table—she sees him as her personal servant and flirts with him to get him to do her bidding. Harold, left out, as usual, will be puttering around, trying to be both useful and out of the way at the same time. Abbie will be next to him, looking up at him with her beatific smile. And Hope, with that slightly hysterical giddiness that's always about to erupt—

I stop walking, seeing Hope right before me. My crazy little bunny, who's been so furious with me over the past year, blaming me for everything that's bad in her life and who's now clinging to Lucille and Lenny with the same ferocity that she was pushing me away. I get such a hit of what this has all been like for her, and it's so strong I have to lean against the car for a moment and just concentrate on breathing. My God—all this silly fortune-telling crap she's been doing at school, these séances—that's not the real Hope. She can be whiny and demanding— and okay, hysterical—but she doesn't believe in going around talking to dead people any more than *I* do. This new side of her—all this has been a kid trying to get attention, to take everybody's mind off the fact that there's a huge uncertain future ahead. Oh, and from her point of view it has been uncertain: parents separating but maybe not divorcing, who knows, because nobody ever says. Mom seeing a guy but then cowering and forgetting all about him when Hope makes a difficult scene. Even Josh—yeah, even Josh made his mark on the situation, taking her mother away, at least emotionally. In fact, it was the night that Josh was there, while we were making love on the deck, when she first starting predicting the deaths of the kids at the sleepover. A cry for help. *I'll get my mother away from that guy.*

I close my eyes and try to get my breathing somewhere back in the normal range, instead of these ragged little half-breaths that feel like a glass broke inside my lungs. And then it comes to me: Hope is just a frightened little kid who's somehow been suddenly given too much power by the adults in her life. She's figured out what it takes to pull all the attention over to her. Make things rough at school, get school conferences scheduled, get the PTA and the principal involved. Use her grandmother's sympathy and her father's flakiness to keep things stirred up as much as possible.

And it sure aided Lucille's plan, to share this little quirky life that I've never believed in, communing with spirits through the Ouija board, talking to the steering wheel, freaking out the schoolgirls with all the unseen world—and I've just left them to it.

I slump down, hold my head in my hands. God, I've left her in the care of Lucille, and clearly Lucille is as insane as she ever was. She may make a decent pot roast and know how to smile and pretend all is well, but she's still got that crazy light in her eyes.

The fact is, she's probably scaring the hell out of Hope, handing over to her that whole powerful, witchy-woman thing, making her believe she's so special and isolated from the rest of the world—making her prove it again and again by being an outcast. I saw this coming. I saw it. And then I simply looked away.

A bead of sweat rolls down my side, gets caught at the waistband of my khakis. It feels like cold, prickly dread.

I open the car door and slide in. I don't know quite what to do next. I realize that I'm cold straight through my very bones, that the sweat has dried on my face and body, and I'm shivering. Everything looks so desolate here—the little houses a block over, with their dark green asphalt siding and lonely porch lights, all hunched together as though they can protect themselves from the powerful ocean, guard their little scrubby bushes and littered sidewalks.

Driving around, I look at different bars with horror at the idea of going in. Once upon a time today, I'd pictured myself tonight in the warm company of strangers, eating seafood at a bar, talking to a roomful of lively people, sleeping in a motel room on the beach, waking to watch the sunrise from a balcony. But now my car swings its way off the beach road and out to the highway.

I stop and get gas at a Mobil station on the way, and then drive through a Taco Bell and order a beef burrito. The lights in the parking lot make me look sickly and yellow in the rearview mirror. My hair is all tangled from the salty wind, and the color has left my face. Somebody who looks like this belongs at home, not out among the people of the world.

I eat my burrito in the car, picking bits of cheese and lettuce out of my lap, and then get back on the highway and turn toward New Haven. The car goes there almost as if it knows the way home by instinct.

# 27

*The house is dark* when I pull up to the curb, with just a blade-sized sliver of weak, pathetic light from the living room windows, visible from around the drawn shades. The bank of windows in the kitchen and dining room is black, and so are the upstairs bedroom windows. No outside lights. And there's something else, too, that seems unfamiliar and out of place. I cut the engine and stare for a moment at the large, dark empty space next to the evergreen trees—a huge chunk of air where the motor home had been parked. Lucille has gone.

I slam my hand down on the steering wheel so hard it hurts, and then I scramble out of the car and run up the sidewalk to the front door. Damn her—and Lenny, too. It's just like them to slip out this way. I don't immediately remember that it's me who's been AWOL all day long. And what does that matter anyway? *I'm* not the perfidious one here. I actually think that—the word *perfidious* springs up into my brain and stays there, repeating itself over and over again. I bang on the door while I'm fumbling to get the right key, and then, when I find it, it's a chore to get it inserted in the lock in the darkness, especially with my hand shaking so hard. And my hand *hurts* where I hit it. Really hurts. *Perfidious* hurting. Then I hear Abbie's voice from inside the door: "Mommy? Is that you, Mommy?"

"It's me, sweetie! I'm coming in! This key is stuck, is all! Hang on!"

Who knows what crazy things have happened? Surely those bastards haven't left her there alone. Did Lenny go, too? And where's Hope? And Hannah? Didn't she come over, like I asked her to? The key sticks in the lock, and I kick the door, and then the tumblers inside the lock give way, and the door opens. Abbie's standing there in front of me, illuminated only by one tiny lamp on the end table, the one with a 40-watt bulb. Her fingers are in her mouth and even in the semi-darkness, I can see that her face is dirty and streaked with tears, but she's trying hard to manage a smile even while her eyes are filling up again—and when I drop my purse, she runs to me and I hug her and rub her hair and say, "Oh, Abbie, Abbie! I'm so glad to see you! Oh, my baby! Where *is* everybody?"

Then I see Harold, lying on the couch with a cloth on his head, struggling to get up. Harold! I'd completely forgotten about him. "Hello, hello," he says in a shaky voice. He sounds short of breath, as if it's the most incredible effort just to sit.

"No, no, stay there! Are you all right?" I say.

"I'm *fine*," he says, but he doesn't sound fine at all. I want to clear his throat for him. "I reckon . . . we've . . . seen a lot of . . . big changes here today, though."

Abbie, still clinging to my leg, nods at me. "Hope's gone with Daddy," she says in a very quiet voice. "And G.G. They went."

"Hope is—*what*?" I look at Harold wildly, and he nods. "Hope's gone? You mean, they . . . took her to Santa Fe? With them?" I feel stupid, as though I can't make the words make sense.

"Oh . . . so you knew . . . about them going . . . to Santa Fe," Harold says. "Well, I'm glad somebody knew." He's sitting by now, with his hands resting on his knees. He reaches over and ruffles Abbie's hair, and she snuggles up to him.

"Wait a minute. Just wait a minute." I need lights on, to hear all this. This is not the kind of news you can absorb in this dimness. As if it can clarify everything, I go around turning on every lamp I can lay my hands on, even the harsh overhead light that we never use, just in case it can bring even more understanding. I turn and look at Harold and Abbie, as if I could make all this sensible if I just looked at them long enough. They're pitiful. "So they . . . just *went*?" A stupid question.

Harold nods and coughs, a deep, retching cough.

"Do you want some water?" I say, but he shakes his head no and keeps coughing.

"When did they leave? Oh, God, they took *Hope*?" I'm scared now. "Did they say anything? Are they just going there and coming right back? Did they say when they'd be back? Oh, my God. Was she upset?"

Harold shrugs. He's having trouble catching his breath. I go over and start massaging his back, trying to help him get whatever it is to come up, but he flinches and pulls away from me.

"Oh, Harold, does that hurt? I'm so sorry. What can I do for you? Can I get you anything—anything at all?"

He shakes his head almost violently. "I'm . . . fine. Just a little . . . tired."

"Have you guys eaten anything?"

"Hannah's son . . . brought . . . us a . . . casserole," says Harold, motioning toward the kitchen. He's stopped coughing, but his face is limned with beads of sweat.

"We didn't eat it," Abbie volunteers, still in a whispery voice. Her eyes are huge, like dinner plates. "We didn't want it. Harold, I mean Grandpa, isn't feeling good, and I didn't like the peas in it."

"Are you hungry?"

They both say no. I sit down in the armchair and, taking a deep, shaky breath, say, "Tell me what happened. When are they coming back?"

It takes approximately forever for them to get the whole story out. All my insides seem to be shaking, like the clear, glistening stuff you see attached to a chicken bone sometimes. Abbie sits on my lap, and the places where her body leans against mine feel like the only solid parts I have. I grip onto her at times so hard that she has to say, "Mommy, not so strong." I feel as though I'm hanging onto her for dear life.

Harold can't supply a lot of details, and he won't tell any of this fast, but what comes out is that around noontime today (when I was with Josh, I note wryly) Lucille and Lenny told Harold they had an errand to do, and then they took Lenny's truck and went to the school and came home with Hope. He said, "Oh, was Hope sick?" and they said no, she wasn't sick. He felt something funny was happening, but he didn't know what. Hope went upstairs. And that's when they sat him down and told him they were leaving, going off to Santa Fe for a while.

They had reasons—oh, they had their reasons, he said—for all of them needing to go, together, and just them. Hope needed a change; some kids at school were giving her a hard time and it would be good, they said, for her to start over in a new place. And Lenny ("I'm sorry," he says, "but I haven't trusted Lenny") wants to start a center or some damn fool thing. Lucille, he sighs, wants to see a man she used to know. Here, he slides his eyes over to me apologetically.

"I know she's your mother, Maz, but there are some things a married woman shouldn't do, in my opinion," he says.

"Mine, too," I say.

He notes that, not looking at me. Then he purses his lips together. "Well . . . but she's had a hard life. Nobody's been very nice to her," he says. "Maybe she doesn't know . . . how you act . . . what it means . . ."

"She knows what it means," I tell him firmly. "She just doesn't care. God, she's taken in so many people. And now, to do this! I can't believe it. I can't believe she'd go and do a thing like this! To you—and taking Hope with her!" I feel tears behind my eyes, but I know I can't let them out. "I've got a good mind to call the police."

"Well," he says. "The police."

"Harold, I really think you're not looking good at all, and it's not doing you a bit of good to relive this horrible day."

"Well," he says, looking away. "I just thought you should know."

It's been about nine hours since they left. They're probably in Pennsylvania or Ohio somewhere. Suddenly I remember that I can call them. I can call them on the motor home telephone, if she kept it hooked up. I can say, "Get Hope back here this minute! Turn that thing around. I did *not* give you permission to take her out of school."

And then, like the tumblers of a lock falling into place, I remember then, Barry saying on the phone this afternoon, "Oh, is it the school thing?" The school must have tried to call me at work to find out if I had okayed Hope's leaving that way. Barry must have figured I'd gotten in contact with them, and that we were working out the problem. God! Why didn't I make him tell me what he meant? Because I was so grateful to have any excuse just to *not know.* Just to leave. Maybe, I think crazily, the school would help me make Lenny bring her back. Me and the Board of Education lawyers: we could sue. We could have the cops stop the motor home and have them arrested for crossing state lines with a kid. *My* kid.

"I'm going to call Lucille," I say. "The motor home phone." I stand up.

"We tried that," says Abbie as Harold stands up and leans against the couch for a moment. "The phone kept ringing and ringing."

"Wait a second," I say to Abbie. "Where's Daddy's truck? Did he go in the motor home, or did he drive?"

Abbie looks at me blankly. Harold says, "They left together . . . in the motor home . . . don't know about the truck . . ."

I stare at Harold. He looks worse and worse, like a Polaroid picture that's going backward: getting dimmer instead of brighter.

"Harold, really. Are you okay?"

He gives me a pained smile. "Just tired."

"I'm going to get you some water," I say.

"I'm okay," he says. "I'm just going to go to the bathroom. I have a pain . . . here." He struggles to his feet and points to his ribcage, and then, seeing my alarmed look, laughs, a short little bark of a laugh. "I hate to be impolite, but I think it's *gas*. I don't want to trouble you ladies—"

Abbie and I go into the kitchen. We can't let go of each other. My heart is still hammering in its jackhammer way, and my teeth feel tight, like they are always going to be in the clenched position. "You must have been so scared," I tell her, turning on the lights. Hannah's casserole is sitting on the counter, with one tiny piece missing. Little green things are poking up through a creamy-looking sauce. My stomach does a dull, slow turnover. Outside the window, the sky is black. I see my reflection, and Abbie's, in the window. We look so small.

"Daddy didn't want me to go with them," Abbie is saying solemnly. I turn my head slowly and look at her, as though I can cement her there by staring at her. Her eyes are so huge and shocked. "Daddy said that somebody had to stay here to take care of you. And that was me."

"What? What did Hope say?"

"She said that she was Daddy's and I was yours. But that isn't true, is it?"

"No, you both belong to both of us," I say. "Did you *want* to go with them?"

She starts to cry and shakes her head. "No, but I miss Hopey already. I think she should come back."

"I know, sweetie. We'll figure this out." I'm biting back tears. My keys are in my pocket. I have this feeling that I could get in the car and take off after them, go blazing across the country in search of them—and that we'd catch them by morning. Find them sleeping and stretching, unaware, stage a raid on the motor home.

"How?" Abbie says. She looks at me as though there's an answer to this, and that she's kindly, patiently waiting to hear just how we're going to be saved.

That's when I hear a crash from the bathroom, the sound of breaking glass, and then a thud, like the front half of the house just collapsed.

# 28

I *let go* of Abbie and run through the kitchen and living room. "Harold? *Harold*? Are you all right?"

The bathroom door's closed, but thank goodness he didn't lock it. I push it open as far as it will go, which is only a crack because he's there on the floor, passed out, and lodged against the door. I can't get in. Through the wedge of the door, I can see his face, which is gray and furrowed, as if he's in pain. His eyes are closed. He's sprawled with his legs jammed over close to the toilet. His pants are unfastened, and there's a trickle of blood on his head and glass—the medicine chest mirror—everywhere. "Harold!" I call. "Harold, wake up!" I push against the door harder, but his weight is lodged firmly against me. Then I remember that at a time like this you're supposed to call 911, that it's not going to do any good to stand there calling his name. He's out cold, and Abbie is screaming somewhere behind me, saying over and over again, "Mommy! Mommy! He's dead, isn't he? Is he dead?" I take her and hold her up next to me while I call, but everything is swimming around in my head. I'm only aware of her arms and legs wrapped around me and her snuffling. We wait for the sirens, which seem to start immediately, and I tell her through a thick voice that takes so much effort to get out, "It's okay. They're just coming to help Harold get better. It's going to be all right."

In minutes, the place is swarming with people. They seem larger than regular people, somehow, and they bring with them such noise that I realize we must have been practically whispering before. They stamp around on the carpet with their boots, and their radios are crackling

with static, and they've pushed open the bathroom door and are working on Harold, hooking him up to electronic devices that they brought
along in their huge bags. They keep calling me "ma'am," as in, "Step
aside, please, ma'am." And: "What happened, ma'am?" That from a
woman with a kind face and a deeply furrowed brow, as if she sees this
kind of thing all the time and it's taking its toll on her facial smooth-
ness. Abbie and I are on the periphery, trying alternately to see what's
going on and to stay far enough away—almost as if we could simply go
into the kitchen and start cleaning up the dishes or drawing a picture,
and that would mean that Harold is fine and that Hope is simply
upstairs. We could just undo everything that's happened if we could act
normal enough.

"Is Grandpa dead?" Abbie keeps asking me, and I tell her that I
don't think so. "They wouldn't be working on him so much if he were
already dead," I say, but I'm not sure that's true. Maybe they're working on bringing him back from the dead, just in case I would be the type
who might say they never tried to revive him and sue them. I don't honestly know how this stuff works. So I keep shuffling things around on
the counter, loading the dishwasher, and then immediately start
unloading it and putting all the dirty dishes away in the cabinet, until
Abbie points out what I'm doing. The buzz around Harold grows
louder at times, and then subsides. I hear a man talking into a walkie-
talkie or a phone or something, and he's saying, "We're bringing him
in." There are beeps and static noise, and the sound of footsteps, people
talking in a suddenly no-nonsense way. They're finished working on
him here. I go out in the living room and stand to the side, my arms
around Abbie. Harold is being loaded on a stretcher. His eyes are still
closed, and his face is pinker now that he's on oxygen. The woman
EMT tells me I can come along to the emergency room if I want. She
says that as if the answer will of course be yes, and I realize with surprise that I do need to go, need to follow Harold. I can't bear the idea
of him waking up and feeling completely abandoned and in a strange
place. I tell the EMT (surprisingly, I come to understand that I can read
her name tag, that she has a name, and that it's Edith) that I need to find
someone to keep my daughter—I almost say "daughters"—and that I'll

follow in my car. I can't think of how I'll drive. I'll call Hannah. Hannah will know what to do about all this.

"Are you leaving me?" says Abbie and she starts to cry again. "Don't go!"

"Sweetie, I've got to go to the hospital, just to make sure Harold is all right when he gets there and they take him to the right place," I tell her. I squat down in front of her and hold onto her arms. "You can go to Hannah's house, and stay there tonight with Rachel. Let me call her." The front door closes with a whoosh, and outside I can hear the stretcher being wheeled into the back of the ambulance. In a minute, the siren will start up. I feel myself tensed for it.

"I don't *want* to go to Hannah's house, I want to stay with you," she says quietly.

"I know, and I'm sorry that you can't." The truth is that I'd love to have her with me, just her warm little body next to mine, sort of a reminder that she's okay and that everything is not lost. "But I'll just be sitting in the emergency room for hours and hours, and there wouldn't be a place for you to sleep. You'll be happier at Hannah's house, and I'll call you and let you know what's happening."

She tucks in her lower lip and nods. "Okay, I'll go to Hannah's." That's the difference between her and Hope. Abbie always backs down, stops arguing, gives in without a fight. I hug her and feel tears springing into my eyes. "Okay, let's get your stuff together, and I'll call Hannah."

The phone conversation with Hannah is more complicated than I want it to be. "Hi, are you calling from Rhode Island?" she says when she hears it's me. "I had Evan take them a casserole—"

"I know, Hannah, and thank you. But lots has happened since then." I tell her quickly about Lenny and Lucille leaving without notice, and then Harold falling over and having what sounds to me like a heart attack. "I've got to go to the hospital behind the ambulance, so can Abbie come over?"

"I'm going with you," she says. "Michael's here, and he can put Abbie to bed with Rachel. He'll just tuck her right in. . . ."

For a moment, I think that I just want to be by myself, to not have to talk to Hannah or anyone else. But then I think of the hospital in the middle of the night, and the frightening stuff they're going to be doing to Harold, and I'm grateful to her for even suggesting it. So I take Abbie over to her house, and Hannah and I head to the emergency room. When the triage nurse tells us that we can't see Harold for a while because they're working on him, we go obediently and sit in the chairs in the waiting area. Hannah brings us Cokes and M&Ms and bags of potato chips from the vending machines. The television set has the evening news.

"What time is it, anyway?" I say to her. "I've totally lost track."

"Eleven ten," she answers.

"It feels like four in the morning."

"It will be, soon." She leans back in her plastic molded chair and looks at me. I feel such a sense of generalized anxiety that I can barely sit there. My mind is jumping all over the place—from Harold's gray face and his body lying on the bathroom floor to Hope riding in the motor home out in the middle of the night in the middle of the United States somewhere. Lucille abandoning Harold. And then, of course, Josh. The whole Josh thing is right there, too.

"This has been a very bad day," I say. About four years later, I add, "What are we going to do?"

She's slumped down in the chair. "About which of our twenty problems?"

"For starters, Lenny taking Hope with him."

"Well . . ."

"No, Harold having the heart attack. I think his heart just *broke* because he trusted Lucille, and then she did this to him. Do you know, he told me that she's been mistreated all her life and that because of that she doesn't know how you're supposed to act? That's what he said. That she doesn't know that you're not supposed to just leave somebody this way and go off looking for somebody else."

"Jeez." She stretches her long legs out in front of her. She's wearing jeans and a purple sweatshirt, and her hair is pulled back in a ponytail that's barely containing all of it from falling all over the place. Periodically she pushes a wad of hair out of her eyes and tries to rewind the rubber band. "So have you called them?"

"I was trying to call them when Harold fell. But then things got just a little bit crazy." I stare at an abstract painting on the wall, all wild, bright colors with lots of glistening reds and pinks, like blood. Who picks this stuff for emergency room waiting areas, anyway? Is that a job somebody gets assigned—"decorate this area for people when they're at their most freaked out"?

"Maybe you should try again," she says.

"I know, I should," I say. I look out across the long expanse of emergency room, to where a little child is stacking some blocks while her mother leans forward and looks gray and worried and scared. Like all of us. I swallow hard. "You know, the truth is, I don't know what to say to them. That's the horrible truth. I feel so empty. What if I said, 'Bring Hope back this instant!' and they said, 'No way, we're not going to,' then what would I say? 'Harold is having a big-time heart attack and it's all your fault'? How would that help any of us?"

Hannah takes my hand and squeezes it. "Maybe it's not about them doing what you say, but you just have to call them because they have to know what effect their actions have had. Maybe that."

"You know what I really, really want? I want you and me to take a helicopter and go out and hover over the roof of that motor home, wherever it is, and then we'll throw down one of those cool rope ladders, and you'll climb down and help Hope get on the ladder and climb up to the helicopter, and we won't tell Lenny and Lucille a single word about Harold," I say to her. "Do you think we could do that—stage a rescue of Hope ourselves, and they wouldn't have to know?"

She stares at me. I see her lip twitch a little. "Why do *I* have to climb down the rope ladder?" she asks.

"Because you're the bravest person I know, and besides that, I would be flying the helicopter."

"I think the bravest person should fly the helicopter," she says. "Besides that, you have no sense of direction, and you wouldn't be able to find the motor home out in the middle of this big country." She idly rubs her elbow. "Also, I think Lucille has to know about Harold, sweetie," she says, "because technically she's his wife. That next-of-kin thing."

"Hannah, you are so letting me down."

"You should go call them anyway. Maybe they'll feel so bad they'll cancel all their plans and be upstanding people again, and we won't have to bother about the helicopter."

"I don't think they could ever feel bad enough."

"I do."

"Could I have some of your M&Ms? I ate my entire bag."

"No, because I want these. If you call Lucille, though, I'll go buy you some more."

"I think I need them for fortification before I call Lucille." I'm holding out my hand, and Hannah laughs.

"They'll be more useful as a reward," she says, just the way I've heard her try to get her kids to do their homework. "Now go make the call, and you'll be glad you did."

I get up and tackle her, wrestle the bag out of her hands. "Give me those freaking M&Ms, you withholding meanie!" I say. I'm weak from laughing. I can barely get them away from her.

She's laughing, too, so hard that tears are rolling down her face. She leans into me, and says in a loud stage whisper, "Maz, I think we need to look at your behavior here, today. You are getting to be such a parasite. Now just because your ex-husband has left with your crazy, schizoid, fortune-telling, scamming mom and your innocent but troubled daughter, and your stepfather is dying in the other room, and your lover broke up with you . . . I do not think . . . that this calls for this kind of outright *begging* on your part, this kind of *shameless thievery*. . . ."

We look up to see a nurse standing in front of us, carrying a clipboard. She's wearing pink scrubs and a shocked expression. Surely nothing they see in the emergency room shocks them anymore, so maybe she's just waiting to see who gets the M&Ms or if a psychiatrist is going to need to be summoned here soon. Hannah and I both try to stop laughing—I can feel us slamming down on the emotional brakes—but it's a little bit like laughing in church. The more you hate yourself for doing it, the harder it is to make yourself calm down. I try taking deep gulps of air, in the hope that will help, but I can feel

Hannah twitching with laughter next to me, and that makes me dissolve again. *Stop it. Harold is probably dying in there. She's come to tell me that he's gone, there was nothing they could do, and I'm in a fit of hysterical laughter.* I compose my face at least. My insides are still heaving themselves around.

"Mrs. Lombard? You can see Mr. Morgenthaler now," the nurse says. She eyes Hannah narrowly. "Are you a relative of Mr. Morgenthaler's, too?"

"No way," I say. "She's just a hanger-on. A groupie." I find my way to my feet. "How is he? Is he going to be all right?"

"Well, he's stable for now, but he had a pretty serious heart attack," says the nurse, and this sobers me up instantly. We start to walk toward the hallway that leads down to wherever they have stashed Harold. "And," she says in a grave voice, "it looks as though he's got some major blockages. The doctor will want to talk to you."

She leads me to a curtained area, where Harold is hooked up to about a million machines, all of which seem to be loudly and industriously measuring and recording the internal facts about him. Lights blink and lines run across screens. For a moment, I can't even focus on him lying in the bed. He seems tiny and incidental to the life of the machines as they carry out their tasks.

His eyes are closed, but when I go over to the side of him, guided there by the nurse, who leaves immediately, his eyelids slowly open, almost like a window shade that's scrolling up slowly, stuck on something unseen.

"Harold? It's Maz," I say, because he doesn't seem to register anything at first when he looks at me. But then he does: he smiles and, with difficulty, waves his hand in the air to indicate all the plastic tubes that are hooked to him. His eyebrows go up and down, almost comically, and I see his tongue poke out of his mouth, try to lick his dry lips, and go back inside, perhaps discouraged or maybe just to see if there's any more liquid inside. It's as though his tongue and his eyebrows have taken on the job of communicating for him.

"Harold, I'm so sorry this happened. How are you feeling? Are you in any pain?" I take hold of his hand. It feels dry and papery, warm to the touch. "God, I can't tell you—I'm so sorry about everything! I'm sorry about Lucille, and I'm sorry I wasn't there sooner to help you."

He manages a little smile and motions me down closer to him. A machine beeps at the movement. "I'm pretty well doped up," he whispers. "And . . . I'm . . . the one . . . who's sorry, Maz."

"Harold, you have nothing to be sorry about. You—"

"No, no," he says. "I should have . . . stopped them . . . with Hope. That's not . . . right . . . what they did."

"Harold, you need to just get well now. Concentrate on getting better. I'll be here. I'll stay with you."

"No, no . . . go on home," he says. "Be with . . . Abbie. I'll be fine."

"Can I bring you anything? Anything from home?"

At that, he emits a little sound, a raspy kind of sound, what's got to be a kind of cousin to a laugh. What would be a full, outright laugh if he weren't a heart patient right now. His eyebrows flicker upward, and the pink tongue comes out again. He motions me to come closer again. I lean in to him, so close I can hear his lungs pumping air—or maybe it's just the wheeze of some machine or other.

"Maz, she . . . your mother . . . took everything . . . with her. All . . . my clothes. Shoes. Everything." He laughs again. "I must not need anything. Madame Lucille says." He's made a joke, I see. A Madame Lucille joke. Then he starts to cough from the laughing, and the nurse instantly materializes next to me. I stand up while she goes over to him and lifts him to a more upright position, gives him a sip of some water but just enough to wet his lips, and then checks the dials on a few machines.

"I think he needs to rest again. I'm about to give him something more for pain. Dr. Heinrich wants to have a word with you, too."

"I'll go," I say. "Harold, I . . . I love you." The words just come out of me. I'm not sure as I'm saying them that I really mean them. A month ago, I didn't even know this guy. But he smiles, and I think, okay, it's true. I do love him. "We're in this together," I say. "We'll get it all fixed up. You work on getting yourself healthy again. I'll do the other part. The getting-them-back part."

He smiles and I see his lips move: "I love you, too."

Dr. Heinrich has kind eyes like those of a golden retriever. He tells me that Harold has extensive damage to at least three arteries, and that they're going to want to do a bypass. But first they have to take a few days to get him stabilized.

"You're his next of kin?" he says.

"He's my stepfather." I clear my throat. "It's a new marriage. I, uh, don't really know him very well."

"Ah. And your mother is . . . here?"

"Um, she's just left," I say, "on a trip. I'll try to contact her. But I don't know if there's anyone else close to him that I should contact."

He frowns. "Well, we'll keep him on medication to get him stable. I don't think it'll take more than a few days. And then he'll be on the O.R. schedule." He looks at me closely. "You should go home now and get some rest. He'll need you more in the next few days. Tonight he's just going to be sleeping."

I start back down the hall to the waiting room, but then realize I didn't ask Harold the main question I needed to know: Is there anyone—a child, an ex-wife, a sibling—that I should call for him? I head back to his room, but by the time I get there, the curtain is closed, and they're working on him again. Giving him something for the pain. I wonder if I crawled in next to him if I could have something for the pain, too.

# 29

"So don't worry, Harold's not goin' to *die*," Lucille is saying into my ear. "It's just more aggravation. A *hell* of a dramatic demonstration. Believe me, Maz, the guides tell me that's all this is."

"How can you *say* that?" I cry. "You really don't care anything about him at all, do you? I can't believe this!"

She sighs. I hear the lighter clicking. She starts in again about how she *does* care about Harold, she *adores* Harold, but the time comes when you just have to reclaim your past, and how can I expect her to turn away from the possibility of reuniting with Jackson Angus and Cassandra? How can I, *of all people*, not know that that's what she has to do? *Hello*, did I somehow miss something through the past thirty years?

"Listen. Where are you?" I say. I look at the clock; it's 8:08. I can't believe I've actually been sleeping. For the whole night, I kept waking up every few minutes, having dreams of misplacing something and searching for it—and then realizing, again and again, with a thunk, just what it is that is gone from me. When the sound of the phone ringing split open the air next to my head, I shot up off the pillow and grabbed for it before I even knew what I was doing. Apparently, after knocking over the alarm clock, a glass of water, and a toy dinosaur, I told her the whole story about Harold without even being fully awake. "Where are you?" I say again.

"God, I just wish I *could* tell you where the hell we are," she says and laughs. "We're out in the middle of goddamn nowhere, is where we *are*, in the most godforsaken place *I've* ever seen in my whole life, and God knows I've been in some real godforsaken territory. You know *that* about me, sweetheart. You were in a lot of those places with me, remember?"

"Lucille, *where—*"

"I tell you, this Lenny of yours acts like it'd be a major sin to get *on* the interstate. He's gotta have *scenery*. You never tole me, darlin', what a goddamn hippie he is. I never woulda considered makin' a cross-country trip with the likes of *this*. My *gawd*." She laughs again, and for a moment I think she must imagine somewhere in that fucked-up mind of hers that what I truly care about right now is whether or not she's having a good time—and thinking that I would want to join in, piling on about Lenny, whom I'm sure she's winking at the whole time.

I try to speak, but she claims the airwaves once again. "And, sweetheart, get *real*. It's not like you avoid any traffic goin' this crazy way. You just wouldn't *believe* the traffic we've been in, even through most of the night on these back roads. I swear, I don't think those truckers take even five minutes off to piss, and they just *roar* at you—"

"Lucille, *stop*," I say. I take a deep breath to steady myself. "Stop it. Tell me right now this minute what is going on." My voice is still croaky. "Why did you take Hope?"

Hannah, much to my surprise, shows up just then at the bedroom door, wearing Lenny's old red robe that I gave him for Christmas the year we got married and that he never once wore. I didn't even know that she had spent the night. Her face is drawn and pale, but she makes a victory fist at me and hands me a cup of coffee. She sits down on the bed in a patch of sunlight and watches me talk to Lucille. "What are you doing here?" I mouth to her. "You need me," she whispers.

Lucille is rambling on again, spinning out words—none of them about Hope. One of her husbands once pointed out that she uses words the way other people use bricks—to build up a wall that nobody can get over, can't even shout over. She's telling me some god-damned thing about the vacuum cleaner not working—the vacuum cleaner!—and then she dips back into the truckers, traffic patterns, blah blah blah, until finally I say loudly, very loudly, "Lucille, for God's sake, stop telling me this crap and answer me. Where are you and why did you take Hope away without telling me? Damn it, she's *my child*."

She stops talking suddenly, and for a few seconds there is only the hissing of the wires. Click, click of the lighter. Her voice slows a little, she takes a drag of her cigarette. I can almost feel the vibe changing. "Why, darlin', she wanted to come, that's why. And to tell you the God's honest, Lenny and I got to talkin' about ever'thing, and, darlin', we think she just needed a little *change*. You know? Those little gals were really gettin' ratty with her, you know how it was, and Lenny says he knows of this great woman in Santa Fe who's homeschoolin' her kids, and that's where he and Hope decided she'd be better off."

The top of my head feels like somebody has just pounded on it. They were taking her for good? For *school*?

"No, no, no," I say. "This is not how this works. She's not going to school there, and you and Lenny cannot just take her, without even telling me."

"Well, darlin', we looked for you ever'where to tell you, and nobody, not even your *boss*, had the slightest idea where you were. By the way, that's some deal you have at work apparently, that you can just leave without tellin' anybody where you're goin'. Nice work if you can git it, sweetheart! I figured you were out with your, ah, gentleman friend? And since you didn't leave us *that* number and your cell phone wasn't workin', how were we exactly supposed to get in touch with you?"

"You're missing the point. I'm her mother, her custodial parent. And this is not how adults act. You don't just do something like this without warning. It was totally out of the blue, it was an act of enormous hostility. . . ."

She sighs loudly. "Oh, sweetie, don't make such a federal case out of everythin', with all that crap about 'enormous hostility.' There was nothin' enormous or hostile about it at all. We just hit on the idea of takin' Hope with us that mornin', so I couldn't have told you any sooner. And as for me and Lenny, I told you days ago that we were goin' and you just about blew a gasket at me. Just flew off the handle."

I clear my throat, speak calmly. "Okay. You've made your point.

Now I want you to turn around right now, and bring her back here. Now."

"To tell you the truth, Maz—and do not get all defensive with me on this—but, sweetie, you have been so preoccupied lately with your own life that I don't even think you've even *noticed* what was bein' said to you. Twice I saw Hope try to talk to you about what's goin' on in school, and you just drifted off into some kind of daydream. It's like you've been *stoned* on that hunk you've been seein'. Nobody could talk to you, sweetie."

*Stoned on that hunk.* I feel a buzzing in my ears. "I have always listened to Hope," I say, but Lucille has smelled blood. She's going for me, like *Jaws*.

"Now, Maz," she says and laughs again, a low, throaty, naughty laugh. "You said so yourself, the other mornin' on the deck. That new lover of yours has just got you all hot and crazy. And, darlin', no one *blames* you for anythin'—my gawd, we've all been there with needin' some love and then finally gettin' some—that's what makes the world go round now, isn't it? But right now we all just think Hope will be happier with her daddy for a while—and with me. That little gal just thinks I put up the moon, you know that."

*You said so yourself.*

My eyes fill up and Hannah shakes her head at me, and raises a fist, even though she has no idea what's being said to me. *Be strong,* she mouths. *You're right, she's wrong,* she says.

But Hannah, bless her, may just be wrong about this.

"Hope will not be happier—" I start to say, but Lucille has gone on talking, doesn't even hear what I'm saying. "Anyhow," she is saying, "I am *not* gonna have this conversation with you right now. I only called because you left so many messages on the answerin' machine that I figured you were gonna have a stroke if I didn't call you back. Plus, you've clogged up our machine somethin' horrible."

"Lucille, please. I'm begging you. What do you want from me? Turn that motor home around and bring her back. I *insist*."

Clicking again. "Sweetheart, *Lenny's* the one drivin' the motor home—I'm not gonna steer this big ole thing out on these back roads—

and I do not believe that as her daddy he believes it's best for her to be in New Haven right now. So even if I wanted to, I don't see how I have much to do with whether she comes back there or not. Now, quick before I hafta hang up—tell me about that Harold. I swear, darlin', with him you don't know whether to call the doctor or the drama critic."

"Actually, his heart gave out in four places," I say coldly. "He might've died."

"Might've, but didn't," she says.

"And when he's strong enough, *if* he gets strong enough, they're going to do bypass surgery."

"Gawd," she says, "he's more dramatic than I gave him credit for. But don't take all this too seriously, darlin'. The guides say he's gonna be just fine."

"Listen to me," I say. "You've got to turn around and come back here."

"*I'm* not comin' back there! You crazy? That'd be even worse for him. If I was there, he'd just have to have a quadruple stroke next time. This heart attack stuff—now that was just to git my *attention*. Next time it's gonna be somethin' *really* big, like all his brain cells spill out on the carpet right on my foot or somethin'—"

"Hope," Hannah whispers. "Talk to Hope."

"Lucille, put Hope on the phone."

"—and I can't take care of him, only ever'body'll be sayin' that's what's got to happen. Believe me, Maz, I'm doin' you a big favor stayin' away right now. The sight a me, and that man will rupture in a million pieces. You won't never get the mess cleaned up after *that*."

"Lucille! Put Hope on the phone."

"Listen to me. You don't have to get stuck takin' care of him, darlin'. Harold has a daughter in Cleveland, I think, named Priscilla or Darlene or some other horrible fifties name like that. Get him to tell you where she is, and then you just call her up and she'll be only too happy to come up there and collect him. She'll just *love* believin' the worst of me. You'll make her day, believe me."

I start pacing with the phone, muster the force around me, try to speak nonthreateningly. "Okay, Lucille. Please. Will you please put Hope on the phone?"

She hesitates. For a wild moment, she doesn't say anything, there's just some buzz from the phone line across all those miles. I close my eyes. Wait for it.

"Honey," she says, so smooth you would swear none of what she's saying is a lie, "I would if I could, but she's asleep right now, and I am *not* gonna wake her up after all the excitement yesterday. God knows that child needs plenty of rest. I've never *seen* anybody who likes to sleep as much as that one. Maybe she's depressed or somethin', is what I think, after that year she's had. But, sweetie, you call us back some other time, and you can talk to her. And, by the way, Lenny says hey." And then she hangs up. Just hangs up. I sit there listening to the dial tone.

I look over at Hannah, unable to speak.

"The police," she says. "Let's call the police."

"No. No, no. That would just make things worse. Hope doesn't want to come back. This has been coming on for a long time, and it's all my fault." My back hurts, and my temples are throbbing. It's all I can do to put the telephone back on its cradle. "Hannah, I've been terrible. Just awful."

She's doing the obligatory friend thing, saying, "No, you haven't, you're a great mom, Hope loves you, you haven't done anything wrong, blah blah blah," when I suddenly look at the clock and feel my hair standing on end.

Oh. My. God. I'm two hours and forty-five minutes late for work. I never called Barry, and nobody made the bread.

*Barry's so sad,* it's as though Eeyore the donkey has come to life as the owner of a natural foods store. He regards me sorrowfully through his huge brown eyes and rubs his bald head.

"I thought I would be a person you'd call when there's trouble," he says in his low singsongy whine. "I knew there was trouble, but I thought we were friends." He shakes his head. "If only you had let me know you weren't coming on time, I could have made other arrangements."

"I know, I'm so sorry," I say to him. I want to get to work, to have as normal a day as I possibly can, to have him stop staring at me. I hurry around the kitchen, opening drawers, pulling out the spatulas and spoons, tying on my apron. I am frantic. And everything's taking twice as long with Barry standing there watching me. My heart is pounding. Somehow all I can do is say, "Barry, I'm so, so sorry," over and over and over again.

Then he starts over again with, "I really would have thought you'd have called me. If someone would have asked me what you'd do, I'd have said, Maz always calls in. She's as reliable as the hills."

"Listen," I say at last. "I've never done anything like this, and I'll make it up to you, I swear. I just—overslept. My stepfather had a heart attack last night, and I was at the hospital until really late—"

"Heart attack. I know. That's where the friendship part comes in," he says, and Eeyore himself couldn't have sounded more desolate. "If you had just let me know—"

"I know. I know. I should have. Please. Forgive me. Now let me get to the muffins."

"It's too late for muffins," he says.

"No, it's not. It's too late for *breakfast,* sure. But if I mix them up now, and get them in the oven, they'll be ready by the time the lunch crunch gets here. Here—let me get to work. Everything'll be fine. You'll see. Just let me do this."

He stands there, watching me, full of gloom. "Do you know what I had to do for bread this morning? Did anybody tell you?"

I get the flour out of the bin and grab for the box of salt, which I then knock over all over the counter. He groans. My hands are shaking as I sweep it up into my hand.

"I had to go *buy* bread from Heart of the Planet." He gives me a long, mournful look. "Heart of the Planet. At least that made them very, very happy, to see me showing up, hat in hand, having to ask for my competitors' bread. But what else could I do?"

"Ouch! That must have hurt. God, Barry. I'm sorry. I'm really, really, really sorry."

He says, "If only you'd called. . . ." and, after a moment of staring at me sadly, he goes back in his office. I sigh, push my hair out of my eyes, pull out the muffin pans from the cabinet with a clatter. Okay, if I can just get these muffins whipped together and into the oven, then I can call the hospital, and then give Hannah a call to make sure Abbie's doing okay and that she knows where I am. *Things are going to be all right . . . don't think about anything but the muffins right now . . . don't think about Hope, out on the road. You can figure out everything another time. Nothing else to do now. Muffins. Muffins.*

I sift the whole wheat flour into the stainless steel mixing bowl and pour in the salt and baking powder. I'm on my way to get the eggs out of the walk-in when I see that Barry has come back. I jump.

"Sorry, didn't mean to startle you," he says. "But just tell me this. What letter is today?"

At first I can't even think of what he means. Letter? Like the mail? Then it hits me. The alphabet menu thing. I smack myself, hard, on the forehead. "Oh, no, jeez, Barry, let's not start with this letter thing again. *Please.*"

He frowns and looks down. "The letter idea was just me trying to be *creative*, to help you get excited about work. That's all it was. If it was such a burden, you should have told me."

"Let me make these muffins," I say, "and we can talk about the letters later. Okay?"

"I don't think you have time to make the muffins. The big mixer's down, you know."

"I do, I do. Just give me a minute. I'll use the hand mixer."

"I don't know if it's working so well, either."

He goes back to his office, and I find the hand mixer in the back of the shelf with the pans, and after a few more minutes of making a satisfyingly horrible noise of clanging around pots and pans and spoons, all put back in the wrong places, I manage even to locate both of the beaters in the dish with the slotted spoons. Damn it, I *am* going to make these muffins. It's as though the whole day now depends upon these muffins getting done before the lunch crowd comes. If I can just make these goddamn muffins, I'll get Hope back, save the free world, Harold will be okay. . . .

I reach over to the back of the counter and plug the thing in, and immediately the mixer explodes into a shower of sparks, like a Fourth of July sparkler. It slips out of my hand and lands in the bowl, clanking around and hissing, while a spray of sticky whole wheat batter splatters over me. I manage to lean over and unplug the thing, and for a moment all I can do is stand there, looking at the gray-beige lumpy mess everywhere. Then I lick my lips where there's a huge lump of chalky, taste-less, good-for-you batter, and I think, *That's it. I'm done. I can no longer work at the Golden Granary. Can't do it.*

I can't make somebody else's recipes that I hate. I can't think any-more about what stupid foods to make for J Day, or R Day, or X Day. I look around me, at the worn wooden counter, the big iron stove that never worked right, the window too high up to let it any real air, the back door that refused to stay open. Nope. None of this is what I want.

I take off the apron and walk into Barry's office, and I tell him. My voice seems very far away. Everything seems as though it's moving in slow motion. I see him hear the news, register it, react. The top of my head suddenly feels cool and tingling, like the first time Lenny and I went skiing, and he took me on the advanced hill by mistake. I stood there on the mountaintop, staring down at the huge rocky cliff I was expected to glide down, knowing that wasn't going to happen, that I'd be lucky to reach the bottom with all my limbs still attached. *How weird,* I think. *I'm quitting my job. How very unlike me, to be walking away from something on my own power.*

He doesn't look surprised. "Well, I've tried with you," he says. He takes off his reading glasses, rubs his eyes, polishes his glasses against his blue shirt. By the time he looks back up at me, we both know how this is going to go. He says heavily, "So this is really what you want—to quit?"

I nod.

"Okay, then," he says, not looking at me. "Listen, I'll do the paperwork so you can get unemployment. Don't want the daughters to suffer just because we can't work things out."

"Thank you," I whisper. There's a whoosh somewhere inside me, like I've just let go of the last thing that held me to the earth, and now I'm flying down the side of the mountain with nothing underneath me. Dry eyed, I gather up the toys from the Daughter Nest and go back home.

# 30

*I go home* and sit in the kitchen by myself—this kitchen that lately was so full of family and conversation and the smells of cooking—and I take a sip of my now-cold coffee and wrap my arms around myself and stare out the window. The world looks so weird without Hope in it, close by. I can look out on the street any day and see the cars parked there in the sunlight, and the evergreen trees hugging the deck, and far down, the way the white plastic table has puddles from the rain on it— but now it looks all different, just from the fact that Hope didn't walk out there this morning and go off to the bus stop. And that I know she won't be there tomorrow, either. And the next day or the next. I can scarcely breathe, thinking about it.

When I think I can walk without falling down, I lug myself upstairs and take a long, hot shower, and I stand there under the running water until the hot water tank is drained and I'm too cold and pitiful to stand there anymore. When I get out, I put on jeans and a sweatshirt and sit for the longest time on the side of the bed, staring at my socks. I can't remember which sock goes on which foot, or even how it is that you're supposed to know. With shoes, it's easy. Why don't they mark the socks? It takes me a long time to remember that socks are interchangeable. That then makes me think of Dan's socks that never matched. Why couldn't he manage that little detail, of all things?

I get up and call the hospital. Harold is sleeping, they tell me. He's stable. No, they don't know when his surgery will be. No, they don't know when he should be waking up. Yes, he can have visitors, one person at a time. He *has* only one person, I say.

I walk over to Hannah's house, and by the time I get there, I feel as though I've walked a hundred miles. She's out in the yard planting petunias, and Rachel and Abbie are sitting beside her, each holding a baby doll. Abbie lights up when she sees me walking from the corner, and runs to throw herself at me. I pick her up in my arms that are so heavy I don't think I can possibly move them, and I bury my head in her neck.

"Did you talk to Hopey? Is she coming back soon?" she says.

"Well, I talked to G.G.," I tell her carefully. "And everything's fine. They're just going to keep Hope for a little while."

"When is she coming back, though?"

"Well, soon, I'm sure. It's just a little vacation," I tell her. And I smile at her. We flop on the grass and watch Hannah digging in the dirt with her plants. The sun feels too bright. I wish I had sunglasses. And I can't seem to sit still. I keep reaching for Abbie, braiding her hair, straightening her shirt, pulling her down on my lap again.

When she finally can't stand being held by me anymore and goes inside to play with Rachel, I sit there for a long while, pulling up pieces of Hannah's lawn and making a careful little pile of grass. She's so busy digging holes to put petunias in that it takes her a while to notice. But then she comes over and sits down next to me. She smells sweaty, like hard work, and her hands are brown from the dirt.

"Michael likes that grass," she says. "He knows each one of those by name, you know. You're going to have a lot of murders to account for."

"Let's talk about something cheerful," I tell her flatly. "Like how I no longer have to go to work every day at the Golden Granary."

"Oh, my God," she says. "What happened?" She narrows her eyes. "Did that bastard fire you?"

"I quit." I see her face register alarm and add, "No, it's good. I don't know much right now, but I am pretty sure this is very good news. I started making the muffins, and the mixer blew up in my hand and started shooting fire all over the place, and I knew I couldn't stay there and make other people's recipes anymore. And Barry was whining about me not being a good friend, and how I forgot that today was supposed to be the freaking letter *H* or something—and then I just saw that I couldn't do it anymore. And I realized that if I can't have what I want, I shouldn't have to have what I absolutely know I don't want. Right?"

"But what are you going to do for money?"

"Well, that," I say, and pull up a few more clumps of her grass, "is a very good question for some other time. Right now, though, I gotta say it's pretty low on the list. I've decided that I'm not going to think about it for a while."

"Wow," she says.

"Yeah. It's pretty wow."

We sit there in silence, and then Michael comes out with three beers and hands them out, and she tells him I've quit my job. He makes little murmuring sympathy noises, and they talk together in low voices about things I might do with my life, as though they just might be in charge. I lie back on what's left of their grass and watch the clouds moving across the sky.

"Hey, Michael, couldn't you let her help you on your barn renovation book? Maz, he's finally picked a title—*Barns Alive.* What do you think?"

"It sounds like a book about mice. What happened to *Darn, I Love That Barn?*" I say. My tongue is thick. "I don't think I can help you unless you're going to call it that."

Michael laughs.

"Maybe you could work in the cafeteria at the school," says Hannah, and I think she might be perfectly serious about this. "You like kids. Or, hey, you could get a job driving the school bus."

"Yuck," I say.

After a while it starts to get dark, and maybe I fall asleep, I don't know. The earth is warm underneath me, and I feel as though I could just lie there forever. I think about Hope out there somewhere in the middle of the country, rattling along in the motor home with Lucille, just as I used to rattle along in the trailer. I think about Lenny, making all his bogus plans and rubbing that little herby thing he wears around his neck and saying maddening things about the cool people in Santa Fe, and how he's going to be a shaman. It hits me that it's just like it used to be—Lucille riding off in her trailer with a guy who has a plan. And a little girl, sitting at the table, probably holding a bottle of Co-Cola, thinking how Lucille is the most amazing person ever—only this time it's not me. Someone else is soaking up all the wild and crazy things they're saying, just as I used to. Full circle. How about that? The thing I'd always been running from, protecting myself from— and here it all is, roaring at me through a whole new channel. The great circle of life.

The next few days are a blur. I keep Abbie with me as much as possible, except when I go to see Harold in the hospital, and then I let her go to day care just for those few hours. Even then, I write a note on the board that says: "NO ONE IS TO PICK ABBIE UP EXCEPT HANNAH, MICHAEL AND ME. SIGNED, MAZ."

"That's, like, pretty paranoid of you, writing that," says Jolie one morning. I don't know why—maybe it's just me—but the vibe at the day care seems very weird lately, although I don't have the energy to talk to anybody about why. Jolie's eyes look puffy, and she's giving me one of her long, intent stares. "I mean, who else *would* be coming to take Abbie, now that those guys have left?"

"Don't know," I say.

"Have you heard from them?" she asks me, and I shrug. I'm not going to get into it with her.

"Listen," she says. "I just want you to know—the Josh thing—I had nothing to do with that, really."

"Oh, please." I hold up my hand. "You and me and men—not a good conversation. Okay?"

She reaches over and pulls a piece of fluff off my sweater. I avoid the urge to smack her. "People at this day care are talking about me," she says. "And I just want you to know. That is one thing I didn't do, tell Josh not to see you anymore."

I walk out and slam the door behind me.

I like going to the hospital, actually. I feel that somebody needs to be there sometimes for Harold, while he waits. He must feel even more

alone than I do. I sit and gaze at all the little machines recording his
every biological process. Most of the time we don't talk. But he knows
I'm there, and maybe I can start to make up to him some of what
Lucille did to him.

When Harold sleeps, I wander down to the family area, where the
other zombies gather. A woman in there says to me, "My gawd! Don't
we all look like a scene from *The Night of the Living Dead?*" When I'm
in Harold's room, I sit and stare out the window. Sometimes I go downstairs and call Lenny's house in Santa Fe on the pay phone. The answering machine doesn't even pick up. They must still be traveling.

So then I dial the motor home phone, praying that Hope will
answer—*just once, please God, let her answer the phone*—but I always get
Lucille's chirpy message with the spooky music playing in the background: "Thees ess Madame Lucille, who sees into your every thought
and emotion . . ." it begins. Sometimes I slam down the phone. But
whenever I can manage to steady my voice enough, I say, "Hope? Baby,
it's Mommy. I miss you so much. I hope you're doing fine. Abbie misses
you, too, sweetie. We want you to come home."

One night I dream that I'm down in the basement doing the laundry when I hear Hope say, "Mommy." I turn and look for her, and she
jumps out from behind the dryer. "I've been here all the time," she says.
"Why didn't you ever come down here and look for me?"

I get up in the middle of the night and go down there, but she's not
there. She's nowhere.

*Friday morning* is my day care turn, and by then I'm glad for the reality of babies and diapers and apple juice and swings, grateful to find
myself reading *Fox in Socks* even, almost in tears at the joy with which
all these little children snuggle up to me on the mattress. Is there any
place better to be than the day care, which smells satisfyingly like little
kids and paste and crayons?

I'm at a particularly tongue-tying part of *Fox in Socks* that takes all
my concentration when I hear the main door open. One of the kids
yells, "Josh is here! Josh! Josh!"

And sure enough, there he is, smiling down at me. I had assumed he'd taken himself off of the day care turn when he broke up with me, but no, here he is. He's wearing his jeans so low I can see the famous hipbones of which we were both so proud. He looks at me with his trademark stricken, hangdog look—the one he used on me when he told me we had to break up. "I heard," he says.

He has trouble getting these two words out because about eight kids are in various stages of climbing on him, and he's slowly being toppled. After he lands on the mattress next to me, he says, his face right up against mine: "You poor, poor thing! I heard what happened, the whole thing. Omigod. How in the world are you holding up?"

In that instant, I am over him. Just like that—the whole of him: the fake-guilty look, the hipbones, the blaring stereos, the stupid pile of quarters, all of it. Who the hell is he calling a *poor thing*? I try not to think about the sex.

"That bastard," he is saying. "Sorry. I should watch my language here, huh? But you poor thing! What can I do to help?"

I can't let myself look at him. "Nothing, unless you've got some magical powers I don't know about and can turn a motor home around. And—oh, yeah—it might be nice if you quit saying 'you poor thing.' You've worked it in twice in the last ten seconds."

He grins. "Feisty. I like that. So what if I came and hung out with you?"

"No."

"Come on. I'll sit by the phone with you and make you cups of tea, and I'll do at least half the worrying so you don't have to do it all. Ouch!" Cameron has just poked him in the eye with his elbow, an unfortunate result of using Josh's left shoulder as a stair.

"What is it with your generation?" I say. "The answer is no."

I get up off the mattress and leave him to do the stories. I go change three poopy diapers and wash my hands and then get the snack ready. While I'm in the kitchen, the telephone rings.

It's Sarah, Jezebel's mom and Jonathan's wife, who's talking so fast I think she must be on speed or something. "I don't have time to talk," she says, rat-a-tat-tat. "Is Jonathan there?"

"Nope. He's not on the turn this morning. Is he supposed to be here?"

"Fucking bastard!" she says, which surprises me. She and Jonathan always seemed kind of happy together—or at least it looked that way to me. But then, any relationship in which the two people weren't constantly bickering looked good to me. Then she says, "And I don't suppose Jolie's there, either."

"Uh, no. Not her turn day."

"So this is the way it's going to be," she says. "Well, thanks. Bye." Then she says, "Wait. You and I gotta talk sometime." And she hangs up.

After snack, when we take the kids outside, Josh comes and sits next to me on the steps and puts his hand on my thigh. I move away. "What if I told you what an idiot I was? Would that help?"

"Nothing much helps right now. I just have to get through this. Alone."

He dangles his hands between his thighs and squints off to the sandbox, where everybody's working on making sand cakes. It's a glorious morning, really, and I try to take a deep breath and think about how blue the sky is and how miraculous it is that everything has leaves again. Life comes back, I think.

"Can I tell you something?" he says and leans close to my ear.

I stay quiet.

"Jolie's doing it again. She's got another one."

"Another one what?"

"Another father in this day care. She's seeing Jonathan now. She has a thing about those married guys. You know?"

I look over at him, wonder idly if right this minute Sarah is tracking them down in some motel room. No wonder she wants to talk to me. *Ugh.* Josh nods, his curly dark hair catches the light, he smiles, widens his eyes at me, gives me a look that's meant to be contrite and sexy all at the same time.

"So—could I come over and make dinner? We could have make-up sex. And revenge sex. And after that, maybe some Josh-and-Maz-are-great-together sex. And you always said we didn't have enough to talk about. But now we do. We could talk about how probably sick Jolie is, and what a fucked-up idiot I was not to see it before."

"God, that's tempting," I say. "But I think I'm going to have to pass."

"Nothing better than sex to get the juices moving again. Good for the heart."

Jezebel, Jonathan's little girl, is crying because someone snatched her bucket. I get up and walk all the way across the yard to the sandbox so I can personally hand it back to her.

"I could be good for you!" shouts Josh.

Jezebel is crying. I pick her up and cuddle her next to my shoulder, rocking her back and forth. "Jezzie, buck up. Let's be strong women together," I whisper.

*Finally,* on the eighth day, Dr. Heinrich, who I think of as Dr. Golden Retriever, calls me on the phone and tells me they can do the surgery the next morning. Harold is apparently strong enough, although you couldn't prove it by me. Whenever I'm there, he's still mostly in and out of sleep, and the skin on his face lies in folds, as though something inside him has just collapsed, and his facial muscles have given up for good. That afternoon I get Hannah to keep Abbie, and go over to the hospital to sit with him.

He's propped up on the pillow when I come in. "So they're going to fix me up after all," he says. "What do you know? The doctors must have taken a vote and decided I'm worth the trouble."

"I'm so glad," I tell him.

He looks at me for a long time and then shakes his head. His face seems to lose several shades of pink. "God, I'm just so sorry I couldn't stop them for you," he says. "You're suffering so."

"Why do you say that? Do I look like hell?"

"Pretty much. Like somebody who doesn't sleep. Who worries all the time."

"Well, I'm more okay than that. And I just want you to know that it's not your fault. The signs were certainly there for me to see what was happening. I should have been paying more attention," I say. "Believe me, I don't think this is your fault in any way."

He smiles at me. "You're an excellent mother. You do know that."

"Oh, yeah! Just terrific. Why, the Mother of the Year people are after me every day."

He closes his eyes again, exhausted, and I turn away from him, and bite down hard on my lip. It's what I do lately—bite hard just to see if the blood will come. He coughs a little.

"Do you need something? Can I get you some ice chips or a cloth?"

"You know what I need?" he says. "I need you to go downstairs and ask the front desk if I died yet. See if my name is on their deceased list." And he laughs.

"I don't think people who are actually dead make jokes. You're probably still legally alive."

We both laugh, but my laugh is hollow and rusty. Then he looks at me and says, "You know what? I'm sick of the two of us sitting around beating ourselves up. We didn't do anything wrong, and we both know it. We've been had. We got *skunked*."

I'm ready to point out what Lucille said—that I've been unplugged and spaced out, and that I've been concentrating more on having a wonderful sex romp than watching out for my kids, that I abdicated my adult life for a while, and that I deserve this, all of it and probably more, too—but why go into all that, just before he goes under the knife? What if he doesn't make it, and the last thing in his head is me poor-mouthing about how rotten and wretched everything has been for me? It's just more of the same, me finding excuses.

Instead I go back and sit down in the visitor's chair and pick for a while at a stray piece of carpet stuck to the sole of my shoe, and then I say, suddenly, "So, Harold, why did you marry her anyway?"

He actually smiles. I hadn't expected that. "God," he says slowly. He licks his dry lips and gazes for a moment out the window, so long I think he's forgotten the question. Then he says, "She's like nobody I ever knew. Just look at her. She's so unpredictable and fun and adventurous and curious. I couldn't believe my good fortune."

"Good fortune!" I say. "Wow. And look at what she did to you."

"Oh, I knew something like that wasn't going to last," he says, and he's got a little smile playing around his lips. "Lucille isn't a keeper. She can't stay with just one person. You know that by now, surely. Some kinds of love just aren't meant to last."

"I don't call it love unless it lasts," I tell him.

"Well, now then, if that's your definition, you're going to miss out on a lot of love that's just floating around out there," he says. "I don't mean to tell you your business, but it seems you and that young man you've been with lately are a good example of that. It's love, but everybody knows it's not going to be the fifty-year kind. You just feel thankful for it while you have it."

Something like a snort comes out of me.

He laughs a little. "Well, maybe that's what you see only when you get old. You see a lot of things aren't going to be right what you want them to be, but you take what you can from them. Sometimes, Maz, the damn thing wasn't even meant to last."

"You're not mad at Lucille? I think you should be furious with her."

"Nah." He shrugs. "She did what she could. She gave all she had to give. It wasn't as much as some people can give, but then she's different from a lot of people."

"I think," I tell him softly, "that I might actually grow to hate her."

"Oh, honey," he says and takes my hand across the blanket. "That could be such a big mistake. You gotta give that one up."

# 31

They do the surgery at 6 the next morning, and at noon a nurse comes to find me in the family waiting room. She says that Harold did fine, and that he's going to be okay. Tears inexplicably start running down my face and I go diving in my pocket for a tissue.

"I know he's going to be all right," I say to her. "I don't know why I'm crying."

"It's okay," she says. "Everybody cries when I tell them the news. Tears of relief."

"I have to go call some people," I tell her, blubbering. My nose is all snotty and of course there's nothing but lint and a red Lego in my pocket. To my horror, I start sobbing. She looks for a tissue, but there aren't any in the room, and in her pocket all she has is a ballpoint pen and a coupon for $1 off for Tampax at CVS. The expression on her face makes me start laughing, and then I sob some more. I keep trying to tell her that I'm okay, but then, while I'm getting the words out, I get overtaken by crying. I try to wipe my nose with the piece of lint. This doesn't work as well as I'd like.

"I haven't—cried this much—the whole time—through all of this," I manage to say. And I sit down and put my head in my hands. Whole chunks of my heart feel as though they're having their ropes untied. Harold is going to be all right—and enough days have gone by now that Hope will get to Santa Fe, which seems so much safer than being on the road. Soon I'll get to talk to her—they surely can't keep her from the phone once they're settled somewhere. There's a *place,* an actual geographic location where she is, and I could find it.

"Hey," I hear a voice say. "It's the Queen of White Bread. I've been looking everywhere for you." I lift up my head and peek through my fingers with dread. Oh, God, it's Dan Briggs, looking healthier and more together than ever—even like a real doctor, wearing a white doctor's coat, and smiling down at me. I have to keep my hands over my face so he can't see the disgusting mucus products that surely must be on my face. Just so he knows I can't talk, I prove it by saying something like, "Hnnnh!"

"Oh, my goodness," he says. "Ohhhhh, dear."

The nurse says, "The Queen of White Bread—is that what you called her?—is kind of in need of a tissue right now. I don't suppose you have one on you."

He fumbles through his pockets and comes up with a cotton handkerchief, which I take only because I have no choice. I mumble something about how it will never be worth using again. He says he doesn't care about that one bit, and I mop up with it while the nurse tells him about Harold's postsurgical condition. I get the idea that he's known about Harold from the beginning, from the sounds of it. As soon as the nurse leaves, he turns to me.

"Please don't look at me," I say. Then I start to sob again.

"Okay." He looks away. "But can you just tell me how you are? One finger for 'basically okay,' and two fingers for 'things are worse than they've ever been.'"

I hold up one finger and then add another one, after thinking it through. But then I reconsider and take down the second finger.

"Hmmm," he says. "I think we have to call that for the undecided category. Is there anything I can do?"

I shake my head, blubbering something about how there is no category. "What are you doing here, anyway? I thought you weren't a real doctor."

He laughs. "Every now and then, I like to play dress-up and come see how the real doctors act." I peek at him through my fingers, and he laughs again and says, "No. Believe it or not, I have patients who get hospitalized, and then I come to see them."

"That's nice of you."

"I suppose. Anyway, it sounds like your stepfather's come through great," he says. There's a silence and then he says, "Hey, would you like to get out of here for a bit and get a bite to eat or some coffee or something? When you stop crying, of course. You probably could use something more than just a hankie."

"I can't. I think I'll just stay here." I blow my nose so loudly it makes a honking noise.

"Well, can I bring something up to you?"

"No, really. I'm fine—just a little mentally ill."

"You don't seem mentally ill to me."

I start to laugh, but I burst into tears again.

"Ohhh, I see," he says. "Well, we'll just sit here together and wait. Just let it all out. Go ahead and just *sob* when you need to. Make noise. And if you want to laugh also—well, you decide." He gets up and I hear him close the door. He sits back down again.

I don't *like* crying in front of other people. I didn't even cry at Big Daddy's funeral—or when Lucille would leave me. But I can't talk, and really, after a while I see that, okay, it might be kind of all right to have him there. Just as a *presence*. As long as he doesn't look at me closely, and doesn't talk. He doesn't. He just waits, as though I could cry for five years and he'd still be there.

Four years and six months go by and I wipe my nose and say, "Wait. I don't think my title was actually the Queen of White Bread, was it?"

"God, I don't remember. You were the queen of something relatively unhealthy—and by unhealthy, of course, I mean by Golden Granary standards."

I look up, and feel my eyes start to leak again. "I quit my job there."

"I heard. I figured it was just you continuing in your tradition of having a more interesting life than I have," he says. He reaches for my hand. The expression in his eyes is so kind that I can't stand it.

I narrow my eyes at him, take my hand away, and dab at my face with the handkerchief. Something's been bothering me through this whole conversation, and now I remember what it is. "Hey, how did you know Harold is my stepfather?"

"Barry told me."

"Wait. You talk to Barry about me?"

"Well, yeah. He's a mutual friend of ours, right? And you gave me a time frame, remember? Call you in three to five years when you weren't so . . . you know . . . having a hard time."

"I don't think three years is up yet. Seems like it sometimes, but . . ."

"No," he says. "But I wanted to know how you are, you know, so in three years when I came back, I'd be caught up. How would that be, showing up on your doorstep in three years' time, and you'd have to spend six months telling me what went on?"

"Oh, God." I put my head down into my hands again.

"By that 'oh God,' are you meaning that you can't believe you told me to wait three years? I believe your thinking was that I was, as you put it, too together for you."

"You were. You still are," I say. I take a deep breath. "Anyway . . . don't you have a girlfriend? Sort of a normal person who takes you out and helps you pick out sweaters?"

He laughs. "Oh, you mean my cousin? I don't really go out with her. It's not legal in all the states, you know."

"She was sure giving me the evil eye that day in the store."

"Uh, you might be just a little sensitive," he says. "I think she was more trying to get me to hurry up. I was taking too long, in her opinion."

"See?" I say. "I'm actually even more screwed up than I used to be. Back then, I was probably a sterling example of mental health compared to now. Just look at me—sobbing in a hospital, unable to stop. And besides being unemployed, I lost Hope . . ."

"You've lost *hope*?" he says. "Don't we all lose hope every now and then?"

I look at him, and see that he was actually kidding; he knew what I meant. He's smiling sympathetically. He comes over and crouches down on the floor in front of my chair and reaches over to touch me. For some reason that makes my eyes fill up with tears again, and I pull away. *No, no, no, I will not hug Dan Briggs just because he happens to show up and think he can be nice to me. I am running my own pathetic little life right now, no matter how badly I keep steering it off the embankments.*

I straighten myself up and look at him. "Okay, listen. You want to know what's going on? You want to hear about this, really? Everything's gotten all messed up since I saw you," I tell him. "Hope hates me now, and she's gone away to Santa Fe with her father and my crazy mother, where they're going to ruin her. And I *can't* go get her, so don't even think that—because she won't come with me. She's made it clear over and over again that she likes them better—and, Dan, I miss her so much that I just have this permanent *ache*." My voice catches, and he reaches out again, but I fling my arm away from his reach and fight to get control of myself again. "No, listen to me! And now, on top of that, I can't go to work anymore and make that food that I detest—I just *can't* bear it—so I quit, and I don't know what I'm supposed to do with my life. Things are now much, much worse, and I really do wish you'd just leave me alone to sort all this out. I need everybody on the planet to just leave me alone." I stare at him. "And you know what else? I may be crying, but this is actually the best day I've had in a long time, just knowing that Harold's going to be all right. These are actually tears of *happiness*," I say to him.

"They are?" he says softly. "This is happiness?"

I bury my head in the handkerchief. "I should be grateful because it's all going to work out. I know it's going to work out. I just can't think of how to make it work out, is all."

"I'd like to help you."

"You can't. What can you do?" I wail. Then I see his face, and I say, "Please. Please just don't—don't be so nice to me. And don't be sappy. If you're nice, I'll just sit here for the rest of time blubbering away. I can take almost anything right now but niceness."

He smiles and looks away, lowers himself from his crouching position to sitting on the floor. He breathes evenly and closes his eyes. I've got to say this for him, he's good at waiting. You can yell at him and he still waits. We sit in silence for a long while. Someone opens the door, looks in, and closes it again. Outside in the hallway I hear the chime that means they're calling a nurse somewhere. Dan studies the tassel on his shoe. I look over quickly to see if his socks match, and am disappointed to see that they do.

"Your socks," I say. "They're the same color today."

He laughs. "It happens."

"But they never were before. The fact that you had two different socks on made me think that maybe I could be—" I hiccup again, can't think of what I mean to say. "Maybe I could be—well, like, maybe *you* could be somebody who wouldn't think I was so totally flaky."

"Hmm," he says. "That's an interesting premise, except for the fact that I never thought you were flaky."

"Oh, but you did. I could tell by the way you looked so rattled when Hope came down that night—and then again when Abbie was licking the window that night at the restaurant."

"Hey, I didn't think anything bad. I liked them. I told you that."

"Oh, but I could tell you were just being nice, and that you'd put in your time with me, but the whole time you'd be shaking your head and telling your friends that I was a total basket case. A fortune-teller's daughter! Left by my husband, and with two psycho kids. You would have left me. I could see it."

"Wait. You *sent* me away, wouldn't even go out with me again, because you were afraid I was going to someday leave you?"

I nod.

"You were worried about me leaving you, when it wasn't even clear yet that we were going to have a relationship?"

"Yeah."

"Wow. You'd written the script for five years in advance."

"Because you would have! I could see how you were looking at everything. You were acting so understanding and like it was all so—I don't know—quirky and novel and *interesting*. When it was my *life*, not some freak show!"

"Maz," he says.

I stop talking. "What?"

"We don't have time for craziness," he says. "You know I don't see your life as a freak show. I see you as a wonderful mother and somebody who's having a *temporary* hard time, and who's doing her best to hold too many things in place—things that you're not even responsible for. Listen," he says, looking at his watch, "Harold's going to be fine for the next few hours. Let's go to the day care and get Abbie and spend the day doing something fun."

At that, I start crying so hard that he has to search his pockets for a whole new handkerchief.

$\mathcal{I}t$ $turns$ $out$ that on a day when you have cried out all the water that you might think your body contains, you still can laugh. Who knew? Dan is just the slightest bit goofy—watching him rummage through the trunk of his car looking for the pieces of a kite, I begin to understand the mismatched socks thing. He always likes to keep a kite on hand, he tells us, just in case there's a day with enough wind in it. He's sure he has the ball of string around here somewhere. He runs around between the trunk and the glove compartment, looking comically frazzled, and finally Abbie finds the string underneath the front seat, and so we are off to Hammonasset Beach—a place, he tells me, where he's heard the wind always blows.

But the kite will not fly on its own. It insists that we run along and do all the work. He claims it has dependency issues, requiring the three of us to run with it, shouting encouragement to it. "Self-esteem!" he shouts. "We'll build up its self-esteem and then it'll take off on its own! You'll see!"

It, of course, does not. It wants to land in the waves—perhaps a subliminal death wish—and Dan is required to keep yanking it upward and running even faster with it. I think we have run miles back and forth across the sand when I remember a technique Pete the Fireman had for kite-flying. I take the string from Dan and, by letting it out a little at a time, unbelievably it takes off and flies just behind me.

He and Abbie jump up and down and cheer for me, and I'm laughing so hard at the sight of them there that the kite takes a nosedive and is in danger of plunging into the sea in a terrible death. Dan comes over and takes the string out of my hand, and I collapse on the sand, laughing, and Abbie comes and tackles me—and we just sit there and watch him. The kite will not stay in the air for him unless he's running back and forth at top speed. "Hey! On top of everything else," he shouts on one of his pass-bys, "I think we're seeing this kite has some loyalty issues!" He looks up at it. "Who bought and paid for you?" he yells. "Who plunked down good money just to show off with you?"

Who wouldn't like a day like this? I tell myself to be careful.

Later, when we're all exhausted, we go to Lenny and Joe's, a seafood place nearby, for lobsters and steamers and ice cream, and Abbie rides on the carousel about a hundred times. I sit at the picnic table with Dan, squinting in the sun.

I have that look-behind-you feeling, and when I turn to him, he's smiling at me.

"Don't get all sentimental and sappy on me," I warn him. "I'm a mom. I can turn sad at a moment's notice."

"All four seasons in one day," he says. "I remember you very well."

"In one hour."

He's about to say something, when my cell phone rings in my bag. It's one of the few times in my life I've ever managed to have it both charged up *and* in my possession at the same time. I pull it out and glance at the number. Lucille.

My heart immediately goes into its jackhammer routine. "Omigod, it's her," I whisper to him.

"I'm having a déjà vu all over again," he says. "Isn't this where I came in?"

"Maybe she'll let me talk to Hope." I can barely breathe.

"So, maybe you should answer," he says.

"Oh, but what if she's just being crazy again?"

"I still think answering would be good," he says.

"Right," I say. "Okay."

"Darlin'!" she screams when I press the button. "How the hell *are* you, you big ole baby of mine?" I hold out the phone so he can hear her, and he rolls his eyes.

"Where are you?" I say.

"Oh, God. I don't have the slightest idea. Somewhere between here an' there, I reckon. Gettin' closer to there by the looks of things. I was just callin' to let you know we're survivin' just fine. Against all *odds,* let me tell you. You know, that Lenny's kind of a nut. He wants to stop and look at every rock between here an' there, like he thinks God's gonna jump out of the earth and talk to him. I think it's just that he doesn't want to get back home, got some complications there he doesn't want to face, if you ask me."

"How is Hope?"

"Oh, you know." She sighs, clicks her lighter. "She's gettin' kind of pissy sometimes, but I can always calm her down with takin' out the Ouija board or lettin' her wear my turban. You know how kids are. And, baby, I swear, ten-year-old girls have got a permanent case of PMS goin' on all the time. They're so bitchy."

"Hey, *I* know a solution to that: bring her back home."

"Oh, *you*," she says. "I can handle her. She's just like you were when you were ten—whiny and bitchy as hell."

I want to say, *You have no idea what I was like at ten—or at any age. I was always playing the part of your companion, afraid of making you mad.* Instead I say, "Why don't you put her on the phone? I'll talk to her."

I look out at the carousel, where a family is helping their toddler get on one of the white horses with red trim. Abbie stands off to the side, looking at them, her fingers in her mouth. She feels me looking at her and turns and smiles and then wiggles her body all over. "Put Hope on the phone, will you?" I say evenly.

"Oh, darlin'. She's not here *now*. She's with her daddy, thank God. I needed a break. They've gone to the store to get us somethin' for dinner. We're all tired of the same old, same old. I'm thinkin' a makin' my fried chicken, like Grandmama used to make—you remember that? She made it so crispy on the outside, remember that?"

*Remember that? Remember that?* I close my eyes, listen to the static of the phone. If I turn my head slightly to the left, the hiss gets louder and louder.

"So, I can tell by the sound of your voice that I'm interferin' with somethin' good, so I'm gonna go now."

"Wait. When will Hope be back? I want to tal—"

"Oops. Sweetie, I think you're breakin' up," she says. "Bye!"

An hour later, when I try to call her back, there's no answer. "She didn't even ask about Harold," I say.

The day curls in on itself after that, and, despite how wonderful Dan is, I can't shake it off. Lucille is out there somewhere, bored and restless, taking it out on Hope. That's what I feel the worst about, I think— although there are so many things to feel terrible about—that Hope is being made to see how she can't keep her grandmother's attention after spending a month having it lavished on her. I remember that feeling so well, of being suddenly shown to be inferior and stale, of suddenly being talked about in a different way—as a *problem child*.

While Dan drives us back home that night, I bite my fingernails and stare out of the car window at the trees going past. He's talking on about lobsters and how great it is to find a place that has a carousel these days, and I try to smile at him, but it's as though I've forgotten how you work those precise muscles without looking pained. It's when he winds down and quits talking that I know he's probably wondering why he even bothered to be nice to me. He turns on the radio, drums on the steering wheel with his class ring.

*A class ring,* I think. *I'm actually on a date with a guy who wears a class ring, and who hangs around the hospital wearing a white coat. What the hell am I thinking? Better yet, what the hell is* he *thinking, hanging out with me?*

When he pulls up to my house, I have my line all prepared. Before he's even had a chance to cut the engine, I jump out of the car quickly and say, "Thankyouverymuchforsuchalovelydaygoodbye!" and slam the door quickly without letting myself look at his face.

It's when I am opening the back door to get Abbie that I realize she's fallen asleep. Damn. This is not going to be the quick getaway the situation calls for. Dan turns off the engine and gets out as I'm trying to quickly scoop her up. He comes around to my side and says quietly, "Here, may I carry her for you? You've got the beach bag and all."

I nod, step back, and he leans in and lifts her out. She opens her eyes for a second, and then tucks her head underneath his chin and cuddles up to him. He kicks the car door closed and heads up the path to the gate, and onto the deck. I follow along miserably. When we get inside, he whispers, "Where do you want her, ma'am?"

I lead the way up to her bedroom, and he puts her down on her bed. I take off her shoes and pull the covers up over her. She murmurs something and turns over in her sleep. When I look up, Dan is tiptoeing out of the room.

I follow him down to the kitchen.

"Well," I say. "Thank you again." This part, I'm thinking, would be better if he would just invent an emergency and run out the door. Then I could stop shaking. Instead, he just stands there, as if he's forgotten how it is that one person manages to disentangle from another, and finally he says, "Lucille's not going to win this one, you know. She really isn't."

"So far she's ahead," I tell him. "And she's not letting up, evidently."

"Yeah, but you've got time on your side. When I see you with your kids—I don't understand how Hope can stand to be away from you for one minute. I *know* in my bones she didn't choose this."

I feel my face crumple. He takes a step toward me and puts his arms around me, and the next thing I know he's kissing me, hundreds of soft tiny kisses all over my lips. And then—well, then, he's *really* kissing me—so much so that when the phone starts to ring and ring, we just let it.


*Later,* I guess that must have been exactly when it happened that Dan became what Hannah calls a member of the cast. He just kind of joins up, and I let him. I stop worrying, little by little, that it's awful if he notices how the dishes are piled up in the sink, or that there's dirty laundry around, and that mostly the beds are unmade, and I can't find my keys and we're out of shampoo. Whenever I get insecure and start apologizing for the chaos, he just rolls his eyes at me and says, "Maz. Get a grip. This is *life*."

Yes, I said to him once, but I don't think it's a particularly well-designed format.

One day it hits me that if a Real Honest-to-God Grown-Up is going to be eating at my house, I can't very well keep living on macaroni boxes and frozen chicken nuggets, so I get out my old cookbooks and start making dishes I used to like, adult foods such as sushi and onion soup and escarole salad. I actually buy shiitake mushrooms and feel no need to apologize for them. It's a break-through moment in Stop & Shop.

He brings over his guitar and lets Abbie teach him some songs she sings at day care: something about a fox in the chicken house and the day care's hands-down favorite, a wistful ballad about peanut butter. He teaches her to play Spit, and they both scream with laughter the first time she beats him at it.

Okay. I'm a sucker for this stuff. And also for the way that he wears boat shoes and the way his ankles sort of stick out underneath his khaki pants, and how sometimes I'll look up and see that he's smiling at me in such a sweet way, and—okay, how he gets my jokes, and that when I'm sad, thinking about Hope, he doesn't say I should snap out of it. I like the deep way he laughs, and how concerned he sounds on the phone when he calls a patient who's having scary symptoms. And, oh yeah, there's the fact that, at night, after Abbie's gone to bed, he asks me questions about Lucille, and how I met Hannah, and what the cooperative day care is really like, what kind of day I had.

And did I mention that he smells good, but not fake-good like you get out of a bottle, but just *good* good?

At first he always goes home at bedtime, but then one night—after we've both had wine and cleaned up the dinner dishes together, and I've folded two loads of laundry, and we've both searched for my keys through the couch cushions—I look over at him and just know I'm so hungry for him that I can't wait one more moment. I drag him upstairs and start taking off his clothes as we make our way to my room. The look on his face is of such pleased surprise that I forget to be scared. And when he undresses me, and we fall together on the bed—well, it's so great to be loved this way, as if every inch of me is some miraculous treasure that only he knows about.

And, okay, so it's not nice to compare guys—but what a nice thing, to be made love to by a man who's probably *not* right then fantasizing about Jolie Whiting.

On *Friday night*, a week after Harold's surgery, Dan and I go to Hannah and Michael's house for dinner. Hannah says she has to get to know him and introduce him to what's going to be his new extended family. "How can he be a member of the cast if we don't know whether he wants Michael's title to be *Barns Alive* or *Darn, I Love That Barn?*" she wants to know. "There are certain protocols that must be followed, and due to all the extenuating circumstances, they simply haven't been. That has to be rectified immediately. For one thing, he's not a Republican, is he?"

"No," I say, and laugh.

"Thank God. Vegetarian? Vegan?"

"No."

"Good. Any outlandish theories we need to know about—JFK assassination theories, any conspiracy stuff in his background? In fact, is he any kind of *buff* on any topic whatsoever—the Civil War, the space program, evolution?"

"I don't think he's a buff."

"Whew. I won't ask about any kinky sex practices. That has to be between you and him."

"Thanks," I say.

"Okay, then, he sounds perfect. There's just the in-person interview to go." And she laughs in delight.

I'm still a little nervous at the idea of an entire evening together. Sometimes people find Hannah a bit much, and I'm afraid she might meet him at the door with a million questions. But no. All goes well. Everybody's relaxed and happy, and Dan fits right in.

We sit at the table long after we've finished eating, picking at the salad, drinking wine, and talking. We talk about the rumblings at day care—how factions are springing up whispering about Jolie and Jonathan, and what, if anything, should be done about them.

Hannah says, "Maybe I'm just reacting to the pain I've seen her bring to you, but I say, how can we keep trusting her with our kids if we can't trust her with our husbands? One time, okay. Modern life is quirky. And I really do think these guys have a responsibility to keep their pants zipped up. But—really, this is starting to feel like she has some kind of problem, you know?"

Dan holds my hand underneath the table, and I feel his toe gently circling my toes. I kick off my sandals and smile at him. When it gets dark, Hannah gets up and lights little white tea lights around the room. I hear the kids playing upstairs, Evan on his skateboard again, the girls chattering while they chase Bustercat for another fashion show. The talk moves lazily from day care to barns to naturopathy, and then, surprisingly, to love. Hannah tells the story of how she and Michael met in college, when he was a disk jockey at the college radio station and she had a public affairs show about feminism. I tell the ridiculous story about how I met Lenny in a fraud situation: how he was advertising for a lead singer for a band he didn't have, and I auditioned even though I'd never sung a note in my life.

Dan clears his throat, smiles at me, and brings our hands up on the table, out in view. Outside, in the twilight, I see little dancing fireflies lighting up all the little dark pockets of the yard.

Hannah sighs suddenly, gazes out the window. "Look at all those fireflies," she says. Then, she says, from out of nowhere: "Of course, if we throw Jolie out, the day care would have to find a new teacher, somebody who really loves it there."

There's a silence. When I look up, they're all smiling at me.

# 32

*Abbie is dawdling* over her oatmeal the next morning. She sticks the spoon in it again and again, stirring it and then sighing. As far as I can tell, not one molecule of oatmeal has gotten to her mouth yet.

"Is it too hot?" I say, and she shakes her head. She leans on her elbow and stares down into the bowl as though the meaning of life will be spelled out in brown sugar. I sip my tea and look out the window. I'm thinking that it's Saturday again, and that I'll go see Harold for a while and then try to call Hope, see if they've ever managed to get themselves all the way to Santa Fe, or if they're still dawdling through the desert. I've talked to Lucille a few times during the week, and it's always been the same—Hope never happening to be right there when we talk. Lucille finally broke down and admitted to me once that it's Lenny who won't let me talk to her.

"Why not?" I'd said. "Put him on the phone this minute."

"He says it's a fragile transition time, and he doesn't want her getting homesick from hearing your voice," she'd said. "He's crazy, you know. *I* disagree with him, of course, but then, I'm not the parent, as he never fails to remind me."

Abbie's talking to me, and I turn my head away from the window at the sudden change in her tone. "I made Hope go," she says in a voice so quiet I can barely hear her. "She was mean to me sometimes, and I wished she would go away."

Ah, I know the answer to this one. "She didn't go away because you wished she would," I say.

She leans over and whispers. "You don't know, Mommy. I wished it and wished it a lot of times."

"People are allowed to think those kinds of things. It doesn't mean they happen."

"Mommy." She stops and looks at me. "I wished Daddy would come home, and he came home. And I wished Hope would go away, and she went away." She stabs her spoon in the oatmeal again. "I didn't wish Grandpa would be sick, but he got sick anyway. It's because I forgot to wish he'd stay all better."

"Oh, sweetie, no, no, no," I say. "Trust me. Hope left because G.G. and Daddy took her away without telling us. And Grandpa got sick because his heart was already ill, and now he's a lot better. None of that had to do with you or what you wished."

She's looking down, and I see a tear running down her cheek.

"Oh, Abbie! My goodness! Oh, honey, come over here and let me hold you."

But she hangs back, looking down at the table.

"Come here, sweetie, and let's have a cuddle."

"I don't want to cuddle," she says.

"Why? What else are you thinking about?"

"I can't tell you." I can barely hear her.

"You can tell me anything," I say.

"Mommy, I can't," she says. "I have to be big."

"Sweetie, you don't have to be big. You can still be little. Come and cuddle with me. Come, tell me what's bothering you. You'll feel better."

She starts sobbing then, and I go over and gather her up. We sit down on the floor in a patch of sunlight, and I massage her little shoulders. They feel like wings underneath her pajamas. I wait.

At last it comes out, haltingly. "Ho-Hope told me Daddy said she had to go with him because you didn't want her anymore, th-that you were mad at her because she wasn't nice at school," she says. She takes a ragged breath. "She said she had to be just Daddy's kid now because you didn't want her here anymore. You were ti-tired of her."

"No!" I say. "No, that's not what happened. Oh, *honey baby*. I *love*

Hope. I didn't want her to go." I smell her hair. "Really? *Daddy* told her that? Are you sure?"

Her sobbing starts up again, and she buries her head in my neck. I can barely hear the next part: "And I was th-thinking . . . I was think . . . thinking . . . that you might get tired of me, too, and send me away."

"Oh, baby." Then it hits me what she's saying, and I remember how good she's tried to be lately, the way I'll come into a room and she paints a big smile on her face, the way she never argues or cries anymore. "Oh, Abbie," I say. "And so you've tried so hard to be perfect because you were scared that you'd have to go away, too?"

She nods, looks down. Her lower lip quivers.

"Darling, Daddy doesn't mean that. I miss Hope so much every single day, and I would *never* want either one of you to go away. Oh, sweetie! It breaks my heart that you worried about that. I wish you'd told me."

She leans her head against me, plays with the buttons on my shirt, her little fingers fluttery and unsure.

I suddenly am filled with the most intense rage, billowing straight through me, as though the air in the room has been suffused with poisonous gas. My hairline is actually tingling.

I almost can't fathom this. *How* could Lenny have been so willing to hurt his own daughter, to tell her such a horrible thing? And aided and abetted by Lucille, who was the original master of Family Destruction! Why in the world would he want to join forces with her, after he'd seen how terrible she could be? Why would he ever want Hope to think I don't love her and want her, just so he can have the satisfaction of getting back at me? I can't stand this, can't bear the fact that Hope has had even one minute of thinking I didn't want her. And, oh my God, from her point of view, riding down the road in that motor home with them—it must feel as though it's *absolutely* true that I don't want her. After all, she never gets to talk to me. I'm almost sure they don't let her know that I've ever even called.

I've let their version of the story be the only one she hears.

My hands get suddenly clammy. I get up and pace around the kitchen, back and forth. *I didn't fight. God, why didn't I fight? Why haven't I ever fought? I didn't fight Lucille for any of the stuff she did to me as a kid. I didn't fight for my marriage when Lenny was sleeping with Jolie—and now, I've just done it again: given up and let them take Hope away. My God! No wonder my friends think I'm crazy and wonder why I won't call the police. Why won't I take any action? Why do I just keep saying it's all my own fault?*

I feel like smacking myself upside my own head.

I open the back door and let the sunlight flood in. My breath is coming in hard little gasps. I start washing the breakfast dishes, staring out at the backyard at a bird hopping aimlessly around on the branch of the maple tree. He stops at the bird feeder, which is empty, and cocks his head to the side, as if he's thinking of where he can go next.

"Abbie," I say, "let's go get Hope."

I call the motor home telephone, and get—of course—the answering machine. But then it occurs to me that they might not be in the motor home anymore. They may have actually arrived in Santa Fe. Maybe they're at Lenny's house by now. I dial his number, barely able to breathe. I don't know what the hell I'm going to say if Lucille or Lenny answers. I'll think of what to say when it actually happens.

It rings approximately twelve hundred times, but I just stand there and listen to the endless series of rings, feeling the blood pumping through my veins, feeling the taste of iron in the back of my throat. I'm just about to hang up, when a small voice answers.

"Hello?" Hope says, almost inaudibly.

I can barely speak. "Hope! It's Mom. Darling, how *are* you?"

She's quiet for too long. Then, coolly: "I'm fine."

"Oh, sweetie, I miss you. It's so good to hear your voice."

"It's good to hear your voice, too," she says. She sounds cautious.

I suddenly don't know what to say. My eyes are filling up. "How was your trip? Oh, my God, how *is* everything?" I want to scream out: How are you managing? Have they really and truly told you that I didn't want you, baby? You didn't really believe them, did you? And are they taking good care of you? Do you miss us? And, oh God, do you want to come home?

"It was . . . okay," she says.

"Hope," I say and try to steady myself. "Hope, I miss you so much! When did you get there?"

Another long silence. "Two days ago," she says quietly.

"I can't believe I'm really talking to you. I feel like I'm going to cry—"

"Don't cry, Mommy," she says.

"Okay. I'm sorry. I won't." I wipe away my tears.

"If you cry," she says slowly, "then that'll make me cry, too."

"Okay. I'll try," I say. I laugh in relief. "We can't both start crying. Or maybe we should. Honey, I've been calling you, but Lucille always says you're busy or something, and I just couldn't stand it anymore. I was calling to tell her that I *must* talk to you, but then you answered!"

"She's not here," she says. "She and Daddy went to get some stuff for breakfast, I think. And to talk to some guy they know. I think."

"Are you by yourself?"

This time, there's a very long silence.

"Are you there all alone?" I say.

"No. Daddy has a . . . there's someone . . . she's here."

"Oh, right. Kimmie," I say. "Daddy's girlfriend."

"Yeah."

"Sweetie, I was so shocked that you left. I mean, I came home and I was just so . . . *shocked* to find out that you had gone back with them. I had no idea you were going."

"You didn't?"

"No! I mean, they didn't tell me anything about it. I was at work and then I went . . . somewhere . . . and when I came home, Harold and Abbie told me that you left."

I hear her sniffling a little, and then she says in such a tiny voice I have to put my hand over my other ear to hear her. "Mommy, I promise

I won't tell people bad stuff anymore. At school, you know. Can I come back home if I promise I won't do that anymore?"

My legs feel as though they won't hold me up anymore. I start crying, and Hope does, too. When I can speak again, I'm blubbering, "Oh, baby, baby, that doesn't matter. I always knew you didn't mean to hurt anybody. It was just a hard time, I know that. I never wanted you to go. Sweetheart, I want you to come back home. I'm coming to get you, and when I get there, I want you to come back with me. We're going to make things a lot better. I've been thinking about our lives, and I think I know what to do to fix things. Everything's going to be all right. I'm coming, baby."

"Okay," she says.

"I'm going to get the first flight I can possibly get."

"Do you want me to tell Daddy and G.G.?" she says.

A squirrel outside the window takes a death-defying jump from one tree branch to the railing of the deck. I feel the whoosh as though it were my own legs.

"No, don't say anything," I say softly. "I'll explain it to them when I get there. You don't worry about a thing. Just sit tight, and I'll be there."

# 33

*Before the hour is up,* I have two tickets on the red-eye for Santa Fe. I think we'll have to change planes approximately fifty times going across country, I tell Dan—once in each state—but as he points out, this is actually good because it'll give the sun a chance to come up in Santa Fe before I land there.

"Also," he says, "you'll have hours of what feels like the most incredibly forward motion. I can't think of anything more healing."

Later in the conversation, he says, "I know you have to do this by yourself, but I just wish I were going with you. I'd love to be there."

"You really will be there," I say. "I'll probably need to call you every couple of hours or so. How's that?"

Then, to rest up for whatever's coming, naturally I spend the rest of the day running around like somebody who's lost her mind. I buy a gold necklace to bring to Hope, and a matching one for Abbie. And then she and I go off to the hospital to see Harold. She tells me on the way that she thought he really died and that nobody wanted to tell her. She laughs while she says this, not knowing she's breaking my heart—my heart, which already has so many cracks in it that the air and light shine through in about ten places.

Dr. Golden Retriever comes into Harold's room and says that Harold can be discharged in three days.

"Good," I say. I turn to Harold, who's got Abbie cuddled up next to him on the bed while she plays with the buttons on the TV remote control. Shyly, I tell him that I'll be back from Santa Fe by then, and that I'd like it if he'd come and stay with us while he gets better.

He smiles at me, and looks embarrassed. "The good thing about being old and sick and having money is that you don't have to inconvenience anybody. I'll go to one of those medical hotel things until I get stronger."

"Please don't," I say. "We want you with us." And Abbie beams up at him.

"Did you know we're getting Hopey to come back with us?" she says. "So I'll sleep in Hope's room with her, and you can have my room. I have a very good window in there, you know."

He grins so hard his eyes squinch up. "You all are too nice to me," he says. When we're ready to leave, he takes my hand and says in a low voice, "I'm really proud of you, doing this. Going there. Now may a crazy old man offer one piece of advice before you go?"

"Sure," I say, although I think I know what it's going to be.

"Forgive your mother," he whispers. His skin feels paperthin. "She gave you a lot—your sense of humor, your way of looking at the world. And even though she doesn't know very much about love, you *are* the one she loves the most."

I'm tempted to tell him all the ninety-seven reasons I have for knowing that he's wrong, but how can you start arguing with an old man who's a heart patient? So I don't. I just kiss him on the cheek and tell him he'd better be close by when I get back home. I'm going to come looking for him, I say, and Abbie grins and does a wiggly dance.

She says, "Will you really come and live with us, Grandpa?" And from the way he smiles at her, I really think he might.


Hannah calls me while I'm packing and says that this is a hell of a day for me to be leaving town. She just got a call from Sarah, who's working her way down the list, calling for an emergency day care meeting for that evening. She's going to spell out for the group exactly what's been going on, and ask them to fire Jolie.

"It's probably good you're going," she says. "You'd probably just be asked to testify against Jolie, and I know how you hate for people to know what a shit Lenny was."

"I don't know why that was ever such a big deal to me," I say. "You should have shaken some sense into me. Maybe none of this would have had to happen."

She laughs. "Ah, I believe you had your own innovative way of dealing with Jolie, didn't you? You started sleeping with her boyfriend."

"Yeah, maybe I should suggest that to Sarah." I throw two days' worth of underwear into my suitcase on the bed. I bite my lip. "Hannah, when they get to the part about how they can't fire Jolie because they don't have another teacher, will you do me a favor? Will you tell them I want the job?"

"Wow, I am sooo glad you said that," she says. "I was going to just volunteer you for the position—and I wasn't exactly sure how I'd break it to you once you got back home." She imitates herself. "'Uh, Maz, you know how you're unemployed? Well, you're not anymore.'"

I have this freaky moment right then when I just want to curl up into a fetal position and start sucking my thumb, audibly, on the phone. I want Hannah to tell me everything's going to be all right. I want her to describe to me just how to talk to Lucille and Lenny, what exactly to say. Surely we could write out a script, and I could just carry it through.

But no. Hannah isn't equipped for this one. This one is all me.


*Dan drives* us to Bradley airport. It's ten at night, but as Abbie says, it feels like about a hundred million at night. My blood is coursing through my veins so crazily it's as though I've had about ten cups of coffee. Honestly, I just keep having these little bursts of adrenaline, and I have to keep jumping up out of my seat and walking around, looking in my purse to see the tickets again and again, and starting sentences that don't have endings. When my cell phone rings, the noise practically sends me into cardiac arrest. Have Lucille and Lenny found out what's happening, and decided to call me up? Did Hope tell, after all?

But no. It's Hannah.

"Well, sweetie cakes, you got the job," she says.

"I did?"

"Jolie's toast as of tonight. Don't worry. We'll cover for you until you get back and get settled. Everybody's real excited about you."

I hear voices and laughter in the background. "I'm still at the meeting," she says. "What an event this was! Omigod, you should have been here. We had cathartic crying, we had laughter, we had accusations for a while, then we had sex talk and a whole he said/she said session. It was the wildest day care meeting ever." Somebody's yelling something nearby. "And, oh, yeah—Sarah and Liz Lawton both say, 'Give 'em hell and don't let that bastard off the hook.' And we all want to hear every single detail when you get back."

"God, I'm sorry I missed this," I say.

"It'll be part of day care folklore for years. And just think—you're in charge of us now."

I can't stop smiling. "I'm—so happy about it. Thank you."

When I hang up, Dan and I take Abbie to one of the little kiosks to buy gum and magazines, although I am sort of counting on her sleeping on the flight. I can already tell I won't be able to sleep one minute.

Dan is looking at me. He clears his throat. "There's just one little thing, and maybe now isn't the time to bring it up."

"No, go ahead," I say. I grin at him. "Are you going to tell me that you think I should forgive my mother?"

He laughs. "No way. I'm more selfish than that. I want to know if you think Hope is going to freak out to see me and you together. She didn't really think much of me before, you know."

I touch his arm. "I think it's going to be fine. I really do."

"I just want to say that if you think we should stay apart while she gets used to the idea, I'll do that."

I give him a pretend-shocked look. "Look at you, already trying to get out of things! I thought I had at least five years with you, until she got to be a difficult teenager."

He laughs. "Hey, I'm giving *you* a way out."

"Forget it, buster."

Abbie has decided on Juicy Fruit, which I have always thought is one of the tackier kinds of gum. I can see I'm going to have to pick out some Doublemint to get me through takeoff and landing. Dan stoops down to Abbie's height, telling her that she should chew very hard when the plane takes off, so her ears will stay clear. "Or you can yawn," he says. "Can you make yourself yawn, do you think?"

She laughs. "Nobody can yawn if they're not tired!"

"Sure," he says. "Like this." And he stretches his mouth open in a big yawn. "This is the Yawn School," he says to me. "It's always important to have a session at the Yawn School when you're flying."

They call us to board. I stoop down next to him and touch his arm. "We're not going to stay apart," I tell him. "It's going to be fine. With Hope."

"Don't say it if you're not sure."

But I know something I didn't know before. Hope's going to sense the difference in me. If I show her that I'm comfortable with him, and that loving him doesn't diminish my love for her—and that we can all be a family, with Harold included, too—then I know she'll follow along. Maybe not right away, but sometime. It's good she's gotten to meet the famous Kimmie and see for herself that Lenny isn't exactly pining for our marriage to go on.

Maybe.

"It might be hard at first," he says.

"Did you say *hard*? Oh, sure, it'll be *hard*," I say. "But I'm not so scared of hard anymore. I just want it to be real. Isn't that how you once described my life? *Real*? I like that. That's now what I'm going for. Not to be scared of real."

"Good," he says. He gives me a long look. "'Cause it could get really, really real."

I've been living in the unreal for so long that real has just got to feel better, I want to say to him. Instead I kiss him good-bye, and he holds onto me for ten seconds longer than is absolutely necessary, while Abbie pulls me from the other direction.

"Come on, Mommy, let's go! They're going to take our plane without us!"

# 34

*Lenny's house* is a cinder block rectangle sitting in the middle of dirt, at the end of a dirt road. Even though it's only nine in the morning, everything already looks brown and used up or blown away, as though the sun has been baking everything for hours and hours. Tumbleweeds have gained temporary custody of the yard by clinging to the house, which is painted a hideous turquoise color. The blinds are down on the windows, giving the whole house a shuttered, desolate look. I shiver in the air-conditioned car and can't sort out whether it's the coldness of the refrigerated air or my own nerves that are making me feel so shaky.

I sit there for a moment after I cut the engine, listening to the car ticking in the dazzling heat, trying to gather myself together. I can't believe how ugly and squalid this place looks, with its garbage cans fallen over in the dry brown dirt. Behind the house, the sky burns a bright, hot blue. The motor home, with its gold-plated script saying "Madame Lucille," looks almost like a mirage rising out of the desert, next to the house. Beyond are gray-brown mountains and jagged cliffs.

"Come on," I say to Abbie, taking a deep breath. "Let's go get her."

She's leaning across the front seat from the back, looking at me doubtfully. "Is this where Daddy lives?"

"This is it, sweetheart," I tell her. "Not much like New Haven, is it?"

"Is Hopey in there?"

"She should be. Let's go see."

"Mommy," she says. "I'm a little bit scared."

*That makes two of us. If this were a movie, there'd be high-pitched violins playing ominously.* We get out and walk carefully through the dusty yard up to the front door. A weed skitters across my shoe, and I jump back in alarm, ready to start screaming. Abbie stares at me.

"No, no, nothing to worry about," I tell her. "I'm not scared at all." Too bad about not getting any healing, nourishing sleep on the plane. My nerve endings could have used a little vacation from me.

The doorbell is broken, hanging from wires, so, after taking a deep breath, I bang on the door so hard my hand hurts. I hold onto Abbie with my other hand, and I'm gripping her so tightly that she pulls away and says, "Ow, Mommy, you don't have to choke my hand."

After a few minutes that seem like an eternity, the door opens, and there's a woman standing there, wearing a knee-length yellow-and-red tie-dyed T-shirt that is stretched tight over her round, pregnant belly. I step back. Is this the famous Kimmie? *Pregnant?* I gulp. She looks like a waif somehow, with long, skinny white legs and long, obviously dyed, shoe-polish-black hair and tired eyes that are all smudged with electric blue eye shadow. She looks at the two of us without a word, and her face looks like it's going to sink in on itself. "Oh. You're his wife and kid, right?"

"Yes," I say. I'd like to say, "You must be the unfortunate Kimmie!" But I don't. I manage to smile at her and hold out my hand, which she looks down at but doesn't take hold of. "I'm Maz, and this is Abbie. Are you Kimmie?"

She barely nods. "He's not here," she says.

"That's okay. Is Hope here?" I say, and just then, I hear a yelp in the background, and see Hope scrambling off a futon in the dark corner of the living room. She comes running over to the door and flies at us. We all get caught up in a yelling, screaming hug. I hold onto Hope so hard that I expect that in a moment she'll turn and insist that I let her go. But she doesn't. She's yelling and jumping around, and she and Abbie both are clinging to me and making odd little yipping noises.

"You might as well come in; the AC is on," says Kimmie.

The three of us crab-walk into the house, which is dark and hot, even though, sure enough, there's an air conditioner huffing away in the window. A television set, sitting on a card table next to the window, is blaring, and Kimmie goes back to the futon and sinks herself down on it and stares straight ahead at the TV set, as though she's exhausted her capacity for conversation. But no—in a moment she stirs herself and says, "Hope, get your mom something to drink, why don't you? I bet she's hot. People always get hot here."

"No, it's fine," I say to Hope in a low voice, hoping that Kimmie will just go back to the television and ignore us. I whisper, "Let's just go get your stuff together."

I have this wild moment of thinking that I can just pack Hope's stuff up quickly and be off with her. We could go back to the airport, get on a plane, and fly home before Lenny and Lucille would ever even know. That would be something, wouldn't it? Do exactly to them what they did to me?

But, oh, what a horrible chain reaction *that* could set in motion! Then I'd have to worry that on any given day, I could just run out to the store to buy *bananas* or something, and I'd come home to find they'd snuck her away again. And then, of course, I'd have to come back to Santa Fe and get her again while Lenny was taking a shower—and it would just go on and on. Years, this way. Expensive, too! I feel a kind of crazy laughter bubbling up inside of me. See? I think. This is where your thoughts end up when you haven't slept. I shake my head, trying to clear it.

We go into a dim back bedroom, where I finally can get a good look at Hope. She's wearing a pair of dark pink shorts I haven't ever seen before and a T-shirt that says "Angel" on it in pink letters. Her hair is a tangly mess, and she looks like she hasn't had a decent bath in a while—but her eyes are shining, and she's jumping around as though she can't contain all the happiness she feels. She shows us the mattress she's been sleeping on, and a couple of magic rocks Lenny's collected, and a pathetic-looking angel doll she bought at a rest stop during the trip. She's opening a drawer to get something, when I hear a noise and look up, startled, to see that Kimmie's standing in the doorway, her arms folded across her big middle.

"So what are you doing here?" she says.

"Um . . . pardon?"

"Why are you here? I mean, are you moving in?" I must look confused because she says, "You are Lenny's wife, right? So did you come to live here, too?"

"No, I—"

"He's always saying you might come," she says as she comes in and sits down on the mattress. She piles up the pillows behind her and leans against them. "Isn't he, Hope? He says you're going to help him open that center thing he's doing. You're a baker, right? He's already telling people you'll come and make bread for the place."

I shift my purse to my other shoulder and look down at Hope, who shrugs at me. "No," I say. "I've told him a million times that I'm not coming here."

"Oh," says Kimmie. She seems to be taking this in. "But—hey, here you are. He was right."

"Not to stay, I'm not." I clear my throat. "So—I see you're having a baby!"

"It's Lenny's baby," she tells me. "In case you were wondering." She giggles. "He's in denial about it. Before he left to go back to New Haven, he told me this baby was all in my imagination."

"Sure looks real enough to me," I say.

"Yeah," she says and pats her stomach. "I think he sees that now. He's kind of a . . . denial kind of person. You know? If I had to pick one word to describe Lenny, it would be what? Uh, *denial*." She looks at me and we both laugh, and I see that she's got a nice spark to her, still burning.

"That's good," I say. "I think that pretty much sums him up. Mr. Denial. Hope, pack, honey."

"Wait. Hope's going back with you?"

"Yeah. It's home, you know. New Haven. Trees. Friends. School. You know."

"Oh, so you just came here to get her? Wow. I didn't know. Lenny said you—" She glances over at Hope and then changes her mind, which I am grateful for.

Hope starts moving through the room, gathering up her stuff, and Kimmie, who is probably so relieved to find out she's not going to have to raise a ten-year-old, now is all loosened up. She sits up on her knees in the middle of the bed and tells me about how the pregnancy is going and that she knows it's going to be a difficult adjustment, having a baby and all with Mr. Denial, but sometimes you just know something's right, and this baby was meant to be. She rubs her belly while she talks, and then suddenly she laughs loudly and says, "Omigod! I just realized—that woman in the trailer out there is your *mother,* isn't she? What a piece of work that one is! Yesterday she was talking on and on about some spirit guides she knows, and how this baby just might be the reincarnation of a cat I had once, because something about how they don't have enough souls now in the universe, and so animals have got to come back as humans. Can you *believe* that?"

We both laugh. "Welcome to my life," I say to her. "You seem to be inheriting the whole slew of them."

The front door closes just then, and I hear Lenny saying, "What the hell?" And then he's standing in the doorway of the bedroom, larger than life, looking from me to Kimmie, and to Hope and Abbie, as if he can't really register what's going on. He's wearing jeans shorts and a black button down shirt open to the waist, with his little herby thing in plain view, and he's rattling the car keys in his hand.

"I saw a strange car out there, and I thought it must be the landlord," he says. Then a huge smile spreads across his face, and he says, "Well, well, well, Miss Maz, it didn't take you too long to change your mind, did it? So, Kimmie, I want you to meet *my wife.*"

*"We've met,"* I say. I lick my lips, which have suddenly gotten dry.

"I was just out getting some food," he says. His eyes are bright. "Come on in and let's get something to eat. For God's sake, why didn't you call and let somebody know you were coming? I could have met you at the airport or something." He smiles at me quizzically, looks at Kimmie, like he's trying to figure out why we're both still half-smiling.

"So can you believe this?" he says to me. "You came to your senses! Is this not a great place, or what?" He grins. "And so you met Kimmie and little Junior here? Eh? Eh?" He goes over to her and pulls her to her feet, yanks up her T-shirt and starts rubbing her belly like she's some good-luck Buddha. She's wearing dark red underpants, and she tries to pull down the shirt in embarrassment. She says, "*Lenny!*"

He laughs. "She's a peach, isn't she? Heeey, so Maz! Did you bring anybody with you—like your little eighth-grade boyfriend? I told you, everybody's welcome here in Santa Fe. We'll just make ourselves a big old happy family with anybody who wants to join us."

"A harem, he means," I say, and Kimmie laughs again.

Abbie has shrunk back behind me. I notice he hasn't even greeted her yet. I say to him cheerfully, "Actually, Lenny, I didn't bring anybody with me, except this little person right here."

He smacks himself in the head. "Abbiekins! Come here and give ol' Daddy a hug, little girl!"

She now puts herself completely behind me, won't even peer out.

"Abbie, do you like my *house*? Did you see all those huge weeds in the yard? Later we can go out and chase them."

"Whoops, we're not going to really have time to chase weeds, fun as that sounds," I say. "Unfortunately, we've got a plane to catch."

"What—you're leaving?" he says. He makes his eyes go round in surprise. "Come on! You can't be serious. You're not even going to look around first—not even going to *consider* this place?"

"Nope," I say. "Considered it already. Decision made."

His eyes narrow at Hope, and he leans over and socks her playfully in the arm. "You rapscallion! Did *you* call your mom and ask her to do this?"

"Of course not," I say. "I had you wired with a transponder, didn't you know? And when it stopped beeping, I knew you'd arrived, and I got on my secret jet and flew out here. Jeez, I thought you *knew* you were wired."

He stares at me. I laugh. Having very little sleep could be a real advantage here. I feel as though I'm moving at regular speed while everyone else is locked in slow motion.

"So," I say. I go over to the corner and get Hope's Winnie-the-Pooh suitcase and hand it to her. "Kimmie and I have gotten to be old friends in just the few minutes we've talked. She's a great gal, Lenny. And she and I do *not* think the baby is a reincarnation of a cat, do we, Kimmie?"

Kimmie laughs.

"Hope, do you have any other clothes here that you need? Do you want to bring along that angel doll? I suppose those magic rocks can stay. Looks to me like the magic might be all drained out of them."

"WAIT!" says Lenny, and I look up from fussing with the zipper of the suitcase.

"This damn thing always sticks," I say. "Lenny, can you make it work? Wasn't that one of your talents—undoing zippers?"

"My God," he says. "I feel like I've walked into the Catskills by mistake. Who *are* you channeling today?"

"It's just me," I say. "Me on very little sleep and with a lot of power-packed *rage*, Lenny." I smile at him, showing teeth. "I don't think you want to get in my way."

He's staring at me.

The zipper suddenly gives way, and I flip open the suitcase. "Put your stuff in here, honey. Come on."

"Wait," says Lenny. "You and I should talk about this. Girls, why don't—? Kimmie, go chase some tumbleweeds with them, will you? I've gotta—"

Kimmie and I both burst out laughing. "I'm not going out in the hundred-degree heat and chase tumbleweeds, Lenny!" she says. "I'm seven months pregnant."

"He was always a little dim about pregnancy," I tell her happily. "Goes back to the denial thing, I think." I walk past him into the hall. "Hope, I don't suppose you've got a toothbrush in the bathroom here, do you? Or—what am I saying?—let's just buy you another one, unless this one is your very favorite or something."

"It's not," she says. She's finished putting two shirts and a pair of shorts into the suitcase. They really hadn't brought her very much. She turns and looks at me.

"Okay, then just zip up, and let's go, sweetie." I smile at her. "Anything else you need? Want to tell Daddy and Kimmie good-bye?"

"I'm not going to stand for this!" he says. "You are *not* going to just walk in here like this and disrupt everything!"

"We'll talk later," I say. "I'll have my lawyer get in touch with yours."

"I don't have a lawyer."

"No? Well, I'd get one, I think. I don't think it looks very good for you to still be married when you're starting a new family with someone else. Congratulations, by the way. I couldn't be happier for you."

"I want to talk to you alone," he says.

"We'll be in touch," I say. I hold out my hand to Kimmie, and this time she takes it. "So glad I got a chance to meet you," I say. "You've got an interesting time ahead of you, don't you? So—is the baby a boy or a girl, do you think?"

She smiles. "As long as it's not a cat, I don't care."

"You're gonna have to watch this one," I say to him. "She's got some gumption to her, I think."

I take Abbie and Hope firmly by each hand, and we start walking to the front door. I can feel the sweat curdling under my arms, starting to trickle down my sides. I'm thinking four more steps—and then we're outside. We could make a run for it by then. We're actually going to be out of here. . . .

And then he goes crazy and starts crying.

I remember this, how he acts when he doesn't get his way. I am so immune, but I know that it's not going to be easy for his daughters to watch. I can picture Hope thinking she needs to run back and stay with him, that she can't leave him after all. That's what he's banking on, I think.

My heart, which apparently has run out of its last two drops of courage, starts skittering around in my chest, and I keep walking with them, straight toward the car. Both girls are looking back at him now, and he's bellowing now, actually kneeling down in the dirt, crying, "Oh, my God! My family! My *family*!"

"He's fine, he's just doing a little act," I say in a low voice. "We should maybe clap for him." But I've got to hand it to him: he's doing a fairly good impression of actual crying. Hope's grip tightens on my hand. Abbie leans into me.

"You don't think he's really crying?" Hope whispers. "What's going to happen to him?" Her voice is shaky. I hold onto her tighter and say, "It's okay. It's really okay. Sometimes he likes a little drama in his good-byes."

She stops walking. "But he's really sad."

Abbie starts crying, and I pick her up and keep walking. "Come on, Hope. We'll talk in the car, honey."

She hangs back. "Kimmie's helping him get up," she says.

"He'll be fine. Now let's just get in the car," I tell her. I open the car door, and slide Abbie inside, disentangle her arms from around my neck. Hope is still standing, watching Lenny, with her fingers in her mouth.

"Maybe I should go hug him," she says. She looks at me with wide, saucer eyes. "What should I do? Mommy, tell me what I should do."

Over by the house, Lenny's decided to take a new tack. "I didn't want you here anyway!" he's yelling. "Just get out of here—and don't expect me to send any more money, either! You're going to see what happens when I get this center up and running without you!"

There's a flash of sunlight reflecting on metal, and the motor home door swings open just then, and there's Lucille standing there wearing a floor-length nylon robe with a big boa-type bright purple collar. Her wig is off, and her hair is sticking up in all directions.

"What the *hell* is the matter with you people?" she says. "Lenny Lombard, have you lost your cotton-pickin' *mind*? Maz—I swear— you cause a ruckus wherever you go, now don't you? Git over here, you big ole baby! Lenny, stop that yellin'!"

He stops. We all stop and look at her.

"Maz, come here!" she commands. "When in the hell did you git in? What's goin' on?"

I say, "Too late. We're leaving."

"Let's get us all some lunch," she says. She makes her way down the motor home's three steps and looks down at her arm, where a watch would be if she ever remembered to wear one. "Isn't it 'bout lunchtime? Well, like Harold used to say about the cocktail hour, it's lunchtime *somewhere* in the world! Let's all pile into that fine-lookin' car a yours and go sit down for a while someplace cool. I do say this is 'bout the hottest place on earth, and I lived in Florida most a my damn life, where it gits so hot and wet that the alligators can't even catch a breath! Can you just hold on a minute while I put my face and my hair on and git outta this gown thing? I'll only be a sec!"

"We're not going to lunch," I tell her evenly. I ease my arm around Hope, and scoot her into the car. "We've got a plane to catch."

"A *plane?*" says Lucille.

"Yeah, Maz woke up this morning making some unilateral decisions for the family," says Lenny. He's standing up now. Kimmie gives me a look, like *Get out while you can.*

"Oh, no. Come on, honey. You're takin' Hope back into that snake pit where she goes to school?" says Lucille. "And Lenny knows such a nice little homeschool right close by! Tell me that's not what you're doin', sweetie!"

I get in the car and turn on the engine and the air conditioner so the kids don't fry. "We're just going to be another minute, girls," I say to them. "I've got a little bit of stuff to talk about with G.G., and then we're going. Everybody okay?"

Their faces are tear streaked and solemn.

"I know," I say. "This is kind of weird today, huh? But—I just want to tell you, it's all going to be fine. Really. Trust me."

When I get back out of the car and close the door, Lucille is sashaying herself across the dirt. I see she's wearing little high-heeled bedroom slippers, the kind with powder puffs on the top, and they're giving her a devil of a time in the dust. She keeps looking down at her feet in dismay, trying to kick pebbles out of them. I could get in the car before she gets to me. I could start the engine, drive away, and never have to do this with her again. But I don't.

Later I think of those showdowns in movies about the old West. All of us standing there in the dirt, me with my hand on the door handle of the car, the girls sheltered inside, Lenny still next to the house, and Lucille crossing from the motor home. She keeps smiling broadly at us all, as though this is all just play-acting and in a minute, we'll pile in the car and get some lunch, tell her that her hair looks pretty, listen to a funny story she has to tell about getting ready in the morning. Her eyes are darting around, from me to Lenny, and you can practically *feel* her antenna trying to pick up signals of what to do next.

"Well, I must say I'm surprised at this!" she says. "First, I'm surprised that you came all this way and didn't let us know. We coulda done us some celebratin' and gettin' ready. Hey, did Lenny tell you we've got a lead on Jackson Angus now, and we're gonna go this afternoon and see if it's him? So if you just waited a little bit, you could maybe stick around and meet the love of my life, and then—who knows?—get to meet your sister."

"I don't have a sister," I say.

"Well, darlin', you *might*." She's smiling at me and tilting her head. "Come on, sweetie. Don't be this way. You know I didn't mean any harm, bringin' Hope here. You make such a big deal out of everythin'. It woulda done Hope some good to be in another part of the country, see somethin' different, be with her daddy for a while. And you coulda gotten a good break, 'cause you look so tired, darlin'. I hate to say it, but you've got those lines formin' around your eyes now, and you need some rest. Lenny and I were aimin' to give you some rest for a while. And now you have to go and make such a federal case of it and be ugly."

"Listen to me," I say. "You don't know one thing about what any one of us needs. I spent my entire childhood being dumped by you with other people whenever it wasn't convenient for you to take care of me, and since then, you've made abandoning people into your lifetime sport. You have only thought about yourself and what *you* wanted over and over again, and now that I'm grown up, I'll be damned if I'm going to let you subject my little girls to that."

She starts to say something, then stops. I hold up my hand. I've got to say this. Even if she freaks out and starts screaming, even if she runs back in the motor home, or comes over and starts pounding me with her fists, I'm going to say this.

"It's taken me years to finally get the idea that it wasn't always my fault that you left me so many times when I was trying to protect you and . . . and *love* you, and be the daughter you wanted me to be. You always let me know that I fell far short of what you were expecting out of me, and that there was *another* mythical daughter you had who would have been perfect, who you would have *kept* with you at all times. I feel like I've spent my whole life trying to be the person who was funny enough and good enough and outrageous enough that *you* would want to stick around." I feel my voice catch, but I go on. "And then—then I grow up somehow, and you try to *take* everything away from me . . . all the people that I love; you need to prove that they love *you* more, and that you are the declared winner. You need to win everything!"

"Oh, darlin', you've got such myths built up about me," she says. "I win because I believe in somethin'. I know what I want, and I git it. You just look around and try to make sure of how everybody's feelin' around you, try to do anything but take a risk. That's no way to live your life, honey. If I coulda taught you anythin', it would be that you need to risk things. You can't just cling to whatever you think is safe for the moment. You need to *live*."

A jet roars overhead, drowning out her words. It's like the television with the sound turned off. She's gesticulating, she's flinging out her arms, she's clicking her lighter as fast as she can. I stare at her. Lenny is rubbing the toe of his boot in the dirt. I look around us, at the sky as blue as banners, at the dirty, scrubby little house, at the way her face is contorting as she talks. She's smiling at me and tilting her head, and her eyes are shooting sparks, trying to bore into me like she's always done. But now—now she looks suddenly so little and so scared—just an old lady standing in the desert sunshine in a bright purple, feathered bathrobe and powder puff high heels.

I can't explain it, but I suddenly feel like laughing. She's right: I never did take risks until now. I feel like getting in the car and riding in doughnut circles all over the yard. I look over at the girls, peering through the back window, their eyes wide and almost frightened and all I can think about is jumping in next to them and saying, "We don't have to worry about this. We're going home!"

I know now what I want to say to Hope, what I *will* say to Hope just as soon as this damned airplane stops spinning and diving around in the sky. We'll drive away, out to the airport, we'll get on the plane for Connecticut, and I'll say, "Hope, darling, we don't know what's going to happen. Life's going to be messy, but we're in this together." I'll say, "I'll never leave you, not as long as you need me." I'll say, "There are so many people for us to love, all through our lives, so many times we get to fall in love and be treasured by someone else. But we'll always remember that we love each other. *Always*."

Or something like that. I'll make it up as I go along. That's the great part: I have years to get it to sound just right. But goddamn, I had so looked forward to yelling at Lucille about Harold, and the other five husbands. I'd thought this could be my chance to make her understand about Robbie, and how mad I still am about the men we had to pick up in bars when I was in high school.

When the jet noise dies down, Lucille is still talking. She's saying, just as though I could always hear her, ". . . and Jackson Angus is just gonna think you're the cutest little thing. If you stick around, you could meet him after lunch. I know you've always wanted to know what he's like. And I really do have a good feelin' about Cassandra. The guides have told me she always *did* know how to appreciate a good risk."

Then I walk across the yard to her. I lean down and kiss her on the cheek, smiling. I say, "Thank you."

She tries to grab my hand. Her eyes are wild, staring at me, and the purple silky material brushes against me as I pull away from her. "What are you thankin' me for?" she says.

I start walking away from her, backward. I shrug at her and smile.

"No, really! What are you *thankin'* me for? Not for what you *should* be thankin' me for, I'm sure of that!"

I stop walking and look at her. "And what's that, Lucille? What should I thank you for?"

"That I taught you to be strong," she hollers. She's a little old lady standing in the dirt, with pebbles in her bedroom slippers, screaming. "I made sure you turned out to be a strong, forceful woman," she says. "God knows, I had to leave you to do it, but I sure as hell did it."

"And that," I say, "that's exactly what I'm thanking you for."

"But you don't even *know* that!" she says.

"Oh, I know it," I say. I stand there for a moment, looking at the wide expanse of sky with just a few little wispy clouds here and there. I pick out a cloud for Lucille, and one each for the kids, and a couple for Lenny and Kimmie. And Harold, of course. And for Dan and me, I find a big comfortable double cloud. Can you wish on clouds? I'm not sure, but I give it a try.

And then I wave good-bye at Lenny and at Kimmie, blow her a kiss because she's going to need all the love she can cling to, and then I open the car door. Five seconds tops, and I'm outta there. Me and my girls.

## About the Author

SANDI KAHN SHELTON is a feature reporter and free-lance writer. Her work has apperared in *Woman's Day, Family Circle, Salon, Redbook,* and *Working Mother.* She is the author of three nonfiction books. She has three children and lives in Connecticut.